LEAVE
NO
TRACE

ALSO BY
D. S. BUTLER

Lost Child
Her Missing Daughter

DS Karen Hart Series:

Bring Them Home
Where Secrets Lie
Don't Turn Back
House of Lies
On Cold Ground
What She Said
Find Her Alive
Before the Dawn

DS Jack Mackinnon Crime Series:

Deadly Obsession
Deadly Motive
Deadly Revenge
Deadly Justice
Deadly Ritual
Deadly Payback
Deadly Game
Deadly Intent

East End Series:

East End Trouble
East End Diamond
East End Retribution

Harper Grant Mystery Series (writing as Danica Britton):

A Witchy Business
A Witchy Mystery
A Witchy Christmas
A Witchy Valentine
Harper Grant and the Poisoned Pumpkin Pie
A Witchy Bake-off

D.S. BUTLER

LEAVE NO TRACE

DETECTIVE KAREN HART SERIES

THOMAS & MERCER

Text copyright ©2024 by D. S. Butler
All rights reserved.

Published by Thomas & Mercer, Seattle

www.apub.com

Amazon, the Amazon logo, and Thomas & Mercer are trademarks of Amazon.com, Inc., or its affiliates.

ISBN-13: 9781662512278
eISBN: 9781662512261

Cover design by @blacksheep-uk.com
Cover image: © Lebendigger, Ghost Bear / Shutterstock; © Robert Brook / Getty Images; © Ildiko Neer / ArcAngel

Printed in the United States of America

Dedicated with lots of love to Auntie Jean

Prologue

Amber Burton's shoes crunched over the gravel as she led her reluctant eleven-year-old son, Tommy, towards Tattershall Castle. It was a gorgeous day, and the air smelled of freshly cut grass. A falconer was setting up, getting ready for his show, and families sat on the lawn waiting for it to start.

'Come on, Tommy,' Amber urged.

She had her husband, Gareth, to help look after Tommy, though he was at work today. She didn't know how people coped as single parents. She was barely holding things together, *and* she had Gareth to help.

He hadn't been much help lately, though. He'd been working longer hours and was more short-tempered, and she was exhausted from trying to juggle everything. She'd put her foot down and insisted he book at least a couple of days off to look after Tommy during half-term next week.

Today was an inset day and yet another day off for Tommy. It had been easier when Tommy was younger. Back then, he'd been ecstatic to have a kickabout with his dad, and getting an ice cream was enough to put a big smile on his face.

Nowadays, he only wanted expensive computer games; otherwise, he sulked.

She *loved* Tommy to bits, but she'd realised that sometimes he really wound her up, and she didn't much *like* him. That was normal, wasn't it? Didn't all parents feel that way occasionally?

Such disloyal thoughts made Amber feel incredibly guilty, so whenever she had them she gave in to Tommy's demands. A vicious circle.

Tommy shuffled along, kicking up dust from the gravel path, his glasses sliding down his nose.

'Don't drag your feet, Tommy,' Amber said automatically.

'But Mum, I told you I don't want to be here. I'd rather be at home playing on my Xbox.'

He was getting on her last nerve today.

Amber stopped and turned to face her son, putting her hands on her hips. She took in the pout on his face and how he crossed his arms over his chest before responding.

'Fresh air and sunshine are good for you. You can't be cooped up inside all the time.'

'You're *so* annoying,' he grumbled, adjusting his glasses and looking around the courtyard with disinterest. He kicked at a pebble, sending it skittering across the ground.

'Look, there's the bird of prey show starting soon,' Amber said, pointing to a sign near the entrance to the castle's main tower. 'Let's watch that together, and maybe get an ice cream afterwards?'

'Whatever,' Tommy muttered, shuffling along beside his mother as they made their way towards the fenced-off display area.

There was a time when the promise of ice cream could get Tommy to do almost anything. Not that long ago, he had *wanted* to spend time with her. He would call out, 'Mum, watch this!' or 'Mum, look at me!' as he attempted a cartwheel or a trick on his bike.

These days, he barely spoke to her. She dreaded to think what he'd be like when he actually reached his teenage years. Amber's interactions with her son usually involved nagging him to make his bed, pick up after himself, do his homework, and get to bed at a reasonable hour. But today was an opportunity for them to spend quality time together. Less nagging, more fun.

'No one else has to do stuff like this,' Tommy continued to moan, his voice taking on a nasally, whiny tone.

'I'm so glad I'm spending money on a nice day out so that you can complain about it non-stop,' Amber snapped back.

She immediately regretted her sharp words.

Amber was the adult. Why was she letting Tommy get under her skin? He could be a selfish little tyke, but he was just a kid. She'd probably put her parents through worse.

She glanced at her phone; the screen was filled with notifications for work emails and missed calls. Her heart sank as she realised something must have gone wrong at the office in her absence. As the logistics manager, her team turned to her when things didn't run smoothly, even when it was her day off.

'Tommy, I need to make a call. Can you please just try to enjoy yourself for a bit?' Amber asked. She motioned towards the falconer. 'Watch the show while I sort out this mess at work.'

'Ugh, you're such a *hypocrite*, Mum. You moan at me about always being on electronic devices. What about *you*?' Tommy grumbled, a scowl twisting his face.

'I'm not doing this because I want to, Tommy. It's my job. It puts food on the table and buys you the computer games you can't live without and—'

'Fine.' Tommy turned his back and stalked off, his hands deep in the pockets of his favourite red hoodie, kicking at tufts of grass as he walked. No doubt ruining the expensive white trainers they'd bought him a few weeks ago.

Amber felt like having a tantrum of her own as she watched Tommy stomp off. He settled beneath a large oak tree, sulking and glaring at the show from a distance.

She sat down on a weathered wooden bench, surrounded by the sounds of chattering tourists and families having fun.

Her phone buzzed again, and she looked down at the screen, her attention torn between work and Tommy. Scrolling through a seemingly endless list of messages, she tried to piece together what had gone wrong. She dialled a colleague, keeping her gaze on Tommy as he sulked. He seemed unimpressed and bored by the majestic birds of prey swooping and diving as the show started.

Tommy's words had hit home. She *was* a hypocrite, and she hated her work intruding on their day out, but she couldn't afford to let things spiral out of control while she was away from the office. She would have to deal with the fallout, whether now or later. But if she nipped the problem in the bud now, it would save her days of work when she got back.

It upset her to see Tommy miserable, even if he was behaving like a brat. His lack of gratitude frustrated her, but it wasn't his fault she and Gareth had to juggle careers and parenthood, was it? She needed to find a better way to balance her commitments.

A huge buzzard glided over the crowd, drawing 'ooohs' from the spectators, and even Tommy seemed impressed as he looked up, his small frame dwarfed by the imposing tree.

She knew her son deserved better, but what choice did she have? They needed her income to make ends meet. Every day seemed to be an endless cycle of compromise and guilt.

As she waited for her call to be answered, she stole one last glance at the oak tree, thinking how much she'd give to go back in time and see Tommy's gap-toothed smile as he gazed up at her adoringly.

It had been some time since Tommy had looked at her with anything more than a moody glare. It was her fault, of course. She needed to try harder. She had to give Tommy what he really needed – her attention.

Sally from accounts finally answered her call.

'Hello Sally, this is Amber Burton. I'm sorry I've been unavailable – I'm on a day trip with my son.'

The piercing cries of the birds of prey echoed across the grounds as Amber listened to Sally explain the logistics catastrophe they were dealing with at work.

While Sally described the data on her screen, Amber was distracted by the birds as they soared over the castle and put on an impressive display for the crowd. For a brief moment, Amber allowed herself to be captivated by the spectacle, imagining what it would be like to be so free and unshackled from the drudgery of her life.

'I'll check my emails and get back to you as soon as I can,' Amber said, unable to keep the resentment from her tone as she ended the call. Today was one of her annual leave days. It really wasn't fair that she was expected to deal with the crisis on her day off.

She sighed, feeling the burden of juggling work and childcare. At least Gareth had booked some days off for the coming half-term. It would be his turn to entertain Tommy. Hopefully, he'd have better luck than her.

Glancing back at the oak tree, she expected to see Tommy still sulking in its shadow, but he wasn't there.

'Tommy?' Amber called out, annoyance edging into her voice. She rose from the bench, scanning the area. The castle grounds were alive with people – families laughing and chattering, children shrieking with excitement – but there was no sign of Tommy.

There was a burst of applause for the end of the show, and the falconer bowed.

'Tommy!' she called again, louder this time, as she walked towards where she'd last seen him.

Was he hiding somewhere to try to teach her a lesson? Attempting to punish her for being on her phone?

But even as those thoughts crossed Amber's mind, a sinking feeling settled in her stomach. Something was wrong.

She reached the red rope separating the bird of prey show from the rest of the grounds. The falconer, a tall man with a weathered face, caught sight of Amber and raised a bushy eyebrow as he removed his thick leather glove.

'Have you seen a little boy? Eleven years old, brown hair, glasses, red hoodie . . . ?'

The falconer shook his head, his eyes sympathetic. 'Sorry, love. Can't say that I have.'

'Right. Thank you.' Amber's mouth was dry, and her pulse had started to flutter.

Amber approached the oak tree where Tommy had been sitting and noticed something out of place: a small, blue teddy bear lying abandoned on the grass. It wasn't Tommy's, but it added to her unease, and she suddenly felt very cold despite the warm sunshine.

'Have you seen my son?' she asked people as they strolled past, giving them a hurried description of Tommy.

They all shook their heads and offered consoling words. *He'll turn up. Have you tried the castle? I'm sure he'll be fine. Maybe he went inside? Shall we help you look?*

But no one had seen him.

How was that possible? Tommy had been under the tree in plain sight of everyone. He knew not to wander off. He *definitely* knew not to talk to strangers. Tommy was eleven. Not five.

And he was pretty streetwise for an eleven-year-old. He'd scream blue murder if someone tried to take him away . . . wouldn't he?

Amber had given Tommy the talk about how he should react if someone ever tried to lure him away. She was absolutely sure that he had understood it. Then, more recently, she and Gareth had sat him down and explained the dangers of being online. Tommy knew there were predators out there, in both the real world and the virtual one.

Amber's eyes darted around the grounds, searching for any trace of Tommy, but he'd vanished. The chatter of people close by faded into the background as anxiety tightened her chest.

A chill ran the length of her body as she looked back at the blue teddy bear, a sense of dread washing over her. To Amber, the toy seemed to be a terrible omen.

Her little boy was gone.

'Tommy!' she shouted, her voice echoing around the castle grounds.

Amber's fear had reached boiling point, and her chest heaved with each breath. She felt light-headed from the all-consuming panic.

'Can I help?' A staff member approached her, his concerned gaze meeting her wild eyes.

He wore an ID tag identifying him as Trevor, and Amber clutched his arm. 'Please. I can't find my son.'

Trevor listened as Amber gave him a description and told him where she'd last seen Tommy.

'Now, don't worry. This sort of thing happens all the time. He's probably gone into the tower . . . or more likely, a boy his age would have gone to explore the dungeons.' He smiled reassuringly. 'Don't fret. I'll get a few people together, and we'll have a proper search for him, okay?'

Amber nodded numbly. She was good at reading people, and though Trevor's words were meant to calm her, his expression showed his concern.

Did he suspect someone had snatched Tommy?

A sob dragged itself from her chest.

Why did I let Tommy out of my sight?

How could I have been so stupid?

Her earlier suspicion that Tommy was playing a cruel trick had evaporated, replaced with a fear so ferocious it threatened to overwhelm her.

Twenty minutes later, Amber and a group of helpful visitors and staff had searched the grounds around the castle, and an announcement had been made over the tannoy system.

Trevor approached Amber again, his face grave. 'I'm sorry. He's not in the castle. I think it's time to call the police.'

Amber looked at him in horror.

This can't be happening.

This. Can. Not. Be. Happening.

Her hands shook as she pulled out her mobile phone and dialled 999. The call connected to the emergency services operator, but Amber's words caught in her throat. Her gaze dropped to the blue teddy bear lying on the ground beneath the oak tree.

'Please help me,' Amber managed to choke out. 'My son is missing.'

Chapter One

Detective Sergeant Karen Hart parked up outside the small bungalow in Metheringham. DC Sophie Jones's parents had moved here, downsizing, just a year earlier. It was a pretty, three-bedroom place constructed from pale yellow bricks, with decorative white shutters on the windows. The front garden had a carefully maintained lawn and mature rose bushes crowded with buds ready to bloom.

Karen glanced at her watch; it was almost one already. She would be cutting it close with her lunch break, but after talking to Harinder this morning a knot of concern had formed in her stomach. Sophie needed her friends around her, even if she didn't want to admit it.

Harinder was the station's resident tech guru and Sophie's boyfriend. They'd been together for more than a year now, and he'd been devastated when Sophie had been attacked a few months ago. They all had. It had knocked the entire team for six.

Despite setbacks after her traumatic brain injury, Sophie had left the hospital determined to recover quickly and return to work. But it hadn't been that simple. Constant reminders her body wasn't the same as it used to be had left Sophie frustrated, and this morning Harinder had told Karen he thought Sophie was depressed.

It had been almost two weeks since her last visit, Karen realised, feeling a wave of guilt.

Sophie's father, Geoff, appeared at the door, his face weary but welcoming. 'Hello, Karen. I just made some tea. Fancy a cup?'

Karen declined the offer as Sophie's mother, Clara, emerged from the kitchen wearing a large floppy sun hat.

Clara greeted Karen, a smile on her lips. 'Thanks for coming.' She shot a worried glance towards the living room. 'We'll be in the garden, feeding the roses, if you need anything.'

The living room – where Sophie now spent most of her time – was dimly lit, thanks to the closed curtains, and smelled faintly of furniture polish and disinfectant. Sophie had contracted an infection shortly after leaving the hospital. Ever since then, her mother had taken to dousing everything Sophie touched with antiseptic.

Karen spotted her friend propped up on the sofa, surrounded by an assortment of cushions. There was a light blue patchwork quilt over her knees, despite the warm weather.

The bruising had long faded, and her curly hair was growing back, but Sophie had lost weight. Her usually dimpled cheeks were now gaunt. There were dark circles around her eyes, and the bright determined spark within them was gone. This wasn't the same woman who had taken on criminals and confidently faced danger more than once.

'How are you feeling?' Karen asked, trying to keep her tone light.

'Fantastic,' Sophie replied, her voice heavy with sarcasm. A smile flickered across her face, but it was strained.

Karen settled into the armchair opposite. Sophie looked so small, so fragile.

'Harinder sent you, didn't he?' Sophie asked, her eyes narrowing. Despite her weakened state, her detective's intuition remained intact.

'No,' Karen said breezily, not wanting Sophie to think she'd been talking about her behind her back. 'I just wanted to check on you and see how you're doing.'

'Really? That's funny, because you usually visit on evenings or weekends, not on workdays.'

'I managed to get away on my lunch break.'

Sophie looked sceptical.

'Rick sends his best, as do Morgan and Arnie and, well . . . everyone. We're all missing you.'

'Rick visited on Saturday,' Sophie said dully. 'He said he's missing me because he can't get my help with his paperwork.' She rolled her eyes.

'The electronic filing system isn't functioning as well without you,' Karen admitted.

Sophie gave a small smile. But her voice was bitter, as if she felt everyone was acting out of pity. 'It's nice to be missed, I guess.' Her gaze flickered away and then back to Karen. 'Are you sure you're not here because Harinder asked you to come?'

'I'm here because I want to help you get through this. How's your progress been this week?' Karen asked, steering the conversation away from Harinder.

'Slow,' Sophie admitted, her eyes downcast as she picked at the edge of the quilt covering her lap. 'The doctors say I'm doing well, considering the injury, but I can't help feeling trapped.'

'Give it time,' Karen urged, leaning forward in her chair. 'You've been through a lot. You need to be patient.'

'Easy for you to say,' Sophie snapped. 'You're not the one who can't live on their own.'

Karen took a deep breath. It was difficult seeing Sophie so bitter. 'I know it's tough. But you're strong. You'll get through this and be back on the job before you know it.'

Sophie scoffed, her eyes filling with tears. 'You're just saying that. I bet Harinder made you come to babysit me. To stop me wallowing.'

'Do you really think I'm only here because Harinder twisted my arm?' Karen asked. She could understand Sophie's frustration, but the thought that her friend believed she was there out of obligation stung.

'Are you?' Sophie challenged, her voice cracking. 'Because if you are, you can save your breath and just go.'

Karen waited for a beat and then nodded. 'If that's what you want, I'll leave. But you should know I came because I care about you, Sophie. Not because Harinder asked me to.'

Sophie didn't reply.

Karen sighed, running a hand through her hair as she glanced around the room. It was a large space, but had a cosy feel. Photographs of Sophie in happier, healthier days hung on the walls, a reminder of the bright and lively colleague Karen used to know.

Seeing Sophie like this – sullen, withdrawn and full of mistrust – was frustrating. Karen wondered if it was just the pain talking, or if Sophie's whole personality had changed. She wished she could catch a glimpse of the old Sophie, with her bubbly laugh and eager energy. The woman in front of her was like a stranger, staring stubbornly down at her lap, avoiding eye contact.

Karen didn't know what else to say to convince Sophie that people truly cared about her and missed her. The injuries had clearly done more than just physical damage. Karen feared Sophie was damaged emotionally too, and she didn't know how to help fix that.

From the tension in Sophie's jaw, Karen could see she was clenching her teeth. 'Do you want me to go?'

'No,' Sophie muttered, finally looking up at Karen with an expression that was equal parts defiance and defeat. 'If you want to help, why don't you pass me my tea?'

Karen stood up and reached for the cup on the table. She held it out to Sophie, who tried to wrap her trembling right hand around the handle. Her grip faltered, and the pain on her face was almost more than Karen could bear.

Sophie cursed, her frustration boiling over as the cup slipped from her grasp, almost spilling the hot tea. Karen kept hold of the cup, narrowly avoiding the scalding liquid splashing on to Sophie's lap.

Sophie crumpled into herself, tears streaming down her cheeks. 'I can't even do that right.'

'It's okay,' Karen said softly, moving to sit beside her.

Sophie started to sob; her left hand balled into a fist as she struggled to regain control.

Karen tried to find the right words. 'I know this is hard. And it's not the same, but there was a time I was scared I'd never feel like myself again, too. It wasn't a physical injury, but after I lost Tilly and Josh, the guilt nearly destroyed me. I was in a bad place, scared I wouldn't be able to go back to work, worried I'd never be the same.'

Sophie's sobs were replaced by quiet sniffles as she wiped her eyes with the back of her hand. Her eyes held a vulnerability Karen had never seen before.

'I . . . I don't know if I can get through this,' Sophie admitted, her voice cracking. 'I've tried so hard, but it's not good enough. Being a police officer is who I am. What if I can't ever go back?'

'Listen,' Karen said. 'We both know how tough you are. You wouldn't have made it this far otherwise. But you need to give yourself time to heal. I promise things will get better.'

'I'm useless.' Sophie shook her head.

'Your job does not define your worth. You are strong, intelligent, and one of the most dedicated officers I've ever met. It will be difficult, but you'll get through this.'

Sophie looked down at her lap again and sniffed. She gave a weak smile. 'One of the most dedicated officers? More than Rick?'

Karen grinned. 'Oh, you're not catching me out there!'

Sophie and Rick had a close but competitive relationship, each always trying to outdo the other at work.

Sophie fidgeted with the corner of the quilt. Her expression was a mix of doubt and gratitude, as though she desperately wanted to believe what Karen was saying but couldn't quite convince herself.

'Thank you,' she said, her voice thick with emotion. 'That . . . that means a lot to me.'

'I wish I could help more, but I think it's time you need.'

'What I need is to stop throwing myself a pity party.' Sophie's face was grim. 'My parents have to tiptoe around me in case they set me off, and Harinder is walking on eggshells. I'm being such a brat.'

'They love you.'

'I know. I'm lucky. It's just hard. I thought I'd be better by now. I'm not a patient person.'

That was an understatement. Sophie was a Type A personality: precise and fastidious, she liked to be in control.

Before Karen could reply, her phone vibrated with an incoming call. She glanced at the screen.

'Sorry, Sophie, I need to take this.'

'Of course.' Sophie settled back on the sofa as Karen lifted the phone to her ear.

A minute later, Karen ended the call and said, 'There's been a report of a missing child, possibly an abduction. I need to get to the crime scene.'

'That doesn't sound good.'

'You'll be okay?'

Sophie nodded and managed a smile.

'Promise me you'll take it one day at a time,' Karen said as she stood up.

'I will.' The earlier bitterness had faded from Sophie's voice, and she almost seemed like her old self again.

Karen headed back to her car, her thoughts divided between the missing-child case and Sophie. The younger officer had been so low recently, her self-belief shattered.

She was determined to find a way to lift Sophie's spirits. A purpose, a way to feel useful – that was what Sophie needed. And it was up to Karen to give it to her.

Chapter Two

Karen got out of her car. It was the first warm day they'd had this year, and the weather had drawn people out of their homes to enjoy the sunshine. Tattershall Castle was up ahead. The old red bricks had taken on a rosy glow in the bright sunlight.

Karen had visited the castle before. A National Trust property, it had been rebuilt by Lord Ralph Cromwell, Treasurer of England, in the fifteenth century. Inside, there was a staircase that led up to the battlements at the top of the tower, which allowed impressive views over the Lincolnshire countryside and the RAF Coningsby air base.

The grounds were usually lively, bustling with families and tourists. But today the place felt sombre.

After crossing the bridge over the shallow moat, Karen walked towards the main tower, which dominated the landscape. A falconer looked up from securing a kestrel in its cage. His face solemn, he gave Karen a respectful nod. 'Afternoon, Officer.'

Though she wore a simple white shirt, neatly tucked into grey trousers, and black low-heeled boots – her usual work attire – he'd still tagged her as a police officer.

The grounds were well maintained, and the grass was thick and soft beneath her feet as she made her way towards the crowd. Seeing Karen approach, a murmur passed through the visitors, their concerned faces showing a mixture of curiosity and dread. They watched her, hoping for answers. Whispers circulated as parents kept their young children close.

Three uniformed officers stood under the spreading canopy of a huge oak tree. They had cordoned off the area and were talking to small groups of people in turn.

Karen's gaze swept over the onlookers. She hoped the incident would turn out to be nothing more sinister than a child wandering off of his own accord, but if the young boy had been abducted, surely someone here must have seen something.

'DS Hart?' a voice called out.

She turned to see a tall, uniformed officer with short blond hair approaching her. His expression was grim. Karen recognised him as PC Richards.

She nodded at him. 'What have we got?'

'An eleven-year-old boy, Tommy Burton, disappeared from the area about an hour ago. His mother, Amber Burton, last saw him sitting by that oak tree.'

'Did any witnesses see Tommy wandering away?' Karen asked, surveying the crowd once more.

'None so far, but we haven't spoken to everyone yet.' Richards sighed, rubbing the back of his neck. 'The castle is now closed to tourists, but we've asked the visitors who were here at the time to stay so we can find out if anyone saw anything, and get their details if we need to follow up.'

'Good work. It might be an idea to ask them to check any photographs or videos they've taken here. Do you have a description of Tommy?'

'White, short brown hair. Five foot tall, slim build, glasses with a round frame.' Richardson flipped open his notebook and continued. 'He was wearing a red hoodie, a green T-shirt with a robot on it, dark blue jeans and white trainers. His mother has some recent photos of Tommy on her phone, so I've been using one when I ask people if they saw him.'

'Good. What about the moat?' Karen suggested.

'We considered that. PC Nicks had a look round but didn't see anything untoward, and with all these people around . . .' Richards gestured towards the crowd. 'It's unlikely he'd have fallen in without anyone noticing. The water is only knee-deep.'

'Who was Tommy here with today? Just his mother?'

Richards nodded.

'Any indication that he might have wandered off?' Karen asked, her mind already racing through possibilities.

'His mother mentioned they'd had a disagreement,' Richards replied, hesitating for a moment before adding, 'but she doesn't think it was serious enough for him to run away.'

'What about the father?'

'He's at work.'

'But Tommy's parents are still together? This isn't a shared custody arrangement?' Karen asked, wanting to eliminate the most likely scenario first. If Tommy's mother and father had had a hostile split, the boy's father would be the first person Karen would want to speak to. Estranged fathers were often the first suspects that needed to be ruled out, and statistics showed immediate family members were often involved in cases of missing children.

'I didn't ask. But she didn't mention any custody battles or anything like that.'

'Okay. Thank you,' Karen said. 'Where is his mother now?'

'Over there, in one of our cars,' Richards said, pointing towards the staff parking area. 'She had a panic attack just after we arrived. So we thought it best to keep her somewhere quiet, away from the gawpers.' He nodded at the crowd.

'All right,' Karen said. 'Keep asking the visitors questions. I'll speak with Amber.'

As much as she'd have liked to give Tommy's distraught mother some space, they didn't have time for that. Tommy needed to be located quickly.

Karen glanced once more at the ancient oak tree, its branches reaching out like twisted fingers grasping for answers. The sun filtered through the leaves, casting dappled shadows on the patchy grass below.

Karen shivered, despite the warmth of the sun. She turned to walk over to the car park and then stopped, thinking of another question to ask Richards. 'Have we asked about CCTV footage yet?'

'Someone is arranging access now. We should have it soon. And . . . just a minute . . . I need to show you something.'

Richards approached a colleague and returned, holding a clear evidence bag. 'It might not be relevant. Probably just dropped by another child . . . but we found this toy bear by the oak tree where Tommy was last seen. Mrs Burton says it isn't his, and he's a bit old for teddies, but we bagged it just in case.'

Karen extended her hand, taking the evidence bag and examining its contents. Inside was a blue teddy bear, its plush fur pristine, as if it had been recently plucked from the shelf of a toyshop. Its black eyes gleamed, and its stitched smile seemed strangely creepy in the circumstances.

'I'm glad you bagged it,' Karen said, snapping a quick photo of the bear with her mobile and then handing back the evidence bag. 'It's best to be cautious. We might need SOCOs.'

'Really?' Richards wiped his forehead. 'You think someone has taken the boy?'

Karen frowned. Richards's voice was too loud for her liking, and she didn't want any onlookers to overhear. 'We can't discount anything yet.'

Of course, she hoped Tommy would be found quickly, but it had now been an hour since he was last seen, and that worried Karen.

'Understood,' Richards replied, his gaze lingering on the blue bear.

As Karen made her way to the staff parking area, she prepared herself for the difficult conversation ahead. She spotted Amber Burton sitting in the back seat of one of the marked cars. The car door was open. The woman's face was pale, and her eyes were red and puffy from crying.

Karen's chest tightened. Cases involving children were always especially hard. Amber Burton was living every parent's worst nightmare.

She introduced herself to the female officer standing beside the car.

'Have you found him?' Amber's voice was hoarse, and her eyes were desperate as she focused on Karen. 'Please tell me he's all right.'

'I'm sorry, Mrs Burton, we haven't found him yet,' Karen said softly. 'I'd like to ask you a few questions about Tommy if that's all right?'

Amber slumped back in her seat. Her mobile phone was on her lap, her handbag on the seat beside her. Make-up was smudged beneath her red-rimmed eyes. 'Sure.' She sniffed, wiping her face with a crumpled tissue. 'Anything to help find him.'

'Has anything like this happened before? Has Tommy ever wandered off or got lost?'

'No, never,' Amber replied, shaking her head. 'He's usually glued to his computer screen at home. He doesn't go out much.'

'Is there anyone he might have arranged to meet here, any friends he could have slipped away to see?'

Amber hesitated for a moment, thinking. 'I don't think so,' she admitted. 'Tommy doesn't have many friends. He's going through a stage where he's more interested in gaming and technology than people.'

'Did you notice anything unusual or different about Tommy's behaviour today, or spot anyone around him who seemed suspicious?'

Amber's eyes widened. 'You think something terrible has happened to him, don't you?'

'Not at all. These are just routine questions I have to ask.'

The woman tried to regain control, clutching the tissue in her hand. 'All right. I didn't notice anyone suspicious. Tommy's been a bit . . . temperamental, but that's usual for him. His teachers say it's because he's so clever. He gets frustrated.'

'Where do you and Tommy live?' Karen asked.

Amber sniffed again and said, 'Washingborough.'

Karen nodded thoughtfully. Washingborough was a village about twenty miles' drive from Tattershall. There were buses that serviced that route, though he'd have to change. 'Would Tommy have been able to make his own way home if he got lost?'

Amber blinked. 'I . . . uh . . . maybe. But he has his mobile, so he would have just called me. Unless . . .'

'Unless what?' Karen prompted.

'He was annoyed with me for making him come here today,' Amber said miserably. 'He might have decided to go home to spite me.'

'Is he familiar with public transport?' Karen didn't voice her concern that Tommy might have tried to get a lift.

'No, not really. I usually drive everywhere, or we walk.'

'Did he have any money on him, or a bus pass?'

'No.' Amber shook her head emphatically but then paused. 'But Tommy is bright. He's resourceful . . .'

21

'Is anyone at home now who could check?'

'No, but a neighbour has our spare key. She's been away but is due back today. I can call and ask her to see if Tommy is home.'

'Good, but first, I just have a couple more questions. Where's Tommy's dad?'

'At work.'

'Have you told him Tommy is missing?'

'I haven't been able to get through.' Amber glared at the phone on her lap. 'It just rings out. Gareth puts his mobile on silent if he's in a meeting.'

'Is there a main switchboard? A receptionist?'

'I think so, but I don't have the number. I always call his mobile if I need him.'

'If you give me the details for your husband's place of work, we'll get in touch with him.'

After Amber provided the details, Karen turned to the uniformed officer and asked her to contact the company.

'One more question, Mrs Burton,' Karen said. 'The blue teddy bear . . .'

'I've already said I've never seen it before. It doesn't belong to Tommy.'

'Are you sure? It was found close to where you last saw him.'

'Positive,' Amber insisted, irritation creeping into her voice. 'I saw it by the tree. I don't know where it came from or who it belongs to, but it's not Tommy's. And right now, I couldn't care less about some toy. My son is missing, and all anyone seems to be doing is asking me about a stupid teddy bear!'

'Mrs Burton, I understand how difficult this must be for you,' Karen said, placing a calming hand on the woman's arm. 'But we have to explore every possible angle to find your son. That includes seemingly insignificant details, like this toy.'

The anger drained from Amber's face as quickly as it had appeared. 'I'm sorry. It's just . . . I can't help but feel this is my fault. If I'd paid more attention to him . . .' Her face crumpled.

'Listen to me, Amber,' Karen said firmly. 'You are not to blame for what's happened.'

As she spoke, a familiar figure approached. DI Morgan, looking characteristically stoic, made his way towards them.

Karen asked Amber to call her neighbour to check if Tommy had come home, and then excused herself to talk to Morgan.

'What's the situation?' he asked.

'Tommy Burton, eleven years old, missing for over an hour now,' Karen reported. 'His mother, Amber Burton, last saw him by that oak tree, and uniform have secured the scene. We're waiting to access CCTV footage, but something is bothering me . . .'

'What?' Morgan asked, his eyes narrowing in anticipation of what she would say.

'A blue teddy bear was found near where Tommy was last seen.' Karen showed him the photograph on her phone. 'Amber Burton insists it doesn't belong to her son. It might be nothing, but something about it just . . . feels off.'

Morgan's eyes locked on to the photo. Karen saw a flicker of surprise, perhaps even shock, pass across his usually inscrutable face. He took the phone from her, zooming in on the photo.

'Where was this found?' he asked, his voice tight as he stared at the screen.

'By the old oak tree,' Karen replied, watching Morgan closely. 'That's where Tommy was sitting to watch the bird show. Why? Do you think it's relevant?'

Morgan hesitated, then met Karen's gaze. 'I worked on a case in Oxford years ago,' he said, his voice low so no one else would overhear. 'Three boys were abducted, and a blue teddy bear was found at each scene.'

It was Karen's turn to feel a jolt of shock. 'You think this is something similar? A message? A link to that crime?' Her stomach knotted with dread at the implication.

'Maybe,' Morgan muttered. 'Could just be a coincidence.' He ran a hand through his hair and handed Karen back her phone.

'I assumed another child had dropped it, but it looks new, doesn't it?' Karen said, looking at the screen. The toy suddenly seemed far more ominous than it had earlier.

'Yes,' Morgan said. 'It does.'

'Tell me more about the Oxford case,' Karen said quietly as she leaned towards Morgan. 'How long ago was it?'

'Fifteen years,' Morgan said, his eyes clouding with memories. 'Three young boys went missing under similar circumstances. In each case, a blue teddy bear was left at the scene.' He hesitated before continuing, his words measured and careful. 'We apprehended the man responsible, Graham Donaldson. As far as I know, he's still behind bars. This detail' – he gestured at the picture on Karen's phone – 'was never released to the public.'

'I remember the press coverage of the Donaldson case. How old were the boys?'

'Between seven and nine.'

Karen nodded thoughtfully. Tommy was eleven – a bit older, but in the same ballpark. She bit her lip, her mind whirring as she processed the new information.

Checking on Graham Donaldson was a priority.

Karen took in a breath and looked back at Amber Burton, who was talking on her phone. Karen hoped for all their sakes that the little blue bear was just a coincidence, but her instincts told her Tommy Burton was in desperate trouble.

She looked past Morgan to the oak, the gnarled branches a silent witness to whatever had happened to Tommy.

'If Donaldson is still in prison,' Karen said slowly, 'this might be a copycat. Or maybe Donaldson has someone on the outside doing his bidding.'

'I hope not,' Morgan said. 'That case was one of the worst I've ever worked on.'

It was disconcerting to see Morgan so visibly rattled; he was usually so cool and controlled.

'What happened to the boys?' Karen asked.

Morgan shook his head almost imperceptibly. 'None of them survived.'

Chapter Three

As the time neared four p.m., Karen rubbed her temples, fighting off the throbbing headache that had been plaguing her for the past hour. She pushed open the door to the stuffy briefing room and was greeted by the drone of voices discussing the details surrounding Tommy Burton's disappearance.

Karen took a moment to observe everyone in the room. Most of her colleagues were already seated, and they chatted among themselves. DC Rick Cooper – his usually cheeky, cheerful face solemn – stared at his laptop screen. Next to him was DC Farzana Shah, her delicate features sharpened with concern. Across from them was Morgan, frowning as he sifted through briefing notes. Beside him was DS Arnie Hodgson, a grumpy, cynical older detective with an uncanny ability to read people.

Team briefings didn't feel the same without Sophie. Karen could almost picture her sitting up straight in one of the chairs, notepad and pen neatly in front of her, always first to volunteer to hand out the briefing notes.

Would Sophie ever make it back to the team? The thought of losing her permanently was troubling. With her Type A personality, Sophie's intensity and enthusiasm could be overwhelming at times, but there was no doubt she brought a warmth to the briefing room and was deeply missed.

'Tommy Burton's parents must be frantic,' Farzana said when she spotted Karen.

'They are,' Karen admitted in a low voice, her thoughts drifting back to her own family – her own loss. The hurt of losing loved ones never truly faded.

During the search, Karen's mind had kept returning to her daughter, Tilly. Though she had lost her child in very different circumstances, she couldn't help thinking this could be a chance to prevent another family from experiencing the same pain. But she knew the statistics – the odds of finding a missing child diminished rapidly as time passed. After forty-eight hours, the chances of recovering Tommy alive would have dropped significantly.

'All right?' Arnie grunted in greeting as Karen slid into the seat next to him. She nodded in response, but DCI Churchill swept into the room before she could reply.

'Let's get started.' DCI Churchill's commanding voice cut through the chatter in the room. Impeccably dressed as usual, he stopped at the head of the table, his eyes zeroing in on Karen. 'DS Hart, you first.'

Karen straightened in her seat, glancing down at her notes before speaking. 'Rachel King, the Burtons' neighbour, has confirmed that Tommy didn't return home under his own steam, so this is looking more and more like an abduction. Uniformed officers are widening the search of the local area and going door-to-door to talk to residents in Tattershall. Rick's heading up the team going through the CCTV, trying to find out where Tommy went and who he was with. A family liaison officer has been assigned to the Burtons. He'll be reporting back directly to me.'

'What do we know about Tommy's family? Any reason someone might target them specifically?'

'Tommy is an only child and lives with both parents at 4 Dahlia Close in Washingborough,' Karen said. 'As far as I can tell, there's nothing unusual about their family life, other than the fact that Tommy is often online.'

'Ha,' Arnie scoffed. 'That's not unusual these days. Seems to me that most kids are practically glued to their electronic devices.'

'Could Tommy have been groomed in some fashion?' Churchill asked, his brow furrowing.

'It's possible. Neither parent believes Tommy was vulnerable to grooming,' Karen replied, a hint of doubt creeping into her voice. 'But as we all know, parents can often be unaware. Tommy is into computers and loves gaming. He might have been targeted by someone online.'

'Then,' Churchill said, tapping his finger against the table, 'we have to look at that angle closely. We need to find out if he has been communicating with anyone online without his mum and dad's knowledge. Also, talk to Tommy's friends and his teachers. They might know more than the parents.' He then turned his attention to Rick. 'What can you tell us about the CCTV footage?'

'We're looking at footage from local venues and buses around the time Tommy went missing,' said the young detective. 'We're also trying to access the security system at Tattershall Castle itself.'

'What's the delay?' Churchill asked, his eyebrows raised.

'Unfortunately,' Rick began, exasperation creeping into his voice, 'a private firm manages the castle's security, and we've been experiencing some difficulties accessing the car park feed. To make things worse, the coverage of the castle grounds is patchy at best – there are several blind spots.'

Farzana muttered a curse under her breath. Karen shared her frustration.

'Has the boy been picked up on *any* surveillance footage?' Churchill asked.

'No, sir,' Rick replied. 'We haven't found any images of Tommy leaving the castle or in the general vicinity yet.'

'Not even when he arrived with his mother?'

'No.'

Churchill's face hardened. 'How is that possible? How do we know he was really there? Do you think Tommy's mother is lying about having Tommy with her? We know she was there.'

'No, sir. The cameras only focus on one small section of the entrance and exit. They could have walked through the area not covered by the cameras.'

Churchill frowned. 'Keep pushing for that car park feed. Stay in touch with uniform and coordinate efforts. Time is of the essence.'

'Understood, sir,' Rick said grimly. He was all too aware of the ticking clock. They all were.

'All right, everyone,' Churchill said, his voice sharp. 'Turn to page four of your briefing notes. I want you to take a good look at the photograph there.'

Karen flipped the pages, and her gaze landed on a photograph of the small blue teddy bear. Its glassy eyes stared back at her.

'DI Morgan,' Churchill said, 'why don't you brief the team on the key details of the Oxford abductions? I know most of you are familiar with the case, but a refresher on the specifics would be helpful.'

Morgan nodded. 'Fifteen years ago, when I was a DC in Oxford, three separate abductions occurred in four months. As many of you know already, the similarities to our current case are striking. All the victims were young boys. One aged seven and two aged nine. Henry Tisdale, Marc White and Stuart O'Connor. A blue teddy bear, just like this one, was found in the area where each boy was last seen.' He tapped the photo on the page. 'A man named Graham Donaldson was arrested, tried, and convicted for the crimes. He's still in jail today.'

Karen felt relief wash over her at hearing Donaldson was still locked up, but it was quickly replaced by frustration. If Donaldson was still in jail, then who had taken Tommy? They were no closer to identifying a suspect.

'Was Donaldson ever suspected of having accomplices?' she asked.

'No,' Morgan replied, shaking his head. 'And he's always maintained his innocence, despite the evidence against him.' His voice grew sombre. 'There's one more thing, which strikes me as unusual. Donaldson was recently moved to Lincoln Prison.'

Questions swirled in Karen's mind. Why had Donaldson been moved? Was it at his request? Was it related to Tommy's abduction? Surely it had to be. The timing seemed too close for comfort.

'Could be a coincidence,' an officer near the front of the room offered.

Arnie cut in. 'If it looks like a duck and quacks like a duck . . .'

'Then it's a duck,' Rick said, looking up from his laptop.

'Or a very confused chicken,' Arnie deadpanned, eliciting a few chuckles from around the room.

Karen smiled at his attempt to use humour to boost their morale, though her thoughts quickly returned to the case and, in particular, how it might connect to Donaldson's crimes.

'I want you to re-familiarise yourself with the Donaldson case, Morgan,' Churchill said. 'I do not like the similarities.'

'I've started on that,' Morgan said, 'And I'd like permission to visit Donaldson in prison. Maybe he knows something about this.'

'Definitely,' Churchill agreed. 'But be careful how much you tell him. Contact the prison service and arrange a meeting with him, and then we'll work through an interview strategy. Considering the serious nature of this case, you should be able to visit the prison today.'

'I've already contacted them, and I'm waiting for a call back.' Morgan hesitated before adding, 'I could also talk to my old boss,

DCI Tranmere. He arrested Donaldson. Maybe he has some theories. Something that could help us.'

'Tranmere?' Churchill raised an eyebrow. 'I'm not familiar with the name.'

'He's retired now, but worked for Thames Valley his entire career. He's a good man. I learned a lot from him.'

'Okay. Give him a call.'

'I'd prefer to see him in person, to go over the details.'

Churchill frowned. 'I don't think I can spare the manpower to send you on an excursion to Oxford.'

'He doesn't live in Oxford anymore. After he retired, he moved to Mablethorpe. It's only an hour from here, across the Wolds.'

Churchill hesitated, so Morgan pressed his point further. 'He might provide some insights we're missing. Tranmere knows the case inside out. If anyone can spot connections we might have overlooked, it's him. Meeting with him is worth the short drive.'

'All right, pay him a visit, but Donaldson remains your priority.'

Satisfied, Morgan nodded, and Churchill turned his attention to the rest of the team. 'DC Cooper, I want you to redouble your efforts to find Tommy on the CCTV and retrace his steps. DC Shah, find out where we stand on tracing Tommy's missing phone. Morgan, keep looking for any possible connections to the Donaldson case. Leave no stone unturned. Karen, I want you to go and talk to Tommy's parents again. I know you said we have a family liaison officer with them, but they might know something they don't realise. And look into any other adults Tommy has come into contact with recently – after-school classes, hobbies, that sort of thing.'

'I'll head there straight after the briefing,' Karen replied.

'Let's keep pushing forward, everyone,' DCI Churchill said, bringing the briefing to a close. 'We'll find Tommy. Just keep focused, and stay sharp.'

◆ ◆ ◆

Karen stepped out of the briefing room and saw Harinder approaching.

'Any word on Tommy Burton's phone?' he asked.

Karen tucked the briefing notes under her arm as she shook her head. 'No sign of his mobile yet, but the search team are looking out for it. Farzana is chasing it up with the phone company. Did you manage to get anything from the cloud?'

'We're still working on that. The phone last pinged the tower at Tattershall just before Tommy disappeared, meaning someone likely removed the battery or SIM card.'

Harinder didn't need to explain to Karen why that was bad news. It added more weight to the theory Tommy had been taken by someone who was carefully hiding their tracks.

'The tech lab has received Tommy Burton's other electronic devices,' Harinder said. 'We're working on extracting information from them.'

'Any luck with social media?'

'Nothing yet. But we're working our way through his messages.' He gently put his hand on Karen's elbow and guided her away from a group of officers passing them. She guessed from the furrows on Harinder's forehead that he was concerned about something other than the case.

'Did you speak to Sophie earlier?' he asked in a low voice – almost a whisper.

'Yes, I did,' Karen replied, remembering the sad, defeated look in Sophie's eyes. 'I managed to pop in at lunchtime, before I got the call about Tommy Burton.'

'Is she okay? I mean . . . she just seems so . . . depressed,' Harinder said. His worried expression made it clear how much he cared for Sophie.

'She's struggling, but she'll get through it. It's just going to take time,' Karen reassured him, though she couldn't dismiss her own nagging doubts.

Harinder sighed. 'I've been researching recovery times and programmes for similar injuries. I've set up appointments with new therapists.' He spread his hands. 'I'm doing everything I can to help, but it just annoys her.'

Karen placed a hand on Harinder's shoulder. 'Sophie has had lots of doctors and medical professionals helping her lately. Maybe she wants you to be there as her boyfriend, not another healthcare professional. She probably needs things to feel normal again.'

Harinder mulled over Karen's words, his expression softening. 'You're right; I hadn't thought of it like that. I've been so focused on helping her recover that I didn't consider what she really needs is to feel like herself again.'

'Maybe ease back on the medical talk and take the focus away from her injuries. Treat her like the old Sophie,' Karen said. 'It might help.'

'That makes sense.'

'Recovering at her parents' house must be difficult for Sophie.' Karen paused, noticing Harinder's solemn expression. 'And for you, too, I imagine.'

Harinder exhaled, nodding. 'It's not easy, but it's the best option for now.'

Karen hesitated before broaching a more delicate topic. 'How are you getting on with Geoff these days?'

Geoff Jones, Sophie's father, had initially suspected Harinder of the assault, and had banned him from visiting Sophie in the hospital during those crucial early days. Even Karen herself had experienced some doubts about the mild-mannered tech guru. She felt her body go cold at the memory, recalling the tension and uncertainty that had shadowed their team following the brutal attack.

'Much better, actually,' Harinder replied with a small smile. 'We've cleared the air, and we've been bonding. He showed me his collection of replica aircraft. You know, the small model planes?'

'Yes, I think I know the type you mean,' Karen said. She hadn't known Geoff was into model aircraft.

'He's quite proud of them. We're going to make one together next week.' Harinder looked slightly bemused by the idea, but Karen thought he was probably welcoming the opportunity to build bridges with Geoff.

It was important that Sophie's support system was united. She imagined Harinder and Geoff working together, carefully assembling the tiny pieces of a model plane. It seemed like a fitting metaphor for the slow, delicate work of rebuilding the trust between them.

'Good. I'm glad to hear that.' Karen leaned against the wall. 'Sophie needs all of us right now. But most importantly, she needs you.'

'I won't let her down.'

'I know.'

As Karen started to walk away, Harinder called, 'Thanks for the advice.'

'Anytime,' she said, her thoughts already returning to the Tommy Burton case, even as concern for Sophie lingered in the back of her mind.

Chapter Four

It was almost five when Karen pulled up in front of the Burtons' house on Dahlia Close. The neat flowerbeds and cheerful hanging baskets gave the impression of a well-tended, happy home, but the drawn curtains hinted at the family's turmoil. She'd been at the house a couple of hours earlier, before leaving Tommy's distraught parents in the capable hands of PC Jim Willson, the family liaison officer.

As Karen approached the front door, it swung open, and Gareth, Tommy's father, stepped out. He was a tall, broad-shouldered man with thinning dark hair.

'Have you found him?' he asked abruptly, his eyes hopeful.

'Not yet, but we're following every lead. Is it all right if I have a quick word with Jim?'

Gareth waved her inside, looking deflated as he turned away. He didn't seem quite as angry as he had earlier.

Karen stepped inside and made her way to the small kitchen, with its wood countertops and bright sunflower-yellow walls. Jim was pouring boiling water into a teapot. The scent of brewing tea filled the room, creating an oddly normal atmosphere despite the tension.

She pushed the kitchen door closed behind her and kept her voice low as she asked, 'How's it going?'

'I've tried to get them talking but had no joy. I didn't want to push them.'

'Sensible,' Karen replied. 'How are they both holding up?'

'They're struggling, as you can imagine. Gareth is still furious at everyone and everything, and Amber blames herself. They're both devastated.' He nodded at the teapot. 'Want a cup?'

'Yes, thank you,' Karen said. 'I'll see if I can get them to open up to me.'

The security cameras at Tattershall Castle hadn't picked up Tommy or Amber. So far, they only had Amber's word to rely on. What if she was lying about taking Tommy to the castle? Could Tommy's parents be attempting some kind of cover-up?

Karen suppressed a shiver as she recalled a case she'd worked on near the start of her career, where the parents had tried to hide the death of their baby by pretending the child had been abducted. She hated to think it, but the possibility that Gareth or even Amber had done something to Tommy at home and was now trying to cover it up had to be considered.

The team had checked the ANPR system, and Amber's car had travelled from Washingborough to Tattershall as she'd described, but that didn't necessarily mean Tommy had been with her.

Gareth's short temper in particular worried Karen. It was a potential red flag. Officers back at the station were looking into his background, but so far hadn't uncovered anything untoward.

Karen was sickened by the thought of any parent being violent to their own child, but it did happen. She couldn't dismiss the possibility. When she'd spoken to them earlier, her instincts had told her that the Burtons were genuinely concerned for their son. But she wanted to make sure.

The liaison officer carried the tea tray into the living room, where Amber and Gareth Burton sat on a cream sofa. Amber clutched a scrunched-up tissue, and Gareth sat with his arms crossed over his chest. The room was small, and cluttered with family photos and knick-knacks. There was a recent school photograph of Tommy in a silver frame on the mantelpiece.

'I'm sorry to trouble you again so soon,' Karen said as she sat opposite Amber and Gareth, accepting a cup of tea from Jim. 'I know this is difficult, but I need to ask some more questions, to help us find Tommy.'

'Of course,' Amber replied, her voice shaky. 'Anything to help bring him home.'

'I wanted to ask you about Tommy's online activities. You told me he spends a lot of time on the computer.'

'Yes, he spends all his spare time on the Xbox or glued to his phone,' Amber said.

'Well, not all the time,' Gareth said. 'We play football at the park at weekends and go for bike rides.'

'It must be at least six months since you did anything like that,' Amber said, tightening her hold on the tissue in her hand.

'I've been working. I took tomorrow off to spend time with him, didn't I?' He glared at his wife.

'Is it possible Tommy could have been communicating with someone online – someone you don't know?' Karen asked, trying to phrase the question as delicately as possible.

'I suppose so—' Amber started to say.

'Absolutely not,' Gareth interrupted, his face reddening. 'Tommy knows better than to talk to strangers. Sure, he plays some online games, but they're harmless things – Minecraft, Roblox, Fortnite, that sort of thing. He isn't involved in any weird communities or anything like that.'

Karen noted the defensiveness in Gareth's posture: his arms tightened over his chest and his muscles tensed. She needed to tread carefully, but getting answers was vital. Tommy could have met someone online who had played a role in his disappearance.

'Gareth, I understand it's difficult to accept, but we have to consider every angle. Kids are naturally more trusting than adults, and sometimes they can be drawn into situations they don't fully understand. Are you sure you don't know any online groups or forums Tommy frequented? He might have believed he was communicating with another child.'

'Look, I've already told you,' Gareth snapped, 'my son wouldn't talk to strangers. We explained the dangers, and he was careful. You should be out there looking for him, not wasting time questioning us again.'

Karen took a deep breath. She knew Gareth's anger was rooted in fear for his son and not directed at her personally, but it still stung.

'Please understand that we are doing everything possible to find Tommy,' Karen said. 'But to do that, we need to gather as much information as we can, even if it's painful to consider. Sometimes gaming communities can foster close connections with other players – people who might know something about where Tommy is now.'

They would get more information about Tommy's online presence from his electronic devices eventually, but if his parents suspected anyone, it could give the team a head start.

Karen searched Gareth's face for any sign of deception. But she only saw a father desperately worried about his son.

Amber wrung her hands together. 'I have to admit, I don't know much about Tommy's online life,' she said, her voice barely above a whisper. 'I've been so busy with work . . . I should have been more involved.'

'Are you serious?' Gareth exploded. 'You're his mother, for pity's sake! You should know what he's doing online!'

'Gareth, please,' Amber pleaded, tears welling in her eyes. 'I didn't think it was a problem. He's always been responsible and advanced for his age.'

'He's only eleven. You should have been making sure that—'

'Tommy is your son, too!' Amber shouted back, her voice cracking under the weight of her emotions.

Karen decided to intervene before things escalated further. She got up and placed a reassuring hand on Amber's shoulder, feeling her trembling beneath her touch.

'It's impossible to watch them every second of the day,' Karen said. 'Children can be targeted online, sometimes leading to dangerous situations. But there's no evidence that this is what has happened to Tommy.'

Yet . . . Karen mentally added. Right now, it seemed to be the most likely scenario.

Gareth scoffed, shaking his head.

In Karen's opinion, Amber was punishing herself enough and didn't need Gareth or anyone else pointing fingers at her. The guilt in her eyes spoke volumes; Amber would do anything to turn back time and keep a closer eye on her son.

Amber dabbed at her eyes with the screwed-up tissue.

'We need to learn as much as possible about Tommy's online presence,' Karen continued as she sat back down. 'This isn't about blaming anyone; it's about finding Tommy and getting him home safely.'

Amber nodded, sniffing. 'You're right; I understand,' she said, her voice still shaky. 'I just wish I knew something that would help.'

'Anything you can remember might be of use,' Karen said, offering an encouraging smile.

Gareth's face hardened, his eyes narrowing as he glared at Karen. 'How about you stop wasting time interrogating us and focus on finding my son?' he said, clenching his fists. 'You're making my wife feel worse. You obviously have no idea what losing a child is like!'

The unfortunate choice of words cut through Karen like a knife. Memories of Tilly's funeral flooded her mind. She pictured the tiny wooden coffin with shiny gold handles and the pink and white flowers spelling out Tilly's name on top. Karen's mother had organised the flowers because Karen hadn't been in the right state of mind. Even though she hadn't been at the scene of the crash, it hadn't stopped her from dreaming about it. The reoccurring nightmare was now less frequent, but no less vivid. She heard the screech of tyres, the sickening crunch of metal against metal, and imagined Josh and Tilly's anguished cries.

Her chest tightened with the familiar pain, but she forced herself to stay composed. This wasn't about her or her loss; it was about Tommy Burton, and her job was to find him.

'Gareth,' Karen began firmly, 'I understand that you're under tremendous stress right now, but I promise we're doing everything in our power to find your son. A team of officers is searching for him in Tattershall and the surrounding area, and more officers are reviewing traffic cameras and other CCTV.' She looked at both Amber and Gareth. 'But it's important to consider all possibilities, including the people Tommy might have encountered online or in person.'

Karen drew from her experience of similar cases. Seemingly innocent connections could prove to be anything but. Children were lured away by someone they trusted more often than by strangers.

She needed the Burtons' help, but didn't want to scare them any more than they already were.

When neither Amber nor Gareth spoke, Karen added, 'Perhaps there was someone Tommy felt close to? Someone he might have confided in or considered a friend?'

Amber glanced hesitantly at Gareth, who remained sullen and uncooperative. But Karen could see the fear in his eyes, the desperate need to find his son warring with his anger.

As the seconds ticked by, the room seemed to shrink around them, suffocating and tense. The muted light from the window cast long shadows, making the space feel even more confined. Gareth got up from the sofa and began to pace the length of the living room, his movements agitated.

'Can you show me Tommy's room again, Amber?' Karen asked, deciding her best chance of getting answers was to get Tommy's mother alone.

Gareth's anger was preventing him from opening up, and Karen suspected that – though he'd been quick to point the finger at his wife – he felt responsible, and the guilt was eating him up. But his earlier explosive reaction might be stopping Amber from confiding something important.

Karen hadn't seen anything to suggest Gareth was physically violent at home, despite his outburst earlier. Amber hadn't flinched when he'd raised his voice. She hadn't cowered when he moved suddenly.

'All right,' Amber conceded, standing up slowly. She led Karen upstairs.

Entering Tommy's bedroom again, Karen was immediately struck by the distinctive personality of the space. The walls were adorned with posters of fantasy worlds and dragons, while a small, white bookshelf overflowed with *Star Trek* novels and fantasy stories. *Star Wars* figurines dotted the shelves, too. A neatly made bed had a duvet cover that matched the curtains: both printed with spaceships and planets. Tommy clearly had a love for science fiction and adventure.

Karen's gaze travelled along the spines of the books, trying to imagine what kind of boy Tommy was – intelligent, creative, perhaps a bit introverted. She wished she could glimpse his online world as easily as his bedroom, but that would take time. The tech team had already taken his electronic devices for analysis, and eventually they would build up a full picture of Tommy's life.

'I'm not sure who he was playing with online,' Amber finally said, her voice breaking through the heavy silence. 'But Tommy did spend time with Adam Foster occasionally. He's in Tommy's year at school and lives at number three.'

'Okay, that's helpful. I'll speak to him,' Karen replied. 'If you think of anyone else, tell Jim, or you can call me directly. You have my card?'

Amber said she did, and they returned downstairs to find Gareth sitting on the sofa.

Karen said, 'Thank you both for your time. As I said, we'll continue to pursue every lead and keep you informed of any developments.'

Gareth gave a curt nod but didn't look up.

Karen stepped into the kitchen before she left. Jim was leaning against the counter, scrolling through his phone.

He smiled. 'Thought I'd give you some space. Any luck?'

'Maybe,' Karen said. 'I'm going to speak to one of the neighbours' sons, Adam Foster. Amber said he sometimes spends time with Tommy, so he might know something.'

Karen intended to speak with all the neighbours. It was only a small cul-de-sac, so it wouldn't take long.

Leaving the oppressive atmosphere of the Burtons' house behind her, Karen stepped out on to the driveway. The air was close and muggy, and the street felt claustrophobic, too. The houses seemed to crowd around her as she headed towards No. 3. There were no vehicles parked outside the house. Suspecting the Fosters were out, Karen pressed the doorbell anyway and waited.

Out of the corner of her eye, she saw the curtains twitch at No. 5.

Karen hesitated for a moment before changing tactics. Rachel King lived at No. 5. They'd checked with her earlier when trying to find out if Tommy had returned home under his own steam, but she thought it might be worth talking to her again, and hopefully, by the time Karen had finished talking to her, the Fosters would have returned home.

As she walked up the paved driveway to No. 5, Karen couldn't shake the feeling that she was being watched.

Her skin prickled as she looked over her shoulder, back towards the Burtons' house. Standing at the window, arms folded across his chest and glowering at her, was Gareth Burton.

Karen turned away. He might not see the point of her talking to the neighbours when Tommy had vanished in Tattershall. But Karen refused to rule anything out. Cases like this one could take unexpected turns, and one of the residents of Dahlia Close might provide information that could unlock the truth behind Tommy's disappearance.

Chapter Five

At just after five thirty p.m., Karen knocked on Rachel King's front door. Rachel had warm, hazel eyes and brown shoulder-length hair. She wore a loose-fitting floral blouse and a long red skirt.

Rachel gave a nervous smile as she gestured towards the interior of the house after Karen asked if she had time for a few questions.

As Karen stepped inside, she smelled lavender and noticed some dried sprigs in a bowl on the telephone table. The hallway walls were decorated with framed pictures of landscapes and flowers.

Rachel led her into the living room. A soft, well-worn armchair and a small sofa were arranged around a low glass coffee table. On the floor, two cats – one ginger and one dark grey – lazily lounged on a rug, eyeing Karen curiously.

'Can I get you a cup of tea?' Rachel asked.

Karen had just had one at the Burtons' and thought she'd be swimming in tea if she said yes, but she agreed anyway. There was something about drinking tea together that softened defences and helped people open up. The ritual cosiness allowed words to flow more easily.

As Rachel was the woman Amber Burton trusted with a key and had asked to check if Tommy had returned home under his own steam, Karen hoped Rachel would know a great deal about Tommy and his parents.

'Please, have a seat,' Rachel said, gesturing towards the sofa as she disappeared into the kitchen.

Karen settled down, her eyes wandering around the room. She noticed a black-and-white family photo on the mantelpiece, and a collection of porcelain ornaments on shelves lining one wall. The cats stretched lazily, their eyes still fixed on Karen as if trying to decide whether she was friend or foe.

'Here you go,' Rachel said, returning with two cups. She handed one to Karen, then sat in the armchair across from her.

Karen thanked her, took a sip, then asked, 'So, how long have you known the Burtons?'

Rachel leaned back, her gaze drifting to the window. 'A long time. They moved to Dahlia Close when Tommy was just one, so that makes it ten years.'

Karen nodded, taking another sip of her tea. 'What's Tommy like?'

Rachel sighed, her eyes clouding with concern. 'He's always been a quiet boy, but I've noticed him becoming more withdrawn these last few weeks.'

'Really?' Karen asked, leaning in slightly. 'In what way?'

Rachel hesitated, as if searching for the right words. 'He used to play in the garden, kicking his football against my fence.' She grimaced. 'It used to drive me mad, but I never said anything because I didn't want to be a bad neighbour, and kids will be kids. Lately, though, he's always indoors. Amber says he's on his computer all the time. I hardly see him in the garden anymore.'

Karen wondered if this was down to a phase Tommy was going through; or had something happened recently that made him want to stay indoors?

'Does Tommy have any friends in the neighbourhood?' she asked as the ginger cat strolled away from the rug and leapt on to the windowsill.

'Tommy used to play with Adam Foster, who lives next door. They were inseparable when they were in primary school,' Rachel said. 'But these days, I don't see them together much anymore. It's a shame.'

Adam Foster. It was the same boy Amber had mentioned. 'I think the family are out at the moment, but I'd like to talk to the Fosters.'

Rachel checked the time on her wristwatch. 'They often take the boys out for an early dinner after one of their activities. I forget which one it is tonight, but they're never home late. They should be back soon.'

'Is there anyone else Tommy was close to?'

'Yes, now that I think about it, you should have a word with Brooke . . .' She broke off, thinking. 'She lives at number two. She babysits Tommy on occasion.' Rachel smiled. 'Not that Tommy would like me using the word *babysits*. He considers himself a young man now, though he's only eleven.'

'Amber mentioned he's advanced for his age.'

'Yes . . .' Rachel hesitated. 'He is very bright. He gets top marks at school and is very talented when it comes to anything related to computers and technology. He has a precocious side, but in other ways he's very much still a child.'

'In what ways?' Karen asked.

'He's not above throwing a strop when he doesn't get his own way.' Rachel smiled to soften her words. 'Like most children really. But he's a nice boy. You might want to have a word with Lyra Hill, at number one, too. She's a teacher at Tommy's school. She might be able to help.'

'Thank you, I'll do that. Have there been any conflicts or issues in the neighbourhood recently?' Karen asked.

'Nothing serious, just the usual petty squabbles over parking spaces and overgrown hedges.' Rachel dismissed the idea with a wave of her hand. 'We all look out for each other here. It's a safe community, and we're proud of it.'

Karen nodded, thinking the close community could be useful. Watchful neighbours noticed things.

'Is there anything else you can tell me about the Burtons? How do they get on usually?' Karen asked, hoping to understand the family dynamics better.

Rachel shifted uneasily in her armchair. Karen guessed this was a little too close to gossip for her liking.

'I think Amber has been struggling lately, to be honest. She's a capable woman and a good mother, but she's been under a lot of stress with her job and trying to keep up with Tommy. Gareth helps sometimes, but I get the sense that most of the childcare falls to Amber.'

'Any arguments?'

'Nothing out of the ordinary,' Rachel said, hesitating slightly.

'What about over the last couple of days?'

'I've been away for a few days, visiting my sister, so I wouldn't know, but every couple has their disagreements, don't they?'

Karen nodded. She wanted to know if Rachel had seen or suspected any domestic violence. On another occasion she'd be more diplomatic with her questions, but skirting around the issue today was wasting precious time.

'I know this might be a tough question, but have you ever witnessed or heard anything that would make you suspect Tommy was being abused?'

'Heavens, no.' Rachel pressed a hand to her chest. 'They love Tommy. What made you ask a question like that?'

'We have to consider all possibilities.'

Rachel pursed her lips into a disapproving line, and Karen guessed she had probably pushed Rachel as far as she was willing to go on the subject.

Karen handed Rachel her card. 'Thank you for your help. If you think of anything else, give me a call.'

'I will. Tommy is a good boy, and his parents are beside themselves with worry.'

As Karen prepared to leave, Rachel's cats followed her to the door, rubbing against her legs. Karen thought their sudden affection – no doubt leaving their scent on her – would likely earn her the silent treatment from Mike's dog, Sandy, later.

As she walked back to her car, Karen considered the information she had gathered from Rachel. The Burtons seemed to have a good relationship with her, and Tommy appeared to be a clever young boy. Both Amber and Rachel had mentioned Tommy becoming more introverted recently, so she needed to work out why that might be. Had something happened to scare Tommy? Was he being bullied? Or possibly stalked by someone online?

She unlocked her car and opened the door to grab the water bottle from the cup holder. Twisting off the cap, Karen took a swig of the now warm water and then pulled a face. Lately, she'd been surviving on tea and coffee at work and had decided to make a concerted effort to drink more water.

She glanced at her phone, checking for any messages or updates on the case. A text from Morgan caught her eye: *Off to visit Donaldson at Lincoln Prison.*

Karen felt a pang of sympathy for Morgan; a prison visit could be an emotionally draining experience, and revisiting Donaldson would be hard for him. She hoped he'd get something useful from the conversation, but from Morgan's description of the child abductor, she didn't think it was likely. Not unless Donaldson wanted to boast.

Karen had never seen Morgan this shaken by an investigation. He was normally so cool and unruffled, but this had got under his skin.

As her gaze shifted from her phone, she noticed a Volvo estate parked on the Fosters' driveway. It seemed the family were finally home.

◆ ◆ ◆

Karen was keen to talk to Adam Foster. Even if he knew nothing about the abduction, Adam would likely be able to provide more insight into Tommy's recent behaviour. Sometimes kids confided in each other while keeping adults at arm's length.

She needed to convince Adam to confide in her, which might be challenging. Getting information from children could be a delicate process.

Karen reached the front door of the Fosters' house and rang the doorbell. A few moments later a woman appeared, wearing jeans and a blue T-shirt. Her hair looked damp, and her face was make-up free and shiny.

'Mrs Foster?' Karen held up her ID.

The woman nodded. 'Yes, Dawn Foster.'

'I'm Detective Sergeant Karen Hart. I'm sorry to disturb you. I'm talking to residents about Tommy Burton. Have you heard . . . ?'

'Yes, Rachel told me. It's awful. How are Amber and Gareth doing? Is there any news? Do you know if someone took him?'

Rather than answer the barrage of questions, Karen asked, 'Would it be okay if I came in for a few minutes and talked to you all? I was hoping to have a word with your sons, too.'

'Of course. The boys are upstairs. My husband is in the kitchen. I'll let them know you're here.' Dawn ran a hand through her hair self-consciously. 'We took the boys swimming and then went for pizza, hoping to take their minds off what's happened.' She led

Karen inside, guiding her to the living room and gesturing for her to sit. 'I'll go and get the boys.'

'Thank you, I appreciate it,' Karen said, sitting down.

Karen heard urgent whispers from the kitchen and suspected Dawn was letting her husband know they had a detective in their living room.

While she waited, Karen took in her surroundings, noting the family photos on the walls and mantelpiece. The room felt lived-in and comfortable.

'Detective Hart, this is my husband, Jerry,' Dawn said as a tall man with short, brown hair entered the room. He offered Karen a firm handshake before taking up a sentry position behind the sofa. The two boys followed closely behind; one looked around Tommy's age and the other slightly older. They sat on the sofa, watching Karen warily.

'This is Adam,' Dawn said, perching on the arm of the sofa and putting her hand on the smaller boy's shoulder. 'And this is Jack.' She nodded at the older boy, who met Karen's gaze briefly and then looked down at the floor.

'Hi, I'm Karen,' she said warmly, giving them a reassuring smile. 'I just wanted to ask you all a few questions about Tommy Burton. Is he a friend of yours, Adam?'

'Sort of.' Adam hesitated, glancing towards his mother. 'We used to play together, but we don't hang out anymore.'

'Can you tell me when you stopped hanging out with Tommy?' Karen asked, trying to coax out information without putting too much pressure on him.

'Umm, I'm not sure,' Adam replied, scratching his head. 'Maybe a few months ago? He just stopped coming over.'

'Did he say why?' Karen asked, paying attention to the boy's body language as well as his words. He seemed open and trusting.

Adam shrugged. 'No, he just started spending more time inside, on his computer or something.'

'Jack, have you noticed anything different about Tommy lately?' Karen turned her attention to the older brother.

'Uh, I don't know,' Jack said, avoiding eye contact. Unlike Adam, Jack's response was guarded. 'I don't talk to him much.'

'Has Tommy made any new friends recently?' Karen asked. 'Or maybe he's mentioned someone he doesn't get along with?' she continued, carefully taking in the reactions of each family member.

'Umm . . . I don't think so,' Adam answered after a moment of thought. 'He mostly keeps to himself.'

'Has Tommy mentioned any problems at home or school?'

'Nothing I can remember,' Adam said, fidgeting with the hem of his shirt.

'What about internet friends? Has Tommy ever mentioned any friends he's made online? Anyone he plays games or chats with?' Karen asked.

'Umm, not really,' Adam said. 'He doesn't talk much about that stuff with me.'

'Do you play any games with Tommy online?'

Jack kept his eyes fixed on his feet.

Dawn gave Adam's shoulder a comforting squeeze. 'They have a PlayStation, but they're not allowed games with an online component without supervision.'

'Which is ridiculous,' Jack muttered.

Dawn gave Karen an apologetic shrug. 'Most games need online access these days, so it does limit how much the boys can play on the console if we're busy.'

'Who does Tommy hang out with at school, Adam?' Karen asked.

'Um, he doesn't really hang out with anyone anymore. He sits in the library at lunchtime,' Adam said, his voice barely audible.

Karen edged forward in her seat. 'Is Tommy being bullied?'

Adam hesitated for a moment, and Dawn rubbed his back. 'It's okay, sweetheart. You just need to tell the truth.'

Adam took a deep breath. 'I don't know. Sometimes kids make fun of him behind his back. You know, because he's into sci-fi and stuff.'

'Has Tommy ever mentioned the names of the kids who make fun of him?' Karen asked.

'No one says anything to his face,' Adam said, looking uncomfortable. 'I don't want to get anyone into trouble.'

'Adam, this is important,' Dawn said sternly.

Jerry leaned forward over the back of the sofa, ruffling Adam's hair. 'You're not in any trouble, mate. Just tell the truth.'

'We're just trying to find Tommy and bring him home safely,' Karen said. 'If Tommy is being bullied, it's important we—'

'But it's not like that,' Adam said, pushing his hair out of his eyes. 'Tommy just doesn't like being around us.'

'Nobody's said mean things to Tommy? Or hurt him?' Karen asked. She was pressing the bullying angle because if Tommy had been bullied, it might have made him more vulnerable online. Someone with ulterior motives could have offered him friendship and understanding, and he'd be more open to that if he didn't have a group of real-life friends.

Perhaps someone connected to Donaldson had communicated with Tommy online.

'He's a weirdo,' Jack burst out.

'Jack!' his father said. 'That's a horrible thing to say.'

Dawn took an audible breath in and glanced at Karen. 'I'm sorry. I think he's just upset by the whole situation.'

Karen took in Jack's scowling face. 'Have you fallen out with Tommy? Did something happen?'

'I barely know him,' Jack muttered. 'He's Adam's friend.'

Adam bit on his lower lip as Karen turned to look at him.

'Neither of you are in any trouble.'

'Why did you say that, Jack?' his father asked.

But Jack remained stubbornly silent.

Instead, Adam spoke up. 'No one hurt Tommy. It's just . . . he's different, you know? He doesn't like the same things as we do and doesn't want to hang out with us. He says he has more interesting things to do. No one actually bullies him or anything.'

Karen appreciated Adam's honesty, even if it didn't provide her with a solid lead. But she was more interested in his older brother's reaction. There had been clear animosity in his voice when he'd called Tommy a weirdo. Had they had an argument or altercation recently? There was obviously bad feeling on Jack's part, at least. But it didn't look like Jack was in the mood to confide in anyone.

'Thank you,' she said to both boys. 'I know talking about all this is tough, but it's helpful. I'm going to leave my card with your mum and dad. If you want to tell me anything else that might help us find Tommy, I can come back for a chat.'

'Okay,' Adam agreed, and Jack nodded. Both boys seemed relieved that the questioning was over.

After the children went back upstairs, Karen turned to Jerry and Dawn as she fished a card out of her bag. 'Thank you for your time. Please don't hesitate to contact me if you or the boys think of anything else.'

'Of course,' Jerry replied as he took the card. 'We all just want Tommy to be found and returned home safely. It's been such a shock to have something like this happen so close.'

Karen said goodbye to the Fosters and returned to her car. She thought through everything she had learned so far: the recent changes in Tommy's behaviour, his social isolation at school, and the tight-knit environment of Dahlia Close. These all seemed to be important puzzle pieces that, if she put them together correctly, might reveal the full picture of what had actually happened to Tommy.

The trouble, of course, was fitting together those pieces in the right order.

She glanced at her phone, noting the time, and wondered how Morgan was getting on at the prison. There was still no news from Rick about the security footage.

Karen's sense of unease had been steadily building since she'd received the call about Tommy Burton's disappearance. Time was a crucial factor in cases like this, and so far, there were still more questions than answers.

Chapter Six

Morgan stood outside the imposing red-brick prison on Greetwell Road and felt the weight of the past case settle heavily on his shoulders. Gathering storm clouds darkened the sky, shadowing every crack and crevice of the high prison walls.

HMP Lincoln was a category B prison, and Graham Donaldson had recently been moved to its wing for vulnerable inmates. Donaldson had requested the transfer to make it easier for his terminally ill father to visit. It sounded feasible, but Morgan didn't trust Donaldson for a second.

Morgan's arrival was outside normal visiting hours, but the governor had agreed to the visitation request immediately after hearing the circumstances. After being escorted through security, Morgan was left to wait in a lobby.

'DI Morgan?' A burly prison officer approached, extending his hand. Morgan nodded, shaking it firmly.

'Right this way.' The guard led Morgan through a labyrinth of corridors.

Faint voices echoed from behind the doors that lined the passageway. They kept up a brisk pace as they moved deeper into the belly of the building.

Finally they arrived at a small, private room, sparsely furnished with a table and two chairs. Already seated in one of those chairs, wearing a grey tracksuit, was Graham Donaldson – the man responsible for the investigation that had given Morgan nightmares fifteen years ago.

'Here we are then,' the prison officer announced, opening the door just wide enough for Morgan to slip through. 'I'll be right outside if you need anything.'

'Thank you,' Morgan said.

His skin crawled as he approached Donaldson, who leered at him, a predatory grin stretching across his haggard face. Time hadn't been kind to him: his once dark hair was now completely grey, and limp strands hung over his forehead. He'd always had a slim build, but now he looked almost skeletal, his cheekbones sharp above hollow cheeks.

'Long time no see, Detective Morgan,' Donaldson sneered, his voice filled with the same mocking sing-song tone that had sent shivers down Morgan's spine fifteen years ago. 'Or should I say . . . old friend?'

'Hardly,' Morgan replied, trying to keep his voice steady. His mind was filling with questions and doubts, but he knew he couldn't afford to let that show. Now was not the time for weakness.

'Have a seat.' Donaldson gestured to the empty chair opposite him with his free hand, the other cuffed and attached to the table. He was enjoying causing Morgan discomfort.

'Let's get straight to the point,' Morgan said, trying to suppress the bile rising in his throat as he sat down. 'We both know why I'm here.'

'No one's told me anything.'

Morgan knew that was a lie. The case – or at least as much of it as DCI Churchill had agreed to disclose – had been explained to Donaldson by the governor over an hour ago.

'Come on, now,' Donaldson drawled, leaning back in his chair with a self-satisfied smile. 'You must admit it's rather amusing that you're here, questioning me again after all these years.'

'I don't find it amusing at all. I'd have preferred never to have to see you again.'

Donaldson pretended to look hurt, then shrugged. 'My solicitor is working to get my case overturned. I could be out soon.'

Not if I have anything to do with it, Morgan thought. 'Enough of these games. This isn't a social call. I want answers.'

Morgan's patience was already wearing thin, and he'd only been in Donaldson's company for a minute. He pulled a photograph from the file he'd been permitted to bring inside the prison, and placed it on the table between them. It was a picture of the blue teddy bear found at the scene of Tommy Burton's disappearance.

Donaldson's gaze settled on the photo, and then he smirked as though savouring a delicious secret. The sight made Morgan's stomach churn with disgust.

'A little boy went missing from Tattershall Castle,' Donaldson mused. 'Tragic. But what does that have to do with me?'

Morgan's jaw clenched as he focused on Donaldson. He thought of Tommy Burton, and imagined the fear and confusion that must have gripped the child as he was taken. He thought of the three boys taken fifteen years ago. They would have been young men by now, living their lives to the full. But thanks to the evil scumbag sitting in front of Morgan, they would never grow up.

There had to be some clue or connection to Donaldson that would lead Morgan to whoever was responsible for this new abduction.

'Think hard, Donaldson,' Morgan said, leaning in closer, his voice low and dangerous. 'Tell me about the people you knew back then. Any associates who shared your . . . interests?'

Donaldson scoffed. 'You think I had friends? People like me don't have friends, Detective. We're lone wolves.'

Morgan knew that wasn't true. Like attracted like. 'Have you heard rumours? Anything at all that could help us find Tommy?'

'Look, Detective,' Donaldson sneered, his grey tracksuit hanging off his bony frame. 'I've been inside for fifteen years. Fifteen! Do you think I get to chat to the men in here without risking a shiv in my back? I'm not safe.'

'You've heard nothing?'

A slow grin spread across Donaldson's face. 'Have you considered maybe Tommy went willingly? Maybe he wanted to go.'

Morgan stared back into Donaldson's beady, bloodshot eyes.

'Let me tell you what I think,' Donaldson said, his lips curving back to reveal his yellow teeth. He leaned closer, his voice low and chilling. 'I think Tommy wanted to go with whoever took him.' He glanced at the file. 'Have you got any photographs of young Tommy?'

Morgan felt his chest tighten, anger flaring like fire. He fought against the urge to lash out. Losing control wouldn't bring him any closer to the truth.

'I'm not here to show you pictures to feed your sick fantasies. You're behind bars to ensure you never hurt another child again,' Morgan growled. 'And I'll make sure you stay here.'

'Is that what you tell yourself?' Donaldson taunted, leaning back in his chair with smug satisfaction. 'That you're the hero copper who put away the nasty monster?'

Morgan took a deep breath, attempting to keep calm. It was unnerving how easily Donaldson could crawl under his skin. He was finding it increasingly difficult to maintain his cool. 'I don't know what game you're playing, but it won't work. I won't let you get to me.'

'Who's playing games?' Donaldson asked, feigning hurt. 'I'm just trying to save my own skin. And yours too. Imagine the scandal when it comes out that you had the wrong man all along . . . You'll be humiliated. I've always maintained my innocence.'

Morgan gritted his teeth, refusing to be swayed by Donaldson's mind games and theatrics. He couldn't afford to let doubt creep in. A child was missing, and every moment wasted could be the difference between life and death. It was time to refocus on what truly mattered. Tommy.

If Morgan had to play along with Donaldson to get answers, he would.

'Then how about any enemies?' Morgan asked. 'Anyone who'd want to frame you, see you take the blame for their crimes?'

'Enemies?' Donaldson mused, his face contorting into a grotesque grin. 'No one comes to mind. At least, not anyone who'd go to such great lengths.'

Morgan felt his frustration bubble to the surface, but he pushed it down. His instinct told him that Donaldson was lying, that there was more to this than met the eye. It was time to try a different tactic.

'Then you're no use to me,' he snapped, anger and frustration creeping into his words. They were running out of time and options. He slid the printed photo of the blue teddy bear into the file and shoved back his chair, preparing to leave.

'Going already?' Donaldson asked, his voice losing its sinister edge and becoming almost pathetic. 'Suit yourself. But remember, Detective, if you're wrong about me and there's someone else out there doing these terrible things, it's on you.'

Morgan's mouth grew dry as those words hit home. Was it possible that he'd been wrong fifteen years ago? Had he missed something, overlooked a crucial piece of evidence? He shook his head, banishing the thought.

'Cut it out, Donaldson!' Morgan barked, his voice loud in the small room. 'We both know you're getting off on this. Another child has been taken, just like fifteen years ago, and I'm sure you know something about it.'

Now Donaldson seemed taken aback by Morgan's ferocity. He withered under Morgan's glare.

Underneath his taunting bravado, Donaldson was a spineless worm – the type who only preyed on those too small and helpless to fight back. When challenged, his sneering mask slipped, exposing the pathetic individual he really was. It was no surprise a man like him had targeted defenceless children.

Donaldson's smug voice had shifted, replaced by a snivelling whine. 'I don't know anything,' he insisted, curling in on himself like a cowering animal. 'I've been in prison! How could I be responsible?'

Morgan stared into Donaldson's eyes, searching for the truth. His mind was filled with doubts, but he couldn't let them take over.

'Prove it,' Morgan demanded, his voice cold and unyielding. 'Give me something that will convince me you're not involved in Tommy's disappearance.'

Donaldson's face twisted. His rubbery lips contorted, but he gave no new information.

'Come on, Detective, please,' he said, his voice wheedling. 'You have to believe me. I'm not evil. You've got me all wrong.'

'All right, let's go back to the case from fifteen years ago,' Morgan said. 'Tell me again how you ended up with young Marc's backpack in your possession. And what about Stuart's shoes? Henry's toy car?'

'Like I've been saying all these years, someone planted them,' Donaldson replied, wiping his nose on the sleeve of his tracksuit.

'Someone planted them?' Morgan repeated sceptically. 'You expect me to believe that? In all my years in the police service, I've never seen a more concrete case than the one we built against you.'

'Look,' Donaldson said, his voice seeming to shake with desperation. 'I didn't hurt those kids. You have to believe me. And I'd never heard the name Tommy Burton before the governor told me about him today.'

Morgan narrowed his eyes. He thought back to the original case and how he and DCI Tranmere had invested all their energy into putting this man away. And yet, here he was, discussing another missing child. The nightmare was repeating itself.

'Give me a name, then,' Morgan challenged. 'Who framed you? Who would want to see you behind bars?'

'Isn't it obvious?' Donaldson said, his voice rising. 'It's whoever took Tommy Burton! They're still out there, and they want me to take the fall for their crime again!'

'Or perhaps,' Morgan countered, his tone dripping with cynicism, 'you're just trying to squirm your way out of this by pretending to be falsely accused. You're working with someone on the outside.'

'No! Please,' Donaldson begged, the desperation in his eyes almost enough to make him seem human. 'There's got to be something you missed – something that can prove I'm innocent.'

'The evidence was solid, and the jury made their decision.'

'Then what do you want from me?' Donaldson asked, his voice a hoarse whisper.

'Answers,' Morgan replied firmly. 'If you're innocent, then help me find whoever is responsible for Tommy's disappearance.'

'Believe me, I wish I could,' Donaldson said, his eyes downcast. 'But I've been locked up for fifteen years, rotting away while the real monster walks free.'

Morgan watched him closely, trying to discern whether there was any truth to his claims. There was so much at stake: the life of a missing child, the verdict from a fifteen-year-old case, and the possibility that he had put the wrong man away all those years ago.

Nagging doubt gnawed at Morgan, but the facts pointed to Donaldson's guilt. The evidence had been irrefutable. He looked into Donaldson's beady eyes and shuddered, sensing the malevolence lurking beneath the surface.

But what if he only saw evil in Donaldson's eyes because that was what he expected to see? Staring into those cold eyes, Morgan looked for signs of the deviant cruelty that had left permanent scars on so many lives.

He considered the facts again – the damning evidence that had convicted Donaldson. Those facts had seemed irrefutable at the time. But what if he had missed something? What if Donaldson was telling the truth, somehow, about being innocent?

Morgan hardened his resolve, forcing the doubts away. No – he knew evil, and it lurked inside this man. Donaldson would never leave prison if Morgan could prevent it.

'I don't believe you're innocent,' Morgan said coldly. 'You're a sick, twisted man. Now, if you have any useful information about Tommy, share it. Otherwise, we're finished here.'

'Just you wait,' Donaldson spat. 'Your career will be over. You'll be a laughing stock when the truth comes out. Embarrassed, humiliated!'

'Goodbye, Donaldson,' Morgan said coldly, rising from his chair. 'I hope I never see you again.'

'Oh, I'll see you again, and I'll laugh in your face when I get out of here.'

The door opened, and the prison officer looked in. 'Everything all right?' he asked Morgan.

'Yes,' Morgan said. 'I'm just leaving.'

'Good luck with your investigation, Detective,' Donaldson said, laughing. 'You'll be back with your tail between your legs when you realise I'm right.'

As Morgan left the room, Donaldson's laughter ringing in his ears, he felt a deep sense of unease. Had he screwed up back then? He'd been confident. He hadn't been reckless, but he'd certainly bent the rules now and then. Nothing dangerous or illegal, but he hadn't been as exacting as he was now.

'Are you all right, mate?' the officer asked.

'Fine, thank you,' Morgan said.

As they navigated the maze of narrow passages, Morgan's thoughts swirled around the confrontation with Donaldson. The man was vile; there was no doubt about that. But was it possible they'd been wrong to convict him all those years ago? That question kept niggling at him.

'Thanks for your help,' he said to the prison officer, forcing a smile before stepping out into the cool evening air.

It had started to rain. Morgan took a deep breath, trying to dispel the claustrophobia he'd experienced in that small room with Donaldson. As he strode towards his car, an idea worked its way into his mind, offering a faint glimmer of hope.

Tranmere.

The name of his old boss brought some reassurance to his troubled thoughts. His old mentor had guided him through some of the darkest moments in his career, and he could help Morgan navigate this too.

Morgan started the car and then reached for his phone. He dialled Tranmere's number.

'Please answer,' he muttered, his voice barely audible above the engine's hum. 'I need your help, old friend.'

Chapter Seven

Karen sat in her car, the window wide open, trying to get some cool air circulating in the muggy heat. She'd spent the last few minutes checking in with the station, but there had been no useful updates.

Tommy should have been home safe with his parents by now. She gazed up at the gloomy grey clouds. The sun would be setting in a couple of hours. She wondered if Tommy was scared of the dark. It made her think of Tilly. Karen's daughter had always wanted a night light to keep the monsters away. Tommy was older, but he was still a child.

Karen shivered, despite the heat, imagining Tommy alone in the darkness, terrified out of his mind.

Her enquiries with the neighbours had yielded little actionable information about the missing boy. Both Rachel King and the Fosters had been polite and well meaning, but ultimately unhelpful. The only interesting discovery had been Jack Foster's animosity towards Tommy. A falling-out between two school kids was unlikely to be relevant, but Karen had made a note of the information anyway.

Next on her list was 2 Dahlia Close. She might get some useful information from Brooke, Tommy's occasional babysitter. Maybe Tommy had confided in her.

She tucked her phone back in her pocket and got out of the car. No. 2 was quiet, no lights on inside despite the darkening skies. Karen lingered for a few minutes and pressed the doorbell multiple times, but there was no response. Karen sighed. She was starting to feel desperate.

Then, with vindictive timing, the rain began to pour down. It felt like an omen. Time was running out, and she couldn't afford to chase dead ends.

Grumbling under her breath, Karen pulled out a card and scribbled a quick note on the back, promising to return the following morning. She slipped it through the letterbox. Frustration gnawed at her as she turned away from the door, the rain steadily increasing.

Just as Karen walked away from Brooke's property, a flicker of movement caught her eye. Next door, a woman was struggling to carry a bulging sack of rubbish. She seemed to stagger under the weight of the bag.

As the woman heaved the cumbersome sack into the bin, she glanced up and noticed Karen standing there, soaked from the rain. She looked momentarily startled before hurrying back into her house and closing the door. Karen squinted through the downpour. That had to be Lyra Hill, Tommy's history teacher.

Karen wanted to get out of the rain and have a hot shower, but she couldn't leave without at least trying to speak to all the street's residents. She approached the house, hoping that even if Lyra couldn't give any insight into Tommy's disappearance, she might be able to provide some additional background.

She rang the doorbell, and after a moment the door creaked open just enough for the woman to peek out.

'Hello, I'm Detective Sergeant Karen Hart.' Karen held up her ID. 'I'm investigating the disappearance of Tommy Burton. Are you Lyra Hill?'

The woman hesitated for a moment before nodding. 'Yes, I'm Lyra,' she confirmed, her voice quivering slightly. She was a petite woman with short, curly brown hair. Her eyes were a deep shade of green, but she avoided direct eye contact with Karen.

'May I come in, please? I'd like to talk to you about Tommy and see if you have any information that could help us find him.' Karen pushed her damp hair back from her forehead.

Uncertainty flickered over Lyra's face, but she eventually stepped aside, opening the door wider. 'Sure, come in.'

As Karen entered the hallway, she noticed Lyra's tense posture and the way her hands were clutched together nervously. She wondered what was making the woman so on edge, but reminded herself not to jump to conclusions. After all, it wasn't every day an officer showed up at your door. And Lyra knew Tommy. His disappearance must have come as a shock.

Karen thanked her as she wiped her wet boots thoroughly on the mat. 'I appreciate your help, Ms Hill.'

'Please, call me Lyra,' she replied, attempting a small smile that didn't quite reach her eyes. 'Let's go into the kitchen where we can sit and talk. I'll get you a towel.'

'Do you want me to take my shoes off?' Karen asked.

'No need.' Lyra led Karen into the open-plan kitchen, which was bathed in warm light from the overhead spotlights. It was a modern space with sleek white cabinets, a white tiled floor, and a gleaming marble island that appeared to be the room's centrepiece. In the far corner, a comfortable-looking seating area offered a view of the garden through rain-spattered bifold doors. Despite its stylish appearance, there was something sterile about the room.

'Please, have a seat,' Lyra offered, her voice barely audible as she gestured towards the grey, high-backed stools surrounding the island. She opened the door to a utility room and re-emerged holding a fluffy grey towel. 'Here,' she offered. 'The weather's awful now. Such a change from earlier.'

'It is. Thank you,' Karen replied, taking the towel and dabbing at her damp hair. She sat on one of the stools, observing Lyra as she grabbed some water from the fridge.

Lyra held up a bottle. 'Want one?'

'No, thank you.' Karen waited for her to take a sip of water, then asked, 'I have a few questions about Tommy Burton, if that's all right?'

'Of course,' Lyra replied, her fingers tapping nervously against the counter. She didn't sit down. 'Anything I can do to help.'

Karen studied Lyra for a moment, noting her evasive body language – the tapping fingers, the way her gaze never quite met Karen's, the anxious shift of her weight from one foot to the other. It was clear that something was bothering her.

'Tell me about your relationship with Tommy. Do you know his family well?' Karen asked.

'Um, not really,' Lyra said. 'I've only been living in the area for ten months. I started teaching at the school around the same time. Tommy's in his first year of secondary school, and I only have him for two classes a week.'

'Have you noticed anything unusual about him or his behaviour recently?' Karen asked. 'Is he close with any other students or staff?'

Lyra hesitated. 'Not particularly. He keeps to himself a lot. But he's a bright kid, always focused on his work.'

'Have you ever witnessed any bullying incidents involving Tommy?'

'Um . . .' Lyra chewed her lip, clearly uncomfortable with the question. 'I can't say I've witnessed any bullying first-hand, but I have noticed that Tommy, well . . . he's a bit of a loner. He doesn't seem to have many close friends in his class.'

'Does that concern you?' Karen said gently.

'Of course,' Lyra admitted, her fingers fidgeting with the label on the bottle of water. 'But he doesn't seem unhappy or distressed about it. He's quite content. As a teacher, you want your students to be sociable and enjoy their time at school, but I don't want to push him if he's comfortable alone. He likes being independent.'

Karen nodded, understanding Lyra's perspective. It was important to respect a child's individuality, but she wondered if there was more to Tommy's isolation than his simply wanting independence.

'Does Tommy participate in any after-school activities or sports?'

'I'm sorry, I wouldn't know. You'd be better off talking to his form tutor about that. I can give you her details if you'd like?'

Karen thanked her, and Lyra grabbed a notepad and pen and wrote down some names, then scrolled for their contact numbers on her phone.

'That's Tommy's form tutor,' Lyra said, pointing at one of the names. 'I've also jotted down the details of the headteacher and his head of year. I'm sure they'll be much more helpful than me.'

'But you live just a couple of doors away from Tommy,' Karen said.

Lyra shrugged. 'I hardly ever see him.'

'Never see him walking to and from school?'

'No, I leave earlier and come home later.'

'Have there been any issues with Tommy's schoolwork recently?'

Lyra shook her head. 'No.'

Karen took a deep breath. Lyra didn't seem to be the great source of information she'd been hoping for. 'It's important for us to understand Tommy's environment and the people who came into contact with him on a regular basis.'

'Of course, Detective Sergeant Hart,' Lyra replied formally. 'I'm sorry I can't be more helpful, and I hope you find him soon.'

'Me too.' As a detective, Karen was trained to read people, and something about Lyra's odd body language told her there might be more going on here than the teacher was letting on. 'Before I go, is there anything else you can think of that might help us in our investigation? Any unusual occurrences or conversations with Tommy?'

Lyra shook her head. 'No, I'm afraid not. I wish I had more to offer, but my interactions with Tommy were fairly limited. I do hope you find him safe and sound, though. If I think of anything else, I'll be sure to get in touch.'

'Thank you for your time, Lyra,' Karen said, standing up from the stool. She could sense the tension and knew Lyra was keen for her to leave. 'I know where to find you if we have further questions.'

Karen shook Lyra's hand, feeling a tremor that betrayed the woman's anxiety.

Lyra led Karen to the front door, and as she stepped out on to the covered porch, her mobile vibrated in her pocket, raising her hopes that it might be a message from Morgan. But when she pulled it out, the screen showed only a low battery warning. Still no news. She was desperate to know what had happened during the interview with Donaldson. Was he cooperating?

Karen stepped back out into the rain and jogged down the driveway. She glanced back and saw Lyra retreating into her house, shutting the door behind her. Then the curtains swished closed, sealing off the brightly lit interior. Karen frowned, making a mental note to delve deeper into Lyra Hill's background – something about the woman's behaviour set her instincts on edge.

The rain lashed at Karen as she sprinted to her car. Sliding into the driver's seat, she quickly shut the door. The windscreen started clouding up, hiding the view behind a thick white veil of condensation. The raindrops hammered against the roof. She switched on the engine and jabbed at the button to turn on the hot air, and then plugged her mobile in to charge.

Karen's shirt and trousers were soaked, clinging to her body like a second skin. The fabric was heavy with water and seemed to steal the heat from her body. Luckily she had a change of clothes at the station.

'Come on, Morgan,' she muttered under her breath, her gaze flickering between the houses on Dahlia Close as the condensation cleared. She knew Morgan was doing his best, but the lack of updates from him and the rest of the team was frustrating.

Karen's desperation was growing. Despite all their efforts, they had yet to uncover any information on Tommy's whereabouts. Donaldson, a known criminal, was their only real lead, and the thought of him potentially holding crucial information about Tommy's disappearance made her feel sick.

She hoped Morgan had managed to extract something from Donaldson, because in the absence of other leads, Tommy's life could depend on it.

Chapter Eight

Raindrops tapped against the windshield as Morgan sat in his car. Flashes of sheet lightning occasionally lit up the dark sky. He hadn't yet moved from his parking spot outside the prison, wanting to process the conversation he'd had with Graham Donaldson. The man's words had left Morgan with a lingering unease. He had remembered the man's evil and deviance but had forgotten how much Donaldson made his skin crawl.

Morgan lowered his mobile phone to glance at the glowing screen. It was ages since he'd last spoken to DCI Tranmere, his former boss and mentor. Now, more than ever, he needed the older man's wisdom and guidance, but the rings seemed to stretch out endlessly.

'Hello?' Tranmere's voice sounded distracted and distant, like he'd been pulled away from something important.

'Tranmere, it's Morgan.'

'Ah, Morgan! It's been too long.' Tranmere's tone shifted from distant to cheerful. 'How have you been?'

'Good, thanks. How about you?'

'Could be better.' Tranmere sighed. 'It was my stepmother's funeral today.'

'Sorry to hear that,' Morgan said, though he sensed irritation rather than sadness from Tranmere.

'Thank you. We never really got on, if I'm honest,' Tranmere confessed. 'She left all of my father's money to Samuel.'

Samuel was Tranmere's son. The last time Morgan had seen him, he'd been just a kid. He remembered the boy's braces and freckles. He'd be in his late twenties now.

'Really?' Morgan wondered if that had caused trouble between father and son. Samuel had been a quiet and introverted young boy who'd worshipped his father and wanted to become a policeman like his dad. 'How is Sam these days?'

'Troubled,' Tranmere replied with a hint of frustration. 'He's not speaking to me at the moment, and I don't know what to do about it.'

'That must be difficult.'

'It is.' Tranmere's gruff voice cracked, revealing a vulnerability Morgan had never heard from him before.

Morgan hesitated, unsure how to broach the real reason for his call. Under the circumstances, it seemed unfair to pile more problems on Tranmere, but maybe his old mentor could use a distraction.

'There's something I need to talk to you about,' Morgan began cautiously, feeling the tension knotting in his stomach again. 'Do you remember the Graham Donaldson case?'

'Of course,' Tranmere replied, a note of wariness creeping into his voice. 'Why?'

'A boy named Tommy Burton went missing today here in Lincolnshire. His mother found a blue teddy bear at the spot where she'd last seen him – similar to the ones from the Donaldson case.'

'Seriously?' Tranmere asked, and Morgan could hear the shock in his voice through the phone.

The rain was now coming down harder, making it difficult to hear. Morgan pressed the phone tightly to his ear. He recounted his conversation with Graham Donaldson and all the details they had so far on Tommy Burton's disappearance.

Tranmere listened intently, his breathing slow and measured. When Morgan finished speaking, there was a moment of silence as Tranmere processed what he'd just heard.

Finally, he said, 'I understand why this is concerning, but we locked up the right man back then. The evidence against Graham Donaldson was overwhelming.'

Morgan stared at the rain-streaked windscreen, watching droplets slide down the glass. What Tranmere had said was true, but he couldn't shake the nervous, nagging feeling that had settled over him. It was like a splinter embedded in his skin, annoying and impossible to ignore.

He closed his eyes momentarily, trying to think logically about what was happening. His old boss had always been unshakeable, even during their most difficult cases. Morgan wanted desperately to believe him, to trust that they had done their job properly all those years ago. But there might have been more to this case – a hidden accomplice they'd missed.

'I always believed that to be true,' Morgan said. 'But after speaking to Donaldson again . . . I don't know. There's something about this situation that feels off. I can't ignore it. Maybe Donaldson was working with someone else.'

'We did our job back then, and we did it well. Donaldson is a sick man, and he's exactly where he belongs.'

'But I can't ignore the similarities between our old case and Tommy Burton's disappearance. It's like history is repeating itself, and I can't help having the feeling that maybe . . . we got it wrong. What if Donaldson wasn't responsible?'

'Nonsense. Now, you listen to me,' Tranmere said. 'We did our job properly. We followed the evidence, and it led us straight to Donaldson. If there's any connection between these two cases, it's likely a copycat or someone who knows details about the original case. Don't let Donaldson get to you. Trust the work we did.'

Trust wasn't something that came easily to Morgan. There had been a time when he'd trusted his instincts. But that was before he'd transferred to Lincolnshire.

In his old job, just after Tranmere had retired, Morgan had been blamed for making a mistake on a case that resulted in the death of a young joyrider. The guilt had weighed heavily on him, reshaping him into a more cautious, precise detective with a near-obsessive attention to detail.

By the time the truth came out, and Morgan realised it hadn't been his mistake after all, it was too late. The experience had changed him. He carried on being methodical and careful to the extreme, because he felt he'd been given a second chance.

It was an approach that sometimes exasperated Karen and the rest of the team, but Morgan couldn't risk working any other way.

'Donaldson still insists he's innocent,' Morgan said.

'Of course he does!' Tranmere snapped back, the aggravation evident in his voice. 'He's a convicted murderer, Morgan. What do you expect him to say?'

Morgan was transported back to the briefing room in Oxford, Tranmere standing over him, his face flushed, voice raised in exasperation.

'But we had solid evidence against him,' Tranmere continued. 'Fingerprints, DNA, and the victims' possessions were found in his house. You know all this.'

'But were we as thorough as we needed to be? Or did we miss something? Donaldson might not have been working alone. Or . . . I don't know, but there's a connection to this case and it could be something we overlooked at the time.'

'Are you suggesting we were careless or biased?' Tranmere shot back, defensive now. 'You know as well as I do that we followed every lead. The case was solid.'

Perhaps Tranmere was right, Morgan thought, his gaze fixed on the rain-streaked windshield. At the time, everything had seemed watertight.

'The way I see it,' Morgan said, 'we either missed something at the time and overlooked an accomplice . . . or we've got a copycat. Neither are appealing prospects.'

Tranmere was silent for a moment, then he sighed, the sound heavy with resignation. 'All right, I understand your concerns and your need to be thorough. Why don't you come over to my place tonight? We can go over things together.'

Morgan hesitated, glancing at the time on the dashboard. 'It's going to be quite late when I get there.'

'Ah, don't worry about that. Sleep is elusive for me these days. The late hour doesn't matter.'

There was a clinking sound on the other end of the line, and Morgan pictured Tranmere pouring himself a generous measure of whiskey. He wondered if his old boss had been drinking more since he retired.

'All right, I'll head over to you now. Do you mind if I bring a colleague along?' Morgan asked, hoping that Tranmere wouldn't take offence. 'She's been working closely with me on this case, and I think her perspective could be really useful.'

Karen didn't have the same close connection to the Donaldson case as they did, and her clear-eyed analysis would be invaluable in helping sift through theories.

'Of course.'

'Thank you,' Morgan said with a small, grateful smile that Tranmere couldn't see. 'I appreciate you letting me sound off and play the what-if game. I don't think we were careless, and I'm equally convinced the evidence is strong against Donaldson, but I need to look at all possibilities with this new abduction.'

'I understand.'

It was good to talk things through with someone who had worked the old case, especially someone as pragmatic and confident as Tranmere.

'It's hard to stop past cases haunting you sometimes,' Morgan said.

'Believe me,' Tranmere replied, his voice touched with weariness. 'I know that all too well.'

◆ ◆ ◆

The sun was low in the sky as Morgan's dark grey Volvo hugged the curves of the narrow country road. The car was a reflection of its owner – sturdy and reliable.

Karen had changed into dry clothes, but her hair was still damp. She sat in the passenger seat, her face turned to the window, taking in the shadowy outlines of the passing countryside.

'Sorry for dragging you out here so late,' Morgan said, his eyes on the road. 'I just need to know if I'm missing anything.'

'No problem.' It was almost eight now, and the storm had passed. 'Tell me more about Tranmere.' She wanted to learn about Morgan's former boss before their meeting.

Morgan paused, as if considering which stories to share. 'He's a character. Stern, but fair.' He grinned.

'What's so funny?'

'I was just remembering an occasion when Tranmere lost his shoes at a crime scene. We were searching a soggy field for a murder weapon. He came over to give us instructions and got his feet stuck in the mud. He ended up carrying his shoes and walking back to the car in his socks.'

Karen laughed.

'And, before he was a DCI, there was the cat incident. We responded to a domestic disturbance, only to find an elderly woman distressed because she'd lost her cat. Instead of brushing it off as a waste of time, Tranmere took it upon himself to search the neighbourhood until he found the cat stuck up a tree. Rather than call the fire service, he had me climb up to rescue it. I'm not sure if I got more scratches from the branches or the cat. He handled Tiddles back to the woman like it was the most important case we'd ever solved.' Morgan gave a nostalgic smile.

'Sounds like he cares about people,' Karen said. 'But why was he sent out to a domestic disturbance? Sounds more like a job for uniform.'

'He's stubborn and had more than a few clashes with senior officers, so we often found ourselves assigned to the worst cases or demoted for a few days. It was explained away as keeping in touch with core policing, but really it was a punishment for Tranmere.'

Karen raised her eyebrows.

'Things were different back then,' Morgan said. 'Tranmere's got a tough exterior, but he's one of the good guys. He always had my back but wasn't afraid to read me or anyone else the riot act if we messed up.'

'I can't imagine you getting into trouble,' Karen teased. 'What were you like as a young officer? Jumping fences and chasing suspects without backup?'

'Something like that.' Morgan glanced at her briefly before returning his gaze to the road. 'I've learned some lessons since then, though. Some of them the hard way.'

Something in his tone caught Karen's attention. She turned to study him more closely and tried to imagine him twenty years ago, as a new detective. She pictured a younger man with fewer lines on his face, his hair not yet touched with grey.

Morgan's lips curved into a wry smile, although he kept his eyes on the road. 'I was quite different back then,' he admitted. 'I didn't used to be so by-the-book.'

The Morgan she knew was always methodical and painstakingly thorough in his work. When they'd first started working together, he had confided that a young joyrider had died and Morgan had been wrongly led to believe it was an error on his part that had led to the tragedy.

Since then, his fear of making the wrong move had made him cautious. Underneath Morgan's cool exterior lay a deep-seated need to always look for mistakes and anticipate errors.

They were silent as Morgan followed the signs for Mablethorpe. Twisted branches from hawthorn trees lined the road, their long shadows stretching across the tarmac.

After a few minutes, Morgan said, 'I'm glad you're coming to talk to Tranmere. I don't want to miss anything. If you think I screwed things up on the other case, you need to be honest with me. Don't spare my feelings.'

Karen looked at him, puzzled. 'Where's this coming from?'

He continued to keep his gaze fixed on the road. 'It's a possibility. And maybe Tommy Burton is in danger now because I messed up the past investigation.'

'Hey,' Karen said softly, touching his arm. 'No one's perfect. But there isn't a reason to think there's a problem with the original case, is there?'

'Well, no.'

'You just want to triple-check everything?'

'Yes.'

Karen smiled. 'That's the Morgan we know and love.'

'You *say* that, but it annoys you. I can tell.'

'Of course it does. But I'd still rather work with you on a case than anyone else. Even if you are pedantic.'

'*Pedantic?*' Morgan shifted in his seat, frowning. 'I prefer *careful.*'

Karen's phone buzzed in her pocket, the sudden noise making her jump. She glanced down at the screen. Mike was calling.

'Karen, where are you?' Mike's voice was tense with concern.

'Sorry, I meant to call earlier. I'm on my way to Mablethorpe.'

'Mablethorpe? Karen, you're supposed to be at the dinner tonight,' Mike said, now sounding more bemused than worried. 'We're all waiting for you at the pub. It's been nearly an hour.'

Her stomach dropped. She had completely forgotten about the family dinner at the local pub, where her parents were supposed to meet Mike's mother and stepfather for the first time. How could she have let that slip her mind?

'Mike, I'm so sorry,' she said, cringing as she pictured everyone waiting, frustrated by her lack of consideration. 'We're working on a child abduction, and I lost track of time.' Her dedication to her job sometimes took precedence over her personal life. She cursed under her breath. 'I completely forgot about dinner . . .'

'That forgettable, am I?' Mike said, but she could tell from the tone of his voice that he was teasing. As he'd worked for the police in the past, he understood the job's demands.

'I really am sorry.'

'If you'd called earlier, we could have rearranged. Now I'll have to fend off World War Three on my own.'

'Is it going that badly?'

'Put it this way – I don't think our mothers are destined to become lifelong pals.'

Karen groaned.

'Why are you going to Mablethorpe anyway?' Mike asked.

'To see a retired DCI. He worked on a similar case years ago.'

'Ah, the glamorous life of a detective sergeant.'

'Again, I'm really sorry,' Karen said. 'I'll make it up to you, I promise.'

'All right,' Mike replied, his tone playful as he added, 'I'll look forward to you making it up to me later.'

'I hope the evening isn't too awful. Tell everyone I'm really sorry.'

'I suppose I should get back inside to act as peacekeeper.' Mike paused for a moment before adding, 'Just keep safe out there, okay?'

'I will.'

After hanging up, Karen's smile faded as she thought about the potential disaster unfolding at the pub. Mike's mother, Lorraine, could be stuffy and difficult, while her parents were anything but. She hoped the dinner wouldn't turn into a complete disaster.

'Everything okay?' Morgan asked, casting a concerned glance in her direction.

'Not exactly,' Karen muttered, rubbing her forehead. 'I was supposed to be at a family dinner tonight. Totally slipped my mind.'

'Ah.' Morgan winced in sympathy. 'That's . . . unfortunate.'

'Yes, very unfortunate,' Karen agreed.

She would be in everyone's bad books, but she couldn't change that now. All she could do was hope that the information Tranmere provided about the case would make Karen standing up her family worthwhile.

Chapter Nine

Karen and Morgan parked outside DCI Tranmere's home and took in the imposing facade. It was a large, elegant, yellow sandstone building, with intricate stonework and large windows. The house was nestled at the end of a single-track road and exuded luxury and privacy.

As they got out of the car, the briny scent of the sea drifted over to them. Karen nodded at the property. 'That's some house. It's huge.'

Morgan turned to Karen as he locked the car. 'Tranmere comes from money.'

The heavy oak front door swung open, revealing a man with a stocky frame. His thick thatch of silver hair was unruly, and his smile was warm. 'Ah, Morgan! Good to see you again. And this must be DS Karen Hart,' Tranmere said, extending his hand. 'I've heard a lot about you.'

'Nice to meet you, sir,' Karen replied, shaking his hand.

'Please, call me Sylvester,' he insisted. 'Come in before it starts raining again!'

They entered the house, and Karen noticed the merry glint in Tranmere's eyes, perhaps aided by the whiskey that lingered on his breath.

'It's been a while, Morgan,' Tranmere said, clapping him on the shoulder. 'Far too long.'

'It has,' Morgan agreed.

Karen took in her surroundings as they entered the grand hallway. The floors were polished hardwood, and what looked to be a very old Persian rug stretched almost the entire length of the hall. The high ceilings and decorative mouldings were complemented by expensive-looking chandeliers. Ornate, gilt-framed oil paintings depicting various landscapes hung on the walls.

'You've got a beautiful home,' Karen said.

'Ah, well, I didn't buy it on a police officer's salary!' Tranmere chuckled. 'Family money.'

'Sorry, I didn't mean to be rude. I—'

'Not at all,' Tranmere cut in. 'My grandfather was quite the entrepreneur. He started a successful shipping company. Our family led a charmed existence, but I always knew I wanted something different, something more meaningful. A bit of a cliché, but that's why I joined the force.'

'Speaking of which,' Morgan interjected, 'we've got a lot to discuss concerning this case.'

'Keen to get down to business as usual,' Tranmere said with a fond smile as he waved them towards the living room. 'Let me pour you both a drink first, though. Whiskey? Or perhaps something less potent?'

'Water for me,' Morgan said, glancing over at Karen.

'Coffee for me, please, if it's not too much trouble,' she replied.

'Coming right up,' Tranmere said, heading off to get the drinks.

As they waited for him to return, Karen looked around the living room. It was filled with travel mementos from various regions. An old, yellow map of the Lincolnshire coast hung on one wall. The furnishings were solid and expensive, with dark leather armchairs and a heavy coffee table at the centre of the room. It was clear that Tranmere had tastes as grand as his house.

Morgan and Karen sat on a comfortably worn sofa as Tranmere returned with a tray bearing their drinks. He handed them out before settling into one of the leather armchairs.

'So,' Tranmere began, sipping his whiskey, 'tell me about the case that's been keeping you both so busy.'

'Sadly, it's looking like a child abduction. I take it Morgan's already mentioned some of the details?' Karen asked.

'Yes, he has,' Tranmere said. 'And those details sounded very familiar. *Donaldson.* I remember when we caught him – it feels like a lifetime ago.'

'It does,' Morgan agreed. 'I hate to say it, but it feels like history is repeating itself.'

Tranmere nodded, his face suddenly sombre. 'It's a sickening thought that someone else out there might be following in Donaldson's footsteps.'

'Or worse,' Morgan said. 'That we didn't catch the right person back then.'

'We did,' Tranmere said firmly. 'There's not a doubt in my mind. But your suggestion that Donaldson has a copycat is not beyond the realms of possibility.'

'It's something we have to look into,' Karen said hesitantly, not wanting to undermine the work he and Morgan had done on the original case. 'It's just . . . that creepy blue bear. No one outside of the investigating team knew about it at the time, is that right?'

'Correct. We kept that detail out of the press. I always expected it to leak, considering the media interest in the case, but it never did.'

'So how would anyone know to copy that aspect of the abduction?' Karen asked. 'Perhaps, rather than a copycat, we're looking for an accomplice. Someone who knew Donaldson and maybe helped him?'

'I've been wracking my brain trying to figure out if we missed anything back then. It's been haunting me,' Morgan said.

Tranmere put his whiskey glass on the coffee table. 'Trust me, we did everything we could. There was no indication that Donaldson was working with anyone else. And if he did have an accomplice, why would they wait fifteen years to strike again?'

'Good point,' Karen said. 'What can you tell us about the original case?'

'I can't tell you any more than Morgan already knows, and you must have all the records of the case files and evidence.'

'We do,' Karen said, 'but I wondered if anything stood out for you. Something that wasn't fully explained at the time?'

Tranmere thought for a moment, then reached for his glass. 'It was a long time ago, but one person always set me on edge. Donaldson's father. He was a real piece of work. Abusive, controlling – I'm convinced he played a part in making his son into the monster he became.'

'Interesting,' Karen said, shooting a look at Morgan. 'Do you think it's worth us talking to the father?'

'I'll do that tomorrow,' Morgan said, looking thoughtful. 'I didn't speak with Donaldson's father at the time.'

'No,' Tranmere said. 'I dealt with him. Bruce Donaldson. We had run-ins going back years, so it made sense that I'd be the one to talk to him. He was a small-time criminal, mostly burglary. He got in trouble a few times for fighting – pub brawls mostly.'

'Maybe there's a connection between Donaldson's father and the current case,' Karen suggested. 'If he knew about the blue bears his son had left at the scenes, then maybe he told someone else about it.'

'Possible,' Morgan said, his brow furrowed in thought.

Karen said, 'We know Donaldson kept trophies from the abductions—'

Tranmere looked up. 'Shoes, a bag and a toy car, if I remember correctly. It's not uncommon for criminals to keep items belonging to their victims as a reminder of their crimes.'

'True,' Morgan agreed, 'but the belongings of the three abducted boys were found in Donaldson's garage. Donaldson shared that house with his father. How sure are we that the father wasn't involved?'

Tranmere drained the last of his whiskey. Then he stood up and walked over to the drinks cabinet to pour himself more. 'I know what you're getting at, but you know we went through every possibility with a fine-tooth comb. Donaldson's father was on holiday, staying in a caravan at Southend-on-Sea, at the time of the first abduction. And we have CCTV footage placing Donaldson himself near the park within ten minutes of the second abduction. I'm convinced he was the sole perpetrator.' Tranmere sank back down in his chair, rubbing his temples. 'CCTV is everywhere these days, so I'm surprised you've had no luck tracking down Tommy Burton.'

'It's unusual,' Karen said. 'Tommy wasn't caught on the security cameras at the castle, and the car park cameras were malfunctioning. We had a hit for his mother's car near Tattershall, but no one saw Tommy leave.'

Morgan looked down at his hands. 'I can't shake the feeling that I may have made an error in the Donaldson case – that I overlooked something important.'

Tranmere heaved himself up from the armchair again and approached Morgan, placing a hand on his shoulder. 'I hoped you would have overcome this self-doubt by now, Morgan. For what it's worth, I'm proud of the detective you've become. I know I can't take all the credit,' he chuckled, 'but I'm proud all the same.'

Karen watched the exchange, noting the genuine affection between Morgan and Tranmere. It was clear that their bond went beyond professional camaraderie; they had a shared history. Morgan's admiration for Tranmere was mutual.

'Thank you,' Morgan said. 'That means a lot, coming from you.'

'Your instincts are better than you realise,' Tranmere continued. 'You'd do well to heed them more often.' After Tranmere patted Morgan's shoulder again, he returned to his armchair.

Tranmere was a real character – old-fashioned and set in his ways, but clearly still as sharp as a tack. He was just as Morgan had described. He was obviously fond of Morgan, so that earned him points in Karen's estimation.

'I'm keen to speak to one of the Burtons' neighbours,' Karen said. 'She used to babysit Tommy, and I'm hoping he confided in her. We're concerned he may have been groomed. He spent a lot of time online. But that doesn't explain how a groomer would know about the blue bears.'

Tranmere grimaced. 'That's a definite possibility. Some nasty predators lurking online.'

'When I asked the prison governor about Donaldson's access to the internet, he told me that Donaldson hasn't shown any interest in computers. But we can't rule out that Donaldson communicated with Tommy somehow. If not himself, then maybe via an intermediary.' Morgan glanced at his watch. 'It's getting late. We've troubled you long enough.'

'Oh, not at all. I wish I could be more help,' Tranmere said. 'In fact, your company cheered me up after a miserable day at that blasted funeral.'

'I was sorry to hear about your stepmother,' Morgan said.

'Thank you, but she wasn't exactly Mother Teresa.' Tranmere offered a tight smile as he stood and led them out of the living room. Despite his words, Karen thought Tranmere's face betrayed a lingering sadness. 'Enough about me. Good luck with this case. I hope you find the poor little lad. Keep me updated if you get the chance.'

They stopped by the front door. The detective chief inspector wore a wide smile as he clasped Morgan's hand firmly. 'It was good seeing you again, Morgan. And it was a pleasure meeting you, Karen.'

'Thank you for your help,' Karen replied, shaking his hand as well.

'Anytime. Safe drive home,' Tranmere said as they stepped out into the cool night air.

As Morgan turned the car around, Karen noticed he seemed lighter and more at ease than before their visit.

'Tranmere seems like a good bloke.'

'He is,' Morgan said. 'One of the best.'

Karen's thoughts turned to one of her old bosses, Anthony, and the great friendship they'd had before his murder. A pang of sadness hit her, as it always did when she remembered his kindness and generosity. What advice would he give her now? *Head down and follow the evidence.*

'Are you all right?' Morgan asked, sensing her mood as he navigated the dark lane.

'Fine. Just tired.'

'Me too,' he said, his gaze fixed on the winding road ahead. 'Tomorrow's another day, eh?'

Another day to find answers and hopefully get to Tommy before the worst happened, Karen thought.

No matter how hard she pushed and how many hours she worked, Karen felt guilty when she returned home at night during time-sensitive cases like this one. She couldn't shake off the feeling that there could be one clue they'd miss or one lead they didn't follow up on because she wasn't there. It was as though she was letting

Tommy down by retreating to the comfort of her own home. But that was self-importance. And, as much as she loathed going home while a little boy was missing, she needed rest.

The team would continue to work at all hours, switching out who was on duty, but there would always be someone handling the phones and running analysis. Officers would work around the clock. They had to. Tommy was counting on them.

◆ ◆ ◆

Karen slipped her key into the lock and turned it as gently as possible, wincing at the scraping sound. She stepped over the threshold into the dark house, exhaustion seeping into her bones. The long day's events lingered in her mind.

Sandy greeted her with a single bark and a wagging tail. Karen held a finger to her lips and glanced up the stairs, hoping that she hadn't woken Mike.

'Shh, Sandy,' she whispered, crouching to stroke the dog's soft fur. 'Let's not wake him.'

Karen felt terrible about leaving Mike to deal with their family dinner alone, and didn't want to make things worse by disturbing him now.

Sandy sniffed around her legs before looking up at Karen with an expression that said: *How could you?* Karen chuckled softly, running her hand along the dog's back. 'Can you still smell Rachel King's cats? That was hours ago.'

'Is everything okay?' a sleepy voice called from the top of the stairs. 'I heard a noise. Thought I'd better check no one was breaking in.'

'Mike,' she said, fighting back a grin. 'You do realise you don't have any clothes on? Did you plan to tackle the intruder in your boxers?'

Rubbing his eyes, Mike shrugged. 'Couldn't find my dressing gown. Besides, it might help scare them off.'

Karen laughed, despite her exhaustion. 'I appreciate your dedication to our home security, but I think you can stand down now.'

'All right.' Mike yawned and stretched his arms over his head. 'Just making sure everything's safe, that's all.' He turned and headed back towards their bedroom.

Karen watched him go with a soft smile. Mike never failed to show his support, even in the most unconventional ways. It was moments like these when she was reminded just how lucky she was to have him in her life. It struck her how easily she'd said *our home* without thinking. Not *my home*, but *our*. It felt nice.

She should have been there for him tonight – their parents had been meeting for the first time, after all.

'I'm getting a glass of water,' she called out softly. 'Want anything?'

Mike called back, saying he was fine, and Karen padded into the kitchen, trailed by Sandy. The cool liquid soothed her parched throat as she took a sip, allowing herself a moment to collect her thoughts. It had been a tiring day, but as worn out as she was, Karen knew it wouldn't be easy to switch off.

She drained the glass and set it on the counter before making her way upstairs, Sandy following closely behind. Karen stopped to make a fuss over her, getting her settled in the dog bed in the hallway. Then she went into the bathroom to strip off her work clothes and brush her teeth before tiptoeing into the bedroom.

Mike was lying on his side, one arm bent beneath the pillow, the same way he always slept. As a floorboard gave a muffled creak, his eyes flickered open.

'Hey,' he murmured, propping himself up on one elbow. 'Tough day?'

'I'm okay,' Karen replied as she slipped under the duvet. 'Sorry, I left you to deal with dinner tonight.'

'Don't worry about it. Missing-child cases are hard.'

'Thank you for handling it,' Karen whispered, snuggling close. The warmth of his body was comforting, making her feel more at ease than she had all day.

'Anytime,' Mike said sleepily, wrapping an arm around her.

'How did it go, anyway?' Karen asked.

'Ah.' Mike chuckled softly. 'Well, it didn't start too badly. But our mothers . . . they're quite a pair.'

'So they didn't get on?' Karen asked.

'Not exactly. At one point, my mum started talking about how she's growing tomatoes this year. Your mother then chimed in, saying she loves gardening and grows tomatoes every year. Of course, my mum took that as a challenge.'

Karen smiled at the idea of their mothers trying to outdo each other. 'I can imagine.'

'Picture them: eyes narrowed, lips pursed, glaring at each other, all over who could grow the best tomatoes,' Mike said. 'My mum said she'll be entering them into her village produce competition this year, but then your mother wasn't about to let my mum steal her gardening thunder. So she told this elaborate story about how she once grew a tomato so large, it made a football look small.'

'I don't remember that!' Karen said, her eyebrows raised in amusement.

'Probably made it up,' Mike replied, grinning. 'But it put my mum in her place. Of course, that only led to them arguing over other things. They started squabbling about which local pub serves the best fish and chips. Apparently, they've both got strong opinions on that, too.'

'Sounds like an eventful evening,' Karen said. 'Sorry you had to deal with it alone.'

'Don't worry about it. It's just the nature of the job. Sometimes you have to miss out on things.' He ran his fingers through her hair and kissed her forehead. 'What I can't forgive, though,' he said with mock sternness, 'is how you can have forgotten about me for even a second. I think I'm pretty unforgettable, actually.'

Karen grinned. 'I don't know what I was thinking.'

'Temporary insanity is my bet.'

'Did you talk to your mum about . . .' Karen trailed off. Mike had been planning to have a conversation with his mother about his birth father, but he kept putting it off.

Mike took a deep breath, his expression serious now. 'I asked her about him. I said it was time I knew more and told her I have a right to know.'

Karen tilted her head to study his face, seeing the hurt and vulnerability that lay beneath the surface. 'What did she say?'

'She didn't take it well. She got defensive and evasive. It was probably one of the reasons she was so argumentative tonight.'

'Maybe she's just scared,' Karen suggested.

'What reason would she have to be scared?'

'Maybe she's worried you'll get hurt. Or she's scared of losing you.' Karen pulled the duvet tighter around herself. 'Or maybe she needs time to think things through.'

'Could be,' Mike said. 'I just wish she'd been more open.'

'She'll come round.'

Soon Mike's breathing slowed and deepened, and Karen wished she could fall asleep as easily. But Tommy Burton's face appeared every time she closed her eyes.

She stared at the ceiling, her thoughts drifting back to the case. Sleep would not come easily tonight.

Chapter Ten

Morgan parked in a vacant space outside the red-brick building, and Karen gazed through the windscreen at the sign where *St Mary's Hospice* was printed in faded letters. The ground was still wet from last night's rain, and the early morning sun struggled to pierce the thick veil of clouds.

Karen smothered a yawn. She hadn't managed to get much sleep last night, and going by the way he looked, Morgan had managed even less than her. She grabbed her bag from the footwell, stealing another glance at him. His frown seemed to be a permanent fixture. He stared straight ahead. This case was going to take its toll.

Karen asked, 'You okay?'

Morgan rubbed a hand over his jaw. 'Ask me again once we leave this place with some answers.' He switched off the engine. 'Ready?'

Karen nodded.

'Then let's get this over with,' he muttered, pushing open the car door.

Karen followed him along the path towards the hospice entrance. Morgan's shoulders were hunched, and his steps were heavy, like he was a man carrying a weighty burden. Karen felt a pang of sympathy for him; they'd both seen their fair share of hard cases, but this one was affecting him more than most.

Apprehension made Karen tense as they stepped inside. Would Bruce Donaldson be as evil as his son?

The foyer of the hospice smelled of antiseptic, but the decor was less sterile than a hospital's. A man behind the reception desk smiled at them.

Karen held up her ID. 'Good morning. We're here to see Bruce Donaldson.'

'Morning, Detectives,' the receptionist said. 'Room twelve, down the hall and to your left. I'll show you.'

Morgan and Karen thanked him, and he stepped out from behind the desk and led the way. They followed him down the brightly lit hallway, and stopped outside the door to room twelve.

The receptionist knocked and poked his head into the room. 'Mr Donaldson, the police detectives are here to see you.'

A gravelly voice responded, 'Send them in.'

The receptionist opened the door fully and stood aside to let Karen and Morgan enter. 'I'll be at the front desk if you need anything else.' He gave them a nod and left, closing the door behind him.

Bruce Donaldson was seated in a chair by the window, a blanket over his knees and an oxygen tube running below his nose. The small room contained standard medical equipment – an adjustable hospital bed, an IV stand and a heart rate and oxygen monitor. But it had been made to look cosier with colourful paintings on the walls and a patchwork quilt on the bed.

Bruce peered at them from his chair. His face was pale, gaunt and hairless. Karen guessed that was from the chemo. They'd been told Bruce had terminal lung cancer and not long left to live. Bruce's eyes were flinty and assessing, and Karen maintained eye contact, trying to get a read on him. The man had raised a monster.

Karen was reminded of the phrase *like father, like son*. Just how much did Bruce Donaldson have in common with his offspring? According to DCI Tranmere, Bruce had been a career criminal who'd had a difficult relationship with the police over the years. Karen wasn't expecting this interview to be easy.

'Mr Donaldson, I'm Detective Inspector Morgan and this is Detective Sergeant Hart. We have some questions about your son, Graham.'

Bruce's mouth twisted into a crooked smile, his breath coming in laboured wheezes. 'What about my boy?' His piercing eyes locked on to Morgan, then slid to Karen, his gaze still sharp and intense despite his wasted frame. 'He's been locked away for nearly fifteen years. What could you possibly want to know now?'

Karen and Morgan pulled chairs over so they could sit opposite Bruce. His rail-thin body shuddered with a wracking cough.

She said, 'We're investigating the recent disappearance of an eleven-year-old boy. We have reason to believe your son may be involved.'

Bruce sneered, the expression distorting his thin face. 'Recent? My Graham? He's been in prison all this time. You're barking up the wrong tree.' He made Karen's skin crawl.

Morgan leaned forward, his own expression hard. 'What do you know about your son's crimes, Mr Donaldson?'

Bruce's sunken eyes flashed with anger. 'I know my Graham is innocent. You lot made a mistake when you locked him up.' His voice was surprisingly forceful, despite his frail appearance.

'Don't give me that.' Morgan's voice was steel. 'You know as well as I do that he murdered those boys.'

Bruce's eyes narrowed to slits. 'My boy isn't some sicko. He'd never do something like that. I didn't raise him to be that way.'

'What about Graham's mother?' Karen asked. 'Where was she when all this happened?'

Bruce gave a disdainful sniff. 'She left – couldn't handle the boy. Always too soft, that one. I was in and out of the nick, but the final straw was when Graham—' He broke off abruptly, eyes sliding away as he took a ragged breath. 'Never mind. It's ancient history now.'

Karen's gaze met Morgan's. 'When Graham did what?' she prompted Bruce. 'What was the final straw for his mother?'

Bruce pursed his lips, his jaw clenched tight. Karen waited, sensing that if she gave him long enough, he might talk.

He finally rasped out, 'Graham did something to her cat in the shed. Said the animal had scratched him and had to be punished. His mum found it and left that night, going on about how Graham wasn't right in the head.'

Karen tried to put the horrible image out of her mind. Graham had shown signs of a deviant personality long before he'd killed those poor boys.

'Did you get Graham help?' she asked hoarsely. 'Counselling, maybe? Or could you have asked his GP for advice?'

Bruce gave an indifferent shrug. 'What would've been the point of that? Lad just needed a firm hand. His mum was always too soft . . .'

Morgan curled his hand tightly around the arm of the chair. 'You're wasting our time. Tell us *exactly* what you know about your son's crimes.'

Bruce choked out a laugh. 'You're wasting *my* time, more like it. And I don't have much of it left.' He took a couple of deep breaths. 'I told you, my Graham is innocent. And you've got nothing on me. I don't know why I let you in. You should be ashamed of yourselves, bullying a dying man. You lot really are scum.'

Karen took over before Morgan lost his temper. 'Something was left at the scene when the boys were taken. Do you know what that was?'

Bruce looked momentarily confused, then cackled gleefully. 'Oh yes, the blue bears. Lovely touch, don't you think? Very theatrical.'

Karen tried not to react, keeping her expression neutral. He knew about the bears. From the state of him, she doubted Bruce could physically walk across the room, let alone have the strength to abduct Tommy. But maybe he had told someone . . . shared that crucial detail.

Morgan cut in sharply, 'The dead boys' belongings were kept in your garage – the one you shared with your son.'

Bruce's face went blank. 'I wouldn't know anything about that. I never went in there.'

'You expect us to believe that?' Morgan shook his head. 'You lived together. Your stuff was in the garage too.'

Bruce shrugged his bony shoulders. 'Believe what you like. I kept out of my Graham's business, and he stayed out of mine. Simple as that.'

Karen noted the sheen of sweat on his brow and the rasp of his breath. As much as she detested the man, it didn't seem like an act. He truly was in a bad way.

Morgan's grip on the chair arm tightened. 'What's the significance of the blue bears, Bruce?'

Bruce feigned boredom. 'How should I know? Stupid things. Maybe whoever took those kids had a thing for cuddly toys.'

'I think you do know,' Morgan said.

Bruce coughed. 'Graham wasn't allowed any toys like that. No boy of mine . . .' He tilted his head to the side. 'Come to think of it, he did have a teddy bear once . . .' He trailed off meaningfully before tilting his head to the side and tapping his chin with his index finger.

Karen studied Bruce's pale face. His expression held the faintest hint of a smile. He was enjoying this.

He looked up at the ceiling as though recollecting a distant memory. 'A neighbour – annoying bloke, always sticking his nose in other people's business – gave Graham a teddy bear. Must've been when he was seven or so. It was only a cheap thing. Sort of toy you get at the arcades. Made for a few pence in China. You know the type. It had black shiny eyes and *blue* fur.' A slow, cruel smile spread across his face as he emphasised the word *blue*. Karen saw through the act. He was toying with them.

'Ugly little thing,' he went on cruelly. 'I burned it. Chucked it on the fire and we watched it melt. The fur caught first, shrinking back from the heat. Then its arms started to warp, stuffing spilling out and bursting into flames. The eyes popped right off.' Bruce gave a wheezing chuckle. 'Graham was wailing the whole time, reaching for it, wanting to save his little friend. I had to hold him back. Stupid kid would have got third-degree burns if it wasn't for me.'

Karen's stomach churned, bile rising in her throat as Bruce Donaldson laughed again – a grating, spine-chilling sound. She stole a glance at Morgan. His face had gone chalky white. It was obvious now why the blue bears held significance for Graham Donaldson. Bruce had to know his actions had helped to turn his son into a monster.

Bruce gave another wheeze, pressing a hand to his chest. 'Then I gave that neighbour a good kicking, and he didn't interfere anymore.'

Morgan rubbed a hand over his face, as if trying to wipe the images from his mind. When he spoke, his voice was hoarse. 'Some father you were.'

'Graham needed a life lesson,' Bruce snarled. 'No softness. No weakness.'

'Did you tell anyone else about the blue bears, Mr Donaldson?' Karen asked.

'I've kept my Graham's secrets all these years, haven't I? Why would I start blabbing now?' Donaldson's eyes gleamed with malice. 'Besides, I don't go around boasting about him. It's not as if he's a fancy graduate or a successful businessman. He's a child killer.' Bruce's face went slack as he realised his slip-up, but he quickly recovered. 'I mean, he isn't – you lot fitted him up. But everyone *thinks* he's a child murderer. People don't like that, so I'm hardly likely to talk about him, am I?'

Morgan shifted forward. 'Has anyone come to visit recently? Asking about Graham or his crimes?'

'I haven't had any visitors. Graham can't come to see me since he's banged up, thanks to you lot. And my old friends don't bother anymore. Went for a pint with them every night for donkey's years, but they forget you quick when you're ill. Not that I care. I don't need them. I've always been fine on my own.'

Karen observed Bruce closely. As vile as he was, underneath his resentment and anger he seemed to be telling the truth. If someone had come asking questions about Graham, he might not want to admit it, though. He had a history of conflict with the police. He might withhold the information out of spite.

'So there's been no one?' she pressed. 'No strangers coming around, asking questions about Graham?'

'I told you,' Bruce said. 'Not a soul. I'm left here to rot in this place while the rest of the world goes on without me.'

He gave another rattling cough then sank back in his chair, his energy seeming to leave him in a rush.

Karen glanced at Morgan. His mouth was set in a grim line, frustration etched deep into his face.

He angled himself towards Bruce. 'There must be something you can tell us. Something you want to get off your conscience before it's too late. You're nearly at the end of the road.'

Bruce Donaldson's eyes flashed with anger. 'You don't need to tell me that, you patronising sod. I can't even take a piss on my own these days.'

Karen thought Bruce was being honest about not talking to anyone. He hadn't seemed to remember the detail about the blue bears until prompted. If someone had come questioning him recently, she thought that detail might have come up.

'Aren't you worried about dying with so much sin?' asked Morgan.

Bruce gave a contemptuous huff. 'I don't go in for all that religious nonsense. Load of old rubbish.' Another grin crept on to his face. 'You should have heard the vicar they sent round to talk to me the other week. He was worried about my soul. Telling me I should repent, make my final confession.' He wheezed out a laugh. 'I told that Bible-basher my only sin was not finishing the bottle of whiskey under my bed. The do-gooder left in quite a hurry after that!'

Bruce chuckled at his own tale, then coughed. Karen frowned, doubt niggling at the back of her mind. His humour felt forced. He was afraid of dying.

Karen chose her next words carefully. 'Mr Donaldson, a young boy's life is at stake here. If there's anything you know that could help us find Tommy Burton, I need you to tell me. *Please.*' She held his gaze, looking into his craggy face, hoping to appeal to any humanity he had left.

But Bruce Donaldson just broke into a ragged coughing fit. He doubled over, gasping for breath between each wracking cough. When the spasms finally eased, he growled, 'You'll get nothing from me. I told you I'll take my secrets to the grave. I don't much like kid killers, but I *hate* coppers. Maybe I'll have that engraved on my tombstone.' He took a few deep inhales through his nose. Then grabbed the clear tube. 'Is this thing even on?'

Bruce pressed the call button, then clutched at the oxygen tube, fumbling to position it properly under his nose. His chest heaved as he gulped in breath after breath.

'Get the nurse!' he croaked.

His chest rattled as he tried to suck in air, his face contorting. 'Get out, the pair of you,' he spat. 'I'm tired.'

A nurse bustled in as Bruce sank back into his chair, spent.

Karen stepped out of the room, her pulse pounding in her ears. Morgan followed with his shoulders hunched. Without a word, they turned and walked down the corridor side by side.

They had gained nothing from talking to Graham Donaldson's father.

As they emerged into the hospice foyer, Morgan paused, turning to Karen with a grim expression. 'He couldn't have taken Tommy himself. He's too weak. He wasn't faking that.'

'No, and I don't think he's told anyone about the blue bears recently either. He seemed to genuinely only remember them just now when we asked him.'

Morgan looked thoughtful. 'Could his medication have made him forget he told someone?'

'Maybe, but I think it's unlikely.'

He sighed, rubbing a hand over his face. 'We're grasping at straws here. We really need a lead.'

'I know. I'll go and speak to Tommy's babysitter. She was out yesterday when I called round. Maybe I'll get something from her.'

'All right. I'll have another word with the receptionist here before we leave,' Morgan said. 'And make sure Bruce Donaldson was telling the truth about no visitors. There has to be something we're missing.'

As Karen walked out into the grey morning alone, worry clouded her mind. Bruce Donaldson's cruelty was one of the faces of wickedness in this case. She dreaded to think what evil they still had to uncover.

Chapter Eleven

After Morgan dropped her at the station so she could collect her car, Karen drove to Washingborough and pulled up in front of Tommy's babysitter's home on Dahlia Close. It was a neat, detached house, just like the others in the cul-de-sac.

As she approached the front door, it swung open to reveal a woman in her early twenties. She was dressed in dark jeans and a loose-fitting black cardigan over a red top. A silver chain with a feather pendant rested at the base of her throat.

Karen introduced herself and showed her ID. 'Brooke Lewis? I left a card for you yesterday. I'd like to have a quick chat if you can spare a few minutes. It's about Tommy Burton, the young lad who went missing from Tattershall Castle yesterday.'

Brooke nodded. 'I was so shocked to hear what happened. Poor Tommy.'

Karen followed Brooke into the spacious kitchen at the end of the hall. It was very similar in design to Lyra Hill's. It had the same bifold doors overlooking the garden, and similar shiny white units.

'I spoke with the Fosters yesterday. They mentioned you sometimes babysit for Tommy,' Karen began as they settled down at the breakfast bar.

'Yes, that's right.' Brooke's expression softened. 'It was such a shock to hear he'd gone missing. I got a WhatsApp message from

Rachel at number five yesterday. She wanted to know if I'd seen him. But we were out all day.'

Brooke lifted her arm to push her fringe from her eyes. The movement made the sleeve of her cardigan shift and revealed a red mark on her wrist. It was just starting to turn into a purple bruise at the edges.

'That looks painful,' Karen commented, nodding towards the discolouration. 'How did you manage to do that?'

Brooke glanced at her arm, tugging down the sleeve of her cardigan to cover the injury. 'Oh, this? I must have knocked it on something.' She gave an awkward laugh. 'I can be quite clumsy.'

Karen thought it looked as though someone had grabbed Brooke's wrist. But she decided not to press the matter.

'You live here with your boyfriend.'

'Yes, that's right. Sam,' Brooke replied, a soft smile appearing on her face. 'We're actually getting married next week.'

'Congratulations,' Karen said. 'Is Sam home?'

'He's in the cabin in the garden, on his gaming rig. He's got a man cave out there.' She rolled her eyes good-naturedly. 'I can go and get him if you'd like.'

'Maybe later. I just have a few quick questions for you first.' Karen leaned forward, resting her elbows on the breakfast bar. 'What can you tell me about Tommy? Did he ever confide in you?'

'Tommy is really into his computer games. He's quite grown-up for his age, but he didn't confide in me when it came to anything serious. We mostly just chatted about school and his games.'

'When did you last see Tommy?' Karen asked.

'Let's see,' Brooke mused, her forehead furrowing. 'It was about a week ago. I bumped into him and his mum at the supermarket. I chatted to Amber for a bit, and then they went on their way. Tommy seemed fed up.' She smiled. 'Not that there was anything unusual about that. What eleven-year-old boy likes going to the supermarket?'

'When did you last babysit for him?'

'Two weeks ago. His mum and dad went into Lincoln; Gareth had a work do.'

'Did he mention anything to you?' Karen asked, watching Brooke closely for any signs of discomfort or hesitation. 'Had he made a new friend perhaps?'

'No, nothing like that.'

'Have you noticed anything different about Tommy's behaviour recently?' Karen asked, her gaze never leaving Brooke's face.

'No, not really,' Brooke answered with a slight shrug. 'He's been just the same as he always is.'

'When you look after Tommy, does he ever come here? Or do you look after him at his house?'

'Usually at his house.'

'Has Tommy ever come here? I thought he might be interested in Sam's gaming rig?'

Brooke's expression darkened, and Karen thought she saw a flicker of fear in her eyes. 'Tommy doesn't really interact with Sam.'

'No? They never speak?'

Brooke nervously tugged at her sleeve and looked down at her hands. 'Well, of course they speak. We live a couple of doors away, but Tommy and Sam don't spend time together.'

'Do you think Tommy would have confided in you if something was bothering him?'

'I . . . I don't know. He's open with me, and because of Sam's hobby, I understand what Tommy is on about when he's chatting about gaming. His parents aren't very tech-savvy. I think they find Tommy hard work.' Brooke looked up suddenly. 'That sounded wrong. I meant they struggle to understand why he's so into his computer. Amber is a brilliant mum.'

Karen made a mental note of the fact Brooke had spoken positively of Amber but not Gareth, but before she could ask another question, the bifold doors opened and a well-built man with short hair and a day's worth of stubble walked into the kitchen. He looked surprised to see Karen there. 'Oh, hey,' he said, his tone casual. 'Didn't know we had company.'

'Sam, Detective Sergeant Hart was just asking me about Tommy,' Brooke explained as he grabbed a glass from the cupboard and filled it with water.

'Ah, yeah,' Sam said, taking a sip. 'Shame about the kid.'

'Can I ask where you both were yesterday?' Karen asked.

Brooke and Sam exchanged a glance before answering.

'We were at a funeral,' Brooke said finally, touching the feather pendant hanging around her neck. 'Sam's grandmother passed away last week.'

'I'm sorry for your loss,' Karen said. She'd picked up on their unease and found it curious, but tried not to let her suspicion show.

'Thanks,' Sam mumbled, avoiding eye contact. 'It was a tough day. Gran was like a second mum to me really.'

'I don't want to keep you long, but I'd like to ask you a few questions about Tommy.'

'Fire away,' Sam said.

'How well do you know him?' Karen asked, and she noticed Brooke stiffen slightly.

But Sam wasn't perturbed. 'Not well. Brooke watches him for his folks sometimes. He's come round here a few times, but only when Brooke wants to watch her reality show. The Burtons don't subscribe to the channel, so Tommy comes around here and plays on his tablet when Brooke watches that daft beach programme with all those people trying to date each other.'

Brooke flushed. 'I only did that once! And Tommy didn't mind.'

Sam shrugged. 'Didn't say he minded, did I? But you really shouldn't watch that rubbish. Gran used to say reality shows rot your brain.'

Brooke narrowed her eyes but made no comment, and Sam seemed oblivious to the bitterness radiating from her.

Karen pressed on, returning to the matter at hand. 'Have you witnessed anything out of the ordinary recently regarding Tommy?'

Brooke shook her head, but Sam looked thoughtful. He looked to be on the verge of confiding something, but to Karen's frustration, he just shook his head and said, 'Nah, doesn't matter.'

'It might,' Karen said. 'You never know what information could help.'

'Well,' Sam began reluctantly, 'it's not really relevant, I'm sure, but I saw Jack, the Fosters' eldest boy, lose his temper and give Tommy a shove the other day when the kids were coming back from school.'

'What?' Brooke's eyes widened. 'You didn't tell me that.'

'It was just kids' stuff,' Sam said with a shrug. 'Tommy was probably being a brat. He could be a little sod at times.'

Karen raised an eyebrow at Sam's choice of words, and Brooke quickly cut in, 'He didn't mean that, Detective. We're worried about Tommy, aren't we, Sam?'

'Right,' Sam muttered sheepishly, rubbing the back of his neck. 'Of course. We just want him to be found safe and sound.'

Karen nodded, her intuition telling her that there was something more beneath the surface here. 'I won't keep you much longer. I just need to take down a few more details for my report. Where do you both work?'

'I run an animal centre,' Brooke said. 'On Sands Lane in Lincoln.'

'Is that a veterinary surgery?'

'No, it's more of a rescue centre, but we also have a small cattery and kennels. The money we get from that helps support the rescue side of things. We do have a local vet who helps us out though.'

Karen turned to Sam.

'Technically, I'm between jobs right now,' he said defensively, leaning against the counter. 'I develop my own games. Not like Call of Duty or anything . . . I work in Unity Engine mostly and just publish on Steam, you know?'

Karen didn't know, but it sounded to her like he was trying hard to defend the fact he didn't currently have an income. 'I see. Can I take your full name, Sam?'

'Samuel Tranmere.'

She looked up sharply. 'Tranmere?' It wasn't a common name. 'Are you related to DCI Sylvester Tranmere?'

Sam nodded, rubbing the back of his neck again self-consciously. 'Yeah, that's my dad, but he's retired now. Did you work with him?'

'No, but I've met him.' She didn't mention she'd seen DCI Tranmere just last night.

Alarm bells were ringing for Karen. Sam lived just a few doors away from Tommy Burton. Sam's father had been the officer in charge of the original investigation into the abductions fifteen years ago. This couldn't be a coincidence. Had DCI Tranmere told Sam about the teddy bears left at the abduction sites? Morgan had said that Tranmere's relationship with his son was troubled.

Sam frowned, uncomfortable under Karen's scrutiny. 'Are we done?'

'Actually, Sam,' Karen said casually, her eyes drifting towards the bifold doors that led into the garden, 'you said you're into gaming. Would you mind if I have a look at your set-up?'

'Really?' Sam perked up, his discomfort seemingly forgotten. 'Sure. Follow me.'

They left the kitchen and entered the small garden. The cabin looked like a big shed with tinted windows. Was that to reduce the glare from sunlight, or did Sam want privacy in there for some reason? Suspicions were forming in Karen's mind. Had their shared interest in gaming led to an opportunity Sam could have exploited to groom Tommy? He seemed open and unthreatening, but she reserved judgement for now.

Sam unlocked the door and ushered Karen inside. The room was dimly lit by the glow of multicoloured LED lights emanating from various pieces of computer equipment.

'Wow,' Karen muttered as she stepped into the cabin, genuinely impressed by the space inside. There was a large, leather recliner beside a high-end gaming chair. Both seats faced three huge monitors mounted on the wall. A whirring computer tower with colourful lights hummed beneath the desk. Even the mouse had a glowing blue strip of lights. This would have impressed a young gamer like Tommy.

A couple of empty beer cans sat beside the keyboard on the desk, the only sign of disorder in the otherwise neat space.

'Pretty nice, isn't it?' Sam boasted, folding his arms and puffing out his chest. 'Built this whole thing myself, piece by piece.'

'It must have taken you a lot of time.' Karen glanced around the room, looking for any signs that Tommy had spent time there, playing games with Sam. 'Has Tommy ever come over? I bet he'd love all this.'

'Tommy?' Sam scoffed, turning away so Karen couldn't see his face. 'No, he's just a kid. This is all too advanced for him.'

'Well, thanks for showing me. It's quite the set-up.'

'No problem,' Sam said as they left the cabin and headed back towards the house.

Karen gave him a sideways glance. Was she in the company of the man who'd abducted Tommy Burton?

Sam would have been a teenager at the time of the original case. Old enough to understand some of what was going on. She needed to talk to Morgan and Churchill about her concerns as soon as possible, and check out Sam's alibi. Had the funeral yesterday taken up the whole day?

Karen said her goodbyes to Brooke and Sam, after handing them her card and urging them to get in touch if they thought of anything else. Brooke led Karen to the door, smiling politely but avoiding Karen's gaze, and Sam hung back in the kitchen.

She was walking away from the house when her phone rang. Arnie was calling from the station.

'Everything okay?'

'We've got a briefing in twenty minutes.' Arnie's voice sounded serious.

'Development?'

'Yes. I don't have the full story yet. They haven't found Tommy, but they've found something.'

'Right,' Karen replied, glancing back at the house. 'I have some news of my own to share at the briefing. Two things, really. I found out that the Fosters' older boy – Jack – got into a scrap with Tommy recently. And you won't believe who I've been talking to – Sam Tranmere.'

'Tranmere? As in the detective who headed the Donaldson case?' Arnie asked, confusion evident in his voice.

'Sam is DCI Tranmere's son,' Karen said, getting into her car. 'He's living with a woman called Brooke Lewis. I've got my suspicions about him, Arnie. He's into gaming and has a cabin in the garden that would really impress a young boy like Tommy, and he lives on the same street.'

'Well, well,' Arnie muttered. 'He's definitely worth a closer look.'

Karen hesitated before going on. She knew how close Morgan was to DCI Tranmere. Part of her didn't want to consider Sam a suspect, but she had to set feelings aside. She couldn't eliminate someone based on who their father was. If anything, Sam being DCI Tranmere's son only made him a more likely suspect. He would know about the old abductions.

'Can you talk to Morgan for me? He's close to DCI Tranmere. I don't want to blindside him with this in the briefing.'

'All right, I'll find Morgan now. See you shortly.'

'Thanks, Arnie,' Karen said, hanging up the call as she started the engine. She had planned to speak with Jack Foster and his parents again, to ask about Jack's hostility towards Tommy, but that would have to wait until after the briefing.

With each new piece of information, the puzzle surrounding Tommy Burton's disappearance grew more complicated, and they couldn't afford to miss any crucial pieces if they wanted to find the missing boy.

One thing was for certain: Sam Tranmere living just doors away from Tommy was a piece of the puzzle they couldn't ignore.

Chapter Twelve

Karen sat in the briefing room, clutching a mug of coffee. Arnie's words echoed in her mind. *They've found something.*

At least it wasn't Tommy's body. That meant there was still a chance of bringing him home safely.

Karen anxiously scanned the briefing notes, acutely aware time was slipping by fast. Criminology studies showed the first hours of a missing persons case were the most vital. The number of leads tended to dry up quickly after the initial few days.

A young blonde officer, DC Cobbs, entered the room. She sat beside Farzana. 'So what's the latest? Are we certain this is an abduction? I still think he could have run off. His mother said he was upset with her.'

'Even if Tommy did go off on his own, he could then have been targeted by someone,' Farzana said. Cobbs started to interrupt but Farzana kept talking. 'It's estimated that twenty-five per cent of children suffer abuse while missing even if they left voluntarily.'

Cobbs's eyes widened. 'That's horrifying.'

Karen agreed. Tommy may have left willingly, but the statistics suggested he could be in danger even if he hadn't been snatched from Tattershall. He was a vulnerable child alone and at grave risk. They had to find him before—

DCI Churchill strode to the front of the room. 'All right, listen up. We've got some news.'

Karen watched as her fellow officers leaned forward, their expressions curious. News about cases like this usually spread quickly, but this time no one had heard what the update was in advance.

Churchill's face was grim as he said, 'Tommy Burton's phone was found destroyed at the bottom of the castle moat.'

There was a sharp intake of breath from some of the officers in the room. This wasn't an unexpected development; when they hadn't been able to get a trace on Tommy's phone, they had suspected someone had removed the battery and SIM card. Destroying the phone was a calculated move – whoever had taken Tommy didn't want them tracking it. Finding the phone was the strongest indication yet that Tommy had been taken by someone clever enough to cover their tracks.

The possibility that Tommy had wandered off or decided to run away from home was now looking extremely unlikely.

As people murmured questions, Karen took one of the handouts that were being passed around, and stared down at an image of the shattered remains of a smartphone. It was a significant discovery, and it didn't bode well for Tommy.

'The search team found it an hour ago,' Churchill said. 'The sheer amount of plant matter tangled up on the bed of the moat, plus the fact that the phone was in pieces, meant it wasn't found on the first sweep.'

Karen looked at Arnie, who was sitting hunched over in his chair, his brow furrowed. He glanced at Karen, and a shared understanding passed between them. Things weren't looking good.

'That moat isn't very deep,' Arnie said. 'Useless for defence, but perfect for hiding evidence.'

The team all understood the implications of this finding: if Tommy had been taken, his abductor was doing everything they could to make it difficult for the police to track them down.

'What if Tommy threw his phone in the moat, then ran off on his own? Maybe he chucked the phone so he couldn't be found?' DC Cobbs suggested, though she didn't sound as confident about the idea now. She continued rapidly: 'Or maybe he had a tantrum and bolted to spite his mum?'

'Then how do we explain the blue bear left at the scene?' Rick said.

Cobbs went quiet and shrugged.

'We can't rule out that he left voluntarily,' Churchill said, 'but we'll proceed as though foul play is involved until we have evidence otherwise.'

He moved on, asking for updates from each officer in turn. Finally, he turned to Karen.

'I spoke to Brooke Lewis, Tommy's babysitter, early this morning,' Karen said. 'She lives two doors away from the Burtons. She couldn't tell me much, but I was surprised to find she's living with Sam Tranmere. They're getting married next week. As you all know, his father, DCI Tranmere, headed up the original investigation.'

Everyone's attention swung to Karen, but her gaze fell on Morgan. She knew Arnie had broken the news to him before the briefing, but this development would weigh on him. Though you wouldn't know that to look at him. His face was blank, impassive. He held her gaze for a moment before looking away.

'I see.' Churchill's tone was neutral. 'This is an interesting development. Did you speak to Sam Tranmere?'

'Yes. He's currently out of work. DCI Tranmere said Sam is due to inherit some money after the recent death of his step-grandmother. He's into gaming, and has a cabin in the garden dedicated to his hobby. All high-end stuff as far as I can tell. No doubt Tommy would have been impressed by it. But he denies saying more than the occasional passing word to Tommy, and is absolutely positive on the fact he didn't allow Tommy to see his set-up.'

Churchill stroked his chin thoughtfully.

'Any chance he has him stashed in the cabin?' Arnie asked.

'I don't think so. He was happy enough to take me out there and show me around.'

'We'll have to look at him closely, but let's not jump to conclusions,' Churchill said. 'Arnie, you can get background on Sam Tranmere and his fiancée. See if anything jumps out at you.'

Arnie grunted and scribbled something on his notepad, his bushy eyebrows drawing together.

'There's something else,' Karen said, leaning forward, resting her elbows on the table. 'When I spoke to Sam and Brooke this morning, I noticed an injury on Brooke's wrist – a bad bruise.'

'An injury?' Rick asked. 'Do you think Sam is knocking her about?'

The question hung heavily in the room.

'I don't know,' Karen admitted. 'There was definitely some tension between them, but it's hard to say for sure.'

She met Morgan's gaze again, but this time he swallowed hard then looked away before saying, 'I can talk to Sam.'

'No,' Churchill said, his tone firm but not unkind. 'There's too much history there. Arnie will do it.'

'I haven't seen Sam Tranmere since he was fourteen. My working with his father years ago won't affect this current case if we need to take it in that direction. I can do my job.'

'No one doubts that, DI Morgan. Nevertheless, I want Arnie to handle it.'

Morgan nodded. 'Fine.'

'One more thing,' Karen said. 'Sam mentioned witnessing Jack Foster, their fourteen-year-old neighbour, arguing with Tommy and shoving him, but Sam doesn't know what the altercation was about.'

Churchill frowned as he processed this new piece of information. 'Have you spoken to Jack Foster?'

'Yes, I spoke to Jack and his brother Adam along with their parents yesterday. Jack was subdued, and denied having much to do with Tommy.'

'Could be relevant. I want you to speak to Jack Foster again.'

'He'll be at school now,' Karen replied, glancing at the clock on the wall.

'Fine, go to the school and talk to him there,' Churchill said decisively. 'Take Rick with you. It's disruptive, I know, but we don't have a huge amount to go on otherwise. We can't afford to wait until he's home. Find out what happened between him and Tommy.'

'I'll go there straight after the briefing.' Karen glanced at Rick, who gave her a nod.

'Speak to the headteacher too,' Churchill continued. 'We need to keep the school in the loop. They held an assembly this morning to explain to the children what's happening.'

'Rick.' Churchill turned his attention to the young detective. 'What have you got on the security footage?'

'Sadly, not much,' Rick replied, running a hand through his dark hair. 'Tommy just disappeared. I think he must have left Tattershall in a vehicle; otherwise he would have been picked up on CCTV at some point in the village.'

An uneasy silence settled over the room as the team absorbed this information. If Tommy had been taken from the castle in a vehicle, he could be miles away by now.

'All right,' Churchill said finally. 'We need to follow up on every lead we have. Karen, see if you can find out more about Jack Foster and his interaction with Tommy. Farzana, I want you to keep looking into where that blue teddy bear was purchased.'

Farzana's face fell. She'd identified the toy manufacturer, but chasing down every supplier and seller would be a long, painstaking job involving a lot of screen and phone time – hardly the glamorous part of any investigation, but it needed to be done.

As Churchill assigned tasks to the rest of the officers, Karen came up with an idea.

Once the team had filed out of the briefing room, she approached Churchill with a request. 'Sir, do you think we could give Sophie the task of chasing down the blue teddy bear stockists?'

Churchill collected his paperwork from the desk. 'She's still recovering, Karen. I don't think it's wise.'

He began to turn away.

'I disagree,' Karen said. 'Sophie needs something to focus on, and she's excellent at research like this. We need all the help we can get, and she won't be working alone. She'll be assisting Farzana.'

Reluctantly, Churchill paused, halfway to the door. 'I don't know, Karen. What if she misses something? She isn't fully recovered.'

'This is Sophie we're talking about. She's precise and meticulous. She was made for work like this. Besides, it will be good for her. I think it might help her get some confidence back.'

After a tense moment, Churchill relented with a sigh. 'Fine, the task is hers if she wants it. But make sure she doesn't overdo it.'

◆ ◆ ◆

Morgan wasn't in his office, so Karen walked through the open-plan main area, her gaze darting from one desk to another in search of him. She couldn't shake the nagging concern that had taken root during the briefing.

A quiet, restrained demeanour wasn't unusual for Morgan, but this case had rattled him, causing him to withdraw even more.

She found him standing beside one of the printers. He looked up as she approached, his eyes guarded.

'I wanted to see you before I left for the school,' she said. 'How are you holding up?'

'Fine,' Morgan muttered, putting fresh paper into the bottom of the machine. 'Just printing off some old case notes.'

'Listen,' Karen began cautiously, 'I'm sorry I didn't get a chance to talk to you about Sam Tranmere before the briefing, but Arnie let you know, didn't he?'

'Yes, he told me.'

'Sam was only a boy when the original case happened, but do you think he could've picked up on any of the background details? Like the teddy bears being left at abduction scenes?'

Morgan frowned, rubbing his temples as if trying to ward off an impending headache. 'It's possible,' he admitted. 'Maybe he overheard his father talking about it. But that doesn't mean he would . . .'

'Re-enact the abduction?' Karen finished for him. 'Maybe not, but we can't afford to rule anything out.'

'Right.' Morgan sighed. 'I just keep picturing him as an awkward fourteen-year-old kid who worshipped his dad. I never expected to have him be a suspect in an investigation.'

'No. It came as quite a surprise to me when he gave me his full name.'

'Ready to go?' Rick's voice came from behind them.

'Almost,' Karen replied, casting one last worried glance at Morgan, but he'd already turned his attention back to the printer.

With Rick in tow, she strode through the station and out into the car park at the front of the building in silence. Her mind was filled with questions, and concern for Morgan.

'Do you think we'll get something useful from Jack Foster?' Rick asked, breaking Karen's train of thought. 'Or do you reckon their fall-out was just kids being kids?'

'Hard to say,' she replied. 'But right now, this lead is one of the few we've got.'

'Do you want to stop off at Sophie's parents' place?'

Karen nodded. 'I'm hoping she feels up to working her way through the list Farzana compiled of the suppliers for that blue bear.'

'I think she'll jump at the chance. She's been bored.'

As they got in the car, Rick said quietly, 'There's still a slim chance that Tommy ran away from home and is hiding out some-where, isn't there?'

Karen empathised with Rick's quiet desperation. She wanted to reassure him and agree that there was still a possibility Tommy was safe after all, though experience told her that was very unlikely.

She understood Rick's need to hold on to hope. She was reluctant to consider the other possibility, too: that they were already too late.

Chapter Thirteen

Karen knocked on the bungalow door, expecting Sophie's mum or dad to answer with their usual offer of tea and biscuits. But Sophie opened the door, her left hand touching the wall for balance. There was no sign of the stick she'd been using to help her get around lately. Her eyes were still dull and her skin was pale, but her face lit up when she saw Karen and Rick.

'I wasn't expecting another visit so soon,' she said with a smile. Then her face tightened. 'You're not here to tell me I'm out, are you? Has Churchill sent you to break the news to me gently?'

'Of course not,' Rick said, leaning in to give Sophie a hug. 'You're stuck with us.'

'How are you feeling today?' Karen asked.

'My right hand is still useless, but I've been trying to get around without my stick. So far, so good. The doctor says my ability to focus should come back in time.' Sophie looked at Rick and gave a weak grin. 'Of course, my focus at fifty per cent is still better than scatterbrained Rick's at one hundred per cent.'

Rick snorted. 'Charming! Seriously though. That brain of yours will be back to normal in no time. You'll be doing sudoku and cryptic crosswords again before we know it.'

'Sudoku and cryptic crosswords?' Sophie grinned.

'Just the sort of activities you love. With your weird obsession with paperwork and highlighters, you're halfway to full-on nerd already,' Rick said.

Sophie tried to look offended but couldn't hide her smile.

'We've actually come with a request,' Karen said, following Sophie into the bungalow. 'Farzana's been compiling a list of manufacturers who produce blue teddy bears similar to the one that was left at the scene of an abduction.' Karen held up a folder. 'We were hoping you might go through the list and see if you can narrow down retailers. We're particularly interested in local shops that sell them. If you feel up to it, of course.'

Sophie's eyes lit up, and Karen glimpsed a spark of her old enthusiasm. 'I'd love to help. It'll give my brain something to chew on.'

'If you need some background information,' Rick said, motioning to the folder, 'the case details are inside too.'

Sophie sank on to the sofa. 'Nothing I like better than a case file. Inactivity is driving me mad. I need to get back to work.'

'You will,' Rick said, 'but there's no rush. Take your time to heal.'

'I know, I know.' Sophie sighed, rolling her eyes. 'I need to be patient.'

Karen sat beside her on the sofa. 'I understand how frustrating this is for you, but try not to overdo it. Let me know if you can't handle this, or if anything's unclear.'

Sophie looked at Karen and Rick, her smile softening. 'Thank you. Both of you. I don't know what I'd do without your support.'

'That's what friends are for,' Rick said gruffly.

Karen squeezed Sophie's hand. 'We need to get going, but you take care of yourself. And remember, I'm here if there's anything you need.'

'I know.' Sophie's fingers tightened around Karen's. 'I'll get started on this list of manufacturers. Leave it with me.'

They left Sophie poring over the folder, her brow creased in concentration. Paperwork was her happy place. It was as if a switch had been flipped, activating the analytical part of her mind. For the first time since the attack Sophie seemed focused and driven, her quick mind already methodically sorting through the details.

The nagging worry Karen had carried since visiting Sophie yesterday eased. Her friend was made of sterner stuff than any of them realised.

◆ ◆ ◆

Karen took in the headteacher's office, noting the MDF bookshelves lining one wall which displayed trophies rather than books. On the opposite wall, framed certificates surrounded a small square window that overlooked the playground.

Ms Harriet Scott sat behind a large desk, her hands clasped on its surface. The headteacher was a stern-looking woman in her late fifties, with greying hair cut short and shrewd blue eyes.

'Thank you for seeing us at such short notice, Ms Scott,' Karen said after they had introduced themselves and sat down.

'Of course. When it comes to the safety of my pupils, I will always make time for the police.' Harriet sighed, glancing out of the window at the empty playground. 'The children have been restless, as you can imagine. We held an assembly to reassure them, but they're scared and upset.'

'Does Tommy have any close friends at school?' Rick asked. 'Anyone we could speak to?'

Harriet shook her head. 'I'm afraid Tommy is rather isolated. He struggles to make friends. In hindsight, perhaps there was more we should have done to make his time here happier . . .' Her voice trailed off.

Karen asked, 'Is Tommy close to any of his teachers?'

'Not really, but you might want to visit the library,' Harriet said. 'He spends hours in there. You should speak with Clark Mills, the librarian. He's rather fond of Tommy.'

'Thank you, we'll do that, but first I wanted to ask you about Jack Foster. We'd like to talk to him.'

'Jack Foster?' Harriet bit her lip. 'Sorry you'll have to jog my memory. It's a large school. Almost two thousand students, and I'm sorry to say, it's impossible to keep track of them all.'

'He's older than Tommy. Fourteen. He has a younger brother, Adam Foster, who's in Tommy's year.'

Harriet's expression cleared. 'Ah yes. I know Jack. Can I ask why you would like to speak to him? I should get his parents' permission first.'

'Of course,' Karen said. 'We understand Jack Foster had an altercation with Tommy recently. Can you tell us anything about that?'

Harriet's brow creased. 'An altercation? I wasn't aware of anything like that. Jack and Tommy aren't friends, as far as I know, and we've had no reports of trouble between them.'

'Our witness said Jack shoved Tommy during an argument,' Rick said.

The headteacher's lips thinned. 'If that had happened on school property, I would certainly have known about it. We have a zero tolerance policy on bullying and violence.'

Karen studied Harriet's face but could detect no sign of evasion in her steady gaze.

'The incident didn't occur at school,' Karen said. 'Would it be possible for us to talk to Jack now? We have a few more questions for him about his interactions with Tommy. We can wait until you have permission from his parents.'

Harriet gave a tight smile. 'I'll ask the school secretary to contact his parents.'

Karen watched her get up and stride from the room.

'She seems pretty convincing,' Rick said under his breath. 'About not knowing anything about trouble between Jack and Tommy, I mean.'

Karen nodded. 'She does. But we need to hear Jack's side of the story.'

A few minutes passed and then Harriet bustled back into the room. 'Mrs Foster has given her permission but requested that I'm present when you speak to Jack.'

'That's good,' Karen said. 'Hopefully Jack will feel reassured with you in the room.'

Harriet gave a brisk nod. 'Jack is in maths at the moment. I will have him brought to my office so you can speak with him.'

A few minutes later, Harriet returned with a sullen-looking Jack Foster. He slouched into the room with his hands stuffed in his pockets.

'Jack, these detectives would like to ask you some questions about Tommy Burton,' Harriet said. 'Please cooperate fully.'

Jack shrugged but didn't reply. His gaze slid to Karen and Rick, then away.

Karen studied him for a moment, noticing the tension in his posture and the way he was reluctant to maintain eye contact — just as he had been last night.

Interesting.

'Thank you, Ms Scott,' Karen said.

Harriet nodded and pulled over a lightweight plastic chair from the corner of the room for Jack, and then sat behind her desk.

Jack fidgeted, eyes fixed on his shoes.

123

'Hello again, Jack,' Karen said. 'I'm DS Karen Hart; we met last night. And this is DC Rick Cooper. We'd like to ask you a few questions about your friend, Tommy Burton.'

At the word *friend*, Jack's head jerked up, his eyes flashing with anger. 'Tommy Burton isn't my friend!'

Karen regarded him calmly. 'You had an argument with him recently. Can you tell us about that?'

Jack paled, his anger fading as quickly as it had risen. He stared down at his shoes again, shoulders hunching defensively. 'We didn't have an argument.' A blush crept up his neck. 'I barely know him.'

'You were seen, Jack.' Karen kept her tone light, but the boy's reaction set off alarm bells. He was lying. Why? Because he thought he'd get into trouble for fighting?

'Who told you they saw us?' Jack asked, a hint of defiance entering his voice. 'They're lying, probably trying to get me in trouble.'

'Come on, Jack,' Rick said gently. 'We already know about the argument. There's no point denying it.'

Jack swallowed, his Adam's apple bobbing. He scuffed his shoe on the floor and crossed his arms over his chest. 'There was no argument.'

'I see,' Karen said, glancing at Rick, who gave a subtle nod. They were on the same page. 'Well, if that's the case, you won't mind coming down to the station to give us an official statement. Just to clarify a few details. We'll ask your parents to come too.'

Jack paled. 'What? No, you can't. My parents will kill me.'

Karen softened her tone and leaned forward. 'Look, Jack, we know you're hiding something. But if you tell us the truth now, this will all be over much faster. It's for Tommy's sake – the longer he's missing, the more danger he's in. You want to help find him, don't you?'

Jack looked at her, eyes wide. 'I didn't do anything to Tommy, honestly.'

The boy was no criminal mastermind. He was upset, and Karen was reluctant to push him too far, but they needed to find Tommy.

'Okay, Jack,' Karen said. 'But you need to tell us why you were fighting with Tommy.'

Jack deflated, shoulders slumping. When he spoke again, his voice was quiet. 'Tommy was teasing me. I lost my temper and shoved him. He deserved it. It was just a little push.'

Karen leaned back in her chair, watching Jack closely. 'What was Tommy teasing you about?'

After a long pause, Jack mumbled, 'About . . . about my ears.' His cheeks reddened. 'Saying they stick out too far.'

'So, you had an argument about it, and you pushed Tommy.'

Jack's head jerked up again. 'He was being *horrible*.'

'Come on, Jack, tell us exactly what happened. We need the full story,' Rick said.

Jack sank back into the chair. He looked utterly defeated.

'Tommy wouldn't stop teasing me,' he said dully. 'He was so loud, and everyone could hear. I told him to shut up, but he wouldn't stop. So, I pushed him. I didn't mean to hurt him; I just wanted him to stop.'

'What happened after you pushed him?' Karen asked.

'Nothing. He fell over, but he wasn't hurt or anything. He shouted at me that I'd be sorry. Then I went home.' Jack shrugged. 'That's it. Nothing else happened.'

Karen studied him, looking for any signs of deception. She didn't think he was lying, but she wasn't sure he was telling them the whole story either.

'All right, Jack, thank you for your honesty,' Karen said. 'You've been very helpful. Is there anything else you can tell us about Tommy?'

He shook his head. 'Not really. Like I said, I don't know him that well.'

Karen nodded. 'You can go back to class now.'

Jack stood up. 'Are you going to tell my parents about this?' he asked nervously.

'I suggest you tell them the truth yourself.'

Jack nodded and left the room without another word, closing the door quietly behind him.

Harriet smiled apologetically. 'Not the breakthrough you were hoping for.'

'No,' Rick agreed. 'But there's still the librarian to speak to. Perhaps they can give us more insight.'

Chapter Fourteen

Harriet Scott escorted Karen and Rick to the school library, then hurried off saying she had a meeting to attend. They walked through the library, scanning the rows of bookshelves and study tables.

The librarian – a balding man in his fifties, wearing round glasses – was reshelving books in the science section. He looked up as they approached and smiled. 'Detectives Hart and Cooper, I presume? The secretary called to say you were on your way here.' He shook their hands. 'I'm Clark Mills.'

As they followed him to the main desk, Karen said, 'We're investigating the disappearance of Tommy Burton. We understand he spent a lot of time here.'

'Oh yes, he did.' Mills sighed, shaking his head. 'Tommy was a regular. Always had his nose buried in a science fiction novel. I was quite worried about him, to tell you the truth. Bit of a loner, that one.'

Karen's gaze landed on a stack of Philip K. Dick paperbacks on the counter. 'You and Tommy share an interest in sci-fi?'

'Guilty as charged.' Mills smiled. 'We often chat about the latest novel he's reading. I think books are a form of escape for Tommy. A way to lose himself in other worlds. He's a keen gamer, too.'

'Are you?'

'No, I stick to books.'

Karen thought of the *Star Wars* figurines and *Star Trek* books lining Tommy's bedroom shelves. 'Did Tommy ever mention his home life?' she asked. 'Any problems with his father, perhaps?'

Mills frowned, glancing away. 'I don't think I should say anything when I don't know for sure.'

'What you tell us could be vital to finding Tommy,' Rick said. 'Please, if there's anything you know that could help, don't hesitate.'

The librarian gave a resigned sigh. 'Last week, Tommy told me a character in the book he was reading reminded him of his father. The character was the bad guy. It was one of Terry Goodkind's *Sword of Truth* books, where the central character, Richard Cypher, discovers that his true father is Darken Rahl, an evil warlord – a man he has dedicated himself to defeating.'

Mills paused, but Karen and Rick stayed quiet, waiting for the librarian to continue. 'It did worry me. The character is pretty nasty, and I found it shocking that Tommy would liken the warlord to his own dad.'

'Did you ask him about it?' Rick asked.

'I did. I asked if his dad was cruel to him, but Tommy said no and that I shouldn't worry about him. He said his dad deserved what was coming to him.' Mills shook his head. 'I put it down to boys' bravado. Tommy has an active imagination. But now I wonder if it really was a cry for help.'

Karen looked at Rick, a chill running down her spine.

What had Tommy meant by that? That his father *deserved what was coming to him*. Did it have something to do with Tommy's disappearance? Would Tommy's father have abducted his own son? It didn't make sense.

'For what it's worth, I've met Tommy's father at parents' evening. He seemed a gentle sort. Hard to imagine him getting angry.' Mills shrugged. 'But I suppose you can't really tell.'

It sounded like Tommy had a difficult relationship with his father. Had Tommy run off to punish him?

'Have you found the person who slashed the headteacher's tyres?' Mills asked, changing the subject.

Rick's eyebrows shot up. 'Someone slashed the headteacher's tyres? Here, at the school?'

'Oh dear,' Mills said, adjusting his glasses. 'Perhaps I shouldn't have mentioned it.'

'When did this happen?' Karen asked.

'A couple of weeks ago. Right in the staff car park. Harriet thought it was probably a student and didn't report it at first. But I thought she would have done now that Tommy's gone missing.' He shook his head. 'Harriet saw the incident as a personal failure. She hates to admit the school isn't running like clockwork. But slashing tyres . . . and now a child disappearing . . . you wouldn't think that sort of thing would happen here.'

Karen couldn't see an obvious connection between the act of vandalism and Tommy's disappearance, but wondered why Harriet hadn't mentioned it.

'You're sure it was deliberate, and not a puncture?' Rick asked.

'Oh, it was deliberate all right.' Mills leaned on the desk. 'All four tyres were damaged.'

'Do you have any theories as to who did it? Or which student Harriet thought was responsible?' Rick asked.

'No, I'm afraid I can't help you there.'

Karen met Rick's gaze and saw concern that mirrored her own. 'Thank you for your time, Mr Mills.'

They left him in the library and headed back to the car.

Karen paused, key in hand, staring across the car park. There was a connection here she couldn't quite put her finger on.

Rick cleared his throat. 'Penny for your thoughts?'

Karen blinked, turning to find him watching her. 'It's just . . . this doesn't make sense. Did Gareth Burton fake the abduction to cover up whatever he'd done to his son?'

'Perhaps Tommy was threatening to tell on him,' Rick suggested. 'Or maybe he just snapped. Abusers don't always follow a clear pattern of logic.'

Karen nodded. 'We need to look very closely at Tommy's father.'

'I've been in contact with social services, but there's nothing on file,' Rick said. 'I know Harriet Scott is in a meeting now, but I'll call later and ask her why she didn't report the vandalism to her car. It could prove to be unrelated, just like Jack Foster's squabble with Tommy, but it seems odd she didn't mention it.'

Karen agreed. She opened the car door and got inside. Instead of turning on the engine, she waited until Rick was in the passenger seat and then said, 'If Tommy's father is responsible for his disappearance, then why the blue teddy bear at the scene? It doesn't fit.'

'No, it doesn't,' Rick said slowly. 'The teddy bear thing gives me the creeps. I just hope this doesn't escalate like it did fifteen years ago. Three victims were taken last time. So far we just have one.'

'Maybe Arnie will get something on Sam Tranmere, but we have to talk to Gareth Burton again,' Karen said, a knot of apprehension forming in her stomach. 'When I spoke to him yesterday, I thought there was something off about him. He kept trying to blame his wife for not looking after Tommy properly, and seemed at pains to tell me he spent lots of quality time with Tommy. But his wife contradicted that.'

'What do you want to do next then? Go back to the station to plan how we'll approach Burton, or head over there now?'

Karen considered this, watching a magpie hop across an empty parking spot opposite. 'Let's go back to the station and talk to Churchill and Morgan first,' she decided. 'We need to be careful with Burton. One wrong move and we could lose our chance to get the truth from him.'

The sun slipped behind a cloud and a chill crept over Karen's skin as she started the engine. They were still some way off solving this case, but perhaps they were getting closer to the truth. She just hoped they wouldn't be too late.

◆ ◆ ◆

Morgan leaned back in his chair and rubbed his eyes. The fluorescent lights in his office were giving him a headache. For what felt like the hundredth time, he glanced at his mobile phone. DCI Tranmere's number glowed ominously on the screen, the green button just waiting to be pressed to connect the call.

His old boss had been good to him. They had worked closely together for over a decade – shared many pints at the local after difficult cases. Tranmere had even encouraged Morgan to aim for the promotion to DI. They were friends, weren't they?

And yet, there was his son . . .

Sam Tranmere lived just two doors away from the missing lad, Tommy Burton. If Tranmere's son was involved . . . Morgan sighed. His loyalties were torn. He wanted to call his old boss and let him know they were looking into a possible connection to his son. But a bigger part of him worried that Tranmere might compromise the investigation. The man could be ruthless when protecting his own, and didn't always stick to the rulebook. As Morgan remembered well.

One case in particular stuck in his mind. Morgan and Tranmere had been questioning Carl Ackley, a suspect with underground connections who'd been accused of money laundering. During the interview, Ackley had leaned across the table and whispered his intent to pay Morgan's family a visit. Morgan had started to sweat, but remained professional despite the panic rising inside him.

It had been the first time he'd been threatened that way, and he was ill-equipped to cope. Being on the receiving end of such threats was never pleasant, but over the years he'd come to realise most of them were bluster.

Tranmere had paused the interview and taken Morgan outside to get some air. Then he'd said the words that had stayed with Morgan: *You don't have to worry. I'll make sure that piece of scum never threatens anyone's family ever again.*

When Ackley had arrived for a second round of questioning, he was shuffling, face red and swollen and split lip bleeding. At the sight of Tranmere, he began to tremble. Tranmere just gave a tight-lipped, satisfied smile.

Later, when Morgan asked what had happened, Tranmere claimed Ackley had got into a scrap with another scrote in the custody suite. But Morgan had never forgotten the raw fear in Ackley's eyes.

Then there was the DS Cameron situation. Cameron had been assigned by Professional Standards to investigate a complaint against one of the team. Tranmere had set out to make him regret that assignment.

The team had trailed Cameron, digging for dirt. They got photos of him with a woman who wasn't his wife. The story went that Tranmere had then dropped the photographs on Cameron's desk and said, *Back off my team, and they disappear forever. Understand?*

A defeated Cameron had quickly dropped the investigation. The team celebrated with a boozy night at their local. Morgan had felt uneasy about threatening a fellow officer, even if he was from what some termed the 'rat squad', but things had been different back then. And at the time, Morgan had been swept along with it all. Young and impressionable, he had admired Tranmere for sticking up for his team. Tranmere was a loyal friend but a terrifying enemy.

Now, Morgan wondered if events had really happened the way he remembered. Or had Tranmere's legendary reputation made him a bigger man in Morgan's eyes?

The door to his office swung open and Arnie strode in, a determined look on his face. 'No criminal records, but it looks like Sam Tranmere has been out of work a while. Living off family money. Your old boss is loaded. Did you know that?'

Morgan nodded. 'Yes, but Tranmere was never one for flashing his cash. He liked to keep his money quiet.'

'You went to his house last night?' Arnie asked.

'Yes, he has a big place out in Mablethorpe.'

Arnie perched on the edge of Morgan's desk, arms folded and eyes narrowed. 'You're not thinking of calling him, are you?' At Morgan's hesitation, Arnie grunted. 'Forget it. That's a bad idea and you know it.'

Morgan rubbed a hand over his face. 'He was my boss, Arnie. My friend. I can't just cut him off without a heads-up.'

'This is an active investigation. Anything you say to Tranmere could compromise it if his son really is involved.' Arnie's stern expression softened. 'I know it's not easy, but you need to keep your distance for now. Promise me you won't call him.'

Morgan met Arnie's gaze, then nodded. 'Okay. I know you're right.'

Arnie visibly relaxed. 'Good. The last thing we need is a retired DCI interfering with an active case.' He leaned back, shifting his position on the desk. 'Do you think his son could be involved? I've been looking into him but can't find anything suspicious. He and his fiancée seem clean.'

'I haven't seen Sam for years. Tranmere always said he was a good kid. It seems they had a falling-out recently, though.'

'Yeah?' Arnie prompted, interested. 'What about?'

'We didn't get into it. At the time, I didn't think it was relevant to the case, and it felt like prying to ask.'

Arnie grunted. 'He must have given you some idea.'

'I got the impression Tranmere thinks Sam is spoiled. They may have had a dispute about money. Sam is the sole beneficiary of his step-grandmother's will.'

'Lucky him,' Arnie mused. 'Then again, they say money is the root of all evil, don't they? Not that I'd know. I wouldn't object to finding out, though.'

Arnie chuckled, but Morgan couldn't even manage a smile. 'It's one heck of a coincidence, Arnie. Sam lives so close to the Burtons. Sam will have known Tommy, seen him around. Not many people knew about those blue bears found at the abduction scenes, but Sam may have known.'

'That's why it's best you don't talk to your old boss, at least until we've cleared his son.' Arnie heaved himself off the desk.

He strode to the door, then paused, looking back at Morgan. 'If you're struggling with all this . . . I'm around. To talk. If you need it.'

Morgan smiled faintly. 'I'll keep that in mind.'

Arnie nodded brusquely and left, closing the door behind him.

Morgan leaned back in his chair again, feeling his tension headache building. Arnie was right – he couldn't call Tranmere. Not yet. But it was good to know he had the backing of Arnie and the team. Their support meant more than Morgan cared to admit, even to himself.

Chapter Fifteen

The desk phone shattered the silence, jolting Morgan from his reading. He snatched up the receiver.

'DI Morgan. It's Governor Briggs,' the gravelly voice said.

What now? Some fresh information about Donaldson? The evil psychopath had better not be trying to use the new investigation to leverage an appeal in exchange for information, which would likely prove useless at best.

'How can I help, Governor?' Morgan asked.

'I remembered something that might be of interest.'

Morgan gripped the phone tighter. 'Go on.'

'A few months before we transferred him to Lincoln, Donaldson received a series of fan letters. They were vetted and copied, of course. There was nothing overtly criminal in the text, but they sounded full of a young man's hero worship to me.' Briggs paused. 'We haven't received any here at Lincoln, but I thought you might want to look into it.'

'I absolutely do,' Morgan said. 'Who were the letters from?'

'A lad by the name of Cody Rhodes. Might have no connection, but in light of the abduction, I thought you should know. Do you want me to send over copies of the letters?'

'Yes,' Morgan said. 'Please send over anything you have on Cody Rhodes. Address, details, whatever's available. This could be a major breakthrough.'

Morgan leaned back in his chair and looked up at the ceiling. The blue bears. Only a few people knew that detail. Had Donaldson boasted to Cody Rhodes and revealed the secrets of his depraved crimes? A theory began to form in Morgan's mind.

'Did Cody Rhodes ever visit Donaldson?' Morgan asked.

'I believe he visited him twice, though not here. I'll send over the dates of the visits.'

'Thank you.'

'I'll email the information straightaway. Good luck, DI Morgan.' Briggs hung up with a click.

Morgan dropped the phone into its cradle. Cody Rhodes. Was he the copycat? If so, that would mean that Sam was innocent, saving Morgan from any issues with Tranmere going forward.

Donaldson had killed the boys he'd abducted within a week. If a copycat had taken Tommy and was sticking closely to Donaldson's original crimes, there was still a chance Tommy Burton was alive.

Morgan's computer pinged, indicating an email had arrived. He opened the message from Governor Briggs to find several scanned letters attached, along with an address for Cody Rhodes. The letters were all handwritten in the same dark scrawl. Morgan clicked on the first one and began to read:

Dear Mr Donaldson,

I hope this letter finds you well. It's been fifteen years since the world was shaken by your deeds. Time hasn't dulled the memories or lessened your impact. I'm reaching out to you, hoping to strengthen a connection that I feel exists between us.

The news was once filled with stories about you, but they painted you in the wrong light. The photographs they used, the headlines they typed . . . it was a disgrace. Optics matter, Mr Donaldson, and the current ones do you no justice.

I've followed your story, your methods, and your reasons. It's a narrative that deserves to be resurrected and retold, not through the distorted lens of the mass media but through the eyes of one who understands.

I see you for who you really are. And it's high time the world sees it too.

They say there's a fine line between madness and genius. I believe you walk that line. Your actions weren't just random events; they were messages. Messages that I believe I am beginning to understand. There's a connection here, a strong bond between us. It's time we explored this further. Between us I believe we can make a lasting legacy.

Looking forward to your reply.

Yours in understanding,

Cody Rhodes

The almost reverential tone Rhodes used in the letter sent a shiver down Morgan's spine. A connection? A lasting legacy? It turned Morgan's stomach. This was fan mail, the words of someone who saw himself linked to Donaldson, someone potentially capable of similar acts.

Morgan moved on to the second letter with a growing sense of unease. Rhodes's handwriting was erratic – looping big letters then tiny marks.

Dear Mr Donaldson,

I had to write to you again. Things are different now. I can see things clearly. You are sending me messages, aren't you? They don't see it, but I do.

We are connected, you and me. It's like a thread, a special thread that only we can see. You did those things as a message for me. I'm trying to make sense of it.

It's hard, but I'm trying. They want to stop me from seeing the truth.

I need to know what to do next. I'm ready to listen. We are linked, Mr Donaldson, in a way no one else can understand.

Please write back. I need to hear from you.

Waiting for your guidance,

Cody

Reading through the disjointed thoughts and simpler language, Morgan was sure Cody Rhodes had the makings of a prime suspect – a man who not only idolised a notorious child killer but seemed to be awaiting instructions.

Morgan scanned the other letters. Rhodes believed he had a personal connection with Donaldson and that they shared some special understanding. He seemed in awe of the man who had murdered three young boys. All the letters reinforced the same sentiments and pointed to a mind obsessed and potentially ready to act.

Morgan uploaded the letters to the database, then jotted down Rhodes's address. The letters were enough for them to bring him in for questioning. They had stopped shortly before Donaldson was transferred to Lincoln Prison. What if Rhodes had decided to finish what Donaldson started? The blue teddy bear at the abduction scene indicated someone with knowledge of Donaldson's crimes.

The letters made Morgan's skin crawl in their sincerity. He looked at the governor's final note at the bottom of the email, highlighting the dates Cody had visited Donaldson in prison. What had they talked about during those meetings? Surely they hadn't planned out a new crime under the noses of the prison officers? Donaldson didn't get privacy with anyone except his legal representatives.

Morgan left his desk. He needed to take this straight to DCI Churchill. He took the stairs two at a time, ignoring the curious glances from the admin staff he passed, and rapped sharply on the doorframe of Churchill's office.

Churchill looked up from a file, frowning. 'What is it?'

'We have a suspect. A lad named Cody Rhodes. I just spoke to Governor Briggs. Before Donaldson was moved to Lincoln, he received a series of letters from Rhodes. The letters stopped before Donaldson was transferred.'

Churchill's eyes narrowed. 'You think Rhodes took Tommy?'

'I think it's highly likely. Briggs emailed me copies of the letters, and it sounds to me like Rhodes admired Donaldson. Maybe Donaldson told him about leaving toy bears at the abduction sites.'

'Right.' Churchill adjusted his tie. 'Do we have a location for Rhodes?'

'Yes, Briggs sent over all the information they have on him. I want to bring Rhodes in for questioning immediately.'

Churchill nodded. 'Agreed. But are you the right person for the task?'

Morgan bristled at the implication but kept his tone level. 'I understand your concerns, sir. But this isn't personal. I just want to do my job.'

It wasn't true though. To Morgan this *was* personal. He was terrified of history repeating itself, and he desperately hoped Sam Tranmere wasn't involved in any of this. That was a can of worms he didn't want to deal with. When Morgan thought of Sam, he still saw the gentle, gawky fourteen-year-old, not the man he would be today.

Morgan didn't want to upset his old boss unless absolutely necessary. Their relationship was complicated, but Tranmere deserved better than his son being involved in a case like this. It would devastate him. Morgan wasn't sure Tranmere would accept Sam's guilt. And he had a history of bending the rules to protect the people he cared about.

But Rhodes was the logical suspect here, not Sam. Morgan needed to get Tommy home – and right now, focusing on Rhodes was the priority.

Churchill said nothing, and there was a long, awkward pause before Morgan said, 'We need to move quickly. I'm familiar with the background of this case. It should be me that brings Rhodes in. He's our first real suspect, and if he is responsible, every second we waste puts Tommy at greater risk.'

After another tense moment, Churchill nodded. 'Okay. Bring Rhodes into custody. But be careful, Morgan.'

'Yes, sir,' Morgan said crisply.

He left Churchill's office and made his way back downstairs to the open-plan area, where he found Arnie.

Arnie spoke first, noticing something in Morgan's expression. 'Development?'

Morgan nodded. 'A big one. You're with me. We're going to pick up a suspect.'

They were close, so close. His mind was already formulating an interview plan. Rhodes would talk, one way or another. Morgan would see to that personally.

◆ ◆ ◆

Morgan turned the car on to the crumbling concrete of a derelict petrol station forecourt. This was the address the governor had given them for Cody Rhodes.

Arnie sat in the passenger seat, a frown on his face. A marked police car pulled up behind them, with two uniformed officers inside.

Morgan scanned the area for signs of life. Weeds had sprung up around the old petrol pumps. The shop windows were cracked and dirty, and a newspaper rack had fallen on its side, blocking the door.

Arnie let out a low whistle. 'If you were looking for a place to hide a kid, this would be ideal.'

Morgan took a deep breath and opened the car door. 'Let's see if anyone's home.'

The petrol station was silent as Morgan and Arnie and the two uniformed officers walked around the perimeter. They announced their presence, but their voices echoed back to them. It was too quiet. No cars driving past. No voices. No signs of life.

Inside the shop, the shelves were empty and covered with dust. Empty drink cans and crisp packets littered the floor. Maybe local kids had been using the place to hang out, or maybe . . .

Morgan spotted a large white cupboard behind where the till must have been when the place was operational. Arnie noticed it at the same time.

'Are you thinking what I'm thinking?' Arnie asked.

Morgan nodded.

They walked over to the cupboard and Morgan tried the handle with a gloved hand. It was locked. He cursed.

Arnie looked over his shoulder, checking the uniforms were still searching outside. 'Hang on.' He fumbled around in his pocket before producing a small set of lock picks. He smiled mischievously at Morgan. 'Permission to go ahead?'

Morgan hesitated, his mind crowding with conflicting thoughts. It went against protocol. There was a chance they might damage evidence, which would risk a later prosecution, and yet . . .

'No, let's wait for the SOCOs. We don't want to disturb evidence.'

'Oh, come on,' Arnie protested. 'It could be ages and any delay might—'

'Go ahead.' Morgan's voice was firm. He didn't want to think about what a delay could mean for Tommy.

Arnie's eyebrows lifted. 'Well, I never thought I'd see Mr Perfect agree to something like this without approval in writing from at least two senior officers,' he teased as he began to work on the lock.

He jiggled it until finally, with a click, the door swung open. Morgan held his breath. Both of them peered into the large cupboard, half expecting to actually find Tommy Burton inside. But all they found was an old-fashioned machine for dispensing cigarettes, clumps of dust and an empty cardboard box.

Disappointed, Arnie shrugged his shoulders and uttered a defeated-sounding 'Worth a try.'

As he pushed the door shut, they heard a faint thump from above.

'What was that?' Morgan asked, heading for the exit.

'Mice?' Arnie suggested. 'Although it would have to be a pretty big one to make a noise like that.'

Morgan walked around to the back of the shop. The area was filled with rubbish and debris. He signalled to the officers outside.

A giggle, a high-pitched sound that set Morgan's teeth on edge, came from the roof.

'Definitely not a mouse,' Arnie muttered.

A rusty fire escape led up the side of the building towards the flat roof. The retractable ladder was down, resting on the ground, which likely meant the roof had been accessed recently.

'Check if there's another way down,' Morgan said to the uniformed officers, who immediately moved to cover the sides of the building. 'I'm going up.'

Without waiting for a response, Morgan gripped the cold metal rungs of the ladder and began to climb slowly. The rusty joints protested under his weight. He emerged on to the roof and glanced around.

A flicker of movement caught his eye, and a figure appeared from behind a large air-conditioning unit.

'Hello,' the man said. 'How nice to see you. I don't get many visitors.'

Morgan's jaw tightened as he stared at the suspect across the roof. He looked scruffier than he had in the photograph Morgan had seen. But this had to be Cody Rhodes.

Up close, he didn't appear threatening. At around five foot three inches, he was dressed in a pair of long shorts that reached the middle of his shins and an oversized white T-shirt with a blue 'Be Kind' logo. He regarded Morgan with pale blue eyes that seemed strangely vacant. His face was plump and unshaven, his hair sticking out at odd angles, as though he'd just rolled out of bed. His clothes were filthy. Near his feet was a cool-box containing cans of beer, and behind him was a folding chair. He'd obviously been intending to spend some time up here.

Morgan raised his hands, palms open. 'Mr Rhodes? We're not here to cause any trouble. We just need to ask you a few questions. I'm Detective Inspector Morgan, and my colleague down there is Detective Sergeant Arnie Hodgson.'

Rhodes shuffled closer and peered over the edge at Arnie, and smiled. 'Am I in trouble?'

Arnie caught Morgan's gaze and frowned.

Morgan gave what he hoped was a reassuring smile. 'Mr Rhodes, we want to have a word with you about your visits to Graham Donaldson.'

At the mention of Donaldson's name, a peculiar gleam entered Rhodes's eyes. 'There's no law against visiting prisoners, is there?'

'No, but we have some questions for you that would be best addressed back at the station.'

'You're arresting me? I'm going to be famous!'

A wave of repulsion shuddered through Morgan as he took in the man's gleeful expression. This was no ordinary suspect. Cody Rhodes was clearly disturbed, and he seemed to find a perverse delight in the prospect of arrest.

Rhodes's gaze shifted to look at Arnie on the ground below them again, and he let out another unpleasant giggle. 'Well, what are you waiting for?' He held out his arms, wrists close together as if waiting for handcuffs. 'Take me away, Detective!'

Morgan exchanged a wary glance with Arnie. This was not proceeding as expected. Rhodes seemed almost too eager to be taken into custody.

'There's no need for handcuffs just yet, Mr Rhodes,' Morgan said carefully. 'Let's get you down the fire escape first.'

Rhodes took Morgan by surprise then, lunging for the ladder and slipping down with practised ease. Then he looked back up at Morgan. 'Are you coming down, Detective?'

Morgan travelled down the ladder more slowly than Rhodes. He reached the ground just as Arnie was saying, 'We only want to ask you a few questions about your relationship with Donaldson. And about the disappearance of Tommy Burton.'

'Disappearance?' Rhodes cocked his head to the side. 'Donaldson's got him?'

Arnie reacted faster than Morgan, clamping a hand on Rhodes's shoulder. 'What do you mean? Where is Tommy Burton?'

'Somewhere private. Somewhere dark. Not telling you. It's a secret.'

Arnie pulled Rhodes round to face him, his expression fierce. 'Enough games. Tell us where the boy is, or—'

Rhodes threw back his head and laughed, the sound echoing around the empty forecourt. 'Or what? It's too late.' His vacant eyes settled on Morgan. 'The boy is caught. And Donaldson's going to gobble him up.'

Morgan stared at Rhodes. However deranged the man might be, his words suggested he knew exactly where Tommy was being held.

'Is he here?' Morgan asked.

But Rhodes just giggled.

Arnie gripped Rhodes's T-shirt. His fist curling into the fabric as if he'd like to throttle him.

'Take him in,' Morgan said to the uniformed officers, putting a calming hand on Arnie's shoulder.

They'd continue the interrogation back at the station and keep at it for as long as it took. Rhodes would talk, one way or another. Morgan would see to that personally.

'Are you all right?' Morgan asked a red-faced Arnie after the two uniformed officers had led Cody Rhodes away.

Morgan got an earful of expletives in return.

'Sicko,' Arnie spat. 'A man like that shouldn't be allowed within a mile of children. Tommy . . . That poor kid.'

Morgan put a hand on his shoulder. 'Rhodes is clearly disturbed.'

'Disturbed?' Arnie repeated incredulously. 'He's an absolute nutcase.'

Morgan stared after the marked police car driving Cody Rhodes away, a chill settling deeper into his bones. If they didn't find the boy soon . . .

He shook off the thought, turning to Arnie. 'We'll question him at the station. We'll get to the truth—'

Morgan stopped talking abruptly, his gaze drifting to the dilapidated petrol station shop. *Somewhere private*, Rhodes had said. *Somewhere dark.*

He frowned. The petrol station was derelict, but the main building seemed largely intact. There was more than one room. And if Rhodes had been living here . . .

'We need to search this place,' he said, already moving towards the shop. 'Thoroughly.'

Arnie didn't argue, following Morgan inside. They separated, combing the area for signs of Tommy Burton. Morgan made his way to the empty storeroom, where everything was covered in a thick layer of dust.

When he turned towards the grimy window at the back, he paused. The dust on the ground in front of the window had been disturbed. There were smudged footprints, faint but unmistakable, criss-crossing the floor. These weren't the clear, deliberate tracks of someone passing through once; they were overlapping, as if someone had been pacing or repeatedly coming in and out of the room. But why? The room was empty apart from dusty shelves.

As he scanned the floor more closely, he noticed something unusual about the laminate flooring. It was a dirty cream colour, 24 by 24 inches square. Near the footprints, two tiles looked out of place. Their edges didn't align perfectly with the adjacent ones.

He crouched down for a better look, noticing faint tool marks along the edges of the squares, suggesting they had been pried open and replaced recently. A chill ran through him as he realised what this meant. Whoever had gone to the trouble of accessing that space beneath the floor had done so for a reason. It could mean they had hidden something – or someone – down there.

He stared at the tiles, his chest tightening.

'Look at this,' he called, his voice strained. Arnie came to stand beside him, cursing under his breath when he saw what Morgan was looking at.

Was Tommy here? Was Cody keeping him hidden under the floor? Somewhere private. Somewhere dark.

Chapter Sixteen

Morgan stared at the area of floor that had been disturbed and said to Arnie, 'Call it in. We need an urgent warrant for a full search and a forensics team here now.'

Arnie's eyes widened. 'There's no time for that. We need to look under there ourselves.'

Morgan wrenched his eyes away from the floor. 'We do this by the book. No mistakes.' He swallowed against the bile rising in his throat. 'We can't risk it.'

Arnie stared at him. 'Sod the book! There's a child's life at stake.'

'I know that,' Morgan replied coolly.

'By the time the SOCOs get here with their cameras and swabs, it could be too late.' Arnie knelt down, his fingers tracing over the subtle, uneven ridges at the seams where a tool had been inserted to pry them off. Then he attempted to grip the edge of one tile, but the laminate didn't budge. It was clear that without a long and narrow tool to lever them apart, the flooring was not going to give way.

'Enough.' Morgan put his hand up. He didn't blame Arnie for his reaction. But they had protocols for a reason. He refused to have another screw-up on his conscience. They shouldn't be disturbing potential evidence. Whoever had been using this hidden spot might have left behind more than just footprints and scratches.

Still, doubt niggled at Morgan as he watched Arnie pace and mutter, stamping occasionally to test the floor for hollow spots. They could be wasting precious time. If Tommy's parents were here, would they want officers going by the book? No. But he couldn't afford to think like that.

Morgan wanted to believe Tommy was here, unharmed, waiting to be found. He wanted to tear up the floor himself. But he couldn't risk contaminating the evidence. He couldn't risk losing Tommy forever due to mistakes and impatience.

Arnie pounded the floor with his fist. 'Tommy! Tommy, can you hear me?'

They were greeted by silence.

Arnie tried again.

'There's no response,' Arnie said finally. His shoulders slumped in defeat. 'I'll call it in.'

Morgan nodded, and as Arnie stepped out of the storeroom to get a signal he noticed the way Arnie's hand trembled as he held the phone to his ear.

He understood Arnie's reaction. He wanted to rip up every last floorboard. And Morgan had already given Arnie the go-ahead to pick the lock, check inside the cupboard before the SOCOs got here, which was very unlike him. But this was a serious investigation. As serious as it got. A positive outcome depended on him doing things according to procedure and keeping a cool head.

Trying to steady his nerves, Morgan inhaled deeply, tasting the dust and mould in the air. They had to get this right.

◆ ◆ ◆

Karen and Rick entered Churchill's office. The door creaked as Rick eased it shut. Churchill was behind his desk, reviewing files, immaculately groomed as always, not a hair out of place.

'Yes?' He didn't invite them to sit down, and tapped a pen impatiently.

'Sir, we believe Gareth Burton may not have been entirely truthful in his initial statement,' Karen said.

Churchill's pen stilled and he raised an eyebrow. 'In what way?'

'The school librarian mentioned Tommy had been reading a fantasy novel featuring an evil father figure. He told us Tommy had remarked his own father was like the villain in the book, and that his father *deserved what was coming to him.*'

Churchill shook his head, frowning. His eyes drifted to his computer screen, and Karen could almost picture the wheels turning in his mind, imagining the media frenzy.

Her frustration simmered.

'That's troubling,' he began slowly. 'But we can't haul the boy's own father in for questioning without good cause.'

Karen bit her tongue to keep from snapping, her nails digging into her palms. Churchill was always so concerned with optics. 'With respect, sir, we think it warrants further investigation,' she said carefully.

Churchill's gaze went back to her. 'I understand your concern, Karen, but we need concrete evidence. The superintendent wants a quiet resolution to this case, not a media circus.'

Karen stared at the floor, fury and frustration warring inside her. Tommy's life hung in the balance, yet all Churchill seemed to care about was negative press.

But before Karen could argue her case further, Churchill said dismissively, 'Besides, Morgan has a much stronger suspect – Cody Rhodes.'

Karen blinked in surprise, exchanging a glance with Rick. This was news to them. She couldn't help feeling out of the loop. Morgan always kept his cards close to his chest, but she thought they had an understanding, a mutual respect. Why hadn't he told her?

She kept her expression neutral. 'That's good news. What evidence do we have linking Cody Rhodes to Tommy's disappearance?'

'Rhodes has been writing fan letters to Donaldson. He even visited Donaldson in prison. Morgan and Arnie will be questioning him soon. He's been living at a derelict petrol station. Seems he's obsessed with famous murder cases, especially Donaldson's.'

Karen took a moment to digest the information. Morgan and Arnie had certainly been busy.

'But no sign of Tommy at this derelict petrol station?' Rick asked.

'No.' Churchill frowned. 'But Morgan's sure he's our man. You two can assist with background on Rhodes. We need to throw everything at this.'

'But we could still talk to Gareth Burton again—' Karen began.

'No. Rhodes is our best lead right now. I need all hands on deck – do I make myself clear?' Churchill's tone left no room for argument.

After a long pause, Churchill said, 'There is still a chance Tommy could be alive if Cody Rhodes is following Donaldson's playbook. I need every officer I have working to figure out where he's keeping the boy. We don't have time to chase maybes. Especially not the boy's own father. The press would have a field day.'

Karen nodded reluctantly, her jaw clenched so tight it ached. 'Yes sir.'

Churchill waved a hand in dismissal. 'Keep me informed of developments. Follow DI Morgan's directions.'

Karen and Rick left the room. Churchill's office door thudded shut, leaving them with the unpleasant truth: they would have to abandon Gareth Burton, at least for now.

Back in the open-plan office, Karen looked at Rick. 'Well, that was short and not so sweet.'

'Sorry. I know you wanted to look into Burton.'

'It's fine. At least we have a solid lead now. That's the main thing, and it sounds promising.'

It still bothered her that Morgan hadn't let her know. Though she supposed it must have happened very quickly, and maybe he hadn't had the chance to call. But Karen didn't like the thought of her and Rick wasting time at the school, talking about car vandalism and Jack Foster getting into a schoolboy squabble with Tommy.

'I suppose this means we drop Sam Tranmere for now too?' Rick asked.

Karen shrugged. 'I think so. He has a pretty good alibi for the time Tommy went missing anyway. He was at his grandmother's funeral. Farzana spoke with the venue that held the wake and confirmed Sam's presence.'

'Right.' Rick sank into a chair by Karen's desk.

She massaged an aching spot at the back of her neck. 'We have to face it – Sam Tranmere living nearby may just be an odd coincidence; a dead end.'

'Or maybe we haven't found the connection yet.'

Karen managed a smile. 'Always the optimist.'

Rick grinned. 'One of us has to be.'

Karen logged on to her computer and accessed the case file, intending to read the latest updates. But her thoughts kept drifting back to Gareth Burton. Something wasn't right there. She was sure of it. And yet they had no solid evidence to justify hauling him in for questioning. Not yet, anyway.

With a quiet sigh, she forced her attention back to the details on Cody Rhodes that had been entered into the database. She had to admit, his behaviour was very suspect.

For now, she'd put Sam Tranmere and Gareth Burton to one side. They needed to follow the evidence and let that guide them.

When it came to Tommy's father, Churchill was right. The evidence was weak at best. For now, she didn't have much more than a gut feeling he was hiding something. And in a case like this, Karen knew feelings wouldn't be enough. They needed proof.

◆ ◆ ◆

On their arrival at the petrol station, Morgan briefed the search team on the situation, highlighting the implications as they changed into protective gear.

One of the officers, a young woman with auburn hair and freckles covering her nose, approached Morgan. She introduced herself as Jane West. 'The warrant's been granted, sir. We have permission to tear up the floor. Should we wait for the SOCOs?'

'Yes, they should be here soon.'

Arnie came to stand at his side. 'You were right to call them in,' he said quietly. 'I'm sorry I reacted like that.'

'Your motives were good.'

'So were yours. You wanted to do this properly.' Arnie sighed. 'I get that.'

Arnie cared, and Morgan couldn't fault him for that. What he couldn't bring himself to say was that Arnie's recklessness mirrored his own, in another life. That he understood, far too well, the impulse to throw caution to the wind when desperate for a result in a case.

Another vehicle rolled on to the forecourt.

'SOCOs,' Arnie said, shading his eyes against the sun.

Morgan's stomach sank at the sight of Tim Farthing getting out of the van. The SOCO's constantly smug expression set his teeth on edge. Of all the scene of crimes officers, why did it have to be him?

After slipping on his protective suit, Farthing rustled over, a bag swinging from his hand. 'DI Morgan and DS Hodgson. Two of my favourite officers.' His gaze slid past them to the shop. 'Found yourselves a body?'

Arnie bristled. 'There's a child missing. We have reason to believe he could be trapped under the floor.'

'Alive? I was told we were looking for a body.' Farthing walked past them, entering the petrol station, and they followed. He sniffed the air. 'Decay would be accelerated in this heat. If there is a body, it must be fresh.'

Arnie stared at him in disgust. 'You really are—' he began, but Morgan silenced him with a look. There was no time for them to rise to Farthing's usual bait.

'The storeroom.' Morgan pointed to where he wanted Farthing to go. 'It appears the floor has been disturbed.'

'Yeah, looks that way,' Farthing said, after he walked into the room and examined the floor. 'What makes you think the boy's under here, then?'

'Our main suspect lives here.'

Tim Farthing grimaced as he looked around. 'He's not much of a housekeeper, is he?'

Jane West approached Morgan again. 'Now that the SOCOs are present, do we have your permission to tear up the floor?'

'Fine by me,' Farthing said.

Morgan nodded. His mouth had gone dry. 'Do it.'

The search team got to work, levering back the laminate and then carefully removing the loose board beneath.

The moment of truth. Morgan hardly dared breathe.

Jane shone her torch into the cavity below. Morgan peered over her shoulder.

No small hand or foot poking from the darkness. No body. Tommy wasn't there. Just dust and rubbish. It looked like the space had been used for storage.

Morgan shook his head in disbelief. He had been so sure. All the signs had pointed here. But he was wrong. Again.

Beside him, Arnie spluttered out a frustrated breath, swearing loudly as he leaned forward to rest his hands on his knees. Morgan put a hand on Arnie's shoulder, as much to steady himself as to comfort his colleague. 'Rhodes is still our main suspect. We'll get him to talk.'

'You're joking?' Arnie straightened. His face flushed red. 'Rhodes won't talk. I doubt Rhodes knows what day of the week it is. He's unstable.'

A chill spread throughout Morgan's body. They were failing.

Just like he had failed those other young boys.

He squeezed his eyes shut against the memory, the weight of it threatening to crush him. It was happening again. He couldn't lose another—

'Sir?' Jane's voice cut through his thoughts. His eyes opened to find her watching him with a mixture of concern and wariness. 'There's no sign of the missing boy here, but . . .' She hesitated. 'There's something you should see.'

'Show me.'

'Look at this.'

Jane shifted, angling the torch. The light shone on stacks of printouts and newspapers.

Morgan's gaze fixed on a local Oxford paper displaying the grinning face of Graham Donaldson. He stumbled back a step, his throat tightening.

Beside him, Arnie let out a low whistle. 'Well, would you look at that. I'd call that more evidence that our friend Rhodes has an unhealthy interest in Donaldson.'

Morgan barely heard him. Graham Donaldson leered up at him from the yellowed pages. Reminding him of the three children Donaldson had taken. Three children lost forever to his darkness.

Henry Tisdale. Marc White. Stuart O'Connor.

And now Tommy Burton was lost, too.

He squeezed his eyes shut again, but Donaldson's face was imprinted on the backs of his eyelids. Sharp cheekbones, gaunt face, and a smile as cold as death.

His hands balled into fists. Not again. He wouldn't lose another—

'Are you all right?' Farthing's voice cut through the fog of memories threatening to engulf him. He opened his eyes to find the SOCO watching him, frowning. 'Maybe you need some air?'

Morgan drew in a sharp breath, pushing back the ghosts of the past. Now wasn't the time. He had a job to do. A boy to find.

'I'm fine,' he said without emotion.

'You don't look fine,' Farthing said.

'Leave him alone,' Arnie snapped. 'This case is bringing up some nasty memories, that's all. He'll be okay.'

Farthing took a long look at Morgan, and then nodded and did something unexpected. He peeled off his gloves and put a hand on Morgan's arm. His voice uncharacteristically soft, he said, 'You're doing a good job. You'll get him.'

Then, without another word, Farthing turned back to his work of bagging and tagging.

Morgan tried to tune everything else out, focusing solely on the debris littering the space beneath the floor. He saw more pictures of Donaldson, and articles Cody Rhodes must have sourced online and then printed out. Rhodes was obsessed with Donaldson's crimes.

Once the team had removed all the items, Morgan turned to Arnie and gave him the nod. They had to get back to the station. They needed answers from Cody Rhodes.

Chapter Seventeen

The interview room had a suffocating atmosphere. The air was hot and stale. The overhead light gave a sickly pallor to Cody Rhodes's round face.

Cody's eyes, wide and unfocused, darted around the interview room as he muttered to himself. Morgan felt uneasy observing him.

'Tell me again about your relationship with Graham Donaldson,' Morgan said, attempting to keep his tone even and conversational.

'Me and Mr Donaldson . . .' Cody mumbled, his wide-eyed, unfocused gaze finding some unseen point of interest on the ceiling, 'I understand him.'

'Is that why you visited him in prison twice?' Morgan probed, leaning forward, trying to recapture Cody's attention.

'I needed to see him and talk to him. I listen, unlike everyone else.' Cody's voice grew stronger, more animated, as if discussing Donaldson somehow anchored him to reality.

'Did the name Tommy Burton ever come up in these conversations?' Arnie asked.

'Tommy who?' Cody asked, blinking. His fingers began to press on the tabletop, as though he were playing a piano that only he could hear.

'Tommy Burton. The eleven-year-old boy who's missing,' Morgan clarified, his patience beginning to fray at the edges.

'Missing? Oh, yes, I saw that on the news. Poor little kid . . .' Cody murmured, his focus drifting away once more.

Morgan exchanged a disheartened glance with Arnie. It was clear they were getting nowhere. Cody's tenuous grip on reality made it impossible to discern whether he genuinely knew nothing about Tommy or if he was simply incapable of providing useful information.

'Tell us more about your visits to Graham Donaldson,' Arnie prodded gently, his voice low and paternal. 'What did you talk about?'

Cody shifted in his seat, his fingers twitching again. 'Mr Donaldson has a story to tell. He knows things.'

Morgan leaned even further forward. 'What kind of things, Cody?'

'Things . . . about life. About people.' Cody's gaze drifted upwards, as though he was searching for something. Then his eyes suddenly focused on Morgan in a disconcerting way. 'Have you found Tommy yet? Poor little thing. Only five years old.'

'Five?' Arnie asked, exchanging a glance with Morgan. 'Tommy is eleven, Cody.'

'Eleven?' The confusion on Cody's face was clear. 'No, no . . . The voice told me five. It wouldn't lie to me.'

'The voice?' Arnie screwed up his face.

But Cody was now staring intently at the red flashing light on the camera in the corner of the ceiling.

Morgan's hopes were fading fast. Cody was far from the key he'd hoped would unlock the mystery of Tommy Burton's disappearance.

'All right, Cody. That's enough for now,' Morgan said, standing up. 'We'll pick this up later.'

158

'Later . . .' Cody whispered, as he stared off into nothing again.

'Let's take a break,' Morgan said, motioning for Arnie to follow him out of the interview room.

They left, the door clicking shut behind them with a sound that felt ominously final.

'Back to square one, I suppose,' Arnie sighed, roughly rolling up his shirtsleeves.

'I'm starting to feel like we're chasing the wrong suspect,' Morgan said, his voice filled with frustration.

Arnie nodded grimly. 'We need to get a mental health team in here, and an advocate for Cody. There's no way any of this will stand up in court if he's this ill.'

'Agreed,' Morgan said, feeling the weight of the case settle heavily on his shoulders. Dead ends were becoming all too familiar.

Farzana appeared around the corner, her eyes searching their faces. 'How've you been getting on?' she asked.

Arnie relayed the news, his voice strained and weary.

Farzana couldn't hide her disappointment. 'I thought we were getting closer.'

'Me too,' Arnie said.

Farzana gave him a sympathetic smile. 'I'm sure you tried your best in there. I've been looking into Cody's background as you requested,' she said, turning to Morgan. 'He has a long history of mental illness, including schizophrenia. Karen and I are trying to get more information from the local mental health unit.'

'Thanks,' Morgan muttered, running a hand through his hair. 'It's starting to feel like we're right back where we started.'

'Not quite. The lab picked up DNA on the blue teddy bear,' Farzana said. 'No match in the database, but now we have Cody Rhodes in custody, we can check to see if his DNA is a match.'

Morgan nodded in acknowledgement. But deep down he didn't think they had the right man for the crime. Cody was disturbed, but Morgan didn't believe he'd taken Tommy. The abduction had been seamless. No one had noticed anything. If Cody had been wandering around Tattershall Castle, people would have noticed him. His behaviour was anything but normal, and he would not have blended in. Even if he'd wanted to, his illness would have made it impossible.

Morgan thought whoever had abducted Tommy had made a careful plan. To snatch an eleven-year-old-boy in public, they'd have to be confident and able to carefully calculate the risk. If Tommy had fought back or called for help, their plan would have been ruined.

He tried to work out what had kept Tommy from crying out for help or trying to escape his captor or captors, and the only answer he could arrive at was that Tommy must have known them. After all, if he'd felt at ease with the person taking him, he wouldn't have resisted.

Morgan felt a spike of doubt. Had Karen's suspect been the right one? Gareth Burton. Tommy's father. Tommy would have gone with him without kicking up a fuss. Was Cody a red herring?

Arnie asked, 'Do you think Forensics will find something useful from what they picked up at the petrol station? If Cody can't or won't talk, maybe it could bring us closer to finding Tommy before it's too late.'

Morgan shook his head. He didn't know – it looked like their case against Cody Rhodes was falling apart before it had even got off the ground.

'Come on,' Morgan said finally, clapping Arnie on the shoulder. 'Let's get a coffee and regroup. We'll find another angle. We have to.'

◆ ◆ ◆

Karen put her phone on the desk and glared at it. She was tempted to hurl it across the room. She'd had so many circular conversations with medical personnel but was no closer to accessing Cody Rhodes's full medical records. Red tape and bureaucracy had never been more infuriating.

Tommy was out there somewhere, frightened and alone. And she was stuck behind her desk, trying to chase down a suspect's medical history. She needed a medical professional with experience of treating Cody to give their opinion on whether he would be able to provide credible testimony.

Morgan believed Cody was unfit for interview, which meant there would now be a lull in the investigation. They would have to wait until they got permission to keep questioning Cody, or were told they had to step back completely. It was bad news for the investigation, and very bad news for Tommy.

Karen believed there were other suspects they should look at. But Churchill had made his point clear. She was to fulfil a backup role, supporting Morgan. Churchill didn't want her chasing down suspects on her own. She understood his concerns. It wouldn't look good if they arrested Tommy's father and he turned out to be innocent.

But Karen didn't care about optics. She just wanted to find the little boy and bring him home safely.

She took a deep breath and picked up the phone again, preparing to take another shot at reaching a social worker or psychiatrist who had treated Cody. She shuffled through the papers on her desk, searching for another contact. But she'd exhausted them all. She flipped back to the first page, deciding to try Cody's GP again.

She ran her hands through her hair as the call connected and rang and rang and rang. With a heavy sigh, she leaned back in her seat. Her gaze fell on Arnie's computer. On the screen, there was a photograph of a smiling Tommy, wearing a baseball cap and standing beside his mother. They weren't supposed to leave their computers logged in while they were away from their desks, but Arnie went by his own rules.

He had been taking this case very, very hard. Karen wondered why that was. Was it personal for Arnie, as it was for Morgan?

Cases that involved abducted children were always difficult. But Morgan had a history linked to this case. He'd felt the loss of those three young boys fifteen years ago. And he didn't want to lose Tommy, too. It wasn't hard to see why the case was affecting him so deeply.

But it seemed to Karen as though Arnie was feeling it keenly, almost as though the case echoed something in his past too.

Come to think of it, she knew little about Arnie's background. He'd come to the station at the same time as Churchill and had become part of the team. Scruffy, outspoken and set in his ways, he was an interesting colleague to work alongside. Sometimes unorthodox in his approach, and often grumpy, he could be challenging. Karen trusted him, though. He had good judgement. And most importantly, in her opinion, a good heart.

But she didn't know much about his background or his family life. She thought he lived alone. But she couldn't remember whether he'd ever mentioned a family in the past. Or even whether he had children. He didn't talk about himself very much.

It was odd. She knew so much about her other colleagues and next to nothing about Arnie.

Her thoughts came back to the case as someone finally answered her call.

'Mansford Road GP surgery,' an officious voice said.

'This is DS Karen Hart. I was hoping to speak to Dr Manisha Jayasinghe. I believe she's Cody Miller's GP?'

'Oh, yes, you called earlier. The doctor hasn't had a chance to return your call yet. She's been very busy.'

'I was hoping she might be free now.'

The receptionist sighed. 'I'll see what I can do.'

A moment later, they transferred Karen, and the line started playing 'Greensleeves'. She groaned. A further two minutes passed before the call connected.

'This is Dr Jayasinghe. How can I help?'

Karen introduced herself, then said, 'Dr Jayasinghe, we have a suspect in custody. I believe he is a patient registered at your surgery.'

She gave the details, and the doctor confirmed Cody Rhodes was a patient of hers.

'In that case, we would very much appreciate it if you could come to the station.'

'Well, I don't know . . .' Dr Jayasinghe said doubtfully.

'It would really help us out. I think Cody is struggling. We don't want to jeopardise our investigation if he's unfit for interview. We're concerned about Cody's well-being,' Karen said. 'There's a little boy missing, and we suspect Cody might have information that could help us find him. So this is very urgent.'

'All right,' Dr Jayasinghe said eventually. 'I'll see if I can shuffle some appointments around.'

'You can come straightaway?' Karen asked, surprised that her many phone calls had finally achieved a result.

'Yes, I'll leave now. I should be with you in about twenty minutes.'

'Thank you,' Karen said gratefully, and gave the doctor instructions on how to get to the station.

It wasn't exactly a breakthrough. But at least it wasn't another dead end.

Chapter Eighteen

Karen leaned on the front desk, her gaze shifting between the clock and the station entrance. It was forty minutes since she'd spoken to Cody's GP. She took a sip from her water bottle, trying to ignore the tempting smell of rich coffee coming from the desk sergeant's mug.

'Still sticking to water?' The desk sergeant raised his eyebrows.

'I'm doing my best,' she said.

He took a long gulp from his mug. 'Delicious.' He smacked his lips.

Karen shook her head good-naturedly. She was jittery enough without the extra caffeine.

A petite woman rushed through the station doors. Karen put the lid back on her water bottle as she approached and extended her hand. 'Detective Hart? I'm Dr Manisha Jayasinghe, Cody's general practitioner. I apologise for the delay.'

Karen shook her hand. 'Thank you for coming. Please follow me.' She led the doctor upstairs to the second floor, where Morgan was waiting outside an interview room.

'Dr Jayasinghe, this is my colleague, Detective Inspector Morgan.'

'Cody Rhodes is in the interview room,' Morgan said, shaking the doctor's hand. 'He seems happy enough for now. Can you give us a brief rundown before you see him? Anything you can tell us about his background would be helpful.'

The doctor glanced at the closed door and then back to Morgan. 'You know Cody has schizophrenia?'

Morgan nodded slowly. 'We do. It was disclosed to one of our colleagues, DC Farzana Shah, a short time ago. We didn't have that detail when we first brought Cody in and began to question him, but it soon became clear that Cody is struggling with some mental health issues.'

Cody's behaviour had led to Morgan putting a pause on his interview. There was no way the CPS or the courts would be happy with information gathered through interview until Cody was approved as fit for questioning.

'You said he's quite calm now?' the doctor asked. 'How was he during questioning?'

'He wasn't outwardly distressed, and in fact seemed quite comfortable and happy to talk to us, but he wasn't making much sense.'

Dr Jayasinghe nodded. 'Cody has been under my care for the past five years for his general medical needs. But you really need to speak to Dr Shepherd, who is his psychiatrist. When properly medicated, Cody's symptoms are manageable. However, if he stops taking his medications, even for a short period, his symptoms often return rapidly. He suffers from delusions, paranoia and disorganised thinking. And during these episodes, he becomes detached and refuses to accept his condition.'

Karen felt her heart sink. They'd been foolish to think they could get medical approval to get back in there and question Cody straightaway. This was going to be a complicated process.

The schizophrenia explained Cody's erratic and confusing behaviour when Arnie and Morgan had questioned him. They were unlikely to get anything further out of Cody for a while, and that meant their chances of finding Tommy were quickly running out.

'Does Cody often refuse to take his meds?' Morgan asked.

'Not often, no. There have only been two other occasions while he has been under my care. The last time was a few months ago, but I must stress that, even while off his medication, Cody has never hurt anyone. May I see him now?' the doctor asked.

Karen nodded and opened the door to the interview room. 'Do you object to us being present?'

Although Cody hadn't been violent since they'd brought him to the station, Karen didn't think it was wise for the doctor to go in alone.

The doctor narrowed her eyes. 'I don't object, as I will only ask Cody simple questions to determine his mental state. But I must insist you do not question him until he is determined fit to be interviewed.'

For a small woman, she had an unusually forceful voice that carried authority.

'Understood,' Morgan said, and he led the way into the room. 'Cody, your doctor is here.'

'Cody?' Dr Jayasinghe said softly as she entered the room. 'It's me, your GP. Do you remember me?'

Cody looked up. His hair hung long and straggly over his eyes. He peered at her, blinking. A few seconds passed before a spark of recognition flickered across his face. 'Oh, Dr J. I remember you.'

'That's right.' She smiled and took a seat across the table from him.

Morgan and Karen remained standing near the door, ready to assist if needed but not wanting to crowd the doctor or Cody.

'Some police officers have been asking you questions. Is that right?'

Cody shrugged. 'I guess.' His gaze dropped to the table, and he used his index finger to trace a big, looping shape on the tabletop. He seemed fascinated by it.

Dr Jayasinghe began with simple questions about the date and Cody's name and address. But Cody struggled to provide coherent answers even to those simple questions. His thoughts were disorganised and illogical.

The doctor was very patient, rephrasing questions and repeating them when Cody seemed confused. But Cody's attention drifted from the table, and he began to stare at the camera in the corner of the room again, even though it wasn't recording.

After a few frustrating minutes where Dr Jayasinghe tried to regain Cody's attention, she finally called off her efforts.

'I have to go now, Cody, but I'll see you soon. Okay?'

Cody didn't respond.

Dr Jayasinghe, Karen and Morgan left the interview room.

Karen looked at the doctor expectantly, but her serious expression told Karen what she had feared. Cody's condition was bad enough that they wouldn't be able to question him anymore today.

Dr Jayasinghe turned to Karen and Morgan. 'It's my professional opinion that Cody has not been taking his prescribed medications for some time. His symptoms are severe. This is the worst I've ever seen him.'

Morgan's expression tightened. 'Do you think once his medications start again, he might stabilise enough to provide us with some useful information?'

'It's possible,' the doctor said. 'When Cody's coherent, he's a pleasant young man. Shy and polite. This current state is very unusual for him. But I recommend you talk to his psychiatrist, Dr Shepherd, who will need to confirm my assessment and prescribe a treatment plan to get Cody's symptoms back under control. I believe she'll advise an inpatient admission where staff can properly regulate his medication regimen. Currently, we can't rely on Cody to take the medications himself.'

A sudden rush of frustration hit Karen. But it wasn't all over. If Cody could be treated, they could question him again when he was stable. There was still a chance they'd get information about Tommy's abduction from him.

'How long does it take for the medications to kick in? When do you think he'll be stable enough to speak to us?' Karen asked.

Dr Jayasinghe thought for a moment. 'It's very difficult for me to say for certain. You'd need to speak with his psychiatrist. But I think at least a few days if not weeks.'

A few days? Weeks? Karen stared at her. If Cody Rhodes was their best chance of finding Tommy, then it was all over.

If he was keeping the boy somewhere without food or water, this could be a death sentence.

'A small boy has been abducted,' Morgan said, his tone icy. 'We have reason to believe that Cody may have been involved. It's imperative we get answers from him as soon as possible.'

Dr Jayasinghe frowned and held up her hand. 'I understand your urgency, but I'm afraid that Cody has a serious medical condition. Stabilising him will take as long as it takes. Rushing the process could be very dangerous to Cody's health. And if he has a setback, you might not be able to question him for weeks.' The petite doctor stared up at Morgan. 'I would like to point out that Cody having schizophrenia doesn't mean he's likely to abduct a child. Cody has been my patient for five years, and he's never displayed violent tendencies. People with schizophrenia can become paranoid and withdraw from their family and friends, but they don't necessarily hurt others. I know Cody well, and I don't think he has taken this child.'

Karen didn't want to reveal too much about the case. But she needed to make the doctor understand their reasons for suspecting Cody's involvement. It wasn't just because he was mentally ill that they had zeroed in on him. They hadn't even known about his schizophrenia until after his arrest.

'Cody has been visiting a serial child murderer in prison. He's been writing this man fan letters.'

Karen watched the doctor's face closely, judging her reaction. Dr Jayasinghe's eyes widened a fraction and then she frowned. 'I find that hard to believe.'

'I assure you it's true,' Morgan said, his tone clipped.

A moment later, her expression cleared. 'I believe you've got the wrong impression from Cody. He's interested in true crime stories. On a couple of occasions, he told me he wanted to create documentaries on famous criminal cases. I grant you it's an unusual career aspiration. But I don't think it makes him dangerous.'

Karen remained unconvinced, and from Morgan's sceptical expression, so did he. Visiting serial killers in prison, keeping newspaper cuttings hidden under the floor, and writing the killer fan mail went beyond a casual interest in true crime. Cody had been obsessed with Graham Donaldson – and that, paired with his current delusional state, was a big red flag.

'With respect,' Morgan said, 'Cody's fascination with a child murderer, along with his present condition, raises serious concerns.'

Dr Jayasinghe sighed. 'I understand your need to investigate. Though I doubt Cody's involvement, once he stabilises you can question him. But I just ask you to keep an open mind and don't judge Cody based on his current mental status.'

Dr Jayasinghe offered them contact details for Cody's psychiatrist, Dr Shepherd, but it was the telephone number Karen had already called, leaving messages with the psychiatrist's secretary.

'I also have an emergency number for the mental health unit that cares for Cody. I believe we should get him admitted as soon as possible,' Dr Jayasinghe said. 'I can arrange that if you're happy for me to . . .'

Karen glanced at Morgan. She could tell from the tension radiating from him he wanted to refuse. He wanted to go back to the interview room and get the truth from Cody, but he couldn't. But the doctor was right. In Cody's current state, they couldn't get anything from him.

Morgan's voice was hard as he said, 'Arrange it, then. And let's all hope this hold-up doesn't lead to the death of a child.'

Chapter Nineteen

DI Morgan was hunched over a stack of case files when his phone rang. He glanced at the caller ID – it was Sophie.

'Sophie, how are you feeling?'

'Much better, thank you for asking. I've been going over the case notes from the old abductions and something caught my eye. I think I've found something interesting.'

Morgan stifled a sigh. As far as he knew, Sophie was supposed to be chasing down retailers of the blue teddy bears, not researching his old case in Oxford. He didn't have time for this. Cody Rhodes was now unavailable for questioning, which meant he had to find a new angle; a way to find Tommy when he couldn't even talk to their prime suspect.

'Sophie, you should contact Karen about this. You're still on medical leave, you shouldn't be worrying yourself about the old case.'

'But this could be important. If you'll just give me five minutes to explain—'

'I understand you want to help, but my plate is rather full at the moment. Why don't you write up what you've found and email it to Karen? She can evaluate if it's worth pursuing further.' His tone was gentle but firm.

There was a pause on the line. He pictured the disappointment on her face and felt his resolve weakening.

'I appreciate your dedication, Sophie, but you need to give yourself time to rest and recover. We've got things handled here for now. Email Karen and try not to worry about work until you're cleared to return, all right?'

'No, wait,' Sophie said. 'I need to talk to you about this directly. Because you know DCI Tranmere.'

That got Morgan's attention. 'Go on,' he said slowly.

'I found discrepancies between two versions of notes on the second abduction, of . . .' She broke off, and he heard rustling papers in the background as she tried to locate the name.

But Morgan didn't need to look it up. The names of those three boys still haunted him after fifteen years.

'The second boy abducted was Marc White,' he said, his voice emotionless, though he felt churned up inside.

'Yes, that's right,' Sophie said. 'The initial notes specifically mention a red Ford Focus parked down the street from the abduction location. But that detail is omitted from the final typed report – the one signed off by Tranmere.' She paused, then continued. 'It could be nothing, but it seemed an odd detail to remove. I thought, with your history, you might have some insight into Tranmere's methods, and you'd know if this was significant or not.'

Morgan's stomach clenched as memories of his old boss resurfaced. He hadn't noticed the discrepancy. He was usually so precise and methodical. He should know the reports backwards, but he'd missed it.

'I can come in,' Sophie said eagerly. 'I'm feeling much better now. I'm sure I can make it into the station.'

Morgan frowned, picturing the last time he'd seen Sophie. She'd been relying on a walking stick for balance and still struggled to grip things properly with her right hand. He felt a surge of fondness for her determination to be useful despite her injuries.

'No, stay home,' he said firmly. 'You're still recovering.' He made a snap decision. 'I'll come to you instead.'

'Oh but—' Sophie began to protest.

'That's an order, DC Jones. I'm leaving now.'

◆ ◆ ◆

Karen walked through the front door and was greeted by Sandy's delighted bark. The dog fussed over her, tail wagging. Karen leaned down to ruffle her soft fur.

She felt some of her stress dissipate as she kicked off her shoes. Sandy padded along behind her as she walked into the kitchen.

'I can't stay for long,' she told Mike. He was standing at the kitchen counter chopping a red onion, looking like the picture of domesticity. 'I just came home to grab some toast and have a shower. I've got to get back to the station. It's been a tough day.'

'You're working too hard,' Mike said. 'I'm making chicken kebabs on the barbecue. They'll only be twenty minutes. By the time you're out of the shower, they'll be ready.'

Karen had to admit it was nice to have someone looking out for her. And chicken kebabs – at least the way Mike cooked them – did sound more appealing than toast. She headed upstairs.

The shower spray was hot and refreshing against her skin, and her mind drifted back to the investigation as she lathered up her hair with shampoo.

Churchill and Morgan were sold on Cody Rhodes as the prime suspect in Tommy's abduction. But Karen wasn't so sure. Dr Jayasinghe had known Cody for a long time, and she'd seemed confident Cody wasn't the perpetrator.

But they couldn't ignore the presence of all the newspaper articles about Graham Donaldson that Cody had stashed under the floor, or the creepy letters he'd sent to Donaldson in prison.

All that was suggestive, but it wasn't conclusive.

Now that they wouldn't be able to question Cody until his condition stabilised, Karen thought they should explore other possibilities and rethink their single-minded focus on him. She understood why Churchill and Morgan had been so adamant about following the lead, but she was personally interested in keeping their net wide at this stage.

The atmosphere at Dahlia Close had been peculiar, as though some of the residents were trying to hide something. When Karen had spoken to Lyra Hill, the woman had shied away and looked uncomfortable. She was Tommy's history teacher, and lived in the same cul-de-sac, so why was Lyra so insistent she knew little about the boy? And Jack Foster's squabble with Tommy was odd, too. Jack had said Tommy had teased him about Jack's protruding ears, but was that really the reason for their fight, or was something else going on? The more Karen thought about it, the more she suspected Jack had made the story up to stop them questioning him further.

Then there was Sam Tranmere, the son of the detective chief inspector who'd worked on the abduction cases fifteen years ago. He lived close to Tommy and was passionate about gaming. He likely had knowledge of the blue bears from overhearing his father talk about the investigation, but did he have a reason for taking Tommy? If it was him, why would he use those same blue bears? That was sure to attract suspicion and link him to the crime.

The aroma from the barbecue drifted through the open bathroom window as she turned off the water and wrapped herself in a towel.

Despite the obvious signs pointing towards Cody Rhodes, Karen couldn't shake the feeling that something else was brewing under her nose. She knew that Churchill and Morgan were zeroing in on Cody for a good reason – his strange behaviour, his letters to the child killer after an almost identical crime years ago – all of it made sense. But she had a feeling that they were barking up the wrong tree – or worse, being led astray. Whatever it was that was nagging at her would need more than just intuition to uncover. She'd have to dig deeper to figure out what was really going on.

Downstairs, Mike had set the small round table on the patio and lit citronella candles to keep away the biting insects. He handed her a plate loaded with chargrilled chicken, red and yellow peppers, and onions.

'Thank you,' she said, spearing a piece of chicken.

It was delicious; smoky with just a hint of garlic. She felt the tension ease from her shoulders as she ate. She hadn't realised how hungry she was.

After clearing her plate, she glanced at Mike and noticed he seemed distracted. The bottle of beer by his plate was still nearly full, the condensation beading on the glass. There was something on his mind, but she'd been too preoccupied to notice until this moment.

She put her knife and fork to the side of her plate and leaned forward, resting her elbows on the table. 'What is it?'

'Nothing,' Mike said.

Karen arched an eyebrow, knowing that something was definitely bothering him.

Finally, he said, 'I went to see my mum today.'

'How did it go?'

'About as well as it usually does.' He sighed, then got up from the table. 'I'll be back in a minute.'

When he returned, he was carrying a battered shoebox. He set it on the table between them. Karen lifted the lid to find the box filled with photographs. 'What's all this?' she asked.

She picked up a photo from the top of the pile. The picture showed a toddler, presumably Mike, standing in front of a man, but the man's face had been scraped off. Karen grabbed another photo, then another, and noticed the exact same thing – the scratched-out face appeared in every single picture.

Gazing at the photos, she shook her head. 'She really didn't like him.'

Mike sighed heavily. 'Clearly. She destroyed my father's face in all the pictures.'

It was strange and unsettling. Karen wasn't sure how to respond.

Mike sat back down, gazing at the darkening sky. 'It's completely irrational. I mentioned not having any photographs of my father, and she said she had some. I thought it was odd she was being so cooperative, until I saw them.'

Karen watched him sympathetically as he leaned back in his chair, struggling with a mixture of emotions – anger, confusion, sadness. There were many unresolved tensions between Mike and his mother that needed addressing. Karen wanted to help but didn't want to interfere.

'It's like she's being deliberately obtuse,' he said, staring at the box of photos.

'Maybe his desertion damaged her emotionally,' Karen suggested.

'Maybe, but I wouldn't know, because she won't tell me what happened between them,' Mike said, exasperated. 'Sorry.' He ran a hand through his hair. 'I shouldn't have shown you these now. It's the last thing you need when you're in the middle of such a difficult case.'

'Of course you should have,' Karen said. 'What are you going to do? Were there any negatives with the photographs? You might be able to get reprints made.'

'To be honest, I'm considering just forgetting about the whole thing.'

'You should try to talk to her again, tell her how this is affecting you. Maybe if you're honest about how you feel, she'll be more helpful.'

'Have you met my mother?' Mike said sarcastically, picking up his beer and taking a long swallow.

He had a point. Lorraine was not the easiest woman to get along with.

'Anyway, I think I'll put it aside for now,' Mike said. 'Dinner's rearranged for tomorrow night, and I don't want to ruin that before it starts.'

Karen winced. She'd already forgotten. Somehow, she would have to make time for dinner. She couldn't stand them up again. She'd never live it down.

'You'd forgotten again, hadn't you?' Mike gave her an accusing look.

'Of course not,' Karen protested unconvincingly.

'You're going to give me a complex,' he said with a grin as he lifted his beer to his lips.

DI Morgan pulled his Volvo up to the kerb outside the Joneses' bungalow. He switched off the engine and checked the dashboard clock – almost nine p.m.

He rubbed a hand over the stubble on his chin, hesitating. He hoped Sophie's parents wouldn't resent him for the late visit, or for encouraging their daughter to work before she was fully recovered.

But Sophie had found something concerning in the old case files and Morgan couldn't ignore that, no matter the hour.

He climbed out of the car, straightening his crumpled suit jacket. He wished he knew Churchill's secret for keeping his clothes so neat and tidy. Although, never going to crime scenes and sitting in an air-conditioned office all day probably helped.

Morgan walked up the narrow path to knock on the Joneses' front door.

A few moments later, Sophie's father opened the door.

'Mr Jones, I'm sorry for calling so late. Is Sophie available?'

'Call me Geoff. No need to stand on ceremony.' He opened the door wider with a welcoming smile. 'Sophie's in the living room. She's been waiting up for you.'

Morgan stepped inside. A row of framed family photos lined the wall of the hall, chronicling Sophie at various ages. His gaze fell on a recent photo of her and her parents, before the attack; in it, she was fresh-faced and laughing, without a care in the world. Before her life was shattered into pieces.

The living room was lit by a lamp on the side table, giving it a cosy atmosphere. Sophie looked up from her spot on the floral sofa. Files were spread out on the coffee table in front of her, and she had a look of determination on her face that Morgan hadn't seen for quite some time. She looked rested, her eyes bright and focused. She smiled at him, dimples appearing in her cheeks.

Perhaps things were finally starting to improve for Sophie.

'Sophie. You're looking well.' He crossed over to take a seat in the armchair angled towards the sofa. 'Now, what's this lead you've found?'

Sophie pushed a file across the table towards him. 'Here, look at this . . .'

Morgan leaned over, scanning the contents.

'It's there. On that page there,' Sophie said, struggling to stand so she could point out the paragraph.

'I'll find it,' Morgan said. 'You don't have to get up.'

'Well, as you can see, the red Ford Focus is mentioned in the initial report, but it's not in the final report Tranmere signed off on . . .'

Morgan listened, but Sophie's words washed over him, because he'd just noticed the name at the bottom of the draft report. It was his. He'd seen that red car. He'd watched hours of CCTV, and knew he'd reported it accurately. But in the final report, the one signed off by DCI Tranmere and carefully typed up on the computer, there was no mention of the red car.

Blood rushed in Morgan's ears. This wasn't his mistake. He remembered that car because he'd asked Tranmere whether they should follow it up. Tranmere had told him that he already had, and that the car belonged to a woman picking up her child from a playdate. Tranmere had convinced him the car was completely unrelated to the abduction.

Morgan felt light-headed. 'I want you to know I filled in that report correctly. I don't know why the red Ford Focus isn't mentioned in the final version.'

'Of course,' Sophie said. 'I didn't doubt you for a second. I just thought maybe I should mention it in case it was important. And well . . .' She tapped on Tranmere's signature at the bottom of the report. 'It seems a bit odd, doesn't it?'

'It does,' Morgan said. 'Very odd.'

'I spoke to Farzana. She told me that DCI Tranmere's son lives not far from Tommy, so I thought . . . well, it's suspicious, isn't it?'

Yes, Morgan thought. *It is.*

But Tranmere's son couldn't really have been involved back then, could he? He would have been fourteen, far too young to drive legally, so it was unlikely Sam had been in the car. But who else would Tranmere be protecting?

Changing a final report like this was a huge risk. If Tranmere had been caught, that would have been his career down the toilet.

Was it simply an omission? An error?

As Morgan read the paragraph again, he noticed that not only had the mention of the red car been removed, but the last sentence had been completely rewritten. It had to be deliberate. Tranmere had been covering up for someone, but who?

'Thank you, Sophie. I hadn't spotted the error.'

'I wouldn't have found it either if Karen and Rick hadn't brought over the draft version. That was unusual. But lucky for us it was kept alongside the final report.'

Morgan nodded. Drafts were usually discarded; there was too much documentation to save everything.

Tranmere must have not realised the original draft was in the file. He would have destroyed it if he had known it was there.

Morgan rubbed a hand over his face.

'Are you all right?' Sophie asked quietly.

'I should be asking you that,' Morgan said. 'How are you getting on?'

'Not too bad. It's been nice doing this, to be honest. I like feeling useful again.'

Morgan smiled, trying not to let on to Sophie how concerned he was about this development.

Tranmere was a good guy. Trustworthy. He recalled how Tranmere would tap the side of his nose and say, *Least said, soonest mended, Morgan,* when he thought Morgan's attention to detail was delaying their work. But Tranmere wouldn't do anything to jeopardise an investigation as serious as the abduction of three young boys. Would he?

'So, what are you going to do about it?' Sophie asked, bringing Morgan back to the present.

'There's only one thing I can do,' Morgan said. 'I'm going to have to confront DCI Tranmere.'

'It could be an honest mistake,' Sophie suggested doubtfully.

But Morgan didn't think this was a mistake. It was deliberate. And that worried him.

He needed to see his old boss and mentor face to face, and ask him why he'd tampered with the report.

Chapter Twenty

Morgan drove up the long gravel driveway towards Tranmere's house, feeling increasingly nervous.

He turned off the engine and took a deep breath. Last time he'd been here under very different circumstances. Then, he'd been asking Tranmere for help. Today, he came with an accusation.

There was another car outside the house. Did Tranmere have visitors?

It was dark, but the lights from inside the house spilled out on to the gravel, illuminating the yew hedge. The trees and shrubs cast dark, shifting shadows. The type of shadows that played tricks with the mind – making him think someone or something was lurking in the darkness.

Was that what he was doing now? Conjuring up a problem that wasn't real? Maybe this was all in his head. Sure, Tranmere liked efficiency, and he'd never liked cases being slowed down by unnecessary details. Had he been rushing while going over the report? Could the absence of the red car in the final version have been a simple clerical error?

Morgan sighed, glancing at the files on the passenger seat. Deep down he knew the omission of the red Ford Focus hadn't been a typing mistake.

He glanced to the left, where the lawn stretched out into the woods at the side of the property. There was a small fountain nestled in the centre of the lawn.

Morgan remembered a time, years ago, when he'd sat on the edge of a similar but much larger fountain in an Oxford park. He'd lost a suspect during a foot chase because of a foolish mistake. But Tranmere hadn't berated him. He'd stood beside him, put a hand on his shoulder and told him that it was a difficult day, but things would get better. He reassured Morgan that he wasn't a bad officer, despite what he'd believed.

And now Morgan was here to accuse his mentor and friend of being just that: a bad officer.

Morgan grabbed the files from the passenger seat and got out of the car, closing the door behind him. As he made his way along the path towards the front door, he reminded himself to stay focused and resist Tranmere's charm. He was here for answers about falsified evidence, and he wouldn't leave here without the truth.

Morgan heard people talking, and winced at the idea of interrupting Tranmere entertaining guests, but this couldn't wait.

Before he could ring the bell, raised voices echoed from somewhere inside the huge house. It didn't sound like a dinner party or a gathering of friends. It sounded like an argument.

Morgan hesitated. Rather than knock on the door, he skirted around the hedge, stepping in the flowerbed to peer inside. Night-blooming jasmine and honeysuckle clung to the brickwork around the window; he brushed them away.

When Morgan had visited Tranmere, they'd spent time in his study or living room. He hadn't seen much of the rest of the house and had never seen this reception room. It was more formal than Tranmere's comfortable old study and grander than the living room. Huge chandeliers hung from the ceiling, but they weren't switched on. Instead, a large Tiffany lamp with colourful glass cast a soft, warm light over the room – just enough for Morgan to see what was going on.

There were two figures facing off. Morgan recognised Tranmere's stocky frame. The other man was taller and slimmer but still broad-shouldered. Morgan could hear them yelling but couldn't work out what was being said. The taller man was jabbing his finger in Tranmere's direction and gesturing wildly.

A moth, attracted by the light, fluttered against the window. Morgan waved it away. He didn't want to get involved in a quarrel that was probably none of his business. But the shouting quickly grew more intense, and the tall man stopped gesturing and violently pushed Tranmere.

Morgan couldn't just stand by. He raced back to the front door and up the steps, ready to ring the doorbell or hammer on the door if necessary; but the door was on the latch.

He pushed it open and called out, 'Tranmere?'

There was no response, so he followed the sounds of shouting. The door stood ajar. Looking in, Morgan saw Tranmere with the taller, younger man, who had Tranmere by the collar and was shaking him.

Tranmere seemed unconcerned. He gave a mocking laugh. 'Is this any way to treat your father?'

So that was Sam.

It had been years since Morgan had seen him.

With a bitter curse, Sam shoved Tranmere away, pushing him back into an armchair.

Before the situation could escalate further, Morgan entered the room.

'That's enough,' he said, physically putting himself between father and son.

'Who are you?' Sam demanded, his eyes burning with anger and his chest heaving.

184

Tranmere rearranged his shirt with an amused expression. 'You must recognise him, Samuel,' he said with a tut. 'This is Scott Morgan. *Detective Inspector* Morgan now. So, Samuel, I suggest you behave yourself. Otherwise, Morgan will have no option but to act in his professional capacity.'

A young woman entered the room. 'What happened? I heard you shouting.'

Sam ignored her question. Instead, folding his arms across his chest and glowering at Morgan, he said, 'I remember you.'

Morgan remembered him too. A gangly, sweet-natured boy who'd thought the world of his dad and wanted nothing more than to follow in his footsteps. Clearly, something had changed along the way.

'You called the police?' Sam said, shaking his head in disgust at his father.

'No, just a lucky coincidence that Morgan picked this moment to drop in,' Tranmere said. 'You always make such a spectacle of yourself, Samuel. I don't know how you became such an embarrassment. You used to be such a—'

Sam looked ready to launch himself at Tranmere again.

The young woman put a hand on Sam's arm. 'Don't. It's not worth it,' she said softly.

Morgan guessed this was Sam's partner, Brooke Lewis, the woman who babysat for Tommy Burton. She met Morgan's eye and gave him a quick, apologetic smile. 'I'm sorry, we didn't come here to make trouble. We were trying to smooth things over.'

Tranmere gave an amused snort. 'I'd hate to see what happens when you come to make trouble, if this is your attempt at smoothing things over.'

'I've had enough of this,' Sam said. 'We're leaving.'

At the door he stopped, turned around, and gave his father a rude hand gesture, then stormed out. Brooke hurried after him.

Tranmere tutted under his breath and winced as the front door slammed. 'Good grief, that boy has got a temper,' he muttered. He ambled over to the window, opened it as wide as it would go, and shouted out, 'I take it I'm disinvited to the wedding again, am I?' He closed the window, chuckling. 'Honestly, I've been invited and disinvited more times than—' He broke off, finally acknowledging Morgan properly. He smiled. 'I'm very sorry you had to witness that. Quite embarrassing. Please, have a seat.'

He gestured Morgan towards an elegantly furnished sofa. The cushions were covered in an expensive-looking floral-print pattern that probably cost a packet. Morgan sank down into it.

'You don't have kids, do you?'

Morgan shook his head.

'Lucky you. More trouble than they're worth.' The smile slipped from Tranmere's face. 'I don't mean that. I love the stupid boy. I just can't seem to get through to him.'

'What's causing the tension between you?' Morgan asked. 'Do you object to them getting married?'

'Gracious, no. Couldn't be happier for them. I imagine this may be his last opportunity to sort his life out and make something of himself, since all he does is play video games.' Tranmere shook his head. 'I warned him about the money, you know. It can be a curse. I held his money back, trying to teach him responsibility. But his grandmother – my father's second wife – spoiled him. Handouts whenever he wanted them. Now she's left him a fortune in her will, and it looks like he'll never learn to stand on his own two feet.'

'I'm sorry. I remember he used to adore you.'

Tranmere looked glumly down at the patterned rug beneath his feet. 'Yes . . . Sadly, things change.'

'Maybe he still wants your approval?' Morgan suggested.

Tranmere smiled softly. 'Let's not dwell on unpleasantness. I must say this is a nice surprise. I've not seen you in over a year, and then I'm honoured with two visits in quick succession.' He relaxed back into the chair. Before Morgan could reply, Tranmere sat up abruptly. 'I should have offered you a drink.' He moved across the room towards a bar cart and picked up a crystal glass.

But Morgan declined. 'No, thank you. I'm here in an official capacity today.'

Tranmere paused and set the glass back down. 'Really?' He walked back and sat in the chair across from Morgan.

Morgan reminded himself not to be distracted by his past friendship with Tranmere. 'Yes, I'm afraid it isn't a social call,' he said evenly. 'It's to do with the Donaldson investigation.'

Tranmere leaned back, steepling his fingers, face impassive. 'Go on.'

'I have a question for you. I want to know why key evidence was removed from my initial report of the second abduction scene.' Morgan held Tranmere's gaze. 'You personally reviewed and edited that report before the final submission. All mention of a red Ford Focus that was at the scene was removed.'

Morgan waited. He wanted to hear an explanation. He longed for Tranmere to say something that would clear up this whole mess.

Tranmere shrugged. 'Must have been an administrative error. Probably a mistake in report processing. A minor detail.'

'A red vehicle seen at an abduction scene is far from a minor detail.'

At the belligerent tone in Morgan's voice, Tranmere's eyes narrowed. But then he leaned forward, resting his hands on his knees. 'I'm sure there's a logical reason behind it.'

'Then I'm sure you can tell me what that logical reason is,' Morgan said, his voice cool.

Tranmere sighed. 'I can't remember. It was a long time ago.'

Morgan picked up the files and handed them to Tranmere. 'Take a look. It wasn't just that the red car was omitted by a typo. The paragraph was reworded.' Tranmere's expression was impassive, and Morgan felt his irritation grow. He wouldn't let this be dismissed as nothing. This was a major omission. 'You changed it. You changed my report.' Morgan could hear the anger in his voice. He didn't want to lose control. He prided himself on being able to keep calm and cool. But this riled him. He'd trusted Tranmere.

Tranmere glanced at the files, only briefly skimming them both. Then he shuffled the pages and put them back in the folder.

He leaned back in his chair, watching Morgan with an amused smile. 'I don't see why you're making such a song and dance about it.'

Morgan's jaw tightened.

A shrewd look entered Tranmere's eyes. 'Come on, Morgan, we both know how these things work.'

'No, I don't think we do,' Morgan said. 'Tell me, how do they work?'

'Morgan, be reasonable. We've all done it.' Tranmere's tone was cajoling.

'I can assure you I've never tampered with a crime scene report.'

'This wasn't tampering. It was just omitting one tiny detail from a report.'

'I don't understand why you'd do it.' Morgan could hear the desperation in his voice. He so wanted Tranmere to come up with a reasonable explanation.

Tranmere covered his face with his hands. For a moment, Morgan thought his old boss looked ashamed, but a second later, he looked up and his smile was back.

'Look, you know I would never have done anything to jeopardise that investigation. But I needed to get Donaldson behind bars, and I wasn't going to let anything mess that up.'

'What do you mean?'

'The red car was nothing, Morgan; you have to believe me. It was completely unrelated to the investigation and had no connection to the abduction at all. I checked it out personally. You know what these investigations are like. I didn't want the presence of the car at the abduction scene leading us on a wild goose chase. Some details are best controlled, to create the right narrative, to ensure a conviction. I was just tidying up. I didn't want anything to jeopardise our case.'

Morgan frowned. He remembered giving his draft report to Tranmere. Maybe time and experience had coloured his recollections, but he was almost positive Tranmere's frown had deepened as he'd read Morgan's report.

Then abruptly, Tranmere had told Morgan he would handle it.

He'd smiled benevolently as he'd ushered Morgan out of his office. *You've done a great job, Morgan. I'll take it from here.* Back then Morgan had been a junior, eager to please Tranmere. Satisfied with the praise, he'd overlooked the red flags.

'What you did wasn't tidying up,' Morgan said. 'You removed all mention of a vehicle at the abduction scene. Don't you get it? We might have missed something. Potentially another suspect. Maybe somebody who was working with Donaldson.'

'No, no, I told you. I checked it out personally. I promise you. We didn't miss anything.'

'Where was Sam on the day of the second abduction?' Morgan asked.

Tranmere's expression changed in an instant, his face now hard. 'What are you implying?'

'You know what I'm implying. I think you're covering for someone. Was it your son?'

'Don't be ridiculous! Sam was fourteen.' Tranmere took a deep breath, trying to calm down. 'I don't know what's got into you. You're not thinking logically. Sam wasn't even old enough to drive.'

Morgan knew that, of course, but Sam could have been in the car with someone else. Sam was someone Tranmere might be willing to bend his morals to cover up for. Despite his attempts to brush this off as something minor, Tranmere hadn't been a careless or reckless officer. He'd changed that report for a reason. He must have felt like he had no other choice.

'Honestly, you're blowing this all out of proportion.'

But Morgan knew Tranmere didn't really believe that. Removing the mention of a car wasn't a decision he would have taken lightly. Yes, he'd been desperate for a conviction. They all had been. Those three little boys had needed justice. But the red car wouldn't have held things up for long. It would have been investigated, accounted for, and they would have moved on with the case. There was something more Tranmere wasn't telling him.

'Those three small boys. We should have done things by the book for them. Do you even remember their names?'

Tranmere sprung to his feet. 'How dare you!' His cheeks grew red and blotchy. 'Henry Tisdale. Marc White. Stuart O'Connor,' he said, his voice low and filled with fury. 'I'll never forget them. I did everything I could to make sure Donaldson was convicted for what he did to those boys.'

Morgan lowered his head, staring at his hands, unwilling to look Tranmere in the eye. That had been uncalled for. Of course Tranmere remembered. After a case like that, you never forgot the victims.

'And now there's another little boy, sir. Tommy Burton.'

Tranmere's fierce expression waned. 'I know.' He sank into his chair. 'Come on, Morgan, you know me. I always have the best interests of the case at heart. If I knew something that would help you find Tommy, don't you think I would tell you?' His voice turned coaxing. 'We worked so many cases together, built so much trust. I value that history between us. Surely my word is good enough for you. I checked out that car. I promise you it had nothing to do with the abduction.'

Morgan shifted uneasily on the sofa. As it adjusted to his body weight, the feather-stuffed cushions enveloped him. He felt like the plush softness was trying to trap him there – pull him back to a time and a place where he'd trusted Tranmere without question.

Morgan was well aware of Tranmere's influence on his career trajectory. He'd given him his first real opportunity to prove what he could do and taught him the ropes, encouraging him when others had doubted his ability. When Morgan was entangled in what a lot of his peers considered to be a career-ending mistake, Tranmere had been in his corner – one of the very few that had.

But Morgan couldn't afford to be swayed by their shared past. 'I'm afraid your word isn't good enough today, sir. Not when Tommy Burton's life is at stake.' He stood up. 'If you won't give me the answers I need, then I'll turn over a full report of our exchange to my senior officer. You'll need to explain yourself to them. I'm too close to this to be impartial.'

Tranmere's mouth tightened into a hard line, and he shot to his feet again. 'What is this?' he hissed. 'You'd throw me to the wolves over a simple error?'

'It's not a simple error,' Morgan said.

'After everything I did for you, this is how you repay me?'

'You had faith in me when others didn't. I'm where I am today in large part because of you. I know that and I appreciate it.' Morgan held Tranmere's angry gaze.

Tranmere scoffed. 'But you turn your back on me when I need your help.'

'Why do you need my help?'

'I've told you,' Tranmere said, waving a dismissive hand. 'I checked the car out. It wasn't important. I decided to omit it so that we could focus on actually catching Donaldson.'

'You forget, sir,' Morgan said quietly. 'I know you. I know your methods. And you would never remove the mention of a vehicle at a crime scene simply to be expedient on a case.'

Tranmere's expression faltered.

'You removed it for a reason,' Morgan continued. 'And if you won't tell me what that reason is . . .'

Tranmere grasped Morgan's arm. 'Wait. Let's not let this get out of hand. We can keep it between us.'

Gently but firmly, Morgan extracted himself from Tranmere's grip. 'I'm sorry, sir, but this has gone beyond us.'

Morgan turned and walked from the room.

He liked Tranmere. But he couldn't let his fondness of his old boss jeopardise this investigation.

'Hang on a minute.' Tranmere chased after Morgan as he made his way down the hall. 'You can't mean this. Not after everything . . .'

Morgan felt a stab of guilt, but he kept walking. He only turned back as he reached the front door. 'I do things by the book now, sir.'

Then he walked out into the darkness. Tranmere stood in the doorway watching him go.

Morgan might have sounded cool and calm, but he felt sick with the magnitude of what he'd just done. Guilt, anger and desperation washed over him, but beneath those swirling emotions, Morgan knew he had to take a stand. He couldn't overlook this, even if it cost Tranmere his reputation.

Morgan got in his car and started the ignition. He had to do what his conscience demanded.

As he turned the Volvo around in front of the house, he saw Tranmere's wounded, desperate expression in the rear-view mirror.

But it wasn't Morgan's job to protect Tranmere. There was only one person Morgan needed to protect, and that was Tommy Burton.

Chapter Twenty-One

Rachel King set the phone back in its cradle. Chatting with her sister usually brightened her mood, but today she couldn't shake the uncomfortable feeling that something bad was looming around the corner.

Next door, the Burtons' house was silent. There was still no word on Tommy. The police had searched the area he'd gone missing in and spoken to all the residents of Dahlia Close, but he hadn't been found. Rachel shuddered. Losing a child . . . she couldn't imagine it.

She'd had a lovely time being with her sister this week, but she'd missed her little house and all her home comforts and was glad to be back. Although, Tommy's disappearance had left her feeling anxious and uneasy.

She scratched Smokey behind his ears, feeling the cat's rumbling purr. Marmalade meowed impatiently, weaving around Rachel's legs and nuzzling her head against her ankles. She opened a tin of tuna-flavoured cat food, wrinkling her nose at the smell.

'Sorry, my loves. I know supper's a bit late today,' she said as she filled their bowls.

A thud sounded from somewhere in the house. Rachel froze, listening. Just the old pipes or the house settling. She was jittery after the recent goings-on in the neighbourhood. Tommy's disappearance had everyone on edge.

Her gaze drifted again to the Burtons'. A mother's worst nightmare, not knowing. Poor Amber. Rachel felt for Gareth too, of course, but if she was honest, she had never really liked Gareth. He was too loud and overbearing for her tastes. And she'd heard him shouting at his wife and child frequently in that horrible booming voice of his.

She could only pray the police found Tommy soon, before . . . But she couldn't finish the thought. Tommy *had* to be all right. He just had to be.

She put the cats' food bowls on the floor.

Marmalade hurried over to her bowl and started munching away contentedly. Smokey sniffed at his dinner, then turned away.

Rachel frowned. 'Not hungry?'

He lifted a paw and began grooming himself. Rachel suspected he'd been visiting another house and using his charms to get food from them.

'I see,' she said. 'You've found yourself another human to boss around, have you?'

Smokey ignored Rachel completely, as was often the way with cats.

She tutted. 'Charming. After everything I do for you. I suppose they feed you something better? Salmon for Lord Smokey, is it? Is that why you now turn your nose up at my supermarket-brand cat food? You used to like it. Marmalade still does.'

Smokey slowly – and, Rachel thought, quite deliberately – turned his back.

She rolled her eyes. When she moved away to the fridge, Smokey leapt up on to the counter.

'Don't you dare!' Rachel said sternly, watching as he reached out a paw to swat at a fork she had left on the counter. 'I said—'

But it was too late. Smokey batted the fork, sending it to the floor with a clatter, then looked up at Rachel with an innocent expression.

'Must you always make a mess?' She sighed, scooping up the fork.

Why couldn't cats resist knocking things over? They were worse than children sometimes.

As she washed up, her thoughts returned to Tommy. He didn't play in the garden anymore, preferring to be indoors with that computer of his. He'd always been a clever boy, curious about how things worked. The kind of child who asked a million questions about anything and everything. A quiet lad, introverted and more watchful than most.

Her gaze drifted to the Burtons' place once more.

Rachel shivered. The ominous feeling swept over her again. She had a dreadful sense of foreboding – that something was terribly wrong – and she couldn't shake it off. Of course she was worried about Tommy, but it wasn't only that. She had a strange desire to run to her car and drive to her sister's place.

But that was silly.

Rachel opened the fridge and took out a bottle of white wine. The wine would help relax her, and maybe a bath would help, too. Then she would log on for her usual late-night game of online bridge. That always cheered her up. As she'd grown older, Rachel had noticed that she slept less. Insomnia had become an unwelcome regular companion, and she suspected tonight would be worse than usual.

Her sister had crystals in her home that she claimed absorbed bad energy, and she kept meditation cushions in the lounge, which she sat on with her legs crossed, listening to whale music.

Rachel considered herself far too sensible for all of that. But today she wished she had some of those crystals. She usually didn't go in for her sister's 'bad energy' nonsense, but today she felt tense and anxious. Though that was hardly surprising given what had happened to the poor Burtons next door.

Rachel might not have crystals, but she did have the next best thing. *Wine*. That would help her relax and get rid of some of the horrible anxiety she was experiencing. She unscrewed the cap and poured a generous glass. The crisp aroma wafted up, already soothing her nerves. She took a sip, enjoying the tartness.

Now, time for a bath. A long, hot soak would be just the ticket. Her sister only had a shower, and while staying there, Rachel had missed her leisurely baths.

Scooping up her glass, she made her way upstairs to the bathroom. Her feline companions could fend for themselves for a bit while she relaxed. A bath and a glass of wine – simple pleasures to take away her worries.

She lit a candle, turned on the taps, and then rummaged in the cupboard for her favourite lavender bubble bath. The familiar, calming scent soon filled the air. Rachel shooed the cats outside – telling them she didn't need an audience, thank you very much – and shut the door.

She sat on the closed toilet seat, swirling her wine glass, as she waited for the bath to fill. Tommy's disappearance had shaken her more than she wanted to admit. She kept imagining herself in Amber's shoes. How could she cope with the not knowing? The waiting?

Rachel turned off the taps, stripped off her clothes and eased into the warmth. The lavender scent soothed her mind, and the hot water relaxed her muscles. She took another sip of wine. Usually, a glass left her pleasantly tipsy, but tonight she thought she might polish off the bottle. Anything to calm these restless thoughts.

There was something niggling at her about Tommy's disappearance. Or, to be more precise, something that had happened afterwards. Something that didn't make sense. She'd gone to the Burtons' earlier hoping to speak to someone about it. But then she'd convinced herself it was probably nothing. She hadn't wanted to be a nuisance. Amber wasn't in any fit state to answer Rachel's questions, and the family liaison officer had seemed terribly efficient and busy, and Rachel hadn't wanted to waste his time.

When she thought it through, it was ridiculous. Rachel couldn't possibly have heard what she thought she had. No – it was very unlikely.

But what if it she had heard correctly . . . ? Somewhere out there – someone had Tommy. What if . . . ? Rachel sank deeper into the bubbles, willing the questions whirling in her mind to go away. She'd deal with it tomorrow. Yes, tomorrow she'd call the officer who'd come to see her after Tommy went missing. Karen something or other. She'd kept the card. Even if it did sound outlandish, at least it would mean that Rachel had told somebody.

Tomorrow. She'd deal with it all tomorrow.

The wine and the warmth were working their magic at last, and Rachel's eyelids were growing heavy in the flickering candlelight.

A few moments later there was a muffled squeak and the bathroom door opened. Rachel gave an irritated sigh, assuming she hadn't fully shut the door and one of the cats had come in. Couldn't she have a single moment's peace?

A draught blew into the room, and the candle flickered out. The skin on the back of her neck tingled.

'Marmalade? Smokey?' she called.

No familiar meow answered her. Rachel sat up in the bath, peering at the doorway. She hadn't left the hall light on, so it was hard to make anything out.

She'd put the matches on the windowsill and couldn't reach them unless she got out of the bath.

Rachel let out a huff. She was thoroughly fed up. First the worries and questions about Tommy's disappearance had invaded her mind, and now one of the cats was demanding attention when all she wanted was a peaceful soak.

'I know you're there, stop playing games,' Rachel called, hoping to spot one of the cats slinking out of the room so she could close the door firmly behind them. But the open doorway remained empty, no marmalade or grey cat in sight.

Had she left the door ajar after all, and a breeze had blown it open? Maybe she'd left the window open in her bedroom, and that had caused the draught. Rachel twisted around in the tub.

Peering at the dark landing outside the bathroom, Rachel saw nothing amiss and no sign of the cats. 'Marmalade? Smokey?' she called again, to no response. She wasn't sure whether to feel relieved or annoyed at the cats for interrupting her bath and then disappearing.

Then she caught sight of a grey tail at the edge of the doorframe. 'Smokey! I should have known it was you.'

Rachel sighed, the calming effects of her bath now faded. She decided to give up on the idea of a relaxing soak. It would be time for online bridge soon anyway.

But before she could get out, a dark shape appeared in the doorway. And this time, it wasn't a cat.

Her breath froze in her throat. Fear stopped her from moving as gloved hands reached out and shoved her under the water.

The air from Rachel's lungs was expelled in a rush as she hit the bottom of the bath, bubbles bursting out of her mouth.

Panic seized her as firm hands kept her under, the water sloshing over her face. Rachel thrashed and kicked, trying to prise the hands from her shoulders.

The water churned around her as she fought against the intruder, But the attacker had an iron grip.

They held Rachel down.

Her limbs slammed into the bath as she struggled against the strong arms submerging her.

She could see only the dark, shadowy figure through the water that distorted her vision. Her hands slid uselessly against the sides of the tub, unable to find leverage to lift herself up.

Her chest spasmed, body fighting to inhale, but there was no air. She kicked out again, but her limbs felt leaden and slow. How long had she been under – seconds or minutes? Her mind clouded in panic as her oxygen-starved body weakened.

She would not give up without a fight.

With a surge of desperate energy, Rachel hit out at the person above her. The attacker let out a muffled yelp and loosened their grip for just a moment. It was enough.

Rachel's head broke the surface of the water, and she gasped, drawing breath back into her lungs. Her body's need for oxygen overrode the logical demand in Rachel's brain telling her to scream. She turned, scrambling to get out of the bath, but she slipped, landing back in the water with a splash.

The dark figure gripped her again. She landed a satisfying kick to their stomach. It wasn't enough, though. They didn't let go.

Rachel's heart hammered as she was thrust back under the water.

Through the swirling water her vision was growing dim, but she saw a swish of grey, and a screech of animal outrage. *Smokey*.

Rachel struggled, but her body was giving up.

A grey paw swatted at the attacker. And a drop of red spilled into the water beside Rachel's head. Blood from her assailant. Smokey was trying to help her.

But Rachel couldn't fight anymore. Her limbs were burning and so heavy. Bright spots danced in front of her eyes.

Her lungs screamed for air but found only water.

Chapter Twenty-Two

Morgan parked inconspicuously at the edge of Dahlia Close and switched off the engine, giving them a view of all the houses in the cul-de-sac. The rain was heavy, drumming on the roof. Morgan glanced at Karen, who was sitting in the passenger seat.

It had been a quiet drive. Morgan had abruptly told Karen he needed her to be present while he talked to Sam Tranmere. The meeting had apparently been okayed by Churchill, which confused Karen, because at the last briefing Churchill had said Morgan was to stay away from Sam Tranmere and had handed the assignment to Arnie instead.

Obviously, something had happened in the interim to change Churchill's mind, but Karen didn't know what that could have been. She hoped it wasn't something she'd have to worry about.

Morgan wasn't in a talkative mood, not that Morgan was ever exactly talkative. But something seemed to be really bothering him tonight, and his fingers had been clenched tightly around the steering wheel on the drive over.

He'd picked her up from home, and during the seven-minute drive to Washingborough had said little about why Churchill had changed his mind – and even less about why they needed to speak with Sam Tranmere again at this time of night.

She'd given him time to brood on whatever was troubling him, but now that they were actually outside Sam and Brooke's house, Karen hoped Morgan would tell her the purpose behind their visit. She undid her seat belt and waited expectantly.

'Sorry for dragging you out so late,' Morgan said eventually, rubbing a hand over his jaw.

'It's fine. I'd had a shower and something to eat. I was ready to get back to work anyway. So, what's happened? Development?'

'Something like that,' Morgan said grimly.

When he didn't elaborate and moved to open the car door, Karen put her hand on his arm. 'Wait a minute. I'm not going in there without the full story. You need to update me on what's happened. Before I went to get dinner, all our focus was on Cody Rhodes. What's changed?'

'You're right. Sorry,' Morgan said, releasing his grip on the handle and leaning back heavily in his seat. 'Sophie discovered something odd in one of the crime scene reports from the previous abductions.'

'Something odd?' Karen repeated with a frown. That didn't sound good. 'What did she find?'

'There was a discrepancy between the report I gave to Tranmere and the report he filed in the official records. He removed all mention of a red Ford Focus that had been near the scene of the second abduction.' Morgan's voice was tight with anger.

'Why would he do that?'

'That's what I wanted to know. I went over to Mablethorpe. I thought I owed him that much. I wanted to ask him about it face to face before turning him in.'

'Turning him in?' Karen repeated in surprise. 'What are you saying? You think Tranmere was involved somehow?'

'I think he was covering up for someone,' Morgan said quietly. He closed his eyes for a moment. 'And I completely missed it at the time.'

Karen stared straight ahead, trying to make sense of what Morgan was suggesting. Who had Tranmere covered up for?

'Do you believe there was someone else at the abductions fifteen years ago . . . someone that Tranmere knew? And now that same person has resurfaced and taken Tommy Burton?'

Morgan ran a hand through his hair. 'I have to admit that is where my mind's going, yes. That's why I want to talk to Sam. If there's anyone Tranmere would have put his career on the line for, it's his son.'

Karen absorbed this, turning possibilities over in her mind. 'Then Sam Tranmere is back on our suspects list.'

Morgan gave a conflicted frown, shaking his head slightly. 'I don't know. He was only fourteen at the time, so it's hard to picture him as the mastermind, and Cody Rhodes wouldn't have been much older.'

'Right. So, we're just going to go in there and ask him some questions. We're not arresting him?'

'That's right,' Morgan said. 'We don't have any evidence against him yet.'

Karen recalled her initial chat with Sam and Brooke. 'When I spoke to Sam and Brooke, some things did feel a bit off. I was concerned about a nasty bruise Brooke had on her arm. And Sam made out as though he barely knew Tommy, when it's quite clear the boy had been at his house on more than one occasion.'

'Interesting,' Morgan said as he peered out of the windscreen. The rain had stopped as quickly as it had started. He nodded in the direction of No. 2. 'Sam and Brooke were at Tranmere's earlier. They were there when I arrived to talk to him. There was a big bust-up, and Sam stormed out. But they must be home now. I can see their car and the lights are on.'

'What was the fight about?' Karen asked as they both got out of the car.

Morgan came around to join her on the pavement, hands in his pockets. 'Tranmere called Sam an embarrassment. Said Sam's done nothing with his life and is just living off his grandmother's money.' Morgan shrugged. 'But I suspect it's more that Sam feels he can't measure up to some impossible standard Tranmere's set for him. He's put his dad on a pedestal and thinks he'll never be good enough. That rejection makes him lash out.'

Karen looked at Morgan with an amused smile. 'Perhaps we should start calling you Dr Morgan. You missed your calling. You should have been a psychologist. That was an impressive analysis.'

'Very funny,' Morgan said dryly, but he managed a smile.

Karen turned to look at the row of identical houses, taking in the symmetrical white uPVC windows and the neat lawns and flowerbeds. Even the doors were the same light grey with chrome handles. Everything looked cosy and safe, but something felt decidedly off to Karen. She couldn't shake the feeling that unseen eyes were tracking their every move from behind closed curtains and blinds.

She took another look around. There was no one about, although interior lights were on in all the houses.

Karen turned her attention back to Morgan, suppressing a shiver. 'Don't you find this place a bit creepy?'

He frowned. 'What do you mean?'

'I get the sense I'm being watched. Look, *there*,' she said, pointing at Lyra Hill's house, where the curtain had most definitely twitched.

Morgan shrugged, unconcerned, as they started to walk towards No. 2. 'That's because we probably *are* being watched. It's a small cul-de-sac. When an unfamiliar car pulls up, the neighbours will pay attention. Especially with one of the local kids missing.'

As he spoke, a curtain moved upstairs at the Fosters' home. Karen bit her lip. 'I suppose you're right. But there's something about this close and the people here . . . They seem oddly wary of the police. Too guarded, like they're afraid saying too much will get them into trouble. It's not normal for a middle-class neighbour-hood like this.'

Morgan looked at her with an eyebrow raised. 'Bit classist.'

Karen shrugged. 'Maybe, but it's true in my experience. The majority of people in a neighbourhood like this don't usually fear or mistrust the police. They have no reason to.'

Morgan stopped walking to look at her. 'You think they know more than they're letting on? I thought the Fosters and Rachel King had been cooperative when you spoke to them.'

'They were, up to a point, but Rachel King shut down when I asked about problems between the Burtons. And the Fosters . . . they seemed helpful on the surface, but Jack Foster was definitely hiding something.'

Morgan crossed his arms over his chest. 'But you and Rick got to the bottom of that, didn't you? Tommy was teasing Jack, and it turned physical. Kids' stuff.'

'That's what he told us,' Karen said. 'But his story was too pat, too convenient. I don't think we have the full truth yet.' She looked around once more at the neat houses, trying to imagine what secrets were hiding behind those doors. She shivered.

Morgan followed her gaze, his expression hardening. 'If anyone in the cul-de-sac knows where Tommy is, they'd come forward. That's what any normal person would do.' His jaw tightened as his eyes fixed on Sam Tranmere's house. 'Anyone who's not a monster, anyway.'

After a moment, Morgan seemed to shake himself mentally, and he gave Karen a sideways glance and a half-hearted attempt at a smile. 'Come on, let's go and speak to them.'

Chapter Twenty-Three

They walked up the paved driveway, avoiding the scattered puddles. They were halfway up the drive when Karen stopped abruptly. A dark figure suddenly stumbled into view, emerging from the side of the house.

Sam Tranmere.

He was wearing a T-shirt and cargo trousers, both of which were drenched. In his clenched fist, he held a long, sharp pair of garden shears. His forearms were raked with scratches.

He swatted at some of the shrubbery in the front flowerbed with the jagged blades. Karen guessed he wasn't a natural gardener.

Morgan said, 'Hello, Sam.'

Sam looked up, his face tight with anger. 'What are you doing here?'

'We hoped we could have a word with you,' Karen said, stepping forward. 'I spoke to you and Brooke earlier, remember?'

His eyes narrowed. 'You were the one who took a look at my gaming kit.'

'That's right.'

'Well, what are you doing back here?' he asked belligerently. 'I don't expect you've come for a multiplayer game, have you?'

'Not exactly,' Morgan said. 'I saw you at your father's a little while ago and—'

'I know.' Sam cut him off irritably. 'I was there, remember, humiliated as usual. He's such a . . .' He flung the garden shears down in frustration, and they clattered loudly on the paving. 'You saw how unreasonable he was being.'

'I got there at the tail end of the argument,' Morgan said calmly. 'Maybe you can tell me about it. Can we come inside?'

Sam glared at them both, then shrugged. 'Suit yourself.'

'What have you done to your arms?' Karen said, looking at the angry red welts.

He brushed a hand over them self-consciously. 'I was trying to clear some brambles,' he mumbled.

'In the rain?' Morgan asked.

'Yes,' Sam snapped, opening the front door and wiping his feet on the mat. 'I came home after that row with Dad and just needed time to chill. I went to the gaming room. But thanks to the weather, brambles were banging against the side of the shed. I couldn't stand it, so I decided to cut them back.'

Karen frowned. 'You could have just put your headset on to block out the noise.'

'I *could* have done, but I didn't *want* to. Anyway, I don't want plants that close to the gaming room. Because then damp gets in, and I don't want that to happen with all the expensive equipment.'

'Fair enough,' Morgan said. 'Is Brooke around?'

'Yeah, somewhere,' Sam said with a shrug, and then he called out for Brooke.

There were footsteps on the stairs. 'Yes?' an anxious voice said. Then Brooke appeared wrapped in an oversized, fluffy dressing gown, her hair still wet. 'Sorry, I didn't realise we had visitors. I've just got out of the shower. I'll put some clothes on.' She smiled apologetically and headed back upstairs.

'Don't take forever like you usually do,' Sam called after her.

He led the way into the large kitchen. 'I suppose I should offer you a drink,' he said, in a tone that suggested he didn't want to.

'Thanks,' Morgan said. 'I'll have a glass of water.'

Sam turned to Karen. 'Same,' she said.

There was a long, drawn-out silence as Sam got the glasses of water and carried them over to the breakfast bar.

'You can sit down,' he said, nodding to the stools. But he didn't sit down himself; instead, he put his hands on the counter and stared down at the angry red marks on his arm.

'You should put some antiseptic cream on that,' Karen said, looking at the scratches.

'Yeah, I will. When you're gone,' Sam said pointedly. 'So, what do you want to know?' He turned to Morgan. 'Do you want to catch up on the family gossip? Or . . .' He faltered, eyebrows lifting. 'Have you found Tommy?'

'Not yet, no, but we're following lots of leads,' Karen said.

'I thought you would have found him by now.'

'Can you tell me how much you remember about the Oxford abductions – the ones your dad worked on,' Morgan asked, leaning in towards Sam.

Sam shrugged, breaking eye contact to look down at the floor. 'I remember them quite well,' he muttered. 'It was probably his biggest case. At least, it was definitely the one that affected him most.' He shook his head, reliving the memories. 'He came home late every night. He missed dinner, which was a big deal when I was growing up. It was just me and Mum for those few weeks.' Sam smiled with a far-off look. 'I was proud of him. Proud of him for trying to catch the evil sod who'd taken those boys.' Then a shadow crossed his face. He frowned, lines creasing his forehead as he looked up sharply. 'Do you think Tommy's abduction has got something to do with the one you worked on with my dad? That was years ago.'

Morgan's voice was calm and steady. 'We're just covering all bases. I'm interested to know how much you remember. Any more details come to mind?'

Sam waved a hand dismissively. 'You'd be better off asking my dad.' Then his face tightened as realisation dawned. 'But, of course, you've already done that, haven't you?' His laugh was humourless. 'You're here because you think I've got something to do with Tommy going missing.' He balled his fists, knuckles whitening. 'I don't believe it. Just because I was angry with my dad, which by the way he deserved, does not mean I'm some sicko who abducts children.' His voice rose in anger. 'As if I'd want to, anyway. Tommy is an annoying little brat. I couldn't imagine anything worse than being stuck with him for a few hours.' Sam stopped talking then, covering his face with shaking hands. 'That wasn't fair. He's just a kid, and he's missing. It was a horrible thing to say. I'm sorry. I've just had a really difficult night.'

'Why's it been difficult?' Morgan asked, studying Sam with a sympathetic gaze.

Sam shook his head, as if it should be obvious. 'The argument with my dad. He always makes me feel so small and pathetic. I don't even know why I bother with him anymore.' He started pacing, unable to contain his frustration. 'Why should *I* make an effort when I'll never be good enough in his eyes?'

Karen shot Morgan a pointed look, recognising this confirmed Morgan's earlier amateur psychoanalysis. But Morgan kept his focus on Sam.

'It's difficult,' he said. 'I understand. I have a difficult relationship with my own father.'

Karen looked at Morgan, surprised. She hadn't known that. They were friends, but he still had some secrets of his own.

'Yeah?' Sam asked, scepticism creeping into his tone. 'I would have thought you'd get on great with your old man. My dad thinks you're brilliant. He wishes I'd turned out like you.' His voice took on a bitter edge. 'You're the type of son he's always wanted.'

Morgan flinched at Sam's words. The weight of accusing his former boss of falsifying a report was clearly taking an emotional toll.

Brooke entered the room, now dressed in a pink tracksuit, her hair still damp. She fiddled self-consciously with the silver feather pendant hanging around her neck.

'Sorry,' she said breathlessly. 'Is this about Tommy – have you found him?' Worry creased her face. 'I haven't been able to stop thinking about him.'

'I'm afraid we haven't yet,' Karen replied gently.

Brooke twisted her hands anxiously. 'I suppose you've still got people out searching for him?'

Morgan gave a solemn nod. 'We have. There's a whole team back at the station as well.'

'Did you find Tommy's things? He had a mobile phone, I think. Did you find that?'

'I'm sure you understand that we can't go into all the details of the case at the moment,' Karen replied diplomatically.

Brooke's cheeks flushed. 'Yes, of course. Sorry.'

An uncomfortable silence settled over the room. Then Sam spoke up. 'It seems wrong to be getting married when all this is going on.'

Brooke's face fell. 'What do you mean?'

Sam gestured vaguely, his eyes downcast. 'Well, Tommy is missing. Dad and I are at each other's throats, so he won't be coming to the wedding. My mum's gone. My grandmother died last week.' His voice dropped to a defeated whisper. 'It just seems . . .'

'That's exactly why it's good to have a wedding now. It gives us something to look forward to.' Brooke grasped his hand gently. 'And we've got the honeymoon. You'll feel better when we get away from here for a little while.' Brooke turned to Karen, as if seeking validation. 'Isn't that right?'

'Where are you going for the honeymoon?' Karen asked.

'The Maldives,' Brooke replied, a note of excitement entering her voice. 'It'll be my first holiday outside of Europe. I'm really looking forward to it.' She glanced at Sam. 'We both are, aren't we?'

Sam didn't meet her gaze.

Undaunted, Brooke lifted Sam's hand, tenderly inspecting the angry red scratches marking his skin. 'These look sore. I'll get the first-aid kit.'

Morgan took the opportunity to lean in close to Sam. 'Can you tell me exactly what you remember about that case with Graham Donaldson? Everything you recall happening at the time.'

'Why?'

'Humour me. It could be important.'

Sam lifted his gaze to the ceiling and let out a long breath as he tried to gather the memories. 'It's a long time ago, I was only a teenager.'

Morgan nodded in understanding. 'I know.'

'It was October, I think, wasn't it?' Sam's brow furrowed as he delved deeper into the memories. 'I remember the first one. Dad said you focused on the ex-husband for a bit . . . and nobody paid attention to the blue bear left at the scene because they didn't realise at the time that it was Donaldson's calling card.'

Karen felt an ominous prickle run down her spine. So Sam *did* know about the blue bears. Would he admit that so freely if he was the one who had taken Tommy? Had he told someone else about the bears? Someone who'd decided it was a good way to misdirect the police?

Sam continued. 'The next one happened two weeks later, and soon after that you found the body of the first boy.' He squinted, trying to recall. 'I can't remember his name.'

'Henry Tisdale,' Morgan said, biting out each syllable.

'It must have been horrible for you,' Sam said quietly. 'You were pretty young yourself then, weren't you?'

Morgan gave a brief nod, his jaw tight. 'Mid-twenties. Feels like a lifetime ago.'

Sam shrugged. 'That's about all I remember. I started having nightmares, so Mum said I shouldn't be around when Dad was on the phone talking about the case. She even stopped me reading the papers.'

'Did you know anyone with a red Ford Focus back then?' Karen asked.

Sam thought for a moment and shook his head. 'Not that I can remember. I think my uncle had a red car, but I can't remember the make or model.'

'Do you have contact details for your uncle?' Morgan asked.

'No, I've not seen him for years. I think he fell out with Dad. Not very surprising. Dad's not the easiest man to get along with.'

'Did any of your friends have a red car back then?'

Sam shook his head. 'No. None of us were old enough to drive.'

'Does the name Cody Rhodes mean anything to you?' Morgan asked, pulling his mobile from his pocket.

'No. Should it?'

Morgan used his phone to show Sam a photo of Cody.

'Don't recognise him. Sorry.'

They continued to press Sam gently, to determine how much he really knew about the old case. He seemed knowledgeable about many aspects. But as far as Karen could tell, he was telling the truth about not knowing Cody Rhodes. Her instincts told her Sam was innocent, at least regarding Tommy's disappearance.

A distant siren sounded. Brooke looked up from dabbing antiseptic lotion on Sam's scratches. 'I wonder what that's about?'

She moved into the hall, peering through the window. 'There's blue flashing lights. I think it's the police.' She paused. 'I mean more police. Were you expecting someone?'

Karen and Morgan stepped outside, taking in the scene.

'It looks like something's happening at Rachel King's house,' Karen said. 'We'd better go and see what's up.'

Morgan's mobile rang. He quickly answered, 'DI Morgan speaking.'

Karen watched as he listened intently to the caller.

'Yes . . . okay . . . I see,' he responded. 'I can get there in about a minute flat. My car's parked just by her house.' After a brief pause, Morgan said, 'Will do,' and ended the call. He turned to Karen. 'Let's get over there now.'

'Should we come with you?' Brooke asked anxiously, hovering nearby. 'Do you think Rachel needs help? Is she hurt?'

Morgan's tone was sympathetic but firm as he replied, 'I don't know yet, but it's best you stay indoors for now.'

Brooke opened her mouth to protest, but Karen and Morgan were already heading out of the front door. Morgan pulled it shut before Brooke could follow.

They walked quickly down the driveway, and as soon as they were out of earshot, Karen asked, 'What's happened?'

'Rachel King's bridge partner reported her missing when she didn't log on tonight.' Morgan shook his head. 'Normally that wouldn't require police attention, but the partner is friends with the chief constable. So, as a favour, he asked for a wellness check. Good thing he did.' Morgan's jaw clenched. 'Rachel King is dead.'

Chapter Twenty-Four

Karen walked to the perimeter of the crime scene, her arms crossed over her chest. She had seen plenty of dead bodies in the course of her job, but it was always hard. Rachel King had been found lying motionless, submerged in the bath. Her hair had been floating around her pale face, and her mouth had been open in what Karen felt was a silent cry for help.

Rachel lived alone, but she had a family and friends, people who loved her and would miss her. Karen pushed back emotion and forced herself to think about the scene clinically.

There had been a half-full glass of white wine on the bathroom shelf. That might suggest an accidental death. It was never a good idea to take a bath after a few drinks; too easy to slip and hit your head or, if you were heavily intoxicated, fall unconscious and drown in the water. But Karen hadn't seen evidence of empty bottles in the house or the recycling bin. There was an open bottle in the fridge, so Rachel had probably only had a glass or two. That, together with the soaked bathmat and puddles on the floor, suggested something more suspicious than an accidental death.

She hunched her shoulders against the gloom of the damp night, all her instincts screaming that something sinister had happened. That Rachel King had been murdered.

Tim Farthing and the other SOCOs were inside now, taking apart the scene, along with the pathologist. It was their time to analyse and collect evidence. Karen and Morgan would wait around to see what their findings were.

Farthing had been his usual charming self. His habitual grumpy mood had been made even worse by the evening call-out. Karen was used to his moaning and complaining now, though it still got under her skin at times. After he'd whinged for the third time about being called out, she had risen to the bait. 'I'm very sorry we had to disturb you, but this *is* what you get paid for.'

Then Farthing had gone back inside muttering about how under-appreciated he was.

There was movement at the front door. Karen turned to see Farthing exiting the house. 'I can't believe I have to work in these conditions,' he grumbled. 'There are two cats running all over the place, contaminating all my evidence.' He rustled towards Karen and Morgan in his blue forensic suit. 'Instead of standing around doing nothing, can you please do us all a favour and find a home for those fleabags?'

'We've called the RSPCA and we're waiting on a call back,' Morgan said. 'I think they've got a lot on tonight.'

'Well, call someone else then. One of my techs has spent the last ten minutes trying to catch that grey one. The little so-and-so keeps hiding under the furniture whenever anyone gets near it.' He looked up at the sky, shaking his head. 'I did not sign up to be an animal handler.'

He trudged off towards the forensics van, muttering under his breath about the indignities of being on call.

It was then that Karen remembered that Brooke Lewis had told her that she worked at an animal rescue centre in Lincoln. 'I wonder if Brooke can help us out with the cats,' she suggested to

Morgan. 'Maybe she could take them in until we track down the next of kin. Or at least keep them clear of the crime scene.'

'Good idea,' he said, turning back towards Sam and Brooke's house. 'The lights are on, so I think they're still up.' He scanned the other houses in the cul-de-sac. 'As are most of the other neighbours too.'

Karen nodded at the crime scene and all the vehicles crammed into the close. 'Not surprising, really, with all this going on and finding out their neighbour's just died.'

'I'll go over now and see if she can help round up the cats,' Morgan said. 'Won't be long.'

A few minutes later he returned with Brooke, who was carrying two plastic cat carriers.

She lifted them up. 'Lucky I had these in the garage,' she said. 'We get a lot of call-outs. I don't have my catcher's pole, though. So I'll have to get them the old-fashioned way.'

'What's the old-fashioned way?' Karen asked.

'Bribery, sweet-talking, and getting close enough to scoop them up with my hands.'

'I hope it works,' Morgan said. 'The SOCO team leader said they're quite a distraction.'

Brooke glanced at the open front door and swallowed hard. 'It's okay to go inside?'

Karen felt a twinge of pity. It was easy to forget that civilians recoiled from crime scenes.

'Let's get you suited up first,' Morgan said, nodding to one of the forensics vans.

As Morgan and Brooke walked away, Farthing emerged from the house, peeling off his gloves.

'What are your initial findings, Tim?' Karen asked.

Farthing scowled, clearly irritated at the interruption. 'We haven't finished yet,' he said, stating the obvious. 'It's going to take some time to process the scene, but I can tell you one thing. This was definitely no accident.'

Karen had thought as much, but she wanted to know how certain Farthing was. 'You're sure? She didn't have one too many drinks and fall asleep in the bath?'

He shook his head decisively. 'No. Though I've seen a few cases like that. Just last month, I attended an incident where a mixture of alcohol and sleeping pills led to a man drowning in the bath.' He moved closer to Karen and spoke in a quieter voice. 'We'll have to wait for the full analysis from the pathologist. But there are signs of a struggle. Markings on the neck and shoulders, and water has been splashed everywhere. Most people don't flail around that much during a bath, even if they're drunk. My guess is she was held under the water forcefully.'

'So you're saying it's murder then?' Karen asked.

'That would be my guess, yes,' Farthing confirmed.

Karen thought back to an hour ago, when she and Morgan had seen Sam Tranmere emerge from the side of his house, drenched. They'd assumed he'd got caught in the rain. His explanation of gardening in the dark struck Karen as unusual.

Maybe they needed to have another chat with Sam Tranmere. Rachel King's killer would have been drenched during the struggle too.

Morgan led a now suited-up Brooke Lewis along the clearly marked-out route into the house.

'Who's that?' Farthing demanded, outraged someone he didn't recognise was entering the crime scene.

'Brooke Lewis. She's a neighbour who works at an animal shelter. She's going to round up the cats.'

'Good grief. You're letting a civilian into my crime scene? I suppose I'll have to watch her, so she doesn't stomp all over crucial evidence. As if I don't have enough to do . . .'

As Farthing raced off after Brooke, Morgan strolled back to Karen.

'I think it might be worth seeing if Sam Tranmere's clothes and shoes match trace evidence from the scene,' Karen said to him.

They both turned as a new car arrived. It parked up behind one of the crime scene vehicles, and Arnie got out. He looked exhausted, with his shirt wrinkled and stubble growth around his jawline. His tired eyes suggested he needed a good night's sleep. He put a hand at the base of his spine, stretching out his back before ambling over to them.

'I've been sent to take over,' Arnie said as he approached. 'I'm to hold the fort until DI Goodridge gets here. He'll be the senior investigating officer when he arrives.'

Morgan's eyebrows shot up in surprise. 'Why? Karen and I are already here. We've been working it for almost an hour already.'

Arnie shrugged. 'Orders from upstairs. Nothing I can do.'

'This is ridiculous,' Morgan said, his voice cold. 'We know the scene. Karen's spoken to the victim before, but we're supposed to step aside for Goodridge?'

'Afraid so,' Arnie said. 'There's no point arguing about it. Goodridge will take over when he gets here.'

Morgan turned and stalked back to his car, fists clenched at his sides. Very un-Morgan-like behaviour.

Karen watched him go. She was annoyed by the abrupt change too, but knew taking her frustration out on Arnie wouldn't help. 'Did this order come from Churchill?'

'No, higher up than that,' Arnie said, running a hand through his messy hair. 'Apparently a friend of Rachel King's knows the chief constable.'

Karen nodded. 'I did hear something about that.'

'How's he handling all this?' Arnie asked in a low voice, leaning in close to Karen. 'I know this is a rough case for him.'

Karen gazed after Morgan, who was now leaning against his car, tapping out a furious message on his phone. 'He's taking it hard, and he's not happy to have this pulled away from us.'

'It's never easy when the higher-ups swoop in out of nowhere and decide to interfere, but maybe it's for the best. This one seems very personal for Morgan.'

Karen nodded. 'It is.'

They both watched Morgan, who was radiating frustration.

'You should keep an eye on him,' Arnie said gently.

'Of course,' Karen said, and then she turned her focus back to the case and gave him a thorough rundown of what they knew so far about Rachel King's death. After summing up, she added, 'Is Goodridge planning to treat Rachel King's murder separately from Tommy Burton's abduction?'

Arnie raised an eyebrow. 'You think they're connected?'

'Well, don't you? It's a bit of a coincidence. Rachel might have known something about Tommy's disappearance. She could have held it back when we first talked to her, or maybe it was something that escaped her until recently. Maybe she saw something. If that's the case, then it could have made her a target.'

Arnie nodded thoughtfully, scratching his chin. 'I'll let Goodridge know. Make sure he checks that out.'

'And we saw Sam Tranmere absolutely soaked earlier. I thought he'd got caught out in the rain, but it might be worth checking his clothing against any trace evidence found at the murder scene.'

Arnie nodded, pulling out his notebook and jotting down a reminder. 'Will do.'

Karen spotted Jim Willson, the family liaison officer who'd been working with the Burtons, approaching. He'd returned, despite the late hour, to support them after Rachel's body had been found.

He walked up to them, clearing his throat. 'Sorry to disturb you, but Amber and Gareth were asking for any updates,' he said. 'They were pretty close to Rachel I think – Amber in particular.'

Karen gave him a sympathetic smile. 'I'm not going to be working this case. DI Goodridge is taking over. Tell the Burtons the investigation is underway, but we can't share the full details yet. Do convey our deepest sympathies though.'

Jim nodded thoughtfully.

'I wouldn't suggest telling the Burtons this yet, but it's looking like a murder,' Arnie said.

Jim's eyes widened. 'Connected to Tommy's disappearance?'

'We don't know,' Karen said. 'How are Amber and Gareth doing?'

'Much the same. Except they're sniping at each other a lot more.'

'Playing the blame game,' Arnie said. 'This sort of thing puts a lot of pressure on a marriage.'

Jim nodded slowly, then hesitated. 'There's one more thing. It may or may not be relevant, but Rachel King came to visit the Burtons earlier today to offer her support, but she seemed distracted. She asked me if she could have a quick word, but then Amber and Gareth started rowing and I had to keep the peace. As she was leaving, I asked Rachel to continue what she was going to say, but she said it didn't matter and rushed off.'

That sparked Karen's interest. 'She didn't give any hints as to what was bothering her?'

'She didn't give any specifics unfortunately,' Jim said. 'She just seemed generally troubled.'

Karen nodded, her mind racing. Had Rachel stumbled across information that had made her dangerous in the eyes of Tommy Burton's abductor?

She shivered, picturing Rachel's final moments, imagining her terror as hands forced her under the water.

Brooke emerged from the house with the two cats in the carriers.

'Good job,' Karen said. 'Did they give you the run-around?'

'For a little while. And Smokey here put up quite a fight. Little devil scratched me. Marmalade walked right in with a little coaxing.' Brooke put the carriers on the floor. Marmalade curled up in a tight ball. Smokey pushed against the back of the cage, his hackles raised, hissing.

Arnie kneeled beside them. 'Shame these little beauties can't talk. Bet they saw something.'

Smokey clearly decided Arnie was too close for comfort and launched himself against the front of the cat carrier with a screech.

Arnie almost toppled backwards. 'Feisty little thing.'

It was hard to believe they were the same cats Karen had seen when she'd visited Rachel. When she'd met them, the cats had been laid-back and affectionate.

'They're both traumatised, poor mites,' Brooke said. 'I'll take them back to mine and put them in the spare room, where it's quiet. I could take them to the animal centre tomorrow, if you like? The cats have been there before. Rachel always left them at the centre when she went on holiday.' Brooke's feather pendant swung forward as she bent down to lift the carriers. She tucked it under the neck of her sweatshirt.

'Thanks, Brooke. That's a great help. I know Rachel has a sister. She might want to take the cats. I'll let you know when we've managed to speak to her.'

'No problem at all.' Brooke looked down at the cat carriers. 'I'm glad I could help. Rachel adored her cats.' Her eyes brimmed with tears, and she blinked rapidly as she set off back to the house she shared with Sam.

Karen looked back at Rachel's home as forensics officers milled around behind the tape. She turned to Arnie. 'I'll leave you to it. Give me a call if you need help with anything.'

'Will do,' Arnie said with an appreciative nod. Then he spotted Tim Farthing and groaned. 'I should have known he'd be on this one. Just my luck.'

Chapter Twenty-Five

The following afternoon, Karen picked up the phone on her desk and dialled the number for the mental health unit. She had called twenty minutes ago and left a message, but no one had responded. They still needed to talk to Cody Rhodes, but his long and complicated medical history was making it impossible.

Now that Rhodes had been sectioned, it meant that if he had actually abducted Tommy and the boy was still alive, then Tommy was still out there somewhere, alone and likely without access to food or water.

Again, the call went through to voicemail. She hung up with a huff of frustration. Karen wanted to be actively investigating Rachel King's murder, not on the sidelines making phone calls. She was sure Rachel's death was somehow linked to Tommy's abduction.

The shrill ring of her mobile pierced the air. She glanced at the screen and snatched it up when she saw the call was from the family liaison officer Jim Willson.

'Jim,' she said. 'What's going on?'

'Karen. You need to come. Come straight to the Burtons' house. Now.' Jim's voice was strained.

She stood up, tucking her phone between her chin and shoulder as she grabbed her linen jacket. 'What's happened?'

'Amber is accusing her husband of hurting their son. She's hysterical, Karen. Absolutely raving at Gareth. I can't get her to calm down. She took a knife from the kitchen drawer . . .'

Karen tensed, a shiver running down her spine. She'd had a hunch something wasn't quite right with the family, but it was horrible to have her suspicions confirmed.

'I'll get a uniform unit there as soon as possible. Hang on, Jim.'

'I managed to get the knife from her, but she's furious. I'm not sure what she's going to do.'

'What is Gareth doing?'

'He's begging her to see sense.'

'Try to get them in different rooms.'

'I've tried that, but they're not listening to me.'

Karen's first impressions of Gareth hadn't been good. He'd come across as a self-important man, trying to shift the blame for Tommy's disappearance on to his wife. He'd accused Amber of not knowing what Tommy was up to. But Amber had been struggling to balance her job and childcare and had already been feeling guilty. It had been cruel and unnecessary.

'What did she accuse Gareth of doing?'

'It was all very muddled. I'm not sure she's thinking coherently.'

In her mind, Karen pictured Gareth Burton again – puffed-up and snapping at his wife when she'd needed his support.

Karen hadn't liked him, but that hadn't been a reason to put him on the suspect list. But after visiting the librarian at Tommy's school, she'd known something was wrong. Gareth's relationship with his son wasn't as he'd made it seem. She should have pushed Churchill. She should have insisted—

'Karen?' Jim's voice cut through her thoughts. 'Are you still there?'

'What did Amber say exactly?' Karen asked, her stomach knotting as she grabbed her bag, getting ready to leave.

Jim hesitated, then said, 'She said her husband killed Tommy.'

◆　◆　◆

Karen almost bumped into Morgan in the corridor. As she looked up at him, she noticed a subtle difference. His face was etched with worry, revealing just how hard this case was hitting him.

Before she could tell him about Jim's phone call, Morgan said, 'Did you have any luck contacting Cody Rhodes's psychiatrist?'

Karen shook her head. 'No, I've left messages with our contact details, but I haven't been able to get through. But listen, I need to go. The family liaison officer at the Burtons' just called, and things have kicked off big-time. Amber has accused Gareth of killing their son.'

Morgan's eyes widened in shock. 'What? How?'

'I don't know all the details yet. Can you update Churchill? I really need to get there now.'

'You need backup?' Morgan said, concern lacing his words.

'I've organised a unit that was already in the area to respond. They should get there ahead of me.'

'I'll walk you out.'

'I don't want to take you away from what you're doing. Don't you need to plan the interview strategy for Cody Rhodes so you can hit the ground running as soon as we have access to him?'

Morgan sighed, a flicker of frustration crossing his face as he walked beside Karen. 'To be honest, I'm not convinced Rhodes is our guy.'

Karen frowned. 'But the newspaper cuttings and his obsession with Donaldson . . . I thought—'

Morgan interrupted her, his voice heavy with disappointment. 'So did I. He has a weird fixation on Donaldson's old crimes, but I don't think Rhodes has the mental capacity to carry out something like this.'

'He might be in a downward spiral,' Karen suggested, as they entered the brightly lit stairwell. 'He might have had more clarity a few days ago.'

'That's why we need to speak to his psychiatrist or someone from the mental health unit. They can tell us how feasible it would be for Cody Rhodes to have snatched Tommy Burton in broad daylight from a busy tourist spot without anyone noticing.'

'The mental health unit must be busy. Maybe they've had an emergency, which is why they aren't checking their messages,' Karen said, her gaze sweeping over the busy front desk at the station as they headed towards the glass doors at the exit. 'Maybe it's worth asking Farzana to visit the unit in person.'

Morgan nodded at Karen's suggestion. 'Good call. I'll do that. I'm waiting for Tranmere to show up. He called a little while ago and wants to meet.'

'Do you think he's finally going to come clean about altering the report?'

'I hope so.'

Together, they made their way across the car park.

Morgan broke the silence, his voice filled with uncharacteristic uncertainty. 'Do you think Gareth is really capable of killing his own son?'

Karen let out a long breath, thinking. Did she really suspect him? There was something about Gareth that was off-putting, but violence? She hadn't witnessed any direct evidence of him being violent towards Amber. However, Tommy's resentment towards his father, as described by the school librarian, was disturbing. 'I don't know,' Karen finally admitted with a shrug.

She clicked the fob to unlock her car and got inside, her eyes meeting Morgan's in the rear-view mirror. Usually he was difficult to read, but today his body language radiated sadness and exhaustion. He lifted a hand and then turned to go back inside.

Gripping the steering wheel, Karen reversed out of the parking space. Was Tommy really dead? Could Gareth be evil enough to have killed his own son? The possibility of a murder fuelled by rage gnawed at her. Gareth's size and strength against the defenceless eleven-year-old would have been insurmountable. Tommy wouldn't have stood a chance.

Maybe Amber had got it wrong, but why would she accuse her husband of something so awful? She must have a strong reason or evidence for such an accusation.

Karen remembered the fear she'd heard in Jim's voice, and put her foot firmly on the accelerator as she sped away from the station.

There was already a marked police car outside the Burtons' house when Karen pulled up. It seemed quiet inside. That was a good sign. At least, she hoped 'it was. Jim must have been looking out for her, as he opened the front door before she reached the path.

Karen looked at him questioningly.

He grimaced. 'Things have calmed down a little bit,' he said. 'Amber's in the kitchen with a neighbour, and I managed to persuade Gareth to stay upstairs until you got here. He wants to talk to you first.'

I'm sure he does, Karen thought. 'No, I'll talk to Amber first. He can wait upstairs. Are you okay?'

Jim gave her a weak smile and nodded. 'I'm all right,' he said, but Karen could see the strain in his eyes. He'd been through a lot over the past half hour. 'It's been wild. Amber flew into the kitchen and grabbed a knife. Then she was screaming at Gareth about how she'd get the truth from him one way or another, and I had to get between them while trying not to get stabbed myself.' He laughed nervously, shaking his head in disbelief at what had just happened.

Jim had managed to talk Amber down and take the weapon away from her without anyone getting hurt, which was no small feat.

'You did well.'

'Thanks, but I don't mind telling you, I've never been so terrified.'

'Which neighbour is with Amber?' Karen asked.

'Brooke Lewis. She arrived shortly before the uniformed officers did. Said she heard screaming. I thought about turning her away, but she seemed to have a calming influence on Amber.'

Jim led the way into the kitchen. Amber was there, her face pale apart from two angry spots of red on her cheeks. Brooke stood beside Amber, her hand protectively on Amber's arm.

PC Carleigh was standing opposite them, her arms behind her back. She met Karen's gaze and lifted her eyebrows. Karen smiled gratefully. She was glad of the quick response from uniform.

'This is absolutely shocking,' Brooke said, her voice quiet yet fierce. 'That Gareth could do this to his own son.'

Shocking didn't even begin to cover it.

'Are you going to arrest Gareth now?' Brooke asked.

Amber let out an anguished sob, burying her head in Brooke's shoulder.

Karen looked directly at Amber before speaking. 'I need to talk to both you and Gareth separately,' she said, gently but firmly. 'Alone.'

Brooke got the hint immediately. 'Oh, you want me to go?'

Karen nodded. 'I'd like to speak with Amber alone.'

'Will you be okay if I leave?' Brooke asked Amber softly, her voice laced with worry.

Amber managed a nod. 'Yes, thank you.'

'Call if you need me.' She squeezed Amber's hand, and with one last anxious look over her shoulder, she headed for the front door.

After Brooke left, Carleigh said, 'Shall I leave you to it?'

'Yes, thanks. I can take it from here.'

Jim gave Karen a nod and left the kitchen with Carleigh, pulling the door closed behind them.

Amber looked up, her eyes burning into Karen's. 'You need to do something. The others aren't listening to me. They're treating me as if I'm some hysterical female. And yes, I might be hysterical, but I know Gareth killed him!'

'Shall we sit down?' Karen asked, motioning to the kitchen table, but Amber shook her head.

'No, I'm too wound up to sit. I can't believe you're not doing anything.'

'We will,' Karen assured her, 'but I need the full story first. Tell me what you told Jim.'

Amber let out a growl of frustration. 'You need to—' she started to say, but Karen cut her off.

They didn't have time for emotional outbursts, even though her heart went out to Amber because, if she was right about Gareth murdering their little boy, this was devastating – something she'd never get over.

'I know this is hard, Amber, but you need to focus. I can only deal with facts. This must be awful and traumatic for you, but I need you to tell me why you're saying these things.'

'I'm saying them because they're true,' Amber said. 'I can't believe I missed it. I trusted him.'

'So,' Karen said calmly, 'tell me what's happened, Amber. Tell me why you think Gareth is responsible.'

'He really pulled the wool over my eyes,' she said, her voice raw. 'I would never have believed it until I saw the video, and then I knew for sure.'

'The video?' Karen asked, confused.

Amber nodded and pulled out her mobile phone from the back pocket of her trousers. 'Silly, really, but I missed Tommy so much. I was thinking . . . hoping . . . that he'd just walk through the front door, come home like he had so many times before. So, I was looking back through the security footage from the doorbell camera. I went back and looked at the recordings with Tommy. Watched all those times he *did* come back home.' Amber took a deep, shuddering breath. 'But in one of those videos, I saw something terrible. Tommy was with his father. And . . . he grabbed Tommy by his shirt and had him pinned against the car.'

'Can I see the video?'

With trembling fingers, Amber scrolled through the recordings and then held out her phone to Karen. 'This one.'

Karen watched the video. Gareth got out of the car first. He stormed around the front, flung open the passenger door, and yanked Tommy out by his arm roughly. The boy stumbled before quickly regaining his balance, but he didn't look scared. Not yet, anyway. He smirked at his father, and in the next instant, Gareth reacted with a flash of anger. He scrunched Tommy's shirt in his fists and lifted him clean off the floor. He shoved Tommy back against the car like a rag doll. Karen flinched, seeing Tommy slam into the metal. It must have hurt. Then Gareth pushed his face close to his son's.

Karen could see Gareth was saying something in the video, but she couldn't hear what it was.

'Can you make the sound any louder?' she asked.

Amber nodded and turned up the volume on the side of the phone. 'But you can't hear what he says. I've already tried to listen.'

'And is this video the only reason you suspect Gareth?'

'The only reason?' Amber stared at Karen in astonishment. 'Isn't that enough? He's manhandling my son. He could have seriously injured him, in view of all the neighbours. So what must he be capable of doing in private?'

'Have you ever witnessed Gareth being violent to Tommy on other occasions?'

Amber shook her head firmly. 'Of course not. I would have left him if he'd done anything like that in front of me.'

'And what does Gareth say was happening when this video was recorded?'

'He said that Tommy backchatted him. But that's no excuse, is it?' Her eyes were fierce as she slapped her hand down on the kitchen counter. 'You don't do that to a child!'

Karen agreed. His behaviour was disgusting. He could have seriously injured Tommy. This was undoubtedly a man who had lost his temper and crossed the line, and it did suggest that he may have taken things further.

'So, what do you think happened when Tommy went missing?' Karen asked. 'Do you think his father took him from Tattershall Castle?'

Karen couldn't see how that made sense. If Gareth had attacked Tommy in a fit of rage and killed the boy, that would be horrific but feasible. But Amber seemed to be suggesting that Gareth had gone to collect their son from the castle and then murdered him, which would suggest premeditation.

But most child murders were the result of fits of rage – uncontrolled, devastating outbursts of anger. A cold-blooded, premeditated murder as Amber was proposing was not common . . .

Perhaps Gareth was very cunning. Having Tommy go missing while under his mother's care was a good way to deflect suspicion away from himself, she supposed. But he would really have to be a cold-blooded psychopath to have plotted something like this.

For the first time, a shadow of doubt passed over Amber's features. 'I . . . I don't know. That's for you to work out. I don't understand the details. All I know is that he hurt my son.'

'I'm not excusing what Gareth did in this video for one second. It's abhorrent behaviour. But do you really think Gareth is capable of killing Tommy?'

Amber didn't hesitate. She looked Karen straight in the eye and said, 'Yes.'

Chapter Twenty-Six

Karen left Amber in the kitchen and met Jim in the hallway, where he was talking with PC Carleigh and her partner. Jim's expression was tense and wary as he fiddled with the neck of his shirt.

'Jim,' she said quietly, 'I'm going upstairs to talk to Gareth.'

He nodded. 'I'll come with you.'

'No, I'll handle this alone,' Karen replied, her tone firm. 'Gareth's in the master bedroom?'

Jim's face creased with concern. 'Are you sure you don't want me to come with you? Gareth seems . . . unpredictable right now.'

'I'll be fine,' Karen said. Her hand rested on the banister. 'I'd appreciate you waiting here in case I need you though.'

Jim nodded. 'Of course. Be careful.'

The house seemed to hold its breath as Karen ascended the stairs. At the top, the master bedroom door stood open. She stopped in the doorway. The walls were painted a deep shade of navy, creating a dark, claustrophobic atmosphere. A large, unmade bed took up most of the room, its dark blue sheets twisted and tangled. A sharp scent of cologne lingered in the air, undercut by a whiff of stale body odour.

Gareth was sitting on the edge of the mattress, elbows on his knees, staring at the carpet. He looked up as Karen entered. His eyes were bloodshot, his hair dishevelled. The picture of a grieving father, or a man with something to hide?

With his face drawn and haggard and dark circles under his eyes, one thing was for sure – he looked like a man at breaking point. Gareth turned away. Sweat beaded on his forehead.

'Mr Burton?' Karen said, stepping further into the room.

'Detective Sergeant Hart,' he acknowledged dully, not bothering to look up again.

'Your wife has made some serious accusations,' Karen said. 'I need to ask you about them.'

'Accusations?' Gareth's voice cracked, then he gave a cold, humourless laugh.

'Amber believes you may have . . . harmed Tommy,' Karen stated cautiously, gauging his reaction.

'Ridiculous!' Gareth exploded, rising to his feet, his face flushed with anger. 'She's distraught, not thinking clearly! I would never hurt my own son!'

'Please, Mr Burton.' Karen held up a hand to calm him. 'I understand this is an incredibly difficult time for your family. But we have to explore all possibilities.'

Gareth's shoulders slumped, and he sank back on to the bed, his anger evaporating. 'I know,' he muttered, staring at the floor once more. 'I can't believe this is happening. Why haven't you found him?'

'Amber said—'

'Amber isn't thinking straight,' Gareth snapped, cutting Karen off. 'I've told you that. Our son is missing and she's lashing out, trying to blame me. It's ludicrous. I'm sure I don't have to remind you that she was the one who was supposed to be looking after Tommy when he went missing.'

'Amber has security footage showing you assaulting Tommy,' Karen said. 'Can you explain that?'

Gareth scoffed, though his hands trembled at his sides. 'I lost my temper for a moment, that's all. Tommy was misbehaving.'

'That's no excuse for violence.' Karen frowned. 'In what way was he misbehaving?'

Gareth said nothing, but he stood up and crossed the room to the window. He stared out at the cul-de-sac below. His shoulders were tense, his hands curled into fists.

'Was this the first time you'd lost your temper with Tommy?' Karen asked.

'Yes. I swear I didn't hurt him. I was angry, but I would never . . .' He shook his head violently. 'I don't know what's happened to Tommy. But I didn't do anything to him.'

'And your wife's accusation?'

'Not true!' Gareth shouted, his voice cracking under the strain of his emotions. 'Amber is not herself with all this stress.'

His denial struck a hollow note. Karen could see fear lurking behind his anger. 'What about the video of you pinning Tommy against the car? What were you saying to Tommy?'

For a moment, Gareth seemed to falter, his bravado crumbling just slightly. But then his shoulders squared, and he faced Karen head-on. 'How am I supposed to remember? It was a week ago.'

'Try.'

'It was . . . nothing. This is all a misunderstanding.' He sat back down.

Karen studied him carefully, weighing his words. There was something off about Gareth Burton. She couldn't shake the feeling that he was hiding something, but she wasn't convinced he was behind Tommy's disappearance.

'Tell me everything,' Karen demanded, her voice insistent. 'No more lies, no more deflections. Just the truth.'

'Are you accusing me of lying? You should be looking for Tommy, not trying to bully me. I've a mind to put in a complaint about you.'

His behaviour didn't fool her. He was afraid and trying desperately to hide it.

'Fine,' she said calmly. 'But this would be easier if you cooperated. There's something you're not telling me.'

'I've told you everything I know.' His voice rose in pitch to a whine. 'My son is missing, and you're wasting time harassing me!' When she didn't react, Gareth surged to his feet, looming over her. But she didn't flinch. After a long, tense moment, he deflated with a sigh and sank back on to the bed.

'All right,' he muttered. 'I'll tell you whatever you want to know.'

His capitulation was too easy. Karen's suspicions deepened, but she kept her face impassive.

'What were you saying to Tommy in the video when you had him pinned against the car?'

'I don't remember.' Gareth looked away, avoiding her gaze. Karen could tell he was hiding something, but she couldn't figure out what. This was like pulling teeth.

She pressed on. 'I don't believe you, Gareth. Something happened. Or do you tend to grab your son by the scruff of the neck and pin him against the car whenever the mood strikes you?'

Gareth's eyes blazed, but then his expression turned sad. He sighed heavily. He seemed to be struggling with himself, debating whether to tell the truth.

'Tommy is . . . gifted,' he began hesitantly. 'But that means he can be hard work at times, and he knows how to press my buttons.'

Karen nodded. 'So what were you arguing about?'

Gareth hesitated again before answering. 'We were arguing about . . . about his pocket money,' he said finally. 'I had taken it away as punishment for him misbehaving, and he was furious.'

Karen studied Gareth intently; something still wasn't adding up here. It was too easy – too convenient – for him to blame their argument on pocket money.

'No, I don't think that's it,' she said slowly. 'What else were you fighting about?'

Gareth's jaw clenched tight as a wave of guilt swept over his face. He averted his gaze from Karen's, unable to meet her eyes any longer.

Finally, after a long silence, filled only by the sound of his laboured breathing, Gareth spoke again in a low voice. 'I told you, it was just a normal argument.'

'A normal argument that ended in violence?' Karen pressed. 'What aren't you telling me?'

'I didn't hurt him!' he protested. 'I never hurt him. I just . . . lost my temper, that's all.'

'Mr Burton,' Karen said, her eyes locked on to his, 'I need to know the truth.'

Gareth's face twisted into an expression of bitter hatred, his eyes narrowing to slits as he glared back at Karen. The master bedroom seemed to close in around them. Karen imagined how scared Tommy must have been of his own father when he'd been pinned against the car.

'All right,' Gareth spat, his voice barely controlled. 'I lost my temper with Tommy because he provoked me!'

'Provoked? How did he provoke you, exactly?'

Gareth looked away, his gaze lingering on a framed family photo on the dressing table – the Burtons in happier times.

'Tommy . . . Tommy wanted more pocket money. He kept asking for more and more, and I told him we couldn't afford it. But he wouldn't let it go, and I . . . I just snapped.'

'I don't think that's all there is to it, Mr Burton.'

'Of course that's all there is to it!' Gareth shouted. 'My son was being difficult, and I lost my temper. It's not like I killed him over it!'

'Yet your wife seems to think otherwise,' Karen pointed out, her gaze never leaving his face. 'Why would she accuse you of something so horrible?'

'I already told you,' Gareth roared, his face contorting with rage. 'She's upset, she's angry, and she wants someone to blame. But I swear on my life I didn't hurt Tommy. I just scared him a bit to get him in line. It wasn't real violence. Not in a way that matters.'

'Every act of violence matters, Mr Burton,' Karen said, watching Gareth struggle to regain control of his emotions. 'Now, I suggest you start telling me the whole truth, or I promise you, things will only get worse from here.'

As the silence stretched between them, Karen could see the battle raging within Gareth: the need to protect his secrets warring with the fear of what might happen if he continued to lie.

'Listen,' Gareth said. 'I've already told you what the argument was about. Why can't you just leave it at that?'

'Because, Mr Burton, I'm not convinced you're giving me the full picture.' Karen paused, watching Gareth closely as she continued. 'You see, I spoke with a member of staff at Tommy's school, and they mentioned that Tommy seemed to have a difficult relationship with you.'

At this revelation, Gareth's face paled, and he looked genuinely shocked. He stared at Karen, his mouth opening and closing.

'That's . . . that's not true. I mean, yes, we have disagreements, but what father and son don't? I love Tommy. He knows that.'

'Does he?' Karen questioned softly.

Gareth's eyes filled with tears. 'I don't know why the teacher would say that,' he whispered hoarsely. 'Maybe he's just trying to stir up trouble. People love a bit of drama, don't they? Tommy's disappearance is probably the most exciting thing that's ever happened to them.'

'Maybe he noticed something about Tommy that worried him, and he was doing the right thing by telling me about it,' Karen countered. 'Mr Burton, it's time to come clean. It's time for you to do the right thing too.'

Gareth stared at her. 'You already know, don't you?'

Karen said nothing, hoping he'd fall for her bluff.

Gareth's face crumpled, and his shoulders sagged.

Karen tensed, wondering if he was finally about to confess. She felt a flare of rage at the idea of Gareth hurting his own son.

'I feel awful.' Tears streamed down his cheeks. 'You have no idea how much I wish I could turn back time and make things right.'

Karen gritted her teeth at the sight of this grown man casting himself as a victim. She took a slow, steady breath and forced herself to push past her aggravation.

'Mr Burton,' she said firmly, 'I understand that this is difficult for you, but we don't have time for this now.'

He bowed his head. 'Tommy . . .' he whispered, his voice barely audible. 'Tommy was . . . blackmailing me.'

'Blackmailing you?' Karen echoed. She had expected many things, but this was not one of them. Her mind raced with questions. What dirt could an eleven-year-old possibly have on his own father?

Gareth nodded. 'He was threatening to tell people about . . . something if I didn't give him what he wanted.'

'Which was?' Karen prompted.

'I can't,' he murmured, shaking his head and wiping away his tears. 'It's too . . . I just can't.'

'Mr Burton,' Karen said, her voice taking on a cold tone, 'if you want me to find your son, you need to tell me everything. The longer you keep secrets, the harder it will be for us to help Tommy.'

But Gareth remained stubbornly silent, his jaw set in defiance. His belligerent expression triggered a strong wave of suspicion in Karen.

She tried to shake off the feeling, telling herself to remain neutral. She couldn't jump the gun on this one. Frustration bubbled inside Karen. She tried another tack. 'You were giving Tommy money. Where did he keep it?'

'In his account. I set up a bank account for him.'

'But Amber told us Tommy didn't have a bank account.'

'She didn't know about it, and technically Tommy doesn't have an account. It's in my name. But he has the cash card to withdraw money.'

Karen stared at him. 'What made you think that was a good idea?'

'He forced me,' Gareth whined.

'He's eleven. You're the parent. How could he force you?'

'He said he'd tell Amber and my . . . my work. I couldn't risk it.'

Karen stared at him and shook her head. 'Do you have access to the account?'

Gareth nodded. 'Yes, I have the app on my phone.'

'Can I see it?'

He reached for his mobile phone on the nightstand. 'No.'

'No? What do you mean, *no*?'

'You can't see it. You can't tell Amber and you can't tell my boss. I told you this in confidence. You have to respect client confidentiality.'

'I'm not a lawyer, Mr Burton, and you're not my client,' Karen said incredulously. 'I'm a police officer. And if you don't show me that app, I'll get a warrant.'

Gareth hugged the phone against his chest.

Karen had had enough of this. She'd tried to be patient and let him tell his side of the story in his own time, but he'd pushed it too far.

She stood in front of him. 'Fine. If you want to play it that way . . . Gareth Burton, I'm arresting you for the abduction of Tommy Burton.'

Chapter Twenty-Seven

Morgan reviewed his notes, waiting tensely for Tranmere's arrival. He'd just had Churchill on the phone, demanding to know why he hadn't been informed of Gareth Burton's arrest before it happened. Morgan had tried to placate him, but he understood Churchill's dilemma. If the press got wind of this and Gareth Burton turned out to be innocent, the optics would not be good.

There was a faint knock and he looked up. Tranmere's craggy face appeared on the other side of the glass. He was with DC Farzana Shah, who pushed the door open.

'Sir, DCI Tranmere to see you,' Farzana said briskly.

'Thank you, DC Shah,' Morgan said, standing up and waving Tranmere in. He held out his hand for Tranmere to shake.

'Morgan, I appreciate you taking the time to see me,' Tranmere said as he took a seat on the other side of Morgan's desk. 'I appreciate we didn't part on the best of terms last time.'

Morgan noted how much his old boss seemed to have aged. Deep furrows lined Tranmere's forehead. But though his eyes were tired, his keen intelligence still shone through. Morgan settled back into his own seat, shuffling the papers on his desk more out of restless energy than necessity. He was surprised to realise his mouth had grown dry.

Tranmere leaned forward, regarding him solemnly. 'I think you know why I'm here.'

Morgan gave a curt nod. 'I hope it's because you want to explain why you removed all mention of the red Ford Focus from my report.'

Tranmere closed his eyes briefly. 'Yes, I falsified that report.' He met Morgan's gaze. 'And I removed all mention of the car because . . . it was my brother's.'

Morgan said nothing. He'd suspected that Tranmere had done this to cover up for someone he cared about. It made more sense than his old boss accepting a bribe. Tranmere was too upright for that. But the admission from Tranmere sent a shockwave through Morgan as he tried to reconcile his behaviour with the man he had admired for so long.

'Why?' he asked finally. 'Why would you risk your career and reputation?'

Tranmere dragged a hand down his haggard face. 'It wasn't done to obstruct justice. I've already told you, that car – and therefore my brother – had nothing to do with the abduction,' he said firmly.

'Yes, but that doesn't explain why you did it. If what you say is true, we could have easily eliminated your brother from our enquiries.'

'I was covering for him.' Tranmere's eyes took on a distant look. 'Ray was an addict, and he dabbled in dealing to support his habit. He was weak. A complete fool, but I was more of a fool for covering for him.'

Morgan stayed quiet as Tranmere continued his explanation.

'He was my younger brother. I thought if I could avoid him getting into serious legal problems and keep him out of jail, that somehow I could save him. I believed I could rescue him from his addiction.' He gave a bitter laugh. 'As if anything could get through to him after he was hooked . . . I saw his car on the CCTV footage and panicked. When I confronted him, Ray admitted that he'd been dealing in the past. He swore he wasn't dealing anymore, that his car was only at the scene because he was picking up drugs for personal use.'

Tranmere paused and looked down at his lap. 'I'm not sure if he was telling me the truth. But there was a crackdown in the area at the time. I thought if Ray got caught up in it, he might go to jail, and I didn't think he'd survive that . . . not with a heroin addiction.'

He focused intently on Morgan again. 'I swear to you, Morgan, if it was pertinent to the abduction investigation I would never have concealed the evidence. I only wanted to protect my family. I know now that was unwise. Ray only got worse over the years. I eventually cut him off.' Tranmere's voice cracked. 'He died of an overdose nine years ago.'

Morgan searched Tranmere's face, seeing the deep remorse. His sense of betrayal and anger began to recede. However misguided, Tranmere's intentions had not been malicious. Though Morgan still couldn't condone them. 'Cutting off your brother must have been very hard.'

Tranmere nodded sadly. 'It was the hardest thing I've ever had to do. It was the inheritance that ruined him. He never had something in his life that made getting up in the morning worthwhile. I had my job, my wife and son. I was the lucky one.'

'But you risked that,' Morgan said. 'You risked your job.'

'If I'd been found out, I'd have been fired. And I would have deserved it.' He looked tentatively at Morgan. 'So what happens now? I suppose you have to tell the powers that be.'

Brushing it under the carpet was inconceivable to Morgan. He played by the rules. 'Yes, I don't know what they'll do about it . . . But it will have to be looked into. I won't be dealing with it. I'm far too involved to be impartial.'

'Haven't you ever been tempted to break the rules?' When Morgan shook his head, Tranmere added, 'Not even to help someone you care about?'

Morgan held Tranmere's searching gaze.

He thought back to how Arnie had unlocked the cupboard at the old petrol station and tried to convince Morgan they should pull up the floor before the SOCOs got there. In those desperate moments, he had been tempted to give the go-ahead. The need to save a young boy had seemed more important than regulations. But Morgan had managed to keep his head and stick by his principles.

He quickly banished those thoughts. 'I understand your desire to protect your brother,' he said carefully to Tranmere. 'I don't agree with your actions, but I can understand them.'

Tranmere nodded slowly. 'I'm sorry I changed the report. Family ties can sometimes drive people to do silly things. There are always shades of grey, Morgan.'

But in Morgan's mind, there weren't. You either did the right thing or the wrong thing, and though his motives had been good, Tranmere had chosen to do the wrong thing.

Rules were needed. If they weren't adhered to, cases fell apart.

'I appreciate you coming clean,' Morgan said.

Tranmere nodded sadly. 'I'll accept whatever punishment is coming my way.'

'Look, I need to ask,' Morgan said, hesitating. 'Could your son have had any involvement with these new abductions?'

'Sam?' Tranmere looked horrified at the suggestion.

'Yes. He knew about the blue bears, perhaps from overhearing you talk about work at home.'

'He was only fourteen.'

'But now he's nearly thirty.'

Tranmere shook his head, vehement. 'No, absolutely not. Sam has had his struggles. But he would never harm a child. He's indecisive, without a true vocation in life. But he's not a bad person.'

'Okay,' Morgan said.

'You do believe me?'

'I believe that you believe Sam isn't responsible,' Morgan replied, avoiding mentioning his own suspicions.

Tranmere looked at Morgan sadly. 'I worry about him. Sam is so like Ray in some ways, just floating through life without any real aim or ambition, and . . . I worry that he could end up the same way.'

'Is he on drugs?' Morgan asked.

'Not as far as I know,' Tranmere said. 'He got in trouble once for smoking weed at school, but I think he's avoided the hard stuff. I'd recognise the signs after seeing it with Ray, but it doesn't stop me worrying about his future.' Tranmere shrugged, then added, 'How are you getting on with the abduction case?'

'I feel like the truth is close, but I'm missing something crucial.'

Tranmere smiled. 'You were one of the finest detectives I ever had the privilege to train. I've always admired your character and your drive for justice. But if I can offer some advice, I'd say you're in danger of becoming a bit too inflexible.'

'Inflexible,' Morgan said, raising an eyebrow. 'In what way?'

'This new, unshakeable integrity of yours. You weren't always this strict with the regulations.'

'I might have been less careful to stick to standard procedure back then, but I never broke the rules.'

'You've always had a strong moral compass,' Tranmere said, a note of impatience entering his voice. 'But you used to be more willing to look at things from different perspectives. You were less stubborn. Less pedantic.'

'I only care about finding the truth.'

'Don't you see?' Tranmere sighed. 'You're following a narrow path. Your focus is now exclusively on what is good and evil, without any acknowledgement of the grey areas in between.'

Here we go, thought Morgan, *we're back to the shades of grey again*. 'I am perfectly capable of acknowledging the grey areas. I'm not a saint. But I would never doctor a report. Not now and not then. The rules are there for a reason. I'd never break them.'

'You can say that for sure, can you?' Tranmere asked.

'Of course.'

'We all have a line that we don't think we can cross. But then something unexpected happens and we find ourselves in a situation where we have to choose. What you think you would do and what you actually do in that moment are two different things.'

Morgan just stared at him.

'One day, it will happen,' Tranmere said smugly.

'What will?' Morgan was irritated at the way the conversation was drifting from the topic.

'One day, there'll be someone that you care about enough to break the rules for.'

Morgan just gave a dismissive shake of his head. 'I don't think so.'

Tranmere simply smiled.

Morgan stood up, signalling the end to the difficult meeting. He had looked up to Tranmere over the years, but today's revelation had muddied that moral certainty. He would need time to reconcile his memories of Tranmere with the man he truly was.

He felt a wave of annoyance wash over him as Tranmere's description echoed in his mind. *Inflexible?* How dare he judge Morgan like that? If anything, it should be Morgan judging Tranmere, not the other way around. He was the one who'd tampered with a crime scene report, after all.

Morgan was man enough to admit that sometimes he could be single-minded when it came to the law. But for good reason – he wanted to ensure justice was served.

He knew his old boss was just trying to offer him advice, but it seemed more like criticism than anything else. It wasn't as though Morgan didn't care or wasn't tempted to bend the rules at times. When Arnie had wanted to pull up the floor at the petrol station, Morgan had wavered. But at the end of the day, justice always had to come first, and that meant being uncompromising about certain things.

Morgan escorted Tranmere out of the station. He felt confident Tranmere had told him the whole truth this time. He'd rewritten the report driven by misguided loyalty to his brother. It didn't undo all the help and guidance he'd given Morgan over the years, but the man Morgan had looked up to was deeply flawed.

At the exit, he extended his hand, which Tranmere grasped firmly in both of his own.

'Despite all this, it was good to see you again, Morgan.'

'It was good to see you again too, sir.'

Tranmere gave Morgan a small smile and a nod before he turned to leave. Morgan exhaled heavily, watching his old boss walk across the car park.

Inflexible, Morgan thought again. What a cheek.

He tried to dismiss them, but Tranmere's words lingered in his mind. Was he really inflexible? Was he too rigid in his approach to the law?

He shook his head, trying to clear his thoughts. He couldn't afford to doubt himself now. He had a job to do.

Chapter Twenty-Eight

Karen studied the hulking man slouched on the opposite side of the table. Gareth Burton dwarfed the petite duty solicitor seated next to him. His shoulders curled forward as though he was trying to make himself look smaller and avoid scrutiny. His bloodshot eyes radiated resentment.

Karen took a slow, deliberate breath. She was sure Burton was guilty. The way he sat, his defensive posture, the way he avoided answering her questions – all signs she recognised. But she had to come at this without preconceptions, free of emotion. She needed to be impartial and follow the evidence.

She folded her hands, meeting his glare with an even gaze. 'Let's try again, Mr Burton,' she said. 'Will you show us your financial records voluntarily?'

Gareth Burton scowled and glanced at the solicitor, who gave an almost imperceptible nod of encouragement. 'I don't see why I should. I haven't done anything wrong.'

Karen tilted her head. 'That's interesting. Earlier, when I was at your house, you told me that Tommy had been coercing money from you and that you had opened a bank account to make regular payments to him. Is that right?'

Burton shifted in his seat, looking distinctly uncomfortable. 'No, it's not right. You must have misheard me,' he blustered. 'None of that's true. You must be making it up.'

Leaning back, Karen regarded him coolly. 'Do you have memory issues, Mr Burton? Because I can assure you that's what you told me.'

Burton bristled. 'I don't like your tone. You can't talk to me like that. Can she talk to me like that?' He turned to the duty solicitor, who said nothing.

Karen bit her tongue, resisting the urge to snap. As well as hurting his son physically, Burton was a liar. She inhaled slowly.

One side of Karen had already tried and convicted Burton, but the other side – the logical, seasoned police officer – knew that without hard evidence all she had was suspicion and an intense dislike of the man sitting across from her.

'Did Tommy run away to avoid further mistreatment at home?' Karen asked.

'Now wait a minute,' Burton shouted, half rising from his chair before the duty solicitor put a hand on his arm to guide him back down. 'I never touched Tommy. Are you really accusing me of that? That's slanderous.'

Beside Karen, Rick gave a sceptical snort.

Burton turned his glare on Rick. 'Have you got something to say?'

Rick smiled mildly. 'Settle down. Answer the questions.'

Burton barked out a harsh laugh. 'Answer the questions? They're all leading questions. I know all about that. You're trying to trick me, get me to say something incriminating.' He crossed his arms. 'I'm no fool. I know my rights.'

Karen pushed across a still shot from the video showing Gareth Burton pinning his son to the car. The image made her feel sick.

Tommy's face was a mask of fear as his father loomed over him. She could only imagine the poor boy's terror.

She reined in her disgust. 'We have reason to believe that Tommy has been extorting funds from you, threatening to expose certain activities.'

'Rubbish,' Burton said. 'I've got no idea what you're talking about.'

'Oh, come off it,' Rick snapped impatiently. 'Once we get hold of your financial records, we'll see it all. What will we find? Payments to gambling apps and bookies? Or something else? We'll also be able to prove you transferred money to another account – the account you gave Tommy the cash card for.' Rick leaned forward. 'Maybe you wanted the extortion to stop? Maybe you got really angry? Angrier than you've ever been before?'

The duty solicitor cleared her throat. 'If you're making allegations, please state them directly.'

But Burton was glaring venomously at Rick. 'You know nothing about me or my finances. And I didn't hurt Tommy.'

Karen pushed the photograph of Tommy pinned against the car closer to Burton. 'Take a look. Are you saying this isn't you with Tommy?'

'I've already told you,' Burton said. 'It was just one time. And I didn't really hurt him.'

'It looks like you're hurting him,' Rick said.

'Yes, well, the camera makes it look worse than it was. He was being a pain, talking back, getting on my nerves. Maybe I was a little rough, but I would never really hurt him.'

'So why not tell us the whole story? How did it all start?'

Burton remained stubbornly silent.

'Come on now, make this easy for yourself,' Rick pressed. 'We've got a warrant coming. We'll have access to your bank records soon enough. Why don't you cooperate? If you didn't hurt Tommy, then let's clear your name.'

Burton barked out a mocking laugh. 'Clear my name? When you've already decided I'm guilty?'

Rick held up his hands, placating. 'No need to shout. Just help us understand.'

'I can shout if I want to. My son is missing, and you're treating me like a criminal!'

'If you have anger issues, we can get you help,' Rick said evenly. 'But we need total honesty for Tommy's sake.'

'I haven't got anger issues,' Burton roared, proving that he did, in fact, have issues with his temper.

Karen decided to take a different angle. 'When did you set up the new bank account for Tommy to use?'

Burton sank lower in his chair.

'It will be easy enough for the bank to tell us, but if you cooperate—'

Burton turned to his solicitor. 'Are you just going to sit there and let them harass me like this?' Before the solicitor could answer, he added, 'I want a new lawyer. This one's useless.'

The duty solicitor sighed, and Rick threw up his hands in frustration.

Karen's grip tightened around her pen. They weren't going to get any productive information at this rate.

They suspended the interview and left the room.

As the door closed behind them, Rick shook his head in disgust. 'It's unbelievable. His son is missing, and he's still only concerned about saving his own skin.'

Karen nodded as she tucked a file of notes under her arm, and they began to walk back to the office. She couldn't understand how a father could show so little concern for his child.

She was appalled by the way Gareth Burton refused to take any accountability and continued to play the victim. He'd lied about hurting Tommy, even though they had video evidence. His self-pity after treating his son so abominably made her feel sick. Thankfully, she knew the bank records would soon reveal the truth, but they were still no closer to locating Tommy.

In the interview room, it had taken every ounce of restraint for her not to give Gareth Burton a piece of her mind. No child deserved such a poor excuse for a father.

Halfway along the corridor they met Morgan. But before Morgan could ask them about the interview, DCI Churchill burst out of the double doors just ahead of them. 'Karen, Rick,' he said, 'I've been watching the interview.'

'It's not going great,' Rick said. 'He's stubborn, but we should have his bank records soon enough.'

'I'm not happy with the way it's going either,' Churchill said bluntly. 'I'm going to put Arnie and Farzana in to question him instead. We need some fresh blood.'

'With respect, sir, I really don't think we do,' Karen said.

'I disagree. He's angry with you. I'm not saying his anger is justified, not at all. But it's holding us back.'

'I assure you I've treated Burton with respect.' *Even though he doesn't deserve it*, she added mentally.

'Of course,' Churchill said, 'but a change of tactics is needed. The clock is ticking for Tommy and we're not making progress.'

Karen was bewildered. 'But it doesn't make any sense, sir,' she said with a steady voice. 'I'm the one who spoke to Gareth Burton. He told me that Tommy was extorting money from him, so why would you take me off the interview?'

'My mind's made up,' Churchill said. 'It's obvious he has some sort of animosity towards you and it's keeping us from getting the facts.'

'But, sir—'

'Don't take it personally.' Churchill strode away, leaving Karen stunned.

She looked at Morgan. 'Can you believe that? He's being thoroughly unreasonable.'

'Well, I can see why you're angry,' Morgan said carefully. 'But there wasn't a planned arrest. Your actions caught us on the back foot.'

Karen stared at him in disbelief. 'I'm not sure I understand your point,' she said, feeling her temper rise several degrees. 'Amber said he killed Tommy. I watched a video of Gareth Burton grabbing Tommy and pinning him against his car. So I think an arrest was appropriate, don't you?' She looked to Rick for backup.

'I would have done exactly the same as Karen,' he offered.

Morgan put his hands up. 'I'm just saying having an interview plan in place before the arrest would have been better procedure. Now we're scrambling for bank and mobile phone records, and we can only hold him for twenty-four hours. It puts us under unnecessary pressure. Churchill was right about that.'

Karen stalked along the corridor with Morgan and Rick following her. She was fuming, but a small part of her suspected that Morgan had a point, which only annoyed her further.

She *had* lost her temper with Gareth Burton. She didn't like the man one bit. But she hadn't arrested him solely due to her dislike. They would have arrested him eventually anyway, given Amber's accusation that he'd killed their son and the presence of video evidence of violence.

Karen gave Morgan a sideways glance. 'I know I took a risk, but it was calculated. If you don't take chances every now and then, you become crippled by indecision, which is even worse.'

'I'm not sure I agree,' Morgan said.

Karen stopped walking abruptly. 'You're making out that I'm reckless.'

'Not reckless exactly,' Morgan said slowly. 'Maybe just a little short-sighted. Interview strategy is important. If you'd spoken and consulted with the team before the arrest, then . . .'

Karen let his words wash over her. Anger didn't even come close to how she was feeling. She couldn't believe that he was questioning her judgement like this.

'I did the right thing,' she said, cutting off Morgan mid-flow as he was quoting a section from a tediously dry police manual. 'What if Gareth Burton had made a run for it before we got all our ducks in a row? Criminals don't just sit around waiting patiently for us to get our interview strategy in order.'

'In this case I don't think Gareth Burton was a flight risk,' Morgan said. 'We should have been more organised before bringing him in.'

Karen narrowed her eyes. 'And I think we should agree to disagree.'

Chapter Twenty-Nine

Two hours later, Karen was still incensed at Morgan and Churchill.

Churchill had unfairly removed her from the interrogation of Gareth Burton before she'd had a chance to obtain any useful information. She was certain that with a little more pressure Gareth Burton would have cracked. Unreasonable and Churchill went hand in hand, so she should have expected the decision from him, but it was Morgan's words that truly stung. He'd as good as said she'd been impulsive when she arrested Burton.

It grated because, although she and Morgan had occasionally clashed at the beginning of their working relationship, they'd grown to work well together; Karen liked Morgan, and his opinion meant a lot to her, so it was even more disheartening to hear him question her actions.

She pulled on her jacket and walked over to Arnie's desk. 'Are you heading back to the interview room?'

'Soon. I'm just waiting for Farzana.'

'I need to disappear for a bit. Mike and I finally have the pleasure of joining both our families for dinner tonight.'

Arnie chuckled, lounging back in his creaky desk chair. 'Oh, then you'll have a smashing evening full of never-ending questions about your career, life decisions, and relationship status. Lucky you.'

Karen couldn't help smiling despite her mood. 'I'm tempted not to go at all. But my last absence was noticed, and they'll start to suspect something if I keep skipping out on family events.'

Arnie's eyes travelled over to Morgan's office. 'How's Morgan doing?'

Karen felt a flicker of annoyance, remembering their earlier conversation. 'Don't ask,' she said.

'That bad?'

Karen nodded.

'Give him a bit of leeway,' Arnie said.

'I always do,' Karen insisted, 'but he's being overcautious. He actually suggested that I'd been too hasty in arresting Gareth Burton. What do you think?'

Arnie shrugged. 'I would have arrested Burton on the spot. The scumbag deserved it.'

Karen smiled faintly. 'Well, Burton's definitely a scumbag. But . . .' She sighed. 'Morgan's probably right – that's what's so annoying. Maybe I should have waited, so we had more time to get an interview plan in place.'

Arnie looked thoughtful. 'When we found Cody Rhodes at the petrol station, he refused to pull up the floor before Forensics got there, and we both suspected Tommy might be under there . . . Sometimes I think Morgan might be a bit too careful. I understand why he didn't want to contaminate evidence by ripping up the floor, but sometimes protocol needs to be broken, especially if a life hangs in the balance.'

Karen nodded in agreement. 'It's maddening when he won't budge at all. It's as though he's some kind of robot.'

'You're not wrong,' Arnie said. 'Maybe it's his way of coping with the stress. He probably needs to loosen up a bit otherwise . . .'

Karen's stomach dropped. Morgan was standing nearby, look-ing wounded, apparently having overheard them analysing his machine-like behaviour.

Arnie stopped talking abruptly, seeing the look of horror on Karen's face.

'Morgan,' Karen said, stepping towards him. 'That didn't come out right. I didn't mean—'

But Morgan was already walking away from them. 'It doesn't matter.'

Karen hurried after Morgan. 'Wait, let me explain.'

He stopped and turned to face her. 'I think I caught enough of what you were saying to get the gist of it.' His voice was calm, but she could tell he was hurt.

'I was frustrated, but I shouldn't have said it,' Karen said, searching for the right words. 'What I meant was that you don't need to keep proving yourself by being so rigid about the rules. The mistake you made in the past doesn't define you, and you don't have to overcompensate by becoming obsessively rule-bound for the rest of your career.'

Morgan recoiled. 'So now I'm obsessive for trying to avoid unnecessary risks? Because I'd like to make the team's lives easier when it comes to interviews?'

Karen held up her hands. She was only making things worse. 'I'm sorry, I didn't mean to be so critical, and I know you're under a lot of strain with this case. All I'm saying is that calculated gambles can pay off. It might mean bending the rules a bit, or relying on intuition rather than a manual because sometimes the rules aren't appropriate.'

'Aren't *appropriate*?' He shook his head. 'Rules are always appropriate.'

But they weren't, not really. The regulations couldn't cover every scenario and situation. To Karen, that was just common sense, but to Morgan, expressing that thought was almost sacrilegious.

Morgan looked past her, his gaze shuttered. 'The rules exist for good reason. We can't just ignore them when it suits us.'

'I'm sorry. Can we forget this ever happened? I shouldn't have spoken about you behind your back like that. It was thoughtless and unprofessional.'

Morgan's face softened, but Karen could still sense the lingering hurt in the tense way he stood.

Glancing at her watch, she silently cursed. She had barely enough time to make it to the dinner. 'I really need to run now, or I'm going to be unforgivably late,' she said. 'This is actually the replacement dinner because I stood up my parents and Mike's last time.' She paused, wanting to make sure they finished their conversation on good terms. 'Can we talk about this later? I don't want to leave things this way.'

'There's no need,' Morgan said, his tone cool and closed-off.

He turned and headed to his office. Karen walked back towards Arnie, who was gathering his notes. He met her gaze with a grimace. 'Accept your apology, did he?'

'Not exactly,' Karen said.

She had a horrible feeling she'd damaged something fragile between them.

Outside the pub, Karen braced herself before entering. Feeling guilty for hurting Morgan's feelings and frustrated over the Tommy Burton case had left her in a foul mood. She was not looking forward to dinner. She didn't feel like being outgoing and playing peacekeeper between her mother and Lorraine.

She entered the pub and was greeted by the sound of laughter and the cheerful clink of glasses. She weaved her way through the busy eating area and spotted her family occupying a large corner table. Her sister, Emma, waved when she saw Karen.

Emma gave Karen a hug, and Mike stood to kiss Karen on the cheek. To anyone else, Mike probably looked relaxed, but she read the tension in his smile. Across from Mike and Emma sat Karen's parents, looking uneasy. Lorraine was seated next to her husband James, Mike's stepfather.

Lorraine's spine was ramrod-straight. She nodded at Karen, but the smile didn't reach her eyes.

Karen slid into an empty seat and tried to force a cheerful tone. 'Sorry I'm late.' She smiled at everyone around the table. 'I hope I didn't miss too much?'

'Not to worry, dear. We've been managing without you,' Lorraine replied. 'Was it work again?'

Karen couldn't miss the undertone of hostility. 'Yes, I'm afraid so.' She shrugged off her jacket and put it on the back of her chair, noting her mother's strained smile and Lorraine's pursed lips.

It was going to be a long night.

Small talk was painful. There seemed to be a silent power struggle unfolding between the two matriarchs. Karen tried to concentrate on the conversation, but her mind was still filled with the case.

As the appetisers arrived, Karen tried to ease the simmering tension by asking what everyone had been up to that day. Lorraine was first to answer, her words dripping with sarcasm.

'Oh, we didn't do anything very exciting. Not compared to you, Karen. You've probably been so busy saving the world with your important job that everyone else's day will fade in comparison.' She gave Karen a tight smile and sipped her wine.

Karen's mother shot Lorraine a sharp look and rose to the bait. 'Actually, Karen's working a very important case at the moment. A missing child.'

Lorraine shrugged dismissively and topped up her glass with more wine. Her flushed cheeks suggested she'd been drinking since earlier that day.

'It must be ever so difficult to have a relationship with a police officer, Mike,' Lorraine said, dabbing her mouth with a paper napkin.

Mike had a mouthful of food so didn't respond straightaway.

Karen stiffened, setting down her glass of water. The cattiness in Lorraine's tone had raised her hackles. 'Police work does require flexibility in emergencies,' she replied, 'and of course Mike knows that very well, having worked for the police himself.'

Lorraine gave a light, tinkling laugh. 'Oh, of course. I didn't mean to criticise your very important job,' she said with fake sweetness. 'I only meant it must be difficult to balance so much work with a relationship. Perhaps that's why you got to the age you are with no family to speak of.'

There was an immediate hush. Karen felt her throat tighten. She put down her knife and fork. 'I have a family, Lorraine. A family I love. My life is good. My job is a part of that.'

The casual cruelty of Lorraine's thinly veiled remark when she was aware Karen had lost her husband and daughter was shocking. Everyone else looked equally stunned. Karen noticed her father's fist clenched tightly around his fork, but before anyone else could spring to her defence, Mike twisted in his seat to look directly at his mother. 'That was out of order. Apologise.'

Around the table, Karen's family voiced sounds of agreement and support.

Lorraine suddenly paled. After an excruciatingly strained silence, she mumbled something indistinct and shoved her chair back from the table. She rushed through the crowded eating area, making a hasty exit to the ladies' toilets.

An awkward atmosphere hung over the group. Karen's mother, her face flushed with indignation, shook her head. 'Well, of all the insensitive and thoughtless comments!'

'It's fine, Mum,' Karen said.

Lorraine's behaviour tonight was over the top. She could be difficult at times, but this hostile pettiness had gone way over the line, suggesting that something was really bothering her.

Coming to a quick decision, Karen stood and looked at Mike. 'I'll go and check on her.'

Karen entered the ladies' toilets and found Lorraine leaning against the sink, blotting her eyes with a paper towel. Their gazes met in the mirror's reflection.

Lorraine sniffed, tossing the crumpled towel into the bin. 'I suppose you've come to tell me off,' she said briskly, 'and I think you'd be justified.'

Karen crossed her arms. 'It was a very cruel comment, Lorraine. Why would you say something like that? Have I done something to upset you?'

Lorraine lifted her chin defensively, but then her narrow shoulders slumped, and she turned to fully face Karen. 'You're right to be angry. What I said was inexcusable. I don't know what came over me.' Her voice took on a desperate, pleading note. 'I'm so sorry. It's just all this stuff with Mike . . .'

Karen waited, keeping her expression neutral.

Lorraine plucked another paper towel and dabbed at fresh tears. 'He's just been relentless lately. Wanting to know about his *real* father.' She put air quotes around the word *real*.

'What's wrong with that?' Karen asked. 'Surely Mike has a right to know?'

Lorraine looked horrified. 'No. Mike can't have anything to do with him. He's not a good man.'

Lorraine could be manipulative at times, but Karen heard real anguish and what sounded like fear in her voice. 'What do you mean?'

She reached out suddenly and grasped Karen's hand. 'I'm not ready to tell Mike yet. Please, just ask him to give me some more time.'

What was Lorraine so worried about? Was it because she thought her relationship with Mike would never be the same if he developed a relationship with his biological father? Or was Mike's father really not a good man, someone he'd be better off not knowing?

Taking in Lorraine's stricken face, Karen chose her next words carefully. 'I can see you're really worried, but the truth has a way of coming out eventually, one way or another. It's better if it comes from you.'

Lorraine looked appalled. 'No, I can't.'

'Look, this is really a conversation that's best kept between you and Mike.'

'You're right. I just need some time. I have to figure out how to tell him.' Lorraine squeezed Karen's hands. 'Please accept my apology for my behaviour in there.'

Karen nodded. 'Okay. Shall we go back?'

Lorraine gave a subdued nod. Together they exited the ladies' room and returned to the table where the others were waiting.

Mike shot Karen a questioning look, and she gave a tiny shake of her head. This wasn't the time to talk about it.

For the rest of the meal, the conversation was stilted. But Lorraine behaved, keeping quiet and occasionally muttering compliments.

Eventually, they all parted ways with mumbled pleasantries and promises to do it all again soon.

In the pub's car park, Karen and Mike stood by her car. 'Well, that was a fun evening,' she said.

Mike gave a surprised laugh. 'I'm not sure I agree with your idea of fun,' he said, but then his smile faded. 'I'm sorry about tonight. I don't know what's got into Mum.'

'She's clearly upset about something.'

'But she shouldn't take it out on you. Whatever her issue is, that was out of line. Did she apologise?'

Karen nodded. She needed to get back to work. There was still so much she had to do tonight, but this was important too. And Mike had a right to know what Lorraine had said.

'I think she's upset because you want to know more about your biological father.'

Mike leaned against the car. 'Did she tell you that?'

'Yes, she seemed very anxious about it.'

'I have been hounding her for details, but why would she take it out on you?'

'She's just lashing out. I don't think there's any logic to what she's doing. I think it's an emotional reaction rather than a calculated one.'

Mike nodded slowly, his gaze distant. 'She's always refused to talk about him. I just . . .' He trailed off, conflicted emotions playing across his face. 'I don't know, maybe I should let it go. It's not always a good idea to dredge up the past, is it?'

'No, but it's understandable to want to know your history.' Karen tilted her head, watching him. 'You need to do what's right for you. At the end of the day, your mum loves you. She'll come to terms with it.'

Mike shrugged. 'Well, maybe it shouldn't be a priority at the moment. I don't need to alienate a mother who's always been there for me, for a father who walked out and never cared about me at all.'

'You could put it on the back burner for a while until you've had time to think.'

Mike nodded and pulled her close. 'You're probably right.' He grinned. 'You usually are. I'll leave it be, for Mum's sake, and see where things stand down the road.' He pressed a kiss to her forehead. 'You're much more understanding than me. I was tempted to walk out tonight.'

Karen smiled against his chest. However misguided and nasty Lorraine's behaviour had been, Karen could see she'd been acting out of an instinct to protect Mike – or maybe protect herself. But it wasn't her business to get stuck in the middle. Mike was an adult, and he could handle things from here.

'Right, well, I'd better get back to work.'

'And I'd better go and collect Sandy.'

Sandy had been left with Karen's next-door neighbour, who had fallen in love with the affectionate spaniel and loved spending time with the dog.

'Sandy's probably had a better dinner than me tonight,' Mike joked.

With a final kiss, they parted ways.

As she drove out of the car park, Karen exhaled slowly, feeling wrung out. She hoped Lorraine would find the courage to communicate honestly with Mike rather than try to hide things from him.

She hadn't told Mike about Lorraine calling his biological father a bad man, and she wasn't sure why. Perhaps it was because she wouldn't put it past Lorraine to say something like that purely to dissuade Mike from looking for his father.

Karen smothered a yawn and glanced at the time. She felt guilty for having spent almost two hours away from work when Tommy

Burton was still missing and Rachel King's killer still walked free. The ticking clock was louder than ever.

But she needed to switch off occasionally, and Mike helped her do just that. He had a knack for pulling her out of her cop's headspace and reminding her there was another side to life. A fun side. Spending time with him recharged her batteries and made her remember what she was working for.

Balancing her job and her personal life was a trick Karen had never fully mastered. It was difficult to walk the line between a career as a dedicated officer and being a normal person. At times, it felt like she was walking a tightrope.

Chapter Thirty

The next day, the briefing room was full of tired voices and the smell of strong coffee. Everyone was feeling desperate; the initial excitement from the start of the case had faded away, and there was still no word on Tommy Burton's whereabouts.

DCI Churchill rapped his knuckles sharply on the wooden table at the front of the room, and the chatter died down as everyone turned their attention to the boss. DC Farzana Shah sat with her files open on the desk in front of her. Rick was next to her, with his laptop open. Karen sat at the back with Morgan and Arnie.

'Right then, team,' DCI Churchill began. 'Let's recap where we are. DC Shah, what's the latest from Forensics?'

Farzana glanced down at the notes in front of her. 'I'm afraid it's not good news. No fingerprints or DNA belonging to Tommy Burton has been found at the old petrol station where Cody Rhodes was residing. Despite an exhaustive sweep and analysis by the SOCO crew, we haven't found any trace of the boy. It's unlikely he was ever there.'

Churchill scowled. 'Could Rhodes have wiped the scene of any evidence?'

Farzana shook her head. 'There's no trace of cleaning chemicals either. Plenty of dust and grime, though. The only areas that looked like they'd been accessed recently were the roof, a small storeroom next to the old toilet block, and the room where Cody Rhodes stored all the newspaper cuttings and articles on Donaldson under the floor. Cody's fingerprints were all over the pages. There's little doubt they're his, but again, Forensics found no sign Tommy Burton was ever there.'

Frustrated, Churchill rubbed a hand over his chin, thinking. 'What about the stuffed bear? Any DNA on that?'

Farzana nodded. 'Yes, there was DNA recovered, but it hasn't given us any hits on the database. We have a sample of Tommy's DNA, but it doesn't match the DNA on the bear. So it's unlikely he came into contact with the toy.'

'We're thinking the toy was just left at the scene as a calling card?' Churchill suggested.

'Yes.'

Churchill turned to Morgan. 'Like the abductions fifteen years ago?'

'Exactly the same. The bears left at the scene were brand new.'

Churchill moved on to the next question. This time directing it at Arnie. 'How's the interview of Gareth Burton coming along?'

'We gave him a break overnight. We've been questioning him again this morning, but he's still playing hard to get, denying all knowledge of what he told Karen yesterday.'

Churchill turned to Rick, who'd been tasked with digging into Gareth Burton's finances.

'It's interesting,' Rick said. 'We got the warrant through, and the banks are cooperating. Gareth Burton had a gambling problem. He has payments going out to all sorts of betting apps. There's a lot of money going into his account – his job pays well. But there's a lot of money going out as well. The joint account he shares with Amber seems above board, but he's got two separate accounts on top of that. One of which he granted Tommy access to; Gareth has been transferring two hundred pounds into it every month.'

'For how long?' Churchill asked.

'Five months,' Rick said. 'There have been gradual withdrawals, presumably by Tommy. A hundred quid here and there.'

'And this money comes directly from Gareth Burton's bank account?'

'It does, but that's not the most interesting thing.' Rick leaned forward, resting his elbows on the table. 'The bank account that Tommy has access to wasn't only getting transfers from his father's account. There are also a number of cash deposits.'

'Do we think they came from Gareth Burton too?'

Rick shrugged. 'It's impossible to say at this point. We know the times and dates of the deposits – a couple of them were last week, so we can certainly look into that. Some banks have banned third-party cash deposits as part of a fraud prevention drive, but not this one.'

Churchill nodded slowly, considering the possibility. 'So there might have been other people paying Tommy?'

The room was quiet as the implications sank in. If Tommy had been getting payments from other people, did that mean he'd been blackmailing them too? And if that was the case, had one of them been prepared to get rid of the boy to end the blackmail?

'You've been quiet, Karen. What's your gut telling you about Gareth Burton? Could he have hurt his own son?'

Karen set down her pen. 'My instinct,' she said slowly, 'is that he's an unpleasant man, but I'm not sure he's the one who took Tommy. He has a nasty temper, but I don't think he would have gone as far as abducting his own son. If Gareth Burton had something to do with Tommy's disappearance, then it would have been down to a sudden outburst of rage – a hot-blooded crime rather than a premeditated abduction.'

Churchill nodded, processing Karen's perspective.

'One point to mention,' Rick said. 'According to the traffic cameras in the area, Gareth Burton's vehicle wasn't anywhere near Tattershall Castle on the day that Tommy was abducted. So, if he took the boy himself, it doesn't look like he used his own car.'

Churchill looked around the room with a solemn expression. 'Let's keep looking into Gareth Burton's finances. We need to find out where this money trail goes. Look into who was paying Tommy.' He looked at Farzana and then Arnie. 'You need to get Burton to talk. If he was giving Tommy these extra cash deposits, that's one thing. If there were more people paying Tommy, then that blows this whole thing wide open, because that means Tommy could have been blackmailing other people – and all those people suddenly have a very good motive for wanting Tommy to disappear.' He paused, frowning down at his notes, then said, 'We need to find out where that toy bear came from. Sophie made a list of stockists in Lincoln. Have we visited them all?'

'Not yet, sir. There's a couple outstanding,' Rick said. 'I can get to those this morning.'

'Good, do that,' Churchill said. 'Because with every hour that passes, Tommy's chances of being found safe and well are diminishing.'

The bell above the shop door jangled as Rick stepped inside. He was immediately hit by the flowery scent of the candles stacked up near the entrance.

Rick glanced around the small gift shop, getting his bearings. This was the last place on his list that, according to Sophie, still stocked the blue bears identical to the one found at the abduction scene.

The place was chock-a-block with scented soaps, inspirational signs and handmade cards. Rick walked up and down the aisles, looking for the blue bears.

A woman in a bright pink dress looked up from arranging fridge magnets. 'Can I help you, lovey?' she asked with a smile.

Rick showed his ID. 'I hope so.'

The woman's eyes widened slightly. 'Oh dear, is something wrong?'

'I'm just following up on a lead,' Rick reassured her.

He pulled out his phone and showed her a picture of the blue bear. 'We're trying to identify the source of this bear, and the manufacturer's records show you carry them in your inventory.'

The woman – Susan, according to her name tag – peered at the photograph, frowning. 'Oh yes, I recognise that one. It was part of our spring collection.' She smiled and then glanced over at the far wall, where other stuffed animals were displayed. 'I'm afraid we're out of stock.'

'But you did have them?'

Susan nodded. 'We had quite a few, yes, but there was an incident.' She paused. 'Some of our inventory went missing. It's a hazard of the trade. We lose quite a bit of stock from shoplifting.'

'I don't suppose you filed a police report or have documentation of what was taken?'

'Unfortunately not,' Susan said. 'I don't own the place, so it's not up to me. The owner just writes it off. Says it's not worth the bother. But I could check with him if that would help?'

Rick thought it over, but said, 'Don't worry.'

It was likely a frustrating dead end. The bear could have come from stolen stock, which would make it practically impossible to trace.

'Sorry I couldn't be more helpful,' Susan said as she walked with Rick to the door. 'Let me know if I can do anything to help.'

'You've been very kind,' Rick said. 'Did you sell any of the bears at all before they were stolen?'

Susan shook her head. 'The blue bears weren't very popular with customers. The owner decided not to restock them.'

'I see. Well, thanks for your help anyway.' Rick started to walk away, heading back to where he'd parked his car.

He'd only taken a few steps when he heard 'Psst.'

Rick turned to see a lanky young man ambling up to him. He held a large holdall. The zip was partially undone, revealing merchandise inside.

'I heard you're looking for something,' the man said with a wink. 'Blue bear, wasn't it? Maybe a little gift for your girlfriend? Ladies love that mushy stuff, don't they?'

With grubby fingers, he slid the zip open wider so Rick could see better. Rick peered into the bag and saw an assortment of items, all undoubtedly stolen. He recognised a trio of the same pale blue teddy bears he was looking for. They looked up at him with beady black eyes.

Rick smiled. His day had just got better. He subtly showed his ID as he said, 'As a matter of fact, I am very interested in those blue bears. Do you mind telling me how you happened to acquire them?'

The man's ferret-like eyes widened. He took a step back, already defensive. 'Hey, that's entrapment that is.'

'No, it isn't,' Rick said. 'Now, where did you get them?'

'It's not what it looks like. I'm just holding them for a mate.'

'Of course you are.'

The man swallowed, glancing around nervously.

'I'm not interested in the particulars of your little enterprise,' Rick said, 'and I might even be willing to overlook this bag of stolen goods if you can give me some information.'

The man shifted from foot to foot, wary but clearly tempted.

'Give us a tenner and you've got yourself a deal.'

Rick frowned. 'No, I make the terms of our deal. It's not a negotiation. Now, tell me about these bears.'

'There's nothing special about them. They're just a bunch of toys.'

Rick pulled out his mobile phone and showed him photographs of Gareth Burton and then Cody Rhodes. 'Did you sell one of the blue bears to either of these men?'

The scruffy shoplifter squinted at the screen of Rick's mobile and shook his head. 'Nah, never seen them before.'

Rick felt a twinge of disappointment. Was he lying? 'You must have sold at least one of these bears though.'

'Maybe I did.'

'Take another look at the photographs,' Rick said, pushing his mobile right up to the man's face.

'It's definitely not them.'

'You seem very sure,' Rick said.

'Of course I am because it was a *woman*, and she paid me to nick 'em too. Gave me a hundred quid, and then she only wanted one of the bears and said I could sell the others. She made my day.'

'Can you describe her?'

The man scrunched up his face. 'I didn't get a really good look. She had quite a posh accent – pretty too, I think, but she was wearing big sunglasses and a hat.'

'Anything more you can tell me about her?' Rick asked. 'Even a small detail could be critical.'

But the man just shrugged. 'I don't want to get her in trouble. She did me a favour.'

'It's really important,' Rick said. 'You're not going to get her in trouble. I just need to find her.'

But the man shook his head. 'That's all I know. But you'll let me walk away from this, won't you? I've been helpful.'

After Rick took down the man's name and details, which Rick hoped – but doubted – were accurate, he said, 'If you get out of here now, I'll forget I saw you.'

The man grinned and hurried off without another word, hauling the holdall on to his shoulder.

Maybe Rick should have tried to convince him to see the error of his ways, but right now he had bigger problems. Who was the mystery woman who'd bought the blue bear? Was she the one who'd left the toy at the abduction scene? Had a woman abducted Tommy?

Rick walked quickly back to his car, his mind whirring through the possibilities. He couldn't wait to get this new information back to the team. This could be the breakthrough they needed. They were looking for a female suspect.

Chapter Thirty-One

Karen stared at her desk. The case files and notes were starting to blur together. She brought the coffee cup to her lips, only to be reminded that it had gone cold.

'Tommy . . .' she muttered under her breath. 'What were you up to?'

She'd been thinking of him as an innocent child, but Tommy was a much more complex character than she'd first believed. It was hard to wrap her head around the fact he'd been blackmailing his own father. Clearly there were multiple sides to little Tommy.

He was cunning enough to have come up with a blackmail scheme, but could an eleven-year-old ever be equipped emotionally to cope with the fallout? He was precocious and bright beyond his years, but at the end of the day, he was still just a child in need of protection.

The revelations from the morning briefing had shocked Karen. She wanted time to process them, as she was certain that the other payments to Tommy Burton were key to figuring out who was responsible for his disappearance.

She stared up at the latticed arrangement of white ceiling tiles, thinking. Who else was paying Tommy to keep quiet?

She ran through the possibilities in her mind, then left her desk and made her way over to talk to Arnie. He was waiting for someone to answer a call and was absently twirling a pen.

'Any news on Rachel King's murder?' she asked, knowing that if there was any positive news, she probably would have heard about it already.

Arnie shook his head, shrugging, 'We've hit a brick wall.' He lifted his stained *World's Greatest Detective* mug and took a sip. 'Rick made any progress tracking those cash deposits?'

Karen perched on the corner of his desk. 'It's not easy,' she said. 'We've been going over the financial records, looking for connections, but cash is hard to trace. We haven't got access to the bank's security footage yet either.'

Arnie gave her a sympathetic pat on the arm. 'Something will turn up soon.'

She wished she shared his optimism. 'I'm sure someone else was paying him.'

Arnie tapped his pen on the scattered files covering his desk. 'Yeah, it's a pity it wasn't transferred directly from another bank account. We could have followed the money trail easy enough then. One option is sifting through the security footage from when the deposits were made – try and ID who was paying the boy. That's if we have no joy from the bank's deposit slips.'

Karen nodded. Tommy's extortion scheme was unnerving. 'A blackmail operation just seems so calculating for a little boy.'

Arnie gave up on the call he was waiting for with a huff. 'Maybe it was Tommy's way of regaining some control after years of enduring his vile father. Smart lad – he saw the chance to turn the table on his abuser.' He took another sip of his coffee. 'Got any theories on who Tommy could be blackmailing?'

'I do, actually,' Karen said. 'I've just been thinking it over and Jack Foster would be top of my list. His story has never sat right with me. All that stuff about Tommy teasing him about his ears.'

'You didn't believe him?'

'No, I knew there was more to it. And there's another resident of Dahlia Close who sets off alarm bells for me: Lyra Hill. She's Tommy's history teacher. She was so jittery when I spoke to her. Every time Morgan and I have visited the area, I've caught her peeking out of windows. Her behaviour is simply odd.'

Karen remembered Lyra's nervous energy and how she'd run indoors when Karen had first seen her, then watched from behind the curtains. She was like a mouse scurrying for the shadows, scared of being discovered. But what did Tommy know about her? What could he have used against her to make her so scared?

'Why don't you go and talk to Lyra and Jack then?'

'I'm waiting on a call back from the bank,' she said, glancing regretfully at the phone on her desk.

'Leave that,' Arnie said, draining his coffee. 'I'll answer the phone if they call. You should go and talk to Jack and Lyra. If you feel those two are worth pressing, I'd say go and have another chat.'

'But where does Rachel King fit into this? Can you imagine either Jack or Lyra killing or abducting Tommy? It doesn't make sense, does it?'

'Stranger things have happened,' Arnie said. 'Nothing would surprise me after twenty-five years in this job. Anyway, the phone calls will keep. I say go and talk to them.'

Karen stood. Arnie was right. She wouldn't second-guess her instincts. 'Okay,' she said, walking back to her desk to grab her things. 'I'll head back to Dahlia Close and try to get some answers.'

Arnie broke into a grin. 'Good luck.'

◆　◆　◆

Karen parked outside the Fosters' home, walked briskly up the driveway and rang the doorbell. Inside, a TV was blaring out sports commentary. It wasn't long before the door was opened by Dawn Foster.

'Who is it, love?' Jerry Foster, wearing a polo shirt and jeans, appeared behind her. 'Oh,' he said, recognising Karen. 'Have you found Tommy?'

'Sadly, not yet,' Karen said, glimpsing both Foster boys sitting on the sofa watching a sports programme on television. 'I'd like to speak to Jack again please.'

The parents exchanged an anxious look. 'Is there a problem?' Dawn asked. 'I thought you'd spoken to Jack at school?'

'I did,' Karen confirmed. 'I've just got a few more questions for him.'

'I'm not sure,' Dawn said. 'This can't be good for either of the boys. They know Tommy. They're upset. We want to help but . . .'

'I've told you everything already,' came a surly voice. Jack appeared behind his mother. His hair fell across his sullen eyes.

Karen fixed the defiant teen with an even stare. 'There are a few discrepancies that I'd like to clarify. Can we have a chat?'

Dawn shuffled her feet, clearly reluctant. 'I really don't know.'

But Karen stood her ground. 'This is urgent, and it might help us find Tommy. It won't take long.'

With a sigh, the woman opened the door wider, and Karen stepped inside the tidy, comfortable home. 'Is there somewhere Jack and I can speak?' she asked. 'You're welcome to be present while we talk, of course.'

Dawn's lips thinned disapprovingly,. and she looked at her husband.

Jerry shrugged and gestured towards a small room off the hall-way. 'You can use my office, but leave the door open. We want to be able to hear what you say.'

'Thank you,' Karen said, and she followed Jack into the small, cluttered office. There were two desks and two chairs. Karen and Jack each took one. Dawn hovered by the doorway.

'What you told me previously doesn't quite add up, Jack. You claimed you fought with Tommy because he was teasing you about your ears . . .'

Karen didn't make any attempt to hide her scepticism.

Jack shrugged. 'Yes, like I told you, he was horrible, teasing me, and that's when I got angry.' His leg jiggled nervously.

Switching tactics, Karen softened her tone. 'Jack, I know you're trying to protect yourself, but if you've got any information that could help us find Tommy, please tell me. This is the time. You need to help us.'

The boy chewed his lip, conflict playing across his face, but then he shook his head emphatically. 'I don't know what you're talking about. I don't know anything else . . .'

Karen exhaled slowly, trying to hide her frustration. Jack was clearly too concerned about getting into trouble to come clean. More pressure was needed.

She turned to Dawn. 'I have reason to believe your son is withholding critical information about Tommy Burton's disappearance, and I need your help to convince him to tell the truth.'

Dawn looked dismayed. 'I don't think he is,' she said. 'He's already told you everything he knows.'

'I'm quite sure he hasn't,' Karen said sharply, 'because I suspect Tommy was blackmailing your son, which means Jack has withheld vital information that could help us locate a missing child.'

She turned back to the squirming teen. 'What was Tommy blackmailing you over, Jack? And where did you get the money to pay him?'

'Jack, is this true?' Dawn demanded.

The boy paled, dropping his gaze to the floor again. 'I don't know . . . w . . . what you're talking about.'

'Where did you get the money, Jack?' Dawn spoke more quietly this time.

Trapped, Jack wrapped his arms around himself defensively. 'Look, I . . . it wasn't my fault. Tommy just had something on me, and I didn't want to drag you all into it, okay?'

Dawn's eyes narrowed. 'Drag us into it? Where did you get the money? Did you steal it?'

Jack lowered his head.

His mother abruptly whirled around and hurried from the room. Baffled, Karen waited as raised voices filtered down the hall. A moment later, Dawn stormed back in, holding up a large, half-empty money jar. 'You've been skimming cash from our holiday savings. How could you steal from us, Jack? From your own family?'

Something seemed to break in Jack then. His shoulders slumped and he dropped his head into his hands. 'I'm sorry, but Tommy was going to show everyone the video if I didn't pay up.'

They were finally getting somewhere. 'What video, Jack?' Karen asked. 'Tell me everything.'

Jerry appeared in the doorway, his arms folded across his chest, his expression stern. 'You'd better come clean, Jack.'

Taking a deep shuddering breath, Jack said, 'Tommy recorded me stealing the mock paper for my maths test. He threatened to send the video to the headteacher if I didn't pay him.'

Jack's parents gaped in dismay.

'You stole an exam.' Jerry looked disappointed.

Jack hung his head, sniffing and wiping his nose on the back of his hand. 'I'm sorry, okay? I was just scared of failing again. No one got hurt.'

'Tell me what happened when you confronted Tommy,' Karen said.

Jack rubbed angrily at his face. 'I got angry with him. I told him to leave me alone. I said I couldn't afford to pay him anymore, but I didn't hurt him.'

'I need the truth, Jack,' Karen said. 'We found out that you and Tommy had an altercation from a witness. You didn't volunteer that information. We know that Tommy was blackmailing you, but you didn't admit that either. So how can I tell if you're telling the whole truth now?'

'I am! I promise. I shoved him a bit but that was all.'

'Did things escalate after that first altercation? Did you hurt Tommy?'

Jack paled, shrinking back into his chair. 'What? No!' His voice dropped to a shaky whisper. 'You don't think I could have . . . could have killed him?'

Karen studied the boy closely. He seemed genuine. He was angry with Tommy, but he was unlikely to be responsible for masterminding the abduction of Tommy from Tattershall Castle.

'I believe you, but I need you to think very carefully. Is there anything else you can tell me?'

Jack shook his head. 'That's all I know, honestly. I stole the exam paper. Tommy had it on video and threatened to tell on me unless I paid him fifty quid a week.' He wiped his eyes, sniffling again. 'I don't want Tommy to get hurt though, and I want you to find him.'

As the boy dissolved into sobs, his mother moved beside him and gave him a hug. 'It's all right, Jack. It's going to be okay.'

As Dawn comforted Jack, she looked at Karen almost pleadingly, as if begging for her boy not to be in any more trouble.

Karen had got everything she could for now. 'Thank you for being truthful, Jack.' She nodded to Jerry and Dawn. 'I'll be in touch.'

Jerry showed Karen out, apologising profusely for his son's behaviour. 'I don't know what's got into him. He had some issues at school last year with bad grades. He's not really academic and I think the stress was getting to him. But I promise you, Jack is not a violent boy. He would not have . . . he wouldn't have hurt Tommy.'

Jerry was babbling, repeatedly apologising for what Jack had done, but as Karen saw it, the boy had made a mistake, and he'd had the courage finally to face up to it.

Maybe there was hope for Jack Foster yet.

Chapter Thirty-Two

Karen left the Fosters', walked past Sam and Brooke's house, and stopped at Lyra Hill's. She rapped sharply on the grey door. She heard the scratch and muffled clink of a security chain being released.

The door swung open to reveal Lyra. Her hair was tousled, and she was clutching a half-empty wine glass. She looked at Karen with over-bright eyes.

Her cardigan had been buttoned unevenly over her blouse.

'Detective,' she said with obviously forced cheerfulness. 'Please come in.'

Karen stepped into the sleek, minimalist home and followed Lyra into the kitchen.

She declined Lyra's flustered offer of a drink and decided to get right to the point. 'Miss Hill, I'll be direct. I have reason to believe you haven't been entirely truthful with me.'

Lyra's tense smile faded, and her gaze skittered away guiltily. She took a deep breath and then a gulp of wine. 'What do you mean?'

Karen fixed her with a piercing look. Time to call her bluff. If she acted like she already knew Lyra was being blackmailed by Tommy and had been paying him money, it could be enough for a confession.

'You know exactly what I'm talking about, Lyra. We have evidence that Tommy was blackmailing you over something serious enough to impact your career. I'm giving you a chance to come clean.'

It was a calculated risk, but Karen's instinct was rewarded. Lyra seemed to crumple, putting down her glass and collapsing on one of the kitchen stools. 'How did you find out?' she whispered.

Karen said nothing and waited for Lyra to continue.

'You're right,' Lyra said, her voice trembling. 'He was blackmailing me. I couldn't tell you. I was so ashamed.' She took a deep breath, trying to calm herself. 'It must sound ridiculous, but I felt trapped. I know I should have told you.'

Karen softened her tone, hoping to get Lyra to open up even more. 'Why don't you start from the beginning? I'm listening.'

Nodding, Lyra took another gulp of wine and then began to speak. 'It started a few months ago. I'd been having trouble fitting in at work, and I did something really stupid. Just my luck that Tommy happened to be watching, and to make it worse, he caught it on video.' She dropped her head into her hands. 'I've been so stupid.'

'What did you do Lyra?'

'I . . . I . . . took a knife to Harriet Scott's tyres. She's the headteacher at the school. She was really tough on me for no reason after I started working for her. But what really made me snap was her telling everyone my marriage had ended because I'd had an affair, something I'd confided to her privately. I hadn't expected her to announce it in the middle of a staff meeting with all the other teachers present! After that, everyone began gossiping about me behind my back.'

Lyra shook her head angrily and took another gulp of wine. 'I just lost it one day after school. I have a penknife on my key ring. I used it to slash her tyres.' She shrugged. 'It was childish and wrong.

But I was so angry. Tommy was recording me, and the next day at school, he told me about the video and said I had to pay him or he'd go to Harriet.'

'How did Tommy approach you?'

Lyra gave a mirthless laugh. 'He just walked right up to me after my history class, smiling in a really unnerving way. And to think, I'd thought he seemed like such a good kid at first.' Lyra scoffed. 'He was quiet, polite and intelligent. He wasn't very popular at school, and I felt sorry for him.' She paused, looking down as her hands tightly gripped the kitchen counter. 'But he was pretty cold about it. It was the last lesson on a Tuesday. I thought he wanted to ask me about the Romans – he'd asked a few questions in class, and I was happy that he was interested and engaged with the subject. But then he showed me his mobile phone. And that's when I saw the video, all zoomed in, clear as day, showing me slashing Harriet Scott's tyres.'

'Why didn't you tell Harriet?' Karen asked.

'Because I was so embarrassed and ashamed. I thought I'd pay him once, but Tommy had other ideas.'

Karen waited a moment before gently asking, 'What made you decide to pay Tommy more money?'

'Because I didn't want to admit what I did. I was a coward. I felt I had no choice but to pay him. I thought Harriet would fire me on the spot. I didn't think Tommy could be so calculating as to demand regular payments. He's just eleven!' Her face twisted bitterly.

Karen felt a pang of sympathy, though she thought Lyra would have been much better off to have come forward immediately.

'How much did you pay Tommy?'

'Fifty pounds, which didn't seem much for a one-off payment to keep quiet. I gave him cash the next day. But then he said he needed more. He told me – you won't believe this – he told me it

286

was weighing on his conscience, so he increased it to seventy-five pounds and kept asking for it every week.' Lyra covered her face with her hands. 'Seventy-five pounds, every week for the last three months. It's a lot of money from a teacher's salary. I've got a mortgage on this place.' She gestured around the room. 'But I started to think I'd have to start tutoring after school to afford the payments. I was terrified of him exposing me.'

Karen gave her a moment before asking the crucial question as gently as she could. 'Did you ever consider a way to stop the blackmail permanently?'

Lyra's head snapped up in alarm. 'No! You don't think I had anything to do with Tommy going missing?'

Karen held her gaze. 'I have to ask, Lyra, did you meet up with Tommy at Tattershall Castle?'

'No,' Lyra said, her voice trembling. 'I was desperate, but I would never have hurt him, no matter what he did.'

'Where were you the day Tommy went missing?'

'I was home. It was an inset day. We were supposed to be doing staff training, but I was feeling poorly . . .' She sounded panicked and flustered. 'Can't you track my mobile or something? Won't that show you I'm telling the truth?'

Karen studied her closely. 'Not if you didn't take your mobile with you. Maybe you left it at home, purely for that purpose.'

'No,' Lyra said, tears welling in her eyes. 'I didn't. I wouldn't.'

Lyra's shock and revulsion seemed genuine. Karen's instinct told her the woman was telling the truth. She had now identified two more people that Tommy had been blackmailing, and yet neither seemed to be responsible for his disappearance.

'I think you're being honest with me,' Karen said finally. 'But it's not unheard of for victims of blackmail to become desperate enough to contemplate violence to bring an end to it.'

Lyra buried her face in her hands. After a few seconds, she looked up. 'Are you saying you think someone might have done something to Tommy to stop his threats? That's horrifying.' She let out a sob.

Karen gave Lyra a moment to collect herself. 'I understand this is difficult, Lyra, but I need you to think really hard about whether Tommy has been blackmailing anyone else.'

'I don't think so. As far as I know, it was only me.'

Karen didn't reply. She was shocked that an eleven-year-old could exert this kind of power over adults.

'It's humiliating,' Lyra said. 'I'm a grown woman, but he reduced me to a terrified mess. I was even thinking of transferring schools next year to escape him.' She looked at Karen despairingly. 'I know I made a stupid, stupid mistake, but I promise I didn't hurt Tommy.'

Karen leaned back and looked out at the garden. The most likely scenario here was that one of the people Tommy was blackmailing had decided they wanted that blackmail to stop. But if it wasn't Lyra, and it wasn't Jack Foster, and it wasn't Tommy's dad, then who?

Karen was still struggling to accept that Tommy had been running this scheme undetected. Tommy was a very unusual eleven-year-old, and far sharper than anyone had given him credit for.

'I really need to find out who else Tommy was blackmailing,' Karen said. 'Can you think of anyone?'

'You mean at school?' Lyra asked, frowning.

'Perhaps, or maybe you noticed something when he was walking home?'

Lyra considered that for a moment, but then shook her head. 'I'm sorry, but I can't think of anyone else Tommy might have targeted. I was so caught up in worrying about myself that I didn't notice anything.'

'And Tommy never mentioned that he had other people paying him money?'

'No,' Lyra said. 'I really thought I was the only one.'

'When was the last time you actually spoke to Tommy?'

'It was Tuesday, the day before he went missing. I'd walked home from school. Amber was standing on the corner with Tommy and a group of mums and a couple of the neighbours. I stopped to talk to them. Only briefly, though. I'll be honest, I hated being in Tommy's presence. He gave me the creeps – the way he smiled as though he would spill my secret at any moment.'

'Did Tommy say anything to you?'

'No, he was very quiet. He just looked at me with a knowing look in his eye.' Lyra shivered and drained her wine.

'And who else was there? What were you talking about?'

Lyra shrugged. 'I can't really remember; it was just general stuff. Probably the weather and . . . Oh yes, I remember. Amber was asking if we could think of anything that Tommy might like to do the next day. She was keen to get him outside, away from the computer. And one of the neighbours suggested going to Tattershall Castle.'

Karen sat up straight. This was new information.

Lyra poured herself some more wine as she went on. 'She told Amber that the bird of prey show was amazing. She insisted Tommy would love it, but then she's always liked birds – especially birds of prey. You must have noticed the feather pendant she wears around her neck.'

Chapter Thirty-Three

Morgan stood in front of the printer as it sputtered and choked out pages in a slow, stuttering rhythm. The office bustled noisily around him. Phones rang incessantly. People strode between desks, and chatter filled the air. But Morgan was lost in thought about the missing boys he hadn't been able to save. If the person who'd abducted Tommy was following Donaldson's method to the letter, then it would soon be too late for eleven-year-old Tommy.

But nothing about this case made sense. Information they'd gathered from Gareth Burton's bank accounts implied Tommy was a juvenile extortionist. Where did that fit in? Or was it a false lead?

Morgan snatched each page angrily as it crept out of the printer, as if punishing it would make it move faster. The printer seemed to sense his frustration and hesitated longer between each sheet, its loud whirring and grinding noises mocking him. He pictured grabbing the clunky machine and shaking it, but restrained himself.

If things weren't already going badly enough, he'd just had a call from Cody Rhodes's psychiatrist, who had not only said Cody still wasn't well enough for an interview, but had provided an alibi for Cody, too. According to the doctor, Cody had been at a hospital appointment reviewing his meds at the time of Tommy's abduction.

Morgan swore at the printer in frustration. His only solid suspect was now a no-go.

'Earth to Morgan.' Arnie waved a hand in front of him. 'I asked if you wanted a coffee.'

Morgan blinked, glancing up. 'Sorry, I didn't hear you. I was just thinking about the case.'

'Yeah, I can see the smoke coming out of your ears from here,' Arnie said, laughing at his own joke, then growing serious suddenly. 'You're really taking this one hard, mate.'

Of course he was. He'd not been able to save the three small boys last time – Henry, Marc and Stuart. And now it looked like he'd have to add Tommy to the list of kids he'd failed to help.

He gave a non-committal grunt and returned his attention to the printer, taking out bits of paper as they spat out of the top.

Arnie was a good detective, if a bit cavalier. Morgan valued order and protocol, and together they were usually a good mix, balancing each other out. He'd thought the same about Karen, too. But apparently she considered him a machine. A *robot*. It was hardly a fair—

'So, do you want that coffee or not?'

'No, thank you.' Morgan's tone was cool. He hadn't forgiven Arnie for talking about him with Karen when they'd thought he was out of earshot.

With friends like that . . .

'Look, I can tell you're still annoyed,' Arnie said, and he scrunched up his eyes as he peered at the control panel on the printer. 'Is that meant to be flashing red?'

Morgan glared at the machine. 'Probably not.'

'I'm sorry for talking about you behind your back with Karen,' Arnie said. 'We're just worried because we care. This investigation has been tough on you.'

'I'm fine.'

'Uh-huh. Course you are.'

At this point, Morgan was 99 per cent certain Arnie was being deliberately irritating. 'I'm just doing my job, Arnie. This case is hard for everyone.'

'Sure, but it's only natural that some cases get under your skin more than others. It might help to talk about it.'

When Morgan said nothing, Arnie tried again. 'Karen might have a point.' He spoke cautiously and took a step back, as though he expected Morgan to spontaneously combust at any second. Did they all think he was really that sensitive?

'Rules are all well and good, but sometimes bureaucracy can slow things down. We all know that.' Arnie seemed to be on a roll. Did the man ever stop talking?

Morgan remained stony-faced, all business. 'Rules create order, and we need them. Especially in a case with a missing child.'

Arnie sighed. 'I suppose you're right. All I'm saying is fear of doing the wrong thing can sometimes prevent you from doing the right thing.'

Was Morgan being treated to some kind of Arnie philosophy class? Maybe if he stayed quiet, Arnie would get bored and go away.

'I'm not sure that makes any sense. I believe we have rules for a reason,' Morgan said, responding despite his intention to stonewall Arnie. Why was he engaging? It would only encourage him.

Morgan's mobile buzzed in his pocket. He pulled out the phone, glanced at the screen, and saw it was Karen. Morgan answered the call, but it kept cutting out. He caught the words *Tommy* and *Lincoln*, but not much else.

He'd hoped Arnie would take the phone call as a signal their conversation was over, but no, that would be too easy. Arnie was waiting expectantly.

After the call failed completely, Morgan tried ringing back, but got an engaged tone. He swore under his breath, then the phone beeped with a voicemail.

Morgan clutched the phone harder to his ear, trying to make sense of Karen's message, which also kept breaking up.

Through crackling interference, he could just make out her saying, 'Going to Lincoln animal shelter. Brooke took Tommy.'

Then the message was interrupted. Morgan's brow furrowed in concentration as he tried to make sure he was understanding the garbled meaning.

He looked at Arnie. 'Karen's gone to an address in Lincoln, an animal shelter. The one where Brooke Lewis works. She thinks Brooke might be the one who's taken Tommy.'

'What?' Arnie said, putting his mug down on a nearby desk. 'Brooke Lewis? Sam Tranmere's fiancée?'

Morgan nodded. 'I can't make out much more of the message. It keeps cutting out, but I think Karen said that Tommy had been blackmailing Jack Foster and Lyra Hill, as well as his father. Jack and Lyra both admitted it.'

Arnie screwed up his face in confusion. 'So why does Karen think it's Brooke Lewis? What does she have to do with it?'

'Because apparently it was Brooke who suggested Amber take Tommy to Tattershall Castle that day.'

Morgan hit the speaker button on his phone, so he and Arnie could listen to the staticky voicemail again.

Just as the message finished, Rick came into the open-plan office looking very pleased with himself.

'I found out where the bear came from,' he said with a wide smile. 'And the person who took it wasn't Cody Rhodes or Gareth Burton. In fact, it was a woman.'

He waited, expecting questions, perhaps a few gasps of surprise and certainly a couple of *well done*s, but instead he was met with silence.

Morgan and Arnie exchanged a look as the implication hit them.

'What?' asked Rick, oblivious.

'No time to explain here,' Morgan said. 'We need to move. Walk with us.'

As they headed out, he explained to Rick that Karen had gone to the animal shelter because she suspected Brooke had taken Tommy.

Arnie let out a low whistle as they raced down the stairs. 'I did not expect this.' He gave Morgan a sideways look. 'Seems like Karen's instincts paid off.'

Morgan was too caught up in thinking through what they were going to do next to respond.

'I mean,' Arnie continued, 'I'm not saying we need to rip up the rule book every day, but success can lie in the middle ground.'

Morgan didn't bother to reply as he strode purposely to the exit. He believed in upholding the law to the letter. Reckless methods caused problems, even if they occasionally got results.

Chapter Thirty-Four

Karen pulled up outside the entrance to the animal shelter on Sands Lane in Lincoln. From the outside, it didn't look impressive. It was a large squat building with small square windows. A concrete parking area surrounded the property, which was encircled by a tall chain-link fence, but the entrance gate was open.

Security cameras were dotted around the building. A dark brown, dilapidated storage shed sat in the corner of the plot. There was a brightly coloured sign displaying the name of the centre and advertising cattery and kennel services at the entrance.

There were no cars in the car park.

She drove into the parking area, stopping at the front of the building. Her instincts were on high alert. There was something very wrong about this. The place appeared deserted.

She stepped out of the car and set off towards the building cautiously.

Then she heard a voice. 'Can I help you?'

Karen turned to see a bald, heavy-set man in a T-shirt and jeans who had come out from the building next door. He peered at her through the fence.

Karen walked over and held up her ID. 'Detective Sergeant Karen Hart. I need to speak to whoever is in charge of this building.'

The man's eyes widened slightly at the sight of her police identification, and he mumbled something about not knowing who owned the place and turned his back.

Karen rattled the fence to keep his attention. 'This is urgent, and I've not finished speaking with you.'

The man turned back round sulkily. 'It's nothing to do with me.'

'I've just got a few questions,' Karen said. 'You're not in any trouble. What can you tell me about this place?'

'It's closed for a few days, I think,' he said.

'What is the building used for?'

'Nothing at the moment. Like I said, it's closed.'

'What's it used for when it's open?'

He nodded at the sign. 'Animal shelter. It's mainly for injured wild animals. But they also house cats and dogs while their owners are on holiday.'

'Do you know why it's closed?'

'Brooke said the other day she's getting hitched. Apparently, they're off to the Maldives for the honeymoon, and it's not easy to get cover for a place like this.' He shrugged. 'That's all I know.'

'Have you seen Brooke here recently?' Karen asked.

'Er . . . I'm not sure. I don't want to get her in trouble.'

'I just need to know if you've seen her this week?'

'She's been popping in and out. Told me she's getting the place sorted before she goes off on her honeymoon. Is that all? Because I've got work to be getting on with.' He pointed to his shop next door.

Karen hesitated, turning back to the animal centre. There was a heavy metal door at the front.

'Almost,' she said. 'Do you have a spare key?'

'Well, look, I can't give you that because that would be . . .' He shrivelled under Karen's stare.

Karen glanced over at his business premises. It was a small household store with buckets, feather dusters, and tubs of batteries on display outside. 'I could always get a unit to come and look at your place of work and make sure everything is above board.'

'It is!' He was indignant. 'I run a legit business.'

'I'm sure you do. Might take a while to make sure though. Probably disrupt your trade for a few days.'

He huffed. 'Fine, I've got a key. Wait there.'

He went inside and brought back the key.

'Thanks, I'll bring it back when I'm done.'

She left him standing at the fence, feeling a little guilty. Threats never sat well with her. But she needed to get inside the building.

Karen slipped on some gloves and slid the key into the lock. The door opened with a creak directly into a reception area. A computer sat on a desk and there was a row of seats, perhaps for people waiting to drop off or pick up their pets.

Flyers hung on the walls. There was a bowl of what looked like wrapped mints on the counter.

Karen walked slowly down the tiled hallway. Doors led off the corridor into small exam rooms. Inside each one she opened drawers and cabinets, and found everything still tidy and neatly arranged. No clues Tommy had been here.

Creeping doubt needled her composure. Had she called this all wrong? No. Tommy could be here somewhere. It was the perfect place to keep him, hidden away from prying eyes.

She had to keep looking.

Karen called out Tommy's name as she searched, but there was no response.

At the end of the hallway, she searched a pristine surgery suite. Medical kits, swabs, and bottles of sterile saline sat on metal trays, as if waiting for the next animal patient.

A prickle travelled down Karen's neck as she saw a vial of xylazine, a powerful sedative, sitting on the metal bench. That should be in a locked medical cabinet. Individually wrapped needles and syringes sat beside a bright yellow sharps bin.

She shook off the chill of unease. She had to focus.

Karen left the medical room and turned into a narrow corridor, momentarily disorientated. She shook her head at the warren-like nature of the building. The corridors and doors were all white and seemed to merge into one.

She entered a cramped passage lined with kennels, amplifying the sense of claustrophobia creeping over her. Everything was empty and clean.

Methodically checking each empty kennel left her clenching her jaw in frustration. Where was Tommy? Was her hunch completely wrong? Just because Lyra had overheard Brooke encouraging Amber to take Tommy to Tattershall Castle, she'd raced here on a wild goose chase.

Morgan would probably have a lot to say about that. He'd be sure to include a detailed description of how the regulations said she should have gone back to the station first and planned out a strategy.

She'd thought about it. But if Tommy was here, she wanted to find him as soon as possible. She'd left Morgan a message, so it wasn't as though she'd gone completely off script.

She entered another, larger room. Sunlight filtered in from a small high window. Karen scanned the space. The cages sat open and empty along the walls. A wide table stood in the centre of the room, with two cat carriers on top.

Karen jumped at a sharp noise and spun around, her heart pounding. But she soon laughed at herself when she saw two furry faces peering up at her from inside the containers. Brooke must have brought Rachel King's cats to the rescue centre.

'Hello again, you two.'

Marmalade meowed sweetly, while the smoky grey one haughtily turned its back on Karen.

There was a large wire cage on the other side of the room with a multi-branched cat tree and assorted toys scattered at the base.

She wondered why Brooke hadn't transferred the cats to the cage and given them a bit more space. Maybe she was intending to come back soon.

Could she have been wrong about Brooke? There was no trace of Tommy and she'd almost searched the entire building.

But the theory made sense.

They already knew Tommy had been blackmailing three people – what if his fourth target had been Brooke?

Brooke was desperate to marry Sam Tranmere, the man who'd just inherited a pile of money from his grandmother. If Tommy had something to threaten her with, something that would make Sam call off their wedding . . . it wasn't unthinkable. Money was a powerful motive.

'Can I help you?'

The voice came from behind Karen. She whirled around to see Brooke Lewis standing in the doorway.

'Sorry, I didn't mean to scare you.' Brooke smiled and put two carrier bags on the floor. One full of bottles of water, the other sweets and crisps. Unless Brooke had a serious junk food habit, Karen guessed they were supplies to keep Tommy quiet. At the thought of the child being alive, Karen's spirits lifted. 'Were you looking for me?'

'Yes,' Karen said. 'What's going on here?' She gestured around. 'I can't see any other animals.'

'No,' Brooke said, looking at Karen's gloved hands and frowning. 'I'll be on my honeymoon next week, and it's mainly me who looks after the animals. So I've been winding things down.' She smiled again. 'Obviously, Rachel's cats are still here. I don't mind caring for them until we leave for the Maldives.'

'You told me Rachel used to keep her cats here whenever she went away?'

'Yes, that's right. She left them here when she went to see her sister recently. Rachel was lovely. She used to help out at the centre as a volunteer occasionally.'

'Did she help out this week?' Karen asked, watching Brooke closely.

'No.' Brooke's eyes showed a hint of apprehension.

Karen leaned in, lowering her voice as if sharing a secret. 'Did Rachel come to the centre this week and see something? Something you didn't want her to see?'

Brooke's expression turned cold. 'I'm not sure what you mean, Detective.'

'I mean, did Rachel see or hear something suspicious, something that tipped her off?'

'You're really not making any sense,' Brooke said as she leaned against the doorjamb.

Karen narrowed her eyes and made a show of exhaling slowly. 'I think she did, Brooke. I think Rachel came here this week, and she saw or heard something. I think she later realised it had something to do with Tommy's disappearance.'

'What?'

'Did you abduct Tommy? Are you hiding him here?'

Brooke huffed out a laugh. 'You're crazy. Why would I have anything to do with Tommy's disappearance? I like him. I baby-sit him.'

Karen stepped towards Brooke, eyeing the bags at her feet. She was taking a big leap here – relying on her intuition, basing her reasoning solely on the fact Brooke had recommended the castle to Amber. What if Karen had this wrong and Brooke was innocent?

Karen hesitated, wondering if she should back down. But she had come this far.

'What's in those?'

Brooke quickly pulled the bags towards her. 'None of your business.'

Karen's confidence wavered. She still couldn't be sure what Brooke's motive was for taking Tommy. Was she making a huge mistake confronting Brooke like this?

Brooke tensed. Was that a flash of panic in the woman's eyes? Karen had to trust her instincts on this. 'It looks to me like water, crisps, chocolate. Are they for Tommy? Are you keeping him here?'

Karen waited for an answer, watching closely as Brooke's confidence slowly drained away. Karen's anger grew at the thought that Brooke could take Tommy and then cosy up to Amber afterwards. Brooke pretending to comfort Amber when she'd accused Gareth of killing their son, when all the time—

'You've lost the plot,' Brooke said, trying to brazen it out.

'I'm going to search every inch of this place, Brooke, so you may as well come clean. If Tommy's still alive, then it's not going to be so bad for you. Tell me where he is.'

Brooke swallowed hard. Then, in a lightning move, she hurled the carrier bag containing the bottles of water at Karen and made a run for it.

Karen sprinted after her, pounding down the hallway. She came to an abrupt halt when she found a white door blocking her path. She tested the handle. Locked.

She swore under her breath. Brooke had locked her in. She wasn't too worried, glancing around. Backup should be here soon, and she still had her phone, even if the mobile service was poor.

She tried to call Morgan, but the call wouldn't connect. Then she tried the station and had the same problem. There had been a landline back at the reception desk, but the locked door prevented her from getting to that.

Morgan would have received her message and would be here soon anyway. Hopefully Brooke wouldn't be able to get far.

Karen began to search the rooms at the back of the building. The only ones she hadn't already searched. She stopped when she came to one that had a shiny bolt across the door.

It looked new.

'Tommy?' she called out, banging on the door. 'Tommy Burton? Are you in there? It's the police.'

At first, there was no response, but then a reedy voice called back, 'Yes, I'm in here.'

'All right, Tommy. I'm going to come in and get you.'

She slid the bolt across and stepped inside a small room. To the right was a large dog crate. Curled up on a tatty blanket in the centre of the crate was a small figure. Tommy Burton.

The boy's head shot up. His eyes were wide.

'It's okay, I'm here to help,' Karen said gently. She crouched down to appear less threatening. 'I'm a police officer, Tommy. Everything's going to be all right now.'

The boy didn't move, but studied her closely. His cheeks were grubby and streaked with tears. His glasses were bent.

It didn't smell too good in the small room. There was a bucket in the corner of the crate that he'd been using as a toilet.

Karen's face heated with rage when she spotted the small padlock on the door. Her blood boiled as she thought of Brooke locking a little boy in a wire cage like an animal.

'Do you know where the keys are, sweetheart?'

He shook his head.

Karen studied the outside of the crate. It was constructed of thin wire mesh. It didn't look strong.

'Are you hurt?' Karen asked. Then she paused. She could smell something else, not just the contents of the bucket. An acrid scent was wafting down the hallway and into the small room. Smoke.

Her pulse spiked. Had Brooke set the building on fire?

Tommy's eyes widened even more and he began to whimper.

'I need to go and find some tools so I can get you out. I won't be long.'

'No!' Tommy's fingers poked through the wire, trying to grab Karen. 'Don't leave me.'

'I have to. I'll come back. I promise.'

He shouted after her as she ran from the room.

Karen searched frantically for something that could help her free Tommy. Finally, under the sink in the bathroom, she found a screwdriver and some other tools. She hurried back to Tommy and knelt beside the cage. Her fingers felt clumsy and awkward thanks to the adrenaline flooding her system, but she managed to unscrew both small hinges with the stubby screwdriver. The metal groaned and protested as she bent the edges of the wire back, until there was just enough room for Tommy to squeeze through.

The smoke was stronger now. It caught in her throat, making her cough. She shoved the small screwdriver in her pocket.

Tommy grabbed on to Karen's arm. He was struggling to stand up straight. The poor child had probably been cramped in there for days.

He looked dirty but otherwise unhurt.

'Help is on the way, Tommy. But we've got to try and get out of here.'

Tommy clung to her like a lifeline as she helped him along the corridor. She knew Brooke had locked the door, preventing them from getting back to the reception and the entrance. But there would be a rear exit, and there should be a fire escape in a building like this.

They stopped by the room with the cat cages and Karen grabbed Smokey and Marmalade, who hissed, yowled, and scratched at the carriers.

'I'm not exactly enjoying this either,' Karen muttered.

Together they headed to the back of the building, and Karen felt a rush of relief with she saw the fire exit sign. 'Come on, Tommy. We're nearly there.'

But when they reached it, the door didn't open. Karen jiggled the door bar. It was locked. Someone must have secured it from the outside.

There was a small picture window beside it. She looked out. She couldn't see anyone. No Brooke Lewis. No backup. But the smoke would soon overwhelm them.

The window was double-glazed. There was no way to open it, and it wouldn't be easy to break.

'Okay,' Karen said, pulling her arm free of the small boy's grip. 'I'm just going to call for help.'

She pulled out her phone, but she still had no signal.

She shoved the phone back in her pocket and squeezed Tommy's hand reassuringly. 'It's going to be okay. Help is coming. Let's go back the way we came and see if there's another way out.'

They hurried to the end of the hall, Tommy rushing to keep up with Karen's long strides. She could see wisps of smoke unfurling slowly from under the door ahead. The fire must be spreading rapidly on the other side. Brooke must have used an accelerant to get it blazing so quickly.

At least the flames seemed to be contained to the front end of the building for now, so they probably had a little time before the whole structure went up.

Karen pulled off her jacket and told Tommy to take off his hoodie and hold it over his nose and mouth.

'We're going to need to stay low to the ground. The smoke will rise to the top,' she said.

Tommy looked terrified but did as he was told, his small face disappearing behind the fabric of the hoodie. He moved closer to Karen's side, clinging to her.

They stumbled back to the room where Smokey and Marmalade had been kept. Karen put the cat carriers down and then shut the door firmly behind them, but thin tendrils of smoke were already creeping in from underneath. She hastily stuffed her jacket along the base of the door to try to slow the spread of the smoke.

'I don't think we'll be able to stay in here for long, Tommy,' Karen said, her voice tight with tension. 'We're going to have to try and get out through that small window as fast as we can.' She put her hands on his shoulders and looked into his frightened eyes. 'I need you to be really brave. Can you do that for me?'

Tommy nodded, his eyes wide and brimming with tears.

Karen grabbed the cat carriers containing Smokey and Marmalade. Smokey hissed and yowled loudly in protest. 'All right, I know this is scary, but I am trying to save you.'

She took both cats out of their cages, then stacked the carriers on top of one another. She climbed on to the wobbly makeshift tower and reached up on tiptoe to open the window.

She yanked on the handle, but it refused to budge. Of course – it had been painted shut. Great. She took out the small screwdriver and used it to scrape at the paint around the window. She kept trying until finally, with a crack, it opened.

Karen's eyes were streaming from the thickening smoke.

Suddenly, there was a tremendous crash from right outside the room.

'Come on, Tommy,' she said, reaching out for him. 'I need to lift you up here, so you can climb through the window.'

He looked horrified and shook his head. He was backing away when an intense roar came from the burning building and seemed to galvanise him into action. His small frame was surprisingly heavy as Karen heaved him up and through the tiny window.

He crawled through the opening and Karen shoved the protesting cats after him. The cats ran off without a backwards glance. Some gratitude.

Karen leapt up, grasping at the edge of the window. She scraped and scratched, boots slipping against the wall as she struggled to pull herself up.

Finally she managed to prop her upper body on the windowsill, but the truth dawned on her slowly, then all at once. The window was too small. With horror, she realised she was too big to fit through.

'Come on!' Tommy cried from outside, his small hands gripping her arms, trying futilely to tug her through. Tears streamed down his smoke-blackened face.

She looked into his eyes. There was no time. 'Go and get help!' she shouted.

He hesitated, then released her and disappeared from view. She hoped he could find someone. But she knew it was likely too late. Even so, at least the little boy wouldn't have to watch her die in here.

Chapter Thirty-Five

The car tyres screamed in protest as Morgan slammed on the brakes outside the animal centre. Arnie braced himself against the dashboard, his eyes growing wide at the sight in front of them.

Wisps of grey smoke curled up from the roof of the single-storey building.

'That's not good,' Arnie said, reaching for his phone.

Morgan's stomach dropped. Had Karen gone in there alone? Of course she had.

He scanned the parking area, noting two cars: Karen's Honda Civic, and a sleek black Audi that belonged to Brooke Lewis, the shelter owner. Were both women inside the burning building?

As Arnie placed a call, Morgan rushed to grab the fire extinguisher from the boot. Looking back at the animal shelter entrance, he already knew one measly fire extinguisher wouldn't be enough.

Arnie had the phone clamped to his ear, shouting into it. After a moment he hung up. 'Fire service are on their way. I've spoken to Churchill. Orders are to wait. Backup is almost here.'

Morgan gave a terse nod. 'I'm going to look around the perimeter of the building.'

He hurried around the side of the animal centre, scanning the white exterior. There were no windows at the back of the building, which seemed odd. As he reached the rear corner, he noticed a green fire escape door that was padlocked shut from the outside. Who would lock an emergency exit like that? It was a major fire hazard.

Jogging around to the opposite side of the building, Morgan spotted a small open window about six feet up.

And then he saw a child standing near the chain-link fence. Morgan rushed over. Eleven-year-old Tommy Burton stood rigidly, tears streaming down his smudged cheeks.

Morgan crouched beside the sobbing boy. 'Tommy, I'm a police officer. Can you tell me what happened?'

Tommy shook his head, choking back sobs. 'The other police officer got me out through the window, but it was too small for her. She's still inside.'

'Whereabouts?' Morgan asked urgently.

'I . . . I think she's still in the same room.' He pointed at the open window. It was tiny. No wonder Karen hadn't been able to get through. He was surprised Tommy had managed it.

'She said we couldn't get to the exit because Brooke had locked the door,' Tommy said between hiccups.

After Morgan got the details from Tommy about which door was locked, he wasted no time in ushering the child back to where Arnie stood by the car.

Though Morgan understood the importance of adhering to police protocol and waiting for the fire service, the urgency of the situation weighed heavily on him. It was Karen who was trapped inside, after all.

Police protocol dictated he should wait for the fire service to arrive. But this was no ordinary situation – Karen's life was at risk. Morgan was torn, his duty as an officer telling him to follow regulations while his instincts screamed at him to do whatever it took to save Karen.

What would Karen do if their positions were reversed? She would throw caution to the wind and barrel inside without a second thought, determined to help him no matter the personal risk. Morgan knew he had to do the same for her. Just this once, protocol had to come second.

By now a crowd of curious onlookers had gathered on the pavement outside the centre. Morgan blocked them out, going back to the open boot of his car to search for something to help him break through the locked door that had trapped Karen inside.

He shoved aside his torch, a warning triangle and an emergency blanket until his fingers finally curled around the cold steel handle of a long pry bar.

'Perfect,' Morgan said to himself, testing the weight of it in his hands.

He turned to Arnie. 'I'm going in.'

'Are you crazy? I just told you, orders are to wait.'

Morgan raked a hand through his hair, still conflicted. His training told him to wait. The firefighters needed to do their job. They were far more qualified than him. Rushing solo into a burning building was stupid, reckless, idiotic even. He'd give the firefighters more work to do because there'd be two people in the burning building, not just one.

But Karen was in there, and he couldn't just wait around outside.

'I can't just leave her,' he said.

Arnie grabbed his arm. 'Wait a minute, Mr Play-it-by-the-rules. Now this is one occasion when you really should follow the rules, Morgan. Don't be an idiot.'

'She might not have time to wait. What if she's only got minutes left?'

'They'll be here soon, mate, they really will,' Arnie said. 'They've got all the equipment, the breathing gear, they'll get her. She'll be all right.'

'No,' Morgan said firmly, shaking off Arnie's hand.

Gripping the bar like a baseball bat, he turned and sprinted towards the entrance of the burning building. Karen was running out of time, and he was done waiting. He had to get to her before it was too late.

It was insane, he knew that.

He ripped off his jacket and wrapped it around his mouth and nose. The door was open, and the acrid smoke invaded his nostrils immediately.

'Get in. Find her. Get out.' He repeated it like a mantra, but he didn't know the layout of this building. The room Karen had been in, the one with the open window, had been on the right. He vaguely remembered from distant training that open windows and doors were a bad idea in a fire – the oxygen fed the flames.

He just needed to find the locked door. Break it down. Find Karen and get out. Simple.

Morgan, you're an idiot, he thought, but he went ahead, aware of the feeble protection of his makeshift mask.

Visibility wasn't good, so he put a hand along the wall, crouching low and groping blindly.

The wall was warm, which didn't fill him with confidence. He felt like he was in a giant cooker. Where was she? Had she already been overcome by the smoke?

He called out, but there was no answer.

Morgan stumbled into a room lined with pens. There were no animals. And no Karen.

As he walked back into the corridor, he heard a loud crack. It sounded like wood splintering. He pushed the jacket tighter against his face, but he was still getting too much smoke coming through the cloth.

His fingers made contact with a dead end; a door. He fumbled for the handle. It was locked. Was this the one Tommy had told him about? He hoped so.

Morgan temporarily dropped his jacket and used both of his hands to grip the pry bar. He wedged the tapered end into the crack between the door and the frame, right above the lock. Bracing himself, Morgan put all of his weight on to the bar, levering it away from him. The wood cracked and splintered under the force, but the door held fast.

Gritting his teeth, Morgan repositioned the pry bar a few inches lower and tried again. 'Come on, come on,' he growled under his breath as he pushed with all his strength.

After three more attempts, the door began to give way with an ear-splitting crack. Morgan could feel the muscles in his arms trembling from exertion as he pushed with everything he had.

Without his makeshift mask, he was inhaling more of the grey smoke. His lungs and chest tightened in protest.

With a final agonised groan, the wood split and the door lurched open. Morgan dropped the pry bar and pressed the jacket to his mouth again to try to prevent the smoke from getting into his lungs. He squeezed himself through the gap, ignoring the splinters tearing at his clothes.

The smoke wasn't as bad on this side of the building. By breaking the door, had he just made things worse? Maybe Karen had been holed up somewhere without much smoke ingress, and he'd just ruined everything. Wouldn't that be a turnaround. Karen making the logical, sensible decision and him rushing in like a crazed fool.

If he didn't make it, they would probably make a police training video of the incident, using him as an example of everything not to do in a situation like this.

He scanned the hazy corridor.

'Karen!' he shouted desperately. 'Karen, where are you?'

Then he heard her respond. The feeling of relief was indescribable.

He called out again.

And then he saw her. She'd opened the door and was crouched down low.

Her face was grubby with soot, and her eyes were streaming. The tears in Morgan's own eyes were definitely just because of the smoke.

Chapter Thirty-Six

Arnie drummed his fingers anxiously against the steering wheel. Letting Morgan enter the animal centre alone had been a mistake.

Trust Morgan. He'd followed the law to the letter most of his career, and now he'd done something stupid like this. It would probably get him killed.

Arnie watched the building intently. The smoke unfurling from the roof was getting darker. What was happening in there?

He looked at the dashboard clock for the tenth time. Only three minutes had passed since Morgan went inside, but each second felt endless. There was no news, no sirens in the distance. Where were they?

'Come on, you two,' he muttered.

He shifted in the driver's seat and glanced at Tommy Burton sitting huddled and shivering on the back seat of Morgan's car. It wasn't cold, so the poor kid was probably in shock. Arnie had given him a blanket he'd found in Morgan's boot.

'It won't be long now. The ambulance will be here soon. They'll take you to the hospital and you'll be able to see your mum and dad again.'

Tommy managed to nod.

Just then, a young woman appeared at Arnie's window holding out a bottled water and a pack of fruit gums. 'Here you go, sweetie,' she said kindly as she handed them to Tommy. 'Thought you could use something to drink. Get your blood sugar up.'

She turned back to Arnie. 'Is there anything I can get for you? I work at the shop just across the road. I'd be happy to fetch you a cup of tea or coffee.'

Arnie gave her a polite smile and shook his head. Offers of refreshment made a nice change from getting abuse from the general public.

'You're very kind, but no thank you.' There was no way Arnie was going to sip tea while his colleagues burned.

Arnie was just about to gently suggest the kind woman head back across the street for her own safety when a movement near the old storage shed caught his eye. Squinting, he watched as a figure emerged from the shed and crept along the far side of the animal centre. As the person drew closer to the burning building, Arnie realised they were carefully pouring liquid from a red plastic canister on to the ground.

His blood ran cold. It was Brooke Lewis – and she was using an accelerant to feed the flames already consuming the building.

'Can you please keep an eye on the boy for a minute?' Arnie asked the shop worker urgently.

As soon as she nodded, Arnie shot out of the car, adrenaline flooding his system.

'Police! Stop!' he bellowed at the top of his lungs.

Brooke's head jerked up in surprise, her eyes wide with shock at being caught. Arnie saw a flash of panic cross her face. The petrol can clattered to the ground as she took off sprinting, away from the burning building.

'I said stop!' Arnie lumbered after Brooke, who had a significant head start. But she wouldn't get away, not on his watch.

She kept running, getting further ahead with every panicked stride. Arnie cursed under his breath. He was no youngster. But he refused to let her escape, not after what she'd done.

Gritting his teeth, Arnie flew after Brooke with every ounce of energy he had. His leather shoes pounded the cracked concrete. He mentally catalogued and regretted every sausage sandwich, doughnut and pint of beer he'd indulged in over the past few years that had slowed him down.

Brooke led him behind the burning building to the chain-link fence. Arnie watched her easily slide underneath a loose section. He got down on his hands and knees, scrambling awkwardly through the narrow gap. His jacket got snagged on the jagged wire, holding him up for precious seconds as he violently wrenched himself free.

Straightening up, Arnie stumbled into a dingy back alley choked with overgrown weeds and discarded fast-food wrappers. Just ahead, he could see Brooke's silhouette as she hurtled down the claustrophobic alley.

At the end of the narrow passageway there was a brick wall. Somehow, Brooke managed to haul herself over it.

Arnie's heart sank as he watched her disappear from view. There was no way he could scale the wall at his age, or with his weight. He'd lost her for sure.

But no, he wasn't giving up. Breathing hard, Arnie scanned the rows of grubby backyards, searching for any movement. Then he spotted a flash of colour.

Rather than climb the wall, Arnie raced laterally to intercept.

They emerged in front of a row of shops. Brooke made a bee-line for the road, but she had to pause for traffic, which gave Arnie a chance.

He launched himself at Brooke, tackling her around the waist. They crashed heavily to the pavement, skinning hands and knees on the rough ground. She thrashed violently beneath Arnie as he tried to subdue her. A well-aimed knee caught him squarely between the legs, making him groan in agonised surprise.

But Arnie held on, fighting the blooming pain and nausea. He managed to wrench one of Brooke's arms behind her back, pulling her into a submission hold. She continued to squirm, but Arnie had the advantage of size and training.

'You're . . . under . . . arrest,' Arnie panted, still trying to catch his breath after the exhausting chase. He looked up to see a small crowd had gathered, gaping at the dramatic scene.

'Get off her, you brute!'

'Stop it! You're hurting her.'

If only they knew.

'Police,' Arnie said, flashing his ID.

That didn't help. The chorus of angry voices changed to: 'Police brutality!'

He gazed down at the woman who had caused so much suffering. The woman who'd snatched Tommy Burton and possibly murdered Rachel King. Brooke glared back up at him with pure hatred.

He hauled her up, ignoring the shouts from outraged bystanders. 'You'd better pray my friends walk out of that building unhurt,' Arnie growled, 'or I promise you'll regret it.'

Sirens sounded in the distance.

The approaching emergency vehicles should have been a relief, but Arnie could only worry it was too late for Karen and Morgan.

By the time they got back to the car, backup was arriving on the scene. But he couldn't see Karen or Morgan. His gut churned with anxiety.

Come on, he thought desperately, *don't let me lose you both.*

Finally, just as Arnie was slapping cuffs on Brooke, he saw them. Karen and Morgan were kneeling on the concrete, coughing their guts up.

Arnie laughed in relief as he stood guard over Brooke. 'It looks like they're going to be okay.'

Brooke scowled and spat at him.

'Aren't you a charmer?' Arnie commented dryly.

He thanked the woman who'd kept an eye on Tommy, then poked his head in the car. 'You okay, lad?'

Tommy nodded. He'd stopped shivering. And curled up in his lap, purring contentedly, was a marmalade cat.

The smell of disinfectant made Karen's nose wrinkle as the nurse dabbed at a graze on her cheek. She winced, resisting the urge to pull away.

'I'm almost done,' the stern-faced nurse said, clutching Karen's chin tightly.

She longed to be out of the hospital cubicle and back home, so that she could have a hot shower and scrub away the smell of smoke.

Arnie sat in a chair next to Karen's bed. 'I'm pretty sure I'm damaged for life,' he said. 'She got me right in the crown jewels.'

'Sounds painful,' Karen commented.

'As a lady, you have no concept of the pure agony I was in. I might never be right again.'

Karen laughed, but the nurse looked decidedly unimpressed with Arnie's antics.

Morgan was in the next cubicle. He caught Karen's eye and gave an amused shake of his head.

Karen winced again as the nurse dabbed at a particularly tender spot on her temple.

Mike appeared at the end of the emergency ward, his face creased with concern as he looked for Karen. His shoulders sagged in relief when he spotted her.

'Are you all right?' he asked, as he walked over and embraced her. 'Churchill called me and told me what happened. He said you rushed into the flames. It sounded very dramatic.'

She was quick to reassure Mike. 'I'm fine. I didn't see any flames, only smoke. We're just waiting to get the all-clear. I feel okay, though, just a little singed around the edges.'

Mike shook his head. 'I think that phone call aged me ten years.'

When the nurse told Karen she was all done and moved away, Mike leaned over and pressed a kiss to Karen's forehead. 'I'm so relieved you're all right.'

'Ugh, get a room, you two,' Arnie said. 'Some of us are suffering real injuries.'

'Don't mind him – he didn't breathe in any smoke, so he's feeling left out,' Morgan said, grinning at the look of outrage on Arnie's face.

'I'll have you know, I'm the one who had to chase down and capture the suspect while these two' – he waved a hand at Karen and Morgan – 'decided to mess about in a burning building.'

'Sounds like you all had a pretty hairy encounter,' Mike said.

'*And* I had to get the cat,' Arnie added.

'The cat?' Mike looked confused.

'Yes. Two cats really. The marmalade one was fine. It got into the car on its own. But the grey one really gave me the run-around. Hid under the car. It took me ages to encourage it out.'

'Arnie did very well to wrangle the cats, but it was Karen who got the boy out in time,' Morgan said.

Mike gave Karen's hand a squeeze. 'I'm glad it worked out, but try not to scare me like that again. Not sure I can take it.'

A doctor approached and addressed Karen and Morgan. 'I'm pleased to tell you both that your lung function tests are normal. So you're all clear to be discharged. Do keep an eye on that cough though, and if the wheezing worsens, come back straightaway.'

Karen nodded, resisting the urge to cough again. Her throat still felt raw. 'Will do. Thank you, Doctor. How is the little boy who was brought in with us? Tommy Burton?'

'He's on the children's ward with his mother. He has a few minor bumps and bruises, but the smoke inhalation wasn't as severe as we'd feared. I'd say he got out just in time.'

Karen exhaled slowly, feeling some of the tension drain away. 'That's good news.'

The doctor smiled. 'I think they'll keep him in overnight for observation. As he's only a child, we like to play it safe.'

Karen decided to pay Tommy a visit after they were discharged. The others waited in the hospital cafe.

Pushing through the heavy double doors, Karen entered the children's ward. It was decorated with bright murals and cheery decorations.

A nurse showed Karen to Tommy's private room. He was sitting up in bed and his mother was perched anxiously at his side.

Tommy smiled when he saw Karen. 'Mum, this is the police officer who saved me.'

Karen chatted to Tommy for a bit, marvelling at how upbeat he seemed, then turned to Amber, whose eyes were red from crying.

'Has Tommy told you everything that happened?' Karen asked.

Amber nodded, looking distraught. 'I can't believe it was Brooke. I trusted her. She tricked Tommy and told him I'd been called into work, and she needed to take him home to look after him until I got back. She'd looked after him before, so Tommy had no reason to think it was a lie.'

Amber reached out to clutch Tommy's hand, as if she was afraid he'd disappear again.

'I tried to get away,' Tommy said. 'I knew something was weird when Brooke took me to that animal place, but she forced me into that room and into the cage. She said she was teaching me a lesson.' Tommy looked down at the white sheets, shame-faced. 'She was having an affair with the vet that used to help her at the animal centre. I recorded them kissing on my phone.' He shot a look at his mother.

Amber gave him an encouraging nod. 'You have to tell the police officer everything, Tommy.'

Tommy fidgeted, not making eye contact. 'I watched a pro-gramme where a kid blackmailed his sister and got money and stuff from her. I thought I could do the same thing.' He looked up at Karen. 'So I told Brooke I would show Sam the video unless she gave me some money.'

Despite his apparently mature scheming, now, in the hospital bed, he looked like a typical eleven-year-old boy. A mop of tangled hair hung over his face as he bowed his head. His skinny arms poked out of the child-sized hospital gown, and an IV line was taped to the back of his small hand. Karen felt a pang of sympathy. Despite his precocious intelligence, he was still just a child – albeit one who had made some very big mistakes.

'What happened then, Tommy?' Karen prompted.

'It just got out of control,' Tommy said miserably. 'Dad paid, Brooke paid, so I decided to try my teacher and Jack Foster. She told me off in class once, and he was always mean to me so . . .' He shrugged. 'I didn't mean for it to go so far.'

'Thank you for being honest, Tommy. But steer clear of black-mail in the future. It's against the law.'

'I've learned my lesson,' he mumbled sheepishly, burrowing down into the sheets.

Karen spent a little more time with them, and then, confident that Tommy was recovering well, she left the ward. Further questions for Tommy could wait until later.

◆ ◆ ◆

She met the others at the cafe, and they left the hospital together. Outside, Karen took a deep breath of fresh air. They made their way towards the car park, but as they neared the ambulance bay, a sudden commotion drew their attention.

The sliding doors into the building burst open and two large security guards forcibly dragged out an angry man. He was unsuccessfully trying to fight them while unleashing a torrent of abuse.

'Get your filthy hands off me!' the man screamed, his red face contorted in rage. He strained against the guards' grip, but they held him tightly.

Gareth Burton. Tommy's father. She felt a flash of anger just seeing him there.

Karen changed direction, heading straight for the enraged man.

'I suggest you calm down, Mr Burton, unless you'd like to be arrested again,' she said sharply when she reached him.

Burton's bloodshot eyes flashed with contempt. 'You've got no authority over me!' He tried again to jerk free of the guards.

Karen stood firm, unfazed. 'You need to leave voluntarily before this gets much uglier for you.' She paused, then added, 'Here's some advice. If you want a relationship with your son, you'd better clean up your act fast.'

Burton glared at her a moment longer before grunting, 'Fine, I'm going.'

The security guards cautiously released their grip as he backed away a few steps. But they remained poised to grab him again if needed.

Satisfied she'd made her point, Karen turned and walked back to where Morgan, Arnie and Mike waited.

'What a lovely bloke,' Arnie remarked sarcastically as Burton gave him the finger.

Karen took one last look back at Burton. His shoulders were slumped in defeat as he skulked away across the car park alone. Karen hoped her words would motivate him to change for Tommy's sake. Only time would tell if he was capable of being a decent father.

Karen felt completely drained of energy as she and the others piled into Mike's car to finally head home. The adrenaline had faded from her system, and she sank gratefully into the passenger seat, every muscle aching.

As Mike pulled on to Greetwell Road, Karen stared silently out of the window. Houses passed by in a blur, but all she could see were visions from the fire flashing through her mind on a loop. The smoke choking her lungs, the fear as the heat started to rise, and Tommy's terrified sobs as she pushed him through the small window. It had been a close call.

She turned and saw Arnie lolling back with his eyes closed. Morgan's gaze met hers. In his eyes, she could see the same bone-deep weariness she felt. But also relief that they'd all made it.

Karen managed a small, tired smile. Right now, she wanted nothing more than to go home and take a long shower. She knew the coming hours and days would be busy with interviews and paperwork as they built a case against Brooke Lewis. But for now, despite being covered in soot stains and reeking of smoke, Karen was simply grateful to be going home.

Chapter Thirty-Seven

Karen stared at the petite woman sitting across from her. Brooke Lewis, with her delicate features and demure manner, appeared more suited for Sunday church than a police interview room. But Karen knew better than to be swayed by appearances.

'Let's go through this again, Ms Lewis,' Karen said. 'You claim to have no knowledge about how Tommy Burton came to be locked in a dog cage at the animal centre you run. You say you had no involvement whatsoever in his imprisonment.'

Brooke turned her large, doe-like eyes on Karen. 'That's absolutely right,' she replied in a syrupy voice. 'The first I heard of poor Tommy going missing was when Rachel sent me a WhatsApp message.' She shook her head. 'I simply can't believe Tommy was there the whole time. It was such a shock.'

Karen maintained an impassive mask, though she would have liked nothing more than to tell this two-faced actress exactly what she thought of her performance.

'Then perhaps you can explain this image from your security cameras at the animal centre,' Karen said evenly, sliding a glossy photograph across the tabletop. The photo clearly depicted Brooke forcefully dragging a reluctant Tommy through the front door of the centre, her face screwed up in determination, fingers digging into the boy's arm in a vice-like grip.

Brooke stared down at the damning evidence, lips parting in surprise. She hadn't been quite as careful in covering her tracks as she'd thought. It would have been easy enough for her to wipe the security footage, but she'd been so arrogantly confident that she wouldn't get caught.

Brooke quickly composed herself, waving a dismissive hand. 'Oh, that must be from a few months ago. I often looked after Tommy, and he came to the animal centre frequently with me.'

Karen's eyes narrowed. 'The recordings are clearly dated and time-stamped. This was the same afternoon Tommy went missing.'

Brooke's polite facade tightened, annoyance flickering across her delicate features. 'All right, well . . . I suppose I should really tell you the whole truth.'

Karen and Morgan exchanged a sceptical look but remained silent, waiting for whatever web of lies Brooke was about to spin.

'You see, I happened to be at Tattershall Castle that day,' Brooke began brightly. 'I was there because I wanted to see the birds of prey show. Anyway, Amber had some sort of work emergency come up unexpectedly. She asked me to take Tommy home with me for the afternoon to help her out.'

'No, she didn't, Brooke,' Karen interjected sharply, her patience fraying. 'We've already spoken with Amber, and she confirms that never happened. Do you really think we're that gullible?'

Brooke tutted. 'It was just an innocent mix-up.'

'Can you *please* tell us the truth?' Morgan said, exasperated.

Brooke huffed out an exaggerated sigh. 'Oh, all right. If you absolutely must know the full story . . . well, the truth is that Gareth – Tommy's father – was abusive. I was very worried about Tommy's welfare, so I decided he would be better off without his dreadful parents for a while. I took him to the animal centre, where I knew he'd be safe.'

Morgan slid another photograph across the table, this one depicting the dark bruises circling Brooke's slender wrist. Self-consciously, she covered the injury with her other hand, rubbing it as if that would make it disappear.

'I'm guessing this was from Tommy fighting back against your . . . help,' Morgan remarked dryly.

Brooke indignantly shoved up her sleeve, displaying the bruise. 'Tommy is the one who hurt me, not the other way around. He threw an epic tantrum, tried to hit and kick me to get away.'

'Yet you still managed to physically overpower him and shove him into that cage,' Karen said.

At the blunt accusation, Brooke dropped all pretence of playing the victim. She leaned back scornfully in her chair, hostility oozing from every pore. 'I'm done talking to you. You can't prove a thing.'

But they were finally getting closer to the truth. This woman was clearly unbalanced, believing her own delusions.

'You imprisoned an eleven-year-old child in a dog crate for days,' Karen said.

Brooke sat up straight, colour rising in her cheeks. 'It was a very large crate,' she said defensively. 'And I made sure he had food and water. I only needed him out of my way temporarily.'

'Out of your way for what purpose?' Morgan asked. 'Was he blackmailing you?'

Brooke chewed her lip, debating how to respond. Finally, she sighed. 'Yes, alright. He had a video of . . . an indiscretion. I wasn't about to let him ruin my future over one foolish mistake.'

'This indiscretion . . . it was an affair, correct?' Karen asked.

Brooke gave an impatient huff, drumming her nails against the tabletop. 'I had a brief fling with the veterinarian who helped out at the animal centre. But it meant nothing. I love my fiancé, Sam.'

'So you wanted Tommy out of the way until after your wedding to Sam Tranmere,' Karen said.

'Why shouldn't I protect my future with the man I love from being destroyed by some snotty-nosed brat?' Brooke shot back angrily.

Karen studied her closely. 'Or maybe it wasn't just about love. Perhaps you also had your eye on the sizeable inheritance Sam had recently come into?'

A slow, sinister smile curled Brooke's lips. 'Well, aren't you the clever detective?'

Revulsion washed over Karen. This woman was utterly ruthless, concerned only with her own ambitions.

'I invested significant time cultivating my relationship with Sam,' Brooke said. 'It wasn't easy getting that layabout to propose. But once we're married, I'll make sure he puts his new money to good use.'

'I don't think you'll be getting married anytime soon, Brooke,' Karen said evenly. 'You're going to prison for a long time.'

Brooke pretended to inspect her manicured nails, bored with the entire interview. 'I'll be out in a few short years. I'll deny everything of course. And I'm sure Sam will stand by me.' She fixed Karen with an insolent, taunting look. 'You don't have any real evidence or witnesses. It's my word against a juvenile-delinquent blackmailer. Who's going to believe him?'

But Karen remained calm and steady. 'Rachel scratched you during the struggle, didn't she? You held her underwater, but she fought back. We found traces of skin cells and blood under her nails. We're just waiting for the DNA results to come back for confirmation, but we'll get them. It's over, Brooke. You may as well come clean.'

Brooke sat back, and Karen watched the dawning realisation creep over the woman's face as she accepted the fact she'd been caught.

Karen opened the case file and withdrew one final damning piece of evidence – a photo of the small syringes and glass vial of xylazine found during the search. Fortunately, they had been found intact after the fire service managed to put out the blaze.

'These were found at the animal centre,' Karen said. 'Did you steal them from Dr Howes, the vet you were having an affair with? Or did he give them to you? Were you planning to use them to silence an inconvenient child witness permanently?'

For the first time, Brooke's arrogance wavered. 'No, of course not,' she said unconvincingly, her face draining of colour.

'You told us you were at a funeral on the day Tommy was abducted. But that wasn't true, was it?' Morgan asked.

'I was.'

'But you left early? Without Sam?'

She shrugged. 'So what? I had a legitimate reason. I had to get back to the animal centre. Rachel needed to pick up her cats.'

'Don't you have other staff?' Morgan asked.

'Yes, but they weren't available.'

'I'll tell you what I think happened,' Morgan said, resting his forearms on the table and leaning in. 'You didn't want any other staff around because you didn't want anyone to know what you were up to. I think you left just after the funeral, telling Sam you needed to take care of business at the centre, but in fact you went to Tattershall Castle and abducted Tommy Burton. Then you took Tommy back to the centre. But when Rachel came to collect her pets, she heard or saw something. What happened? Did she arrive earlier than you were expecting?'

Brooke blinked rapidly, shaking her head.

'You killed Rachel King because she suspected you,' Karen said bluntly.

'You think you're so clever. But you're wrong. Rachel didn't hear a thing when she came to pick up her cats.' Brooke flattened her palms on the table, a sheen of sweat glistening on her skin. 'And you can't prove anything,' she insisted through gritted teeth.

Karen held her gaze steadily. 'We can and we will. When the DNA test results come back, we'll have definitive proof; they found traces of DNA on the blue bear at the abduction scene, and I'm certain it will match yours.' Karen smiled. 'And your car was at Tattershall Castle the day Tommy was taken. All that, plus Tommy's account of events, has given us a very strong case against you.'

Brooke slumped back in her chair, the defiance seeming to drain from her body. 'All right, maybe we did argue when Rachel accused me of hiding Tommy. She said she heard a child shouting when she came by to pick up a cat toy she'd left at the centre. But I didn't hurt her, I swear it! When I left, she was still very much alive.'

'Nice try,' Karen said.

Brooke's chest began to rapidly rise and fall. Her eyes grew wild, like a trapped animal's. 'Okay, yes, she suspected me of taking Tommy, but I convinced her she was wrong. I told her it wasn't Tommy, just a voice on the radio. She believed me. I never laid a finger on Rachel.'

'You're lying, Brooke,' Karen said with absolute certainty. 'The truth is you murdered Rachel to keep her quiet. And I believe you intended to kill Tommy too, once the urgency of the search had died down. You couldn't let him go free to talk about what he'd witnessed.'

Utterly defeated, Brooke began to tremble. Karen watched the ugly truth creep over the woman's face – she knew she'd been caught at last.

Given enough time after getting rid of Tommy, Brooke likely had another murder planned.

'Tell me . . . after marrying Sam Tranmere, how long did you intend to let him live?' Karen asked coldly. 'Were you impatient to get your hands on all the inheritance money? Why settle for half when you could have it all to yourself?'

Brooke glared at her with pure hatred. In that look, Karen had the confirmation she needed. This woman was a ruthless predator who would have killed again and again to get what she wanted.

Chapter Thirty-Eight

Morgan sat at his desk reviewing the notes from Brooke Lewis's interview, the pages spread out haphazardly in front of him. It was looking like they had a strong case against her. A sharp rap at the door drew his attention away from the files.

'Sorry to interrupt, sir,' DC Farzana Shah said, poking her head in, 'but there's someone here asking to speak with you. Sam Tranmere.'

Morgan straightened in his chair, surprised. After the events of the last couple of days, he could only imagine the shock Sam must be feeling. Did Sam want to accuse Morgan of unfairly targeting Brooke? He'd heard from the others at the station that Sam had shown up earlier, demanding they release Brooke immediately, insisting it had all been some terrible mistake.

Was Sam now here to try to convince Morgan that Brooke was innocent?

'Thank you, send him in,' Morgan said.

He entered the office. Despite Sam being almost thirty years old now, Morgan could still see the gangly teenager in him – the boy who'd idolised his father.

The intervening years had filled out Sam's once wiry frame, and he was now tall and broad-shouldered, yet today he slouched with his hands jammed in the pockets of his faded jeans. Sam's gaze remained fixed on the floor, and when he finally glanced up at Morgan briefly, his eyes held a weary, wounded look.

'Have a seat, Sam,' Morgan said, with a small wave towards the chair across from his desk.

Sam sank heavily into the seat. Crossing his arms over his chest, he radiated discomfort.

It looked like Morgan would need to start the conversation, since Sam hadn't uttered a word.

'Good to see you, Sam. What can I do for you today?'

Fidgeting in the chair, and straightening his jeans, Sam opened his mouth several times only to close it again, seemingly at a loss for where or how to start.

Morgan resisted the urge to press him, instead giving Sam time to gather his thoughts.

Finally, with one hand covering his eyes, Sam said, 'It's about Brooke.' Dropping his hand, he looked up and met Morgan's gaze. 'They're telling me she only wanted to marry me for my grandmother's money, and she kidnapped Tommy to stop him telling me she was having an affair. And that she . . . she killed Rachel King?' Sam's voice had grown hoarse, and he paused before asking quietly, 'Is it true? Is she really a murderer?'

Morgan heard the desperate plea in Sam's question. He wanted – *needed* – Morgan to contradict the horrible accusations against his fiancée.

There wasn't an easy way to handle this that would make Sam feel better, so Morgan settled on the direct approach. 'I'm afraid it is true. We have strong evidence against her. I'm sorry you had to find out this way, Sam. It must have come as a shock.'

That should win Morgan some kind of prize for understatement of the year.

As if to drive home his inadequacy in situations like this, Morgan realised he hadn't even offered Sam a cup of tea. How very un-British of him. Tea and sympathy might not be in Morgan's wheelhouse, but he felt desperately sorry for Sam.

Staring down at his hands, Sam nodded numbly. To Morgan, he suddenly looked like the vulnerable boy of fourteen again, awkward and lost.

'I can't believe it,' Sam said, almost to himself. He lifted his head, brow creased. 'She really killed Rachel?'

Morgan hesitated, wrestling over how many gruesome details to provide, but Sam had a right to the facts, however brutal. 'We think so. We've got solid forensic evidence.'

'What does that even mean?'

Morgan inhaled slowly. This next part would be difficult for Sam to hear. 'We found Brooke's skin cells beneath Rachel's fingernails. It suggests Rachel fought back while Brooke held her under the water.'

Sam's face drained of colour, and for a moment Morgan thought he might actually be sick.

'Why?' Sam asked.

'We believe Rachel had grown suspicious of Brooke in regards to Tommy's disappearance. We think that when Rachel dropped by the centre, she heard something that alerted her to the fact Tommy was hidden there. Brooke wanted to silence her before she could voice her suspicions.'

'But why didn't Rachel say something sooner if she thought something was wrong?' Sam asked hoarsely.

'I don't know for certain,' Morgan admitted. 'Perhaps she was unsure at first, lacking solid proof. Maybe she believed Brooke's excuse that the noises Rachel heard were from a radio. But Brooke wasn't willing to risk being exposed.'

When Sam didn't respond, Morgan decided to ask a question of his own. 'Did you tell her about the blue bears from the Donaldson case?'

Sam looked up and grimaced. 'Yes. I know I shouldn't have. I was telling her about Dad – boasting, I suppose. She was so interested. I should have guessed that wasn't normal.' He made a strangled noise, halfway between a groan and a sob, dropping his head into his hands. 'I was going to marry her, and she . . .' He trailed off, unable to continue.

'Don't blame yourself,' Morgan said gruffly. 'She fooled everyone. She kept all this hidden remarkably well.' He felt extremely awkward. Was he supposed to comfort Sam? Pat him on the back, perhaps?

Several moments of silence passed before Sam spoke again. 'There's something else. I'm not sure I should tell you this . . .'

'If you have information that will help the case against Brooke, I'd urge you to do so. You don't owe her any loyalty.'

'Brooke's old boyfriend contacted me when we first started dating.'

'What did he say?'

Sam gripped his hands together, clearly struggling. 'He told me I should dump her. That she was evil. I thought he was just being a jealous ex-boyfriend. A sore loser.' He bit his lower lip and stared down at the floor. 'But now I'm not so sure.'

Morgan waited, nodding encouragingly.

'He was rambling, not making much sense. He insisted she was dangerous. He said . . . that she'd got him to take out a life insurance policy and then tried to poison him.' Sam looked up. 'He said she used anti-freeze.'

Morgan tried to hide his shock. 'Do you have this man's name or contact details?'

Sam pulled out his mobile. 'I saved the number. I guess part of me was never really sure. His name is Oliver Wells.'

Morgan took down the name and number, hoping Oliver Wells could provide information to strengthen their evidence against Brooke. 'Thank you, Sam. I know this isn't easy.'

Sam suddenly looked up sharply. 'The blue bear . . . do you think she was trying to frame me? She must have wanted the police to connect the two cases.'

'Honestly, I'm not sure. I think she used it as a distraction, a way to muddy the waters.'

'Good job I didn't follow Dad's career path. Some detective I'd have made, eh? I couldn't even spot the fact my own fiancée is a homicidal maniac.'

'Sam, she took elaborate steps specifically to deceive you.'

Sam just nodded again, seeming to retreat into himself. Morgan wished he was better at this. Karen would make it look easy. Maybe he could get her in here. Let her comfort Sam. But, no, that was a cop-out. Sam had come here to see Morgan, even if he was terrible at this sort of thing.

He didn't have the right words to ease the pain Sam was experiencing, so instead, Morgan opted for his default setting: keeping his mouth shut and being a patient ear, letting Sam talk as he processed the brutal betrayal.

Morgan sat quietly with Sam as the young man unloaded the jumble of thoughts swirling through his head.

After a while, Sam took a deep, shuddering breath and scrubbed his hands over his face before offering Morgan a weak smile. 'Thank you,' he said. 'I appreciate you being straight with me.'

'Of course.'

As Sam slowly rose, some of the tension seemed to leave his broad shoulders. 'One good thing has come out of this mess,' he said. 'It's brought my old man and me back together again.'

Morgan raised an eyebrow. 'Glad to hear it.'

Sam shrugged. 'We've still got a mountain of issues left to sort through, but it's a start.' Then he hesitated briefly before blurting out, 'Look, I know you and Dad probably see me as some dead-beat, just frittering away my inheritance.' Sam met Morgan's gaze defiantly. 'But the truth is, I've actually made something of myself. I started designing video games, and I just sold the latest one for six figures.' Sam lifted his chin proudly. 'I'm not the waste of space my dad makes me out to be. I've got a new career that I'm really good at.'

'I'm sure your dad is proud of you.'

Sam smiled. 'I thought I might invite Tommy to work on some game development with me. If you think that would be okay? I feel so guilty I didn't see what was happening right under my nose.'

'You aren't the guilty party, Sam, but if it's all right with Amber, I think it's a great idea to have Tommy channel his intelligence into something productive.'

In Morgan's opinion, the blackmail scheme had likely stemmed from the boy feeling powerless. Ostracised at school for being different and preferring computers and books to people, and intimidated by his father at home, it wasn't hard to see why Tommy had acted badly. Developing a game with Sam would benefit them both. It would be a creative outlet for Tommy and would hopefully allow Sam to ease some of the guilt he felt for not realising what Brooke had been up to. Maybe working alongside Sam, designing a virtual world where he made the rules, would allow Tommy to gain confidence and keep him on the right path.

Morgan had underestimated Sam. A lot of people had. He'd been written off as a trust fund kid who would bum around for the rest of his life, when, in fact, he'd used his skills and talent to make a career out of something he loved.

Morgan stood and extended a hand. 'It was good seeing you again, Sam. I'm sorry it had to be under these circumstances. Take care of yourself.'

Sam shook Morgan's hand firmly. 'Thank you.'

Morgan walked Sam to the front of the station. Glancing outside, he spotted Tranmere leaning against the side of his car, looking anxious. But his face transformed when Sam emerged, and he strode quickly forward to envelop his son in a fierce, crushing hug.

Morgan observed a ripple of emotions play across Tranmere's craggy features – relief, joy, regret. The older man clearly loved his son, and it seemed Sam was ready to meet his father halfway. Morgan hoped they could repair their relationship.

As Sam climbed into his own car to leave, Tranmere approached Morgan, smiling. 'Thank you for everything,' he said, pressing a hand to his mouth briefly before continuing. 'If not for your diligence on this case . . .' He trailed off, unable to give voice to his unspoken thoughts.

But Morgan understood. Sam had come perilously close to ending up married to Brooke Lewis, a cold-blooded killer. It was likely she would not have stopped her murderous schemes with the death of Rachel King, but gone on to despatch Tommy, and possibly even Sam himself.

Tranmere gripped Morgan's shoulder. 'I know there's friction between us now, but I hope in time you might find it in you to forgive an old fool.' His eyes searched Morgan's face. 'I acted dishonestly, but from the heart. Surely you understand that?'

However misguided Tranmere's past actions had been, Morgan accepted they came from a desire to protect his family.

'It's in the past. I've forgotten it already.' It would be out of Morgan's hands if an investigation was opened into Tranmere's handling of the Donaldson case. But the last thing Morgan wanted was for the case to be re-examined. The thought of Donaldson exploiting the fact Tranmere had tampered with a crime scene report filled him with dread.

Tranmere smiled and gave him a knowing look. 'It must be easier to see things from my point of view now.'

Morgan frowned. 'What do you mean?'

'Word around the station is that you ran into a burning building to save a colleague, completely disregarding procedure. It seems you finally found a reason to bend the rules a bit yourself.'

Morgan stiffened. You couldn't escape station gossip. 'Word travels fast.'

Tranmere chuckled. 'There's the Morgan I remember. A big old softie at heart.'

At this, Morgan bristled. First Karen had called him a *robot*; now, according to Tranmere, he was a *softie*. He wasn't sure he liked either description. But he certainly didn't want Tranmere going around telling everyone he was soft.

'There were extenuating circumstances,' Morgan said.

Tranmere's eyes twinkled. 'I'm sure there were.'

Morgan huffed, trying to look stern, but felt his lips twitching. Tranmere knew him too well, the smug so-and-so. Morgan would never admit it to anyone, but it had felt good to throw the rulebook out the window for once. Still, he had a reputation as a hardened, by-the-books detective to maintain.

'Just don't go spreading rumours. I've got an image to uphold.'

Tranmere grinned and mimed zipping his lips. 'Wouldn't dream of it. Thanks again, Morgan. You're one of the good ones.'

With a final handshake, the two men parted ways, and Morgan watched the Tranmeres drive off.

He sighed. Tranmere's teasing words echoed in his mind, bringing the hint of a smile to Morgan's face. *Old softie?* Morgan shook his head. That was definitely worse than a robot.

Chapter Thirty-Nine

Karen set the cat carriers down with a clunk, eliciting an indignant yowl from one of the cats inside. Across the steel lab counter, Tim Farthing eyed the container dubiously.

'You cannot be serious,' he said. 'You want me to do what?'

Karen smiled. 'I need you to get DNA samples from these cats. Specifically, I need you to scrape under their claws for any skin cells or blood residue that may be caught there.'

Tim's eyebrows shot up towards his receding hairline. 'And why exactly am I acting as a feline manicurist?'

'We have reason to believe these cats may have scratched Brooke Lewis,' Karen explained patiently. 'If we can match her DNA to any biological traces caught beneath their claws, it will help the case against her.'

Comprehension slowly dawned on Tim's round face, swiftly followed by undisguised disdain. 'Brilliant plan, except Brooke will just claim she sustained those scratches while getting the little beasts into their carriers, since *you* invited her to help us after Rachel King's murder.'

In hindsight, that had been a mistake. Karen conceded his point with a slight nod. 'True, but we still need the samples collected and analysed.'

With a huff, he turned and began solemnly assembling the necessary supplies – tiny containers, plastic utensils, tweezers and gloves. All the while muttering under his breath about the indignities of his job.

Karen bit back an amused smile. She knew Tim secretly relished forensic challenges, though he would rather suffer a thousand deaths than openly admit it. His prickly personality was grating at times, but he was good at his job. Despite his constant moaning.

Donning blue nitrile gloves with an exaggerated, martyred sigh, Tim gingerly unlatched the first cat carrier door.

'Good grief!' Tim recoiled as the grey cat took an angry swipe at his arm, just missing the fabric of his lab coat. He turned to Karen with thinly veiled irritation. 'You might have warned me they were psychotic.'

Karen raised her hands apologetically. 'I thought you'd remember. You were the one demanding their removal from the crime scene, after all.'

The puffed-up grey cat had taken refuge at the back of the carrier, safely out of reach. But the marmalade cat perched warily at the front of its box.

Eyeing the cats sourly, Tim selected a plastic scraper. 'Right then. Best get this over with quickly before they scratch me to ribbons.'

He began to cautiously approach the marmalade cat. It hissed out a warning, taking an angry swipe that just barely missed the hand Tim prudently yanked back in time. He recoiled with a growled curse.

Karen couldn't suppress an amused chuckle, earning herself a sharp scowl from Tim.

'Having some trouble there, Dr Doolittle?' she asked, trying not to laugh.

'You're enjoying this far too much,' Tim said, though Karen thought she caught a hint of humour in his eyes. 'Is this an elaborate form of retaliation?'

'Of course not,' Karen replied, plastering on her most innocent expression. 'We need to be extremely thorough. You know that. Got to dot those I's and cross those T's.'

Tim let out a disbelieving snort at this, clearly unconvinced of her motives. But he turned his attention back to the cat, resuming his cautious approach.

Karen pretended to focus on a pile of lab reports, listening with amusement to Tim's inventive cursing and cajoling.

'Come here, you devil . . . hold still!' There was a crash, a thud, and an indignant feline shriek. Karen hid her smirk behind a case file, keeping up the charade that she wasn't closely following the struggle occurring in front of her.

It fell quiet after a few minutes, and Karen chanced a discreet glance. Tim had managed to partially wrap the marmalade cat in lab blue roll, immobilizing it long enough to scrape beneath its claws. Karen had to grudgingly give him credit for an effective strategy.

She watched as Tim carefully worked on each claw in turn, and deposited samples into neatly labelled tiny containers. When Tim abruptly glanced up, catching her studying him, she hastily ducked behind the case file again.

A moment later, Tim cleared his throat. 'One set collected,' he announced. 'Now to catch the slippery grey rascal.'

Risking another discreet glance over the folder, Karen saw that Tim had a scowl on his face as he peered into the carrier sheltering the grey cat. As a peace offering for her earlier joking, she fished a bag of cat treats out of her pocket and handed it over to the glowering technician. Tim accepted the treats grudgingly, and cautiously placed one beside the cat.

It worked like a charm. Seconds later, the grey cat was purring contentedly as Tim got to work.

'You could have told me about those treats earlier,' Tim grumbled.

'Where would the fun be in that?'

She caught the barest upward lift of the corners of his lips before he arranged his expression back into a scowl.

When Tim was finished, and Karen approached to help him get the cats back in their carriers, he asked, 'What happens to them now?'

'Rachel's sister is taking them in. She's picking them up in an hour.'

'I could always look after them until she gets here, if you're busy?' he offered.

Karen hadn't had Tim down as a cat fan, and she was taken aback by the offer. She asked him if he'd like her to leave them. He shrugged nonchalantly, but Karen could tell he'd warmed to the cats.

Karen had to bite her lip to keep from grinning. 'I suppose it couldn't hurt.'

As she made her way over to the door, she heard the treat bag rustle.

'Don't give them too many treats,' she warned. 'They have a long journey ahead.'

Tim guiltily shoved the treat bag behind his back. 'Of course I won't. I'm not sure they deserve any treats anyway, ferocious little beasts.'

Karen gave him a knowing smile. 'Mm-hmm. Sure.' Those cats had Tim wrapped around their claws already.

'Do let me know if you require more . . . interesting sample-collecting,' Tim called after her as she departed. 'Wrangling psychotic cats really livens up my day.'

Pausing at the door, Karen glanced back over her shoulder. 'I can tell.'

Tim gave a derisive snort, and Karen headed out the door still grinning.

◆ ◆ ◆

Superintendent Murray's voice cut through the bustling open-plan office. 'I want to congratulate you all for recovering Tommy Burton safe and sound.'

In the background, DCI Churchill was practically buzzing with excitement, which made Karen wonder what he was up to.

'Yes, well done, everyone,' he said. 'Now, let's head outside. The *Lincolnite* is sending a photographer to capture this celebratory moment.'

Karen suppressed a groan as Churchill herded them out of the office. Typical Churchill, seizing any opportunity for positive press.

They assembled outside on the steps, in front of the waiting photographer.

'Let's have the superintendent in the centre,' the photographer said, waving her over.

Murray obliged, standing on the top step. Churchill hurried the detectives into place. 'Let's get everyone together.'

They were awkwardly shuffling into formation next to the super when a car pulled up. Tommy Burton emerged, followed by his mother.

Churchill ushered them over. 'What a great image this will make. Probably front-page stuff.'

The photographer merely grunted.

Tommy grinned as he trotted up the steps. Amber shot Karen a look of amused commiseration.

Churchill arranged them in a row, stepping back critically. 'Superintendent centre, mother and son beside . . . hmm, Karen, stand just there please.'

Karen shifted into position, flanked by Morgan and Arnie. Farzana and Rick had broken out into giggles on the step behind them. She noticed Morgan studiously trying to ignore Churchill's fussing, though his jaw was clenched.

Arnie looked ready to tell Churchill exactly where he could shove his 'inspirational image'.

Tommy was enjoying the excitement though, whispering to his mother as the photographer angled his shots.

Churchill frowned. 'Arnie, if you could shift slightly to the left . . . No . . . no, *my* left please.'

Arnie huffed and shuffled sideways. Churchill's forehead remained furrowed. 'Perhaps you might be better in the back row? We'll have the more photogenic officers at the front.'

'Ouch!' Rick called from behind them. 'That's an epic burn.'

Karen tensed, seeing Churchill's insult register on Arnie's craggy face. Before he could erupt, she shot Churchill a look. 'I think we're arranged perfectly. Let's wrap this up. I'm sure the photographer has other jobs to do today.'

Churchill flushed, but backed off with a murmured 'You're right. Sorry, Arnie. Of course you're photogenic. It's just the light today . . .'

Leave it to Churchill to turn Tommy Burton's rescue into a PR photo op. The photographer had everyone say 'Cheese' and captured the required shots. Karen hoped her grin looked more natural than it felt. At least Tommy seemed to be enjoying the novelty, hamming it up beside the superintendent.

Finally released from the ordeal, Karen breathed a sigh of relief as everyone started to disperse.

Superintendent Murray approached Karen, smiling. 'DCI Churchill does get carried away with the press angle, but try to humour him. The publicity does our department good overall.'

'Yes, ma'am.'

The super offered Karen a final congratulations before following DCI Churchill inside.

Amber came over and gave Karen a grateful smile. 'I've never had my photo taken for the paper before.'

'It was certainly an experience,' Karen said. 'I'm glad you're here, though. I wanted to have a quick word.'

Amber's eyes filled with concern. 'Is something wrong?'

'No, I wanted to talk to you about Tommy. I know he seems to be in a buoyant mood, but he might experience after-effects from the abduction later.'

'I did think that might happen. What should I look out for?'

'It's difficult to say. Everyone is different, but he might have nightmares, difficulty sleeping, or become withdrawn. Sometimes, children who've been through traumatic experiences develop behavioural changes or exhibit signs of anxiety.'

Amber nodded. 'He's going to be spending some time with Sam Tranmere. They're designing their own game. Tommy can't wait, and I think looking forward to that has really helped keep his mind off what happened. But I'll keep a close eye on him all the same. Is there anything specific I can do to help him through this?'

'It might be an idea to consider counselling or therapy. A professional can guide you both through any challenges that arise.'

'I'll do everything I can to make things easier for him . . . He's seeing his dad next week.' Amber's expression hardened. 'Supervised visits only, but Tommy wanted to see him.'

She stopped talking as Tommy wandered over. She brushed the boy's fringe back from his face. 'I think you wanted to say something, Tommy?'

Tommy flashed a toothy grin at Karen. 'Oh yes. Thanks for saving me.' He leaned closer. 'You're going to be famous.'

'Sorry?'

'I'm meeting a publisher. They want to put my story in a book. I might even end up on TV. You'll be in it too, of course.' His eyes shone with excitement.

Karen should have known their pint-sized blackmailer would leap at the chance for profit and possible fame. The calculating glint in the boy's eye made her suspect he hadn't quite learned his lesson.

Amber tutted. 'Tommy, I said we could talk to them about it. We haven't agreed to anything yet. I'm not sure it will be good for you to relive it all.'

Tommy scuffed his shoe sulkily. 'I want to do it.'

Karen noticed the quick shift in Tommy's demeanour from cheerful and full of plans to moody and childish. One moment he seemed wise beyond his years, scheming and manipulating, and the next he was a petulant little boy not getting his way.

Shaking her head, Amber guided him away with a mix of fondness and exasperation. 'Let's go and say thank you to the other officers now.'

Karen watched them approach Farzana, both amused and slightly concerned by Tommy's mercurial nature. That child would need to be watched closely in the years to come.

Morgan appeared next to her. 'Tommy will have an interesting future. Whether it'll be fame or infamy remains to be seen.'

'He's bold as brass, I'll give him that. Did you hear him say he's in talks with a publisher to write an account of his story?'

Morgan pulled a face. 'I'm not sure that's the best idea.'

Karen agreed.

'If looks could kill . . .' She nodded at Arnie, who stood glaring at Churchill and grumbling under his breath as he brushed imaginary fluff from his rumpled jacket. Karen felt a pang of sympathy.

Meeting Morgan's eye, they came to a silent agreement. Together, they walked over to Arnie.

'So, what do you say we head to the pub tonight to celebrate properly, Arnie?' Karen suggested. 'I think it's Churchill's turn to buy the first round.'

Morgan clapped a hand on Arnie's shoulder. 'Too right. We'll drink to our success, whether Churchill thinks you're photogenic or not.'

Arnie gave them both a scowl, but it quickly melted into a smile. 'Sounds good to me, and we can drink to Tommy's memoir, too. That ought to be a page-turner. I'd better get a mention. After all, it was *me* who actually cuffed Brooke Lewis.' He slung his arms across their shoulders. 'Let's get back inside. There's a sausage sandwich calling my name.'

Chapter Forty

Karen sighed as she sank back in her chair, closing her eyes to bask in the warm afternoon sun. A light breeze wafted the rich aroma of freshly brewed coffee over the crowded patio where she sat with Morgan. The city around them bustled with activity, pedestrians and cars taking full advantage of the sunny weather.

She was glad to take a break from the mountain of paperwork on her desk. The Tommy Burton case had been exhausting, and she welcomed the return to more routine cases that were less harrowing.

The investigation had been an important lesson in looking beyond superficial impressions. Hardly anyone involved was who they had first appeared to be.

The sweet, friendly act Brooke put on didn't reflect reality. DCI Tranmere had initially appeared to be an upstanding ex-officer, when in fact he'd broken the law to protect his brother. Karen's impression of Sam Tranmere had been that of a lazy layabout, living off family money, when he was actually a talented games designer. It was a good reminder for Karen not to judge people so quickly. First impressions could be flawed.

Even Tommy Burton himself hadn't matched her initial perceptions. He wasn't just an innocent little boy as she'd first thought, but a complex youngster engaging in blackmail against those around him.

'Gorgeous day, isn't it?' Morgan said from across the small metal table as he lifted his steaming mug. He leaned back comfortably in his chair, stretching out his long legs and crossing them at the ankles. 'And here I was thinking the words *England* and *gorgeous day* were mutually exclusive.'

Karen smiled. 'I know. I feel as though I'm suddenly on holiday in the Mediterranean, not sitting in the middle of Lincoln.'

After leaving the mental health unit at Lincoln County Hospital, they'd stopped at the sunny cafe for a much needed break. Their conversation with Cody Rhodes had been . . . intriguing, to say the least.

'It was strange seeing Cody so lucid today,' Karen remarked, opening her eyes to glance at Morgan.

'He was considerably more coherent than I would have expected, given my previous interview with him.' Morgan shrugged and took a sip of his coffee. 'Seems that his medication has worked wonders.'

Cody had given them detailed information about his prison meetings with the notorious serial killer Graham Donaldson. He had been experiencing a delusional episode when he contacted Donaldson, believing the child killer was communicating with him telepathically. His obsession had been a manifestation of his disordered thinking. Cody's brain had linked his research for a documentary into Donaldson's crimes with a twisted belief that Donaldson was some kind of special messenger.

The Cody they'd met today and the one who had written the letters were like two different people. She hoped the details Cody had provided would be enough to stop Donaldson from making a successful appeal.

'Let's hope Cody's information is enough to keep Donaldson behind bars for the rest of his miserable life,' Karen said.

She knew Morgan felt the same. Over the last few days, he'd seemed almost . . . relaxed. With this gruelling case finally wrapped up, it was simply a matter of tying up loose ends and preparing the mountain of paperwork for prosecution. Karen was confident they'd get a conviction.

Morgan took another sip of coffee before answering. 'Did you hear Gareth Burton is having counselling?'

Karen nodded. 'He's already earned supervised visitation rights with Tommy. I suppose it's a good thing for him to rebuild that relationship.'

'Did you also hear that the CPS are pursuing the case against Dr Howes?'

'Good.' Howes was the vet Brooke had been having an affair with – the one who had provided her with the sedative Karen suspected Brooke had planned to use on Tommy. Of course, Howes was denying any such thing and had lawyered up, hoping to squirm out of the charges.

'Looks like he'll be struck off the register and lose his practice at the very least.'

Karen shook her head, thinking back over the details. 'He ruined his marriage and his career over the affair – what was he thinking?'

'He wasn't. Or, if he was, he believed he was untouchable. He'll likely serve jail time as an accessory.'

'It's a shame Oliver Wells refused to press charges,' Karen said.

'He's married now with a baby. He just wants to forget he ever knew Brooke.'

'Can't blame him for wanting to move on with his life.'

'No, and with the other evidence against Brooke, his testimony isn't critical anyway,' Morgan said. 'She'll be put away for a long time.'

The scrape of a chair being dragged over the pavement made Karen turn. She lifted a hand to shield her face, squinting against the bright sun.

'Sorry we're late,' Rick said as he finished pulling a couple of chairs over to their table. 'Traffic's an absolute nightmare today. Seems like the whole city has decided to get out and enjoy the heatwave.'

Karen's smile widened as she spotted Sophie emerging carefully behind Rick, one hand resting on her ornately decorated folding cane for balance. The pink glittery swirls and patterns adorning the stick were just her style.

Rick pulled a chair close to the table for Sophie to sink into, making sure she was comfortable. Though Sophie waved off his fussing, Karen knew she was grateful.

'Right, shall I go inside and put some food orders in?' Rick asked, rolling up his sleeves. 'I don't know about the rest of you, but I'm famished.'

They gave Rick and Morgan their lunch selections, and the two men headed indoors to place the order.

Karen looked at Sophie. There was colour in her cheeks and the spark was back in her eyes.

'It's good to see you out and about,' Karen said.

Sophie smiled as she folded up the cane and put it in her bag. 'It feels good.'

Her journey to reclaim her independence after the violent attack was inspiring. Despite various setbacks, she was determined to get back to her former self. Or as near to it as possible.

'I hope making the list of toy stockists wasn't too much too soon,' Karen said. 'We appreciated your help but didn't mean for it to turn into so much work for you.'

'It was just what I needed. It gave me something productive to focus my energy on.' She gave Karen a smile. 'I should be thanking you.'

'Your attention to detail was impressive – you not only compiled a list of places that sold the blue bears, you also caught that mysteriously vanishing red car in the case notes from the Oxford abductions.'

Sophie's expression clouded. 'I know, but I'm not entirely convinced that was a good thing. Didn't that cause some serious friction between Morgan and his former DCI?'

'I think the truth coming to light was for the best.'

Just then, Morgan made his way out of the cafe, balancing a tray loaded with sandwiches, packets of crisps, and drinks. 'All right, who had the chicken salad?' he asked, passing out the wrapped bundles.

As they ate, Sophie happily filled them in on her most recent MRI results and successful check-up with her doctor. Karen ate her sandwich, enjoying the easy flow of conversation.

'I've got some good news to share,' Sophie ventured, putting her sandwich down. She paused for effect. 'I'll be officially returning to work next week. Only part-time, mind you, but it's a start.'

Karen grinned. 'Sophie, that's fantastic.' She reached over to squeeze her arm. 'I know how hard you've worked for this.'

'Hear, hear,' Rick said. 'Best news I've heard in ages. It hasn't been the same without you cracking the whip and criticising my paperwork.' He grinned playfully.

'This calls for a toast,' Morgan said, lifting his coffee mug. 'To the old team, back together again.'

They clinked their mugs and glasses around the table, and Karen caught Morgan's eye and smiled. He seemed to have forgiven her for calling him a robot.

They'd never have the same working style. Morgan would always be a stickler for the rules, wanting to hold back until they'd gathered every last shred of evidence, whereas Karen was guided by gut feelings and instinct. But they understood each other. And, Karen thought, more importantly, they complemented each other.

She looked around the table. It was the friendship between all four of them, despite their disagreements and differences, that truly made them all work well together. And she was proud to be a part of the team.

ACKNOWLEDGEMENTS

Writing this novel has been a journey filled with challenges. Most of those challenges resulted because I wrote this book while moving house. What a mistake that was!

I have to extend my deepest gratitude to Doreen. When the clock was ticking, she ensured our house sale and purchase crossed the finish line.

To Therese, Maureen and Pam, I am so grateful for all your support and our daily chats on WhatsApp. I am thankful the move has brought me closer to my family. Despite the stress associated with moving, having my brothers now living only minutes away is fantastic and more than makes up for the hassle of relocating.

To my editors at Amazon Publishing, past and present, who have all been a joy to work with – thank you! Thank you, Kasim, for your encouragement and commitment to the series. It's been a pleasure to work with the amazingly talented people in various departments. Thanks also to Russel McLean for his help in making this story the best it can be. And I'm indebted to the copy-editing genius of Gemma Wain, who picks up on my silly mistakes.

And of course, deepest thanks to Chris for supporting everything I do, even my first crazy idea to write a book.

To Jim, I hope you're pleased to see PC Willson make his comeback as a family liaison officer!

Finally, to my readers, my heartfelt thanks for embarking on this journey with me. Your support, encouragement, and love for my characters are what keep me writing.

Thank you all for making this book possible.

ABOUT THE AUTHOR

Born in Kent, D. S. Butler grew up as an avid reader with a love for crime fiction and mysteries. She has worked as a scientific officer in a hospital pathology laboratory and as a research scientist. After obtaining a PhD in biochemistry, she worked at the University of Oxford for four years before moving to the Middle East. While living in Bahrain, she wrote her first novel and hasn't stopped writing since.

Follow the Author on Amazon

If you enjoyed this book, follow D. S. Butler on Amazon to be notified when the author releases a new book!

To do this, please follow these instructions:

Desktop:

1) Search for the author's name on Amazon or in the Amazon App.

2) Click on the author's name to arrive on their Amazon page.

3) Click the 'Follow' button.

Mobile and Tablet:

1) Search for the author's name on Amazon or in the Amazon App.

2) Click on one of the author's books.

3) Click on the author's name to arrive on their Amazon page.

4) Click the 'Follow' button.

Kindle eReader and Kindle App:

If you enjoyed this book on a Kindle eReader or in the Kindle App, you will find the author 'Follow' button after the last page.